Amy rolled Kelly onto her back. She kissed her eyelids and then the tip of her nose. "I've missed kissing these lips," she said as she felt Kelly's mouth open. Her tongue found Kelly's. She reached down and pulled up Kelly's top. "I've missed kissing these," she said as her tongue lingered first on one and then the other of Kelly's nipples. She could hear Kelly's breath quicken. "I missed kissing all of this." Her tongue trailed along Kelly's stomach.

Visit

Bella Books

at

BellaBooks.com

or call our toll-free number

1-800-729-4992

The Tides of Passion

Diana Tremain Braund

Bella
BOOKS

2005

Bella Books, Inc.
P.O. Box 10543
Tallahassee, FL 32302

Printed in the United States of America on acid-free paper
First Edition

Editor: Christi Cassidy
Cover designer: Sandy Knowles

ISBN 1-59493-048-1

This book is dedicated to all those women who truly understand its premise. To love and be loved is assumed in a relationship. To cherish and be cherished is something we all have to work at. To all those women who value their partners, this is your book.

But this book is specifically dedicated to six women who live its theme every day: Bonnie Potter and Linda Stern, my tennis partners and friends; Lynn Earnest and Laura Nusen, my traveling buds and friends; and Dee Boughner and Jill Carson, who are not only my friends, but my Maggie Beth and Terry.

This book is also dedicated to Jean Symonds—you are my Elizabeth, you capricious curmudgeon you.

You may write to the author at: dtbtiger@yahoo.com.

Acknowledgments

First I would like to acknowledge the wonderful work of writer Erma Bombeck. (1927–1996). I grew up reading her work and often wonder what her take on the world would be today if she were alive. I embraced her philosophy from what she wrote in "If I Had My Life to Live Over."

I would also like to acknowledge the work of Darthe Jennings whose music I quoted from. She is a consummate singer and song-writer. Her CDs can be obtained at darthe@catsout.com.

Chapter One

It was their last night together. The next day Kelly was off for a weeklong conference.

To celebrate they had gone to a restaurant where the lights were soft and the talk even softer. There was a candle on the white tablecloth. Romantic music played in the background. There was a tasteful gentleness and air of delicacy to the place.

Their waitress, Celeste, introduced herself. She was young and blond with staring seal-gray eyes.

They'd ordered wine. A fine Riesling, to go along with the extraordinary night. Celeste brought it along with a basket of bread wrapped in a white linen napkin. She set the basket on the table along with some whipped butter and a small dish of olive oil.

With her right hand she inserted the corkscrew, gave it one twist and the cork popped. She poured a glass for Amy, one for Kelly. They savored the fruity flavor, let it roll gently over their tongues.

Then they ordered grouper bathed in a special blend of spices and sauce and buried under fresh asparagus. Kelly was thinking about leaving and how much she was going to miss the woman she had loved for the past five years.

Kelly reached for the basket and uncovered the bread. She could smell the heat. She broke off a piece and handed the basket to Amy.

She spread whipped butter onto the bread.

She put the bread in her mouth and savored the spongy texture melded with the butter. It was delicious.

"You really lack class, you know," Amy murmured.

The words at first confused Kelly. Then they scalded her like steaming water.

"I'm just kidding, Kelly." Amy clearly noticed the reaction on her face, the distress and bewilderment. "We've got to whip you into shape, kid. When you're served bread at a fine restaurant like this, you don't butter it and pick it up and take a bite out of it. You break it in pieces and butter each piece and put it in your mouth. I don't know where I learned class, but I did," Amy said as she tugged at her bread, broke a piece off and dipped it in olive oil. "Better yet, you should dip it in olive oil."

Obediently she broke the bread into pieces and dipped one piece in oil and put it in her mouth. The constant criticism had made her pliable; it was never predictable and always a shock. It was interspersed between days of fun and togetherness.

Most of the time Kelly would say nothing. She knew it was criticism born of Amy's insecurities. Or so she had convinced herself. Other times she felt like Amy wanted to bite her ego like a coyote gnawing at the haunches of a deer.

Then Kelly had a major flashback. "Sit up straight. Don't slouch. Eat slowly, not like a pig. You're so lazy you could lie down next to dirt and sleep in it." Her dad's words clanged in her brain, like the distinctive sound of prison gates being slammed shut.

The verbal abuse that had been so much a part of her life with her father came back, only this time it was twice as biting because

2

she had been so unprepared for the verbal assault. And the words came again from her lover.

Kelly looked across the table and wondered, did Amy love her? At that moment, five years became a specter of uncertainty.

"You're sulking. I'm over it," Amy said in the car, the restaurant just a diminishing image in Kelly's side mirror. And she was.

In the past, her outbursts of anger or the sharp words that flowed from her tongue felt like a rapier cutting into Kelly's heart. She thrust forward and then parried. She got over it quickly.

But Kelly found it more and more difficult to forget the prick of her words. So Amy had found a word for it. *Sulking*.

"I'm not sulking," she answered obliquely.

"You are. I told you I was just kidding. Ya gotta toughen up, woman."

Just kidding, she thought. Kidding to cover her truth. Kelly lay her head against the headrest and closed her eyes. Memories were like life's bookmarks. Lately she didn't like the pages they were marking. She was remembering more of the acerbic parts of their relationship; she found it harder to remember the bookmarks that had separated the loving parts of their journey together. She sighed inwardly, remembering only the pain of their relationship, not the pleasures. Is that where these memories were being stored? She wondered.

Chapter Two

Amy could tell by the way Kelly hugged her when she was leaving for the conference the next morning that there was something wrong. Her hug was indifferent; Kelly had been quiet after they had returned home from the restaurant.

When they got home, Amy thought they might have a glass of wine and talk, but Kelly had gone upstairs, brushed her teeth and gone to bed. By the time Amy had followed, Kelly was turned away from her, her heavy breathing a sign she was asleep.

Now this morning, Kelly had gotten out of bed, taken her shower and dressed. Amy heard her go down the stairs and she was almost out the door by the time Amy had gotten to the kitchen. Amy had hugged her; Kelly had seemed distracted, unresponsive. Then she'd left with a curt good-bye.

Amy shrugged to no one in particular as she stared at herself in the bedroom mirror. She couldn't figure out what had gone wrong. They had had dinner Sunday night at a wonderful restaurant. The food had been tasty, the service perfect, and they'd talked about everything from what Kelly hoped to learn at the nurses' conference to what they planned to do for the following weekend.

Amy searched for her favorite blue slacks in their closet. She had selected her powder blue blouse and now she wanted her navy blue slacks. She loved the way the powder blue contrasted with the dark blue of the slacks. She even looked on Kelly's side of the closet, although Kelly's longer legs would not have fit into the slacks. *Hmm*, she thought, *maybe they're in the dryer.*

She walked into the bathroom and picked up her brush and ran it through her brown hair, unconcerned that gray, was already poking through. *Forty*, she thought. By the time her mother was forty, her hair was completely gray for which she affectionately blamed Amy. Said when she wasn't turning strands of hair gray, she was adding new wrinkles to her face. Amy smiled as she thought about her mother. Amy's father had died when she was four years old. She remembered them not having a lot of money, but she never felt poor. Her mother went to work at Webster's grocery store first as a checker, finally as the store manager. Amy was raised by her grandparents. She adored her grandmother and tried to put her grandfather out of her head. Mostly she remembered the yelling and the constant criticisms leveled at her mother and her. Amy could never do anything right.

She splashed on some perfume and looked at her face, noting she had fewer wrinkles than her mother did, but then again she didn't have a kid to deal with. Only Jasper, the cat. She knew Kelly had fed him before she left because Jasper wasn't bugging her to eat.

Amy clicked off the bathroom light, went downstairs to the laundry room and pulled her blue slacks out of the dryer.

Her thoughts turned back to Kelly. Definitely sullen, she thought. In the kitchen she poured herself a cup of coffee. She opened the refrigerator and took out a package of English muffins, selected one, cut it in half and put it in the toaster. Picking up the newspaper Kelly had left on the table she scanned the headlines, then turned to the local pages. She was more interested in what was happening on the island than in what George W. Bush had to say about Iraq, again.

When the toaster popped, she spread butter and jam on the muffin and bit into it as she carried the plate to the table. She set the plate down next to her coffee and resumed reading. The town selectmen had held a meeting the night before and judging from the lead paragraph, not much had happened. According to the police report, Jack Martin was arrested for operating a vehicle after suspension. He was always getting caught driving without a license. She doubted Jack ever held a license very long. He had been their neighbor while she was growing up. He must be in his seventies, she thought.

Amy rinsed her dish and cup and put them in the sink. She left the newspaper open on the table, where she'd read it when she got home. She smiled. When Kelly read the newspaper, she would put it back in the order she had found it, each section carefully tucked inside the other. Amy knew she drove Kelly crazy when she got to the newspaper first and left it strewn on the table. But that's just who she was, she thought. Straightening newspapers was not her thing.

In the car, Amy again thought about what had changed Kelly's mood. It couldn't have been anything she'd said. She scowled at the road as she tried to remember all the things they'd talked about the night before, but everything seemed pretty innocuous.

Amy brightened. Maybe Kelly was just upset because she was leaving. Although they had been apart for several days before— either because Kelly was at a conference or Amy had to go on a buying trip for the store—maybe this time Kelly was sad about leaving. Amy turned right onto Stillson Street, just off the Bleu Island town square.

That makes sense, she thought. *I'll just have to cheer her up when she gets home*, Amy decided as she parked in the driveway behind the store. *Make it up with a nice dinner, some good wine and a backrub.* Her concern about Kelly stopped as soon as she turned on the store lights. She could see the red light blinking on her message machine. She punched the button and began to listen to her messages. She picked up a piece of paper and pen and began to jot down names and numbers. Definitely going to be a busy day, she thought.

Chapter Three

"Amy Day," she said by way of introduction. "Welcome to my shop."

"It's lovely," the woman enthused. Dressed in white slacks and a bright pink golf shirt, Amy knew she was a summer tourist who was there to just look and not buy.

"Thank you." She turned back to the shelf she was straightening. When she had opened her gallery and frame shop ten years earlier, she was optimistic that those who entered would buy something. She featured well-known Down East artists and sculptors and carried everything from paintings that were as big as a wall to small postcards.

But as she became more seasoned, she would play a game with herself. When new customers entered the store, she sized them up and could guess if they would buy or not. Most of the time she guessed right. No point following this chicky around, she thought. No sale there.

Amy ignored the woman and sorted through the brochures that highlighted the area. Tourists would pick them up as they strolled from picture to picture.

A brochure on the Down East Heritage Museum Amy stacked in one pile. The museum had opened the year before and focused on the rich historical and cultural history of the area.

Next came a brochure on eco-tourism. Many of the brochures had pictures of the Atlantic Ocean, and more importantly the pristine Passamaquoddy Bay. A favorite picture usually captured some aspect of Maine's bold coast, with its craggy slate cliffs and rugged stone and rock beaches. Her section of the bay was just a few feet from her shop.

One of her favorite brochures showed a picture of a three-masted schooner on the front. Her friend Jim Bows had refurbished the ship, and on most summer days she watched it sail past her store and out into the bay, the tourists packed in and eager to chase after whale tails or spend a romantic night on board with only the soft swish of wind through the sails.

Amy looked up as the door opened. "Hey, my friend."

"Hey, yourself," Elizabeth said as she closed the door behind her. "Oops, sorry, you've got a customer."

"Come in, come in." Amy waved her over to where she was sorting. "Just straightening some brochures."

Elizabeth's salt-and-pepper hair was cut short and tucked under a Boston Red Sox cap. She always looked slightly rumpled. Her white polo shirt hung loose on her and was sloppily tucked into khaki shorts. Aside from that, she looked like an old Irish matriarch. Her turquoise eyes sparkled and distracted from her short and slightly hooked nose and thin lips. She had an engaging face highlighted by hundreds of wrinkles that she called the "mementos" of her life. Amy smiled. Elizabeth was self-deprecating about her looks. She said her ancestors mixed in a tiny bit of British and she had bought into the stiff upper lip of her British ancestry, thus her "Brit lips." She refused to answer to Liz or Lizzie. Introduced herself in a straightforward manner and told people her name was

9

Elizabeth and she would not welcome any substitutes. She wasn't as big as a minute. She used to tell everyone she had to stand on a rock to kick a duck in the ass. After Amy's mother died, Elizabeth had become her mentor and best friend. They talked about everything, including loves lost. Lois, Elizabeth's partner of fifty-one years, had died several years earlier.

"Kelly at the conference?"

"Yes."

"How long?"

"She's back Friday."

Elizabeth smiled. "Great. Wanted to invite you two over Saturday for a lobster feed. Maggie Beth and Terry will be there and a few others. It's just casual. I woke up this morning deciding I wanted to have a lobster feed."

"Terrific." Amy straightened the last of the brochures. "What can I bring?"

"Your great cucumber salad."

Amy made a salad everybody liked that had cucumbers and red onion bathed in mayonnaise and sour cream. Amy knew her friends liked it because the salad contrasted nicely with the rich flavor of the lobster.

"I love it with lobster." Elizabeth leaned against the counter. "Heard the scuttle?"

Amy turned her attention fully to Elizabeth. If there was gossip to be had on Bleu Island, Elizabeth knew it. She was the oldest town clerk in the state. "What's going on?"

"Been a bunch of men in to see Gary." Gary Crandall was the town manager. "He's been tight as a clam. Last night they were back, had a meeting with the selectmen. They held it in executive session. Been hush-hush. Some kind of development deal, but I haven't been able to find anything out. Gary's been carrying everything around in his briefcase. I can't even snoop his desk."

Amy chuckled.

"I'm not ashamed of it." Elizabeth stuck her chin out. "He knows I snoop his desk. He snoops mine. What's the fun of working at the center of what's happening in the town and not knowing what's going on?"

"I haven't heard a word— 'course, you know me, I'm usually the last to know what's going on. If I didn't have you, things would come and go and I wouldn't know a thing about it." Amy watched as the tourist made her way toward the door. "Thank you for coming in," she said to the woman. "Come back again."

"I will." The woman waved as she closed the door behind her.

"You guess her right?"

"Oh, yeah." Amy had told her friends about the guessing game she played in her head about her customers. "It's okay, it's June and it's been a good year so far. Next month's going to be a corker with the Fourth of July festivities. It's always my biggest month."

"I heard we're going to get a bunch of new marching bands. Some coming from as far away as Moncton and Saint John."

"I don't know what we'd do without our Canadian neighbors— heck, they provide half the participants in our parade. But I love it. Brings lots of folks home and even more just to watch. Biggest parade Down East."

"Gotta run. Have to get back to the town office. Maybe I'll know more of what's going on and can tell you later. Definitely some kind of development deal. Got a feeling it's big 'cause Gary's not usually this tight-lipped."

"Wouldn't that be a kick. We could use some kind of new industry down here." After the sardine factories closed, she thought they were going to go under as a town. It didn't impact her gallery business much, because she depended mostly on the tourists for that, but it had impacted her framing business for several years. "People aren't paying to have their pictures framed when they can't figure out how to put food on the table," she said.

"I know. Gary and the selectmen have been doing everything they can. He's working closely with the state office of Economic and Community Development. Last time the governor was down here, Gary told him to send just one business prospect this way and he'd make certain they set up shop here. Maybe that's what's happened."

11

"Better here than in the other Maine," Amy said. She sported a bumper sticker on her car that said, "I live in the other Maine." There were those who lived along the state's northeast coast who felt that all state aid stopped at the Bangor city line.

Amy had grown up on Bleu Island. A ferry was the only link from the island to the mainland, also known as Port Bleu. Amateur historians speculated that the port and island got its name because of the huge Maine wild blueberry fields that in the fall made the countryside look like an extension of the ocean, only dark purple-blue. Those same historians acted like they had a head full of lice when it came to why blue was spelled the French way. A real mystery because Maine had been settled by the British. Elizabeth maintained that there was a closeted Frenchman in the mix who named the island. Or, some believed, one of the island ancestors just had a wicked good sense of humor.

When Amy's parents were growing up there wasn't any ferry and they had to get to and from the island by small boats. Sometimes, when the weather turned nasty, they'd be stuck on the island for weeks. Then the state introduced ferry service in the early '70s and the island population exploded.

In the winter, the population shrank to about a thousand locals. Come Memorial Day, throw in a mix of summer folks and tourists and the tiny island's population blossomed to around four thousand. At one time the town was a bevy of business activity. Amy remembered walking past one of two car dealerships on her way to school. There had been a movie theater and a bowling alley. She used to buy all of her clothes locally.

Then the sardine businesses began to fail. The federal and state regulations that put pressure on the industry to clean up its act and not pollute the ocean were partly to blame as was the change in the American diet. Sardines were the favorite fast food of the 1950s only to be replaced by McDonald's. The movie theater burned and no one wanted to invest money in a dying town. The bowling alley closed and one of the owners of the car dealership got into trouble with some rebate deals that ended up in his pocket rather than that of the buyer.

Bleu Island had been struggling ever since.

Elizabeth said, "Gotta get back to the office. Give my love to Kelly. See ya Saturday."

"Looking forward to it."

On Friday, Amy closed the shop at the usual five o'clock and drove to the grocery store. She wanted to pick up some steaks. Kelly said she'd be home around suppertime and Amy wanted to cook something simple. Kelly had been gone a week and Amy could feel the stirring between her legs as she thought about what they would do after they'd eaten. She chuckled to herself. The first year they would have done the deed immediately and then eaten. Now, they settled for food first, love second. Maybe this time, she thought, they'd make love first.

She noticed the state liquor store up ahead and stopped. A bottle of wine would go well with the meal, she decided.

Good food, delicious wine and a night of lovemaking, she decided as she turned her 1992 black Saab into the driveway leading to their house. She never tired of looking at the 150-year-old white Cape. It sat high on a hill and sported a 360-degree view of the bay. She parked the car next to the house she had inherited from her grandparents. She and Kelly slept in the same room she had grown up in.

When she opened the door, Jasper greeted her. He purred as he wrapped himself around her legs. "Let me set this down, fella, and I'll feed you," she said as she put the packages on the counter. She picked him up. Jasper had been a present from Kelly. She had always wanted a six-toed cat and Jasper had not been a disappointment. He rubbed his head against her chin. She caressed his paw. "How was your day?" He was a ball of white fur with just one or two inky splashes on his coat. The paw she was holding had a tiny black spot on it. "Catch any dinner?" She set him down on the counter and reached for his dish. "How about tuna delight tonight?" she asked. Jasper rubbed against her arm as she opened the can. "In a hurry, huh?" Amy laughed. She poured the food into his dish and set him and the food on the floor. "Gotta shower. Mama number two is coming home," she said to the now disinterested cat. Jasper had his head buried in the food.

A half-hour later, Amy opened the bathroom door, the steam from her shower following her down the hallway. Kelly's bag sat on the floor next to the bed. "You're home!" she yelled down the stairs.

"I'm in the kitchen."

"I'll be right down," Amy said as she pulled on her running pants. She felt a slight twinge of disappointment. She had expected Kelly to come up and give her a hug. Probably tired from the drive, she thought. Boston was more than seven hours away.

"How was the trip?" Amy said as she entered the kitchen. She walked over and took Kelly in her arms.

"Tiring. The last few hours were hard, really, really hard," Kelly said as she returned her embrace. "Steak for supper. Good."

Amy stood back. "Everything okay?" She studied Kelly's face, which was drawn, and her tired eyes. She and Kelly had met five years earlier, not long after Kelly had been hired at the Bleu Island Hospital. Elizabeth had introduced them at a party. Kelly was slender to Amy's more solid build. Kelly's hair was blond, her eyes cobalt. Amy's hair was brown, her eyes chocolate. She had always loved the contrast in their appearance. Amy was forty, Kelly four years younger than her. They had clicked first as friends and then as lovers.

"Sure." Kelly stepped back. "How about I start the grill," she said as she picked the steaks up and headed out to the patio.

"So tell me about the conference," Amy yelled through the screen. She pulled lettuce and tomato out of the refrigerator, thinking she'd make an oil and vinegar dressing.

"Not much to tell. Some good presenters, some not so good."

Amy could hear the grill cover being lifted followed by the *clunk-clunk* of the charcoal as it hit the metal bowl. "You were so looking forward to that one presenter. Something about ethics and nursing? Was that good?"

"Excellent," Kelly said as she came back inside, brushing the charcoal off her hands.

"So tell me about it. Did you learn new stuff? Were the presenters interesting?"

"Not much to tell. Mostly longs days. We had some good group discussions after the presentations. I'm glad I went."

"Your friend Laurie called while you were gone and left a message on the answer machine. Asked you to give her a call." Kelly and Laurie had been in nursing school together. Although they were best friends, they'd seen little of each other after Kelly left Portland. Laurie had been in a relationship, and taking the time to even spend a weekend together had never worked out. One year turned into two and soon Laurie and Kelly weren't doing much more than occasionally chatting on the telephone. Amy spooned dressing on the salad. "Elizabeth stopped today before I closed. She invited us to a lobster feed tomorrow after I close the shop. Maggie Beth and Terry will be there, and she didn't say who else, but I expect it'll be the usual group."

"Good," Kelly said as she picked up the tongs and went back outside. "Should be fun," she called over her shoulder.

"Some things going on at the town office."

"What kind of something?"

"She wasn't sure. Said there've been several meetings between Gary and some strangers. Said they met with Gary and the selectmen. I just love Elizabeth." Amy laughed. "Said she even snooped through Gary's desk but couldn't find a thing. Not even a hint of embarrassment, said she regularly snooped through his desk for information. Sounded like they kinda made a game of it."

Kelly laughed. "That's our pal. No sneaking around, just put it out there. This is what I do and this is who I am." She carried the steaks into the kitchen and began to set the table. At the last, she grabbed two sheets off the paper towel roll and put them next to the plates.

Amy put the salad bowls on the table and sat down. The steak smelled delicious. "Could be good," she said, thinking about the activities at the town office. "I'd love to see some kind of development that will get us back on our feet. Would help my business, not yours so much. You got a job whether you're treating one sick person or twenty."

"Don't be too sure. Last hired, first fired. We lose any more businesses in this town and it could mean cuts at the hospital."

Amy frowned. "I'd be surprised. We've been through tough times like this before. The hospital just keeps perking along."

"Even so, I'd hate to see another business close," Kelly said as she cut her steak and put a piece in her mouth.

"Me too," Amy said, taking a bite of the rare steak. "Wow, these are good. Nice and tender." She picked up the breadbasket and handed it to Kelly. "Bread?"

"No, thanks." Kelly stared at her as she buttered a piece and then bit into it.

Amy put the bread down and studied her lover's face. "Everything all right?"

"Sure, just tired. It really was a long drive from Boston. The first two hours seemed to just zip along, but the last three hours were a real bugger. I could feel my energy level dropping."

"Well, a hot shower and a bit of a rest and you'll feel terrific," Amy said as she finished her steak. "I'll do the dishes, you relax."

Two hours later, Amy stretched out on the bed. She could hear Kelly in the bathroom, the sound of the faucet being turned on and then off, the squeak of the medicine cabinet door. When Kelly came into the room Amy said gently, "Come here." She patted the bed. "Let me just hold you."

Kelly turned off the light.

The bed moved ever so slightly as Kelly sat down on the edge. Amy pulled the sheet back and eased Kelly into the bed. "I missed you."

"Me too," Kelly said against her shoulder.

Amy rolled Kelly onto her back. She kissed her eyelids and then the tip of her nose. "I've missed kissing these lips," she said as she felt Kelly's mouth open. Her tongue found Kelly's. She reached

16

down and pulled up Kelly's top. "I've missed kissing these," she said as her tongue lingered first on one and then the other of Kelly's nipples. She could hear Kelly's breath quicken. "I missed kissing all of this." Her tongue trailed along Kelly's stomach. Kelly smelled of Palmolive soap.

Amy slipped between her legs. She parted her lips and she heard Kelly's sharp gasp. It was always like this when they made love. She could taste Kelly's excitement. She could feel her hips vibrate first gently and then rapidly as she reached higher and higher, finally peaking. And then the exhalation of air as Kelly floated over the top.

Amy rested her head against Kelly's shoulder. "That was wonderful," she said.

"It was," Kelly murmured.

Kelly turned to Amy and kissed her gently. "Okay if I don't make love to you? I am really tired."

Amy could not keep the disappointment out of her voice. "It's okay. You had a long drive." She rolled onto her back. They lay in silence next to each other. Then she felt the bed move as Kelly turned toward her.

"That's not fair of me," Kelly said delicately. She kissed Amy's lips. "Not fair of me at all," she said as she kissed her way toward Amy's nipples.

Chapter Four

Kelly turned her white Ford SUV onto Shin Pond Road. She had rushed to leave, gulping her coffee and choking down her English muffin. She had not even sat down at the table like she ordinarily would, but rather stood at the sink. Amy was still in the shower when she yelled she was leaving.

She had gotten up at six. She knew Amy thought they would laze around in bed for a few hours, making love again. Amy had to open the store, but not until nine.

Her excuses sounded feeble even to her. Even though it was Saturday and she had the weekend off, she said she wanted to check her mail, check on some of her patients. She rubbed her eyes as she drove past Slater's Autorama and the Dunkin' Donuts.

She had lingered long after the conference was over talking with other people. Somehow going home seemed more like a duty, rather than a desire. She wondered how often she had lied to ignore the truth. She was tired because all she could think about while she was gone was the ache she had felt their last night together. She had ordered herself to get over it and had even tried to bury it in discussions and work. But it kept coming back to her like an evil spirit. Lately, she wished her life was more like her computer, just hit escape and the garbage disappeared. Now she was running as fast as she could to work. How strange, she thought, the first year they were together, making love had been like catching lightning in a bottle, fiery and intense. They used to linger for hours feasting on each other's bodies. She believed that Amy's body spoke to her when they made love and she understood Amy's language and she responded to Amy's unspoken sounds. Amy had told her she was the best lover she'd ever had. Kelly used to chuckle, but one night Amy had taken her face in her hands, looked her in the eyes and said, "Believe it."

Last night, it had felt mechanical and programmed. She had gone through the motions, Amy fell asleep afterward and Kelly spent a sleepless night counting criticisms. She felt like she had hit shuffle on a CD player—she could hear Amy's words, only in different sequences.

Five years of deflecting, ignoring or being hurt by all the things she had not done right. How many times would she have to listen to how she had failed to measure up? In all those years, Amy never once complimented her on what she wore when they dressed up to go out. She never mentioned the positive things Kelly did for her like drawing a hot bath for her after a long day at work because Amy loved to luxuriate in the bathtub. Instead, Amy complained because she didn't like Kelly's blouse, or her lipstick was too red or the bathwater was too hot or too cold. She recalled one time she'd sent Amy an animated e-mail card telling her how much she loved her. Amy never acknowledged the card and days later when Kelly had asked her if she'd gotten it, Amy had complained that the sound on her computer was not loud enough for her to hear it. She never acknowledged the sentiment of the card. After that Kelly had stopped sending *I Love You* cards. Not on purpose, but somehow it no longer seemed important.

19

Elizabeth had introduced them.

Kelly had gone into the town office soon after she had been hired at the hospital. Elizabeth had been at her desk. Kelly smiled as she thought about that day. Elizabeth had been intense, answering her questions, giving her advice about housing and the like. Kelly liked her immediately and she sensed it was mutual.

Elizabeth had invited her for coffee.

She had accepted the post at the hospital after years of working in a large facility in Portland. She had grown weary of the big-city hospital politics. She and Laurie, her best friend, had agreed to run away.

After months of talking and planning, they decided to abandon the big city and move to northern Maine where they could do some real nursing. Laurie had a friend in a nearby town who had convinced her to move Down East where people were really who they seemed to be

By the time Kelly handed in her notice, Laurie had fallen in love with a woman named Heather, whom she had met on the Internet. Kelly decided to stick with her plan to move to Bleu Island; Laurie moved in with the woman in Portland.

A week later, when she was ready to go, Laurie helped her pack. Days earlier she had helped Kelly move her furniture into storage. The next morning, she was to leave for Bleu Island. Laurie handed her a CD and quoted lines from the title song, "If I could give you something to keep your dreams in sight, I would illuminate this path you're walking and hang another star across your night." She remembered Laurie's hug and her words. "I would do that for you, my friend. Listen to this CD and think of me." The song was from Darthe Jennings' album *Lessons of the Heart.* They had discovered the singer/songwriter through friends. When she got to the island, she played the CD a lot. She missed her best friend.

The first few weeks on the island were lonely. Days at the hospital went fast and she actually was glad she had made the move. She liked the community spirit of the small hospital. But nights were dismal and dreary. The apartment she was in was over a pizza restaurant across from the marina. After just two days of smelling cooked pizza, she decided she had lost her appetite for it. Housing on the island was impossible with few apartments to rent and even fewer houses. She was told she would have to wait for a house rental and that was what she was doing. She spent a lot of time talking long-distance with friends or feeling sorry for herself. She made a point of talking with her mom in Lewiston or her sister in California at least once a week. She spoke less often to her brother in Texas. It was hard talking with Laurie, because Heather had not warmed to her. She got the feeling that at times Heather had not given Laurie the message that she had called. So the days and weeks turned into months and after a time they rarely talked.

Then she'd met Elizabeth, Elizabeth with the dazzling eyes and the accelerated discourse. Even Elizabeth admitted she liked to talk, mostly about herself. Then Elizabeth had introduced her to Amy and three months later they had moved in together.

Kelly turned into the hospital's parking lot. The building was small. Everything was confined to two floors. The emergency room was to her right. There was only one doctor there, compared with the half-dozen who worked on emergency patients brought in day and night in Portland. In her five years on Bleu Island, there had never been one gunshot victim.

Her office was in the main hospital where fifty beds, including the four ICU beds for the critically ill, took care of the needs of the island. Everything was a microcosm compared with where she had been. But she loved it.

Promotions came easily and before Sandra Belton, the aging director of nursing had retired, she'd recommended Kelly for the job. At first, she had refused to take it, fearing it would upset those who had been at the hospital a long time, but Sandra had convinced her that nobody else really wanted the job. She had been the director of nurses for exactly one month.

"Good morning," Kelly said to Loraine. Loraine had been the hospital's switchboard operator and receptionist for years.

"Kelly, welcome back. How was the conference?"

21

"Good." Kelly paused. "No, better than good. It was excellent. Things quiet here?"

"Absolutely. No crises, just everyday stuff."

"Good, that's the way I like it."

"Here let me get you your mail," Loraine said as she got up and reached behind her to a number of wooden cubicles. "You're going to be busy for a while." She chuckled, handing two huge stacks over.

"Looks like it." Kelly frowned. "Oh well, better now than trying to do it on Monday when I'm answering the telephone and dealing with hospital issues."

"And here"—Loraine reached down to a stack of pink papers on her desk—"are your messages."

"Thank you." Kelly quickly shuffled through the papers. "How's Frank?"

"Good," Loraine said. "Thanks for asking. He got out of the hospital yesterday. The docs said it was only a mild heart attack, thank God."

"That's great, Loraine." Kelly set the messages on top of her mail. Loraine's husband had been brought in the day before she had left. While working construction with some other men he'd fallen off a ladder. No broken bones, but definitely suffering from chest pains. "I'll be in my office." She added, "Loraine, if anyone calls, just take a message."

"Sure, Kelly."

Kelly walked down the hall to her office. She stopped at the nurses' station where Joyce Kilkie was on duty.

"Kelly, welcome back," Joyce enthused.

"Good to be back." Kelly smiled. "And before you ask, it was a great conference. I'm glad I went. How are things here?"

"Quiet, really quiet."

"Good."

"Did Loraine tell you? Frank got out yesterday. She was one happy woman."

"I saw it in her eyes. Thank God he was in town when it happened. If he'd been out in the boonies . . ." Kelly paused. "Well, it might have been a different ending."

"Agreed."

"Who else is on duty?"

"Susan and Janet. They're in with patients right now. Want me to get them?"

"No, just curious. I'll be in my office," Kelly said as she turned down a side hallway.

"Glad you're back," Joyce called.

"Me too."

A few moments later, Kelly turned on her computer and let it jitterbug through its various screens. She separated her mail into piles—things she knew she would have to address immediately, notices from agencies, the state and federal governments and junk. The junk mail she dumped into the trash.

She sorted through her messages. There was one from Laurie. She picked up the telephone and dialed. She looked at the clock— eight thirty in the morning. Good, she thought. She hoped the call would get her out of bed.

Laurie answered on the first ring. "Good morning."

"Darn, I was hoping I'd wake you up."

"Rat that you are." Laurie laughed. "Back from the conference, good."

"How'd you know I was at a conference?"

"Your receptionist told me, no mystery."

"And you called me earlier this week because?" Kelly glanced at the pink phone message.

"Because I wanted to talk with my best friend."

"And?"

"What do you mean by and?" Laurie dragged out the last word.

"You don't usually call me at work."

"Well." There was hesitancy in Laurie's voice.

"Everything okay with you and Heather?"

"No, we've sorta broken up. You could say she is now my ex."

"Oh, Laurie, I'm so sorry."

23

"Me too, I still love her—somewhat."

Kelly grinned. Laurie, who had spent most of her adult life in love-'em-and-leave-'em situations, had settled in with Heather. Kelly thought this time it was going to work. But Laurie, after a breakup, had so many levels of love, depending how hard the separation, from *somewhat* to desperately. "Did it just happen?"

"No, it's been a month. I didn't call you because, I don't know, I was probably more embarrassed than anything else. Plus we haven't talked." Kelly heard the unspoken message in Laurie's words. They hadn't talked because of Heather. "There were lots of tears, from both of us. But I hope we're going to be friends," she said lightly. "Actually, we *will* be friends. It's going to just take a while."

"What happened?"

"I don't know."

"Is there—"

"Someone else? No. We just seemed to come apart." Her voice broke and Kelly sensed she was fighting back tears. "I'm . . ." Laurie paused and cleared her throat. "Not going to cry. I promised myself I would tell you all this without crying."

"You can cry, my friend."

"I know." Laurie hesitated. "But I spent a lot of time crying the last couple of weeks."

"Maybe you can fix it."

"No, actually this isn't the first time we've broken up. We've essentially broken up at least once every year since we've been together. Then we'd decide we could make it work, so we'd get back together." Kelly heard the weariness in her friend's voice. "This time we agreed we wouldn't even try. It just takes too much of an emotional investment and we decided we don't want that. That's why eventually I think we could be friends." Laurie gave a short laugh. "Although Heather does kinda hate me right now because I ended it. But I'll tell you one thing—"

"What's that?"

"In the future I'm going to bed them and not wed them. It uses up too much of my heart to fall in love."

Kelly smiled. "Well, that will keep you busy."

"You bet. Anyway, let's talk about you, not me. How's Amy?"

"Great, busy at the store." Kelly glanced at her watch. Amy was probably reading the newspaper.

"And you?"

"Fine, Laurie, but that's not the reason you called me a few days ago. I don't get the sense you're up to chitchat."

"I'm thinking of moving Down East." Laurie rushed on, "I'm not really happy here at the hospital. I thought about all our talks and how much I really don't want to be here in this big hospital, and I was wondering if you're looking for any good nurses down there?"

"We're always looking for good nurses down here. Do you know any?"

"Low blow, Kelly. Low blow." Kelly could hear the relief in Laurie's laugh.

Kelly chuckled. "So when do you plan to make the move?"

"Whenever. I would want to give at least a month's notice here. They've been good to me."

Kelly frowned. "You realize that you'd be working for me. That's different than when we worked side by side there."

"I thought about that, but I can handle it. Unless, of course, you turned into Nurse Ratchet."

Kelly laughed. "Only with you, my friend, only with you." She turned serious. "Send a résumé. I'll run it past the CEO, although he pretty much leaves the hiring of the nursing staff to me. I do like him to see the résumés."

"Look in your mail, it should be there."

"Pretty confidant."

"I figured you'd hire me."

"We can't afford to pay what you're getting down there."

"I figured, but it also won't cost me as much to live. And, if I'm lucky, they'll make me some kind of muck-a-muck after five years like they did you."

Kelly laughed. "You never know."

"Kelly, thanks. I see this as a great move for me. We haven't

25

seen much of each other in the past couple of years. That's my fault because I've just let life come between us. I don't know, Kell, when we were in nursing school and the time we worked together afterward, we had such a bond. Now, instead of grabbing hold of what's most important—our time together as friends—we've grown apart, and I've been kicking myself because time together is for building memories," Kelly heard Laurie laugh uncomfortably. "Listen to me, I sound downright sappy. By the way, I went to another of Darthe's concerts this year. I thought about all the concerts we went to together. It made me sad you weren't there. I have one of her CDs for you."

"I'd love it. I've just about worn her others out." Kelly hesitated. "Getting back to that lost time, I'm just as responsible, my friend. I've been so preoccupied with my relationship with Amy and my job and I've been just as absent from your life. I've thought of you often and now . . ." Kelly paused. "Well, we can't put Humpty Dumpty back together again. All we can do is promise we won't let time and distance get between us again. So let's see what I can do with this résumé."

"By the way, I'm looking forward to getting to know Amy. You two sound like you're just so connected, I doubt anything would break you up. Anyway, pal take care and get that résumé to your boss. I'd like to think I can start packing."

"Start packing." Kelly laughed. "It'll be fun having you here. I miss you."

"I miss you, too. It'll be like before, only you have a partner."

"And so will you," Kelly replied, thinking Laurie could meet someone on the island.

"No way. I'm not going to fall in love ever again. Sorry," Laurie said soberly. "I don't do that well."

"You will." Kelly said seriously. "Laurie, it hurts now but if it isn't right then all you end up doing is putting in time on a relationship that isn't working and that's wrong. So Heather had to become a thing of the past." Kelly paused. "Only, next time go slowly."

"I will," Laurie said. "You know what I missed most after you left? After a shift, it didn't matter if it was day or night, we'd go have coffee and just talk. I missed that."

"Me too. It's going to be great having you here."

They said good-bye and Kelly hung up. She rested her chin in her hand. She and Laurie had gone through nursing school together and were so excited when they had both been hired at Portland's largest hospital. Over the years, they had helped each other through good relationships and, after the relationships shattered, broken hearts. In their first year of nursing school, Kelly's partner at the time, Robin, had not been happy about her friendship with Laurie. She was jealous. Three years into their relationship, Robin had ended it, and Laurie was there to help her pick up her life. Kelly had done the same for Laurie, although it had become a joke between them because Laurie's relationships rarely lasted longer than a year. The fact that Laurie and Heather had made it for more than five years was some kind of record—even Laurie had admitted that. So now the record was broken.

Kelly spent the next few hours looking through her mail and reading her e-mails. She'd found Laurie's résumé and had put it on a side pile to show to Don. She crinkled her brow when her telephone buzzed. "Yes."

"Sorry, Kelly, you said not to bother you but Amy called, said it was important. I told her you were out of your office, but I did take a message."

"Thanks. How long ago did she call?"

"A few minutes. I debated whether or not to bother you."

"It's fine. Thank you." Kelly hung up and dialed the store number. Amy picked up on the first ring. "Hi, you called?"

"Oh, glad you called back."

Kelly hesitated. "And?"

"Just wanted to see when you're coming home?" Amy said hurriedly.

Kelly looked at the clock. "You called to see what time I'd be home." She tried to keep the impatience out of her voice. "You're

27

not going to close the store until five o'clock, so you can figure I'll be home around that time."

"Well, you don't have to get testy."

Kelly inhaled. "I'm not *testy*. I was just in the middle of some things."

"I just thought if you got done early you might like to come over here. I've missed you," Amy said softly.

"I'll see."

"I love you," Amy purred.

Kelly stared at the square tiles on her ceiling. She closed her eyes. "That's nice." *Put the restaurant thing behind you*, she told herself as she hung up. *There's more to this relationship then just that night at the restaurant.*

Chapter Five

"Wow, look at the cars. Elizabeth isn't having a lobster get-together. It looks like five o'clock at the local seafood house." Amy parked the Saab behind a large SUV.

"Elizabeth does love a party," Kelly said as she opened the door. Spike greeted them with tiny yips and lots of jumps. He reminded her of a bouncing ball. "Hey, Spike." She picked him up, scratched his belly and rubbed his head. When she put him down he kept jumping at her leg.

"Here." Amy handed her the cucumber salad. "Let her think you made it."

"Fat chance," Kelly said as she took the plate. "Come on, Spike, let's go find your mama." She could see Elizabeth smiling at them from the porch. Her hair was standing at weird angles, evidence of the number of times she had run her hands through it.

"Spike, settle down," she yelled at the dog. "Hey, you two." Elizabeth walked across the yard and hugged first Kelly and then

Amy. "Don't you just love a party. I just started inviting people and look what happened." Her arm swept through the air as if she was embracing all of the people there.

"How many did you invite?" Amy asked.

"Well, with you two, I think we topped twenty. Thank God lobster is cheap here. If we were in the city I would have had to have given the lobster dealer my firstborn." She linked her arms through Amy's and Kelly's. "Not that I have a firstborn." They walked into the house. "Some folks are in the house, others are in the backyard. I think you know everyone here."

Amy stopped before they joined the first group. "You learn any more about that project?"

"Nada," Elizabeth said. "I tried. I cajoled, begged and pleaded with Gary. I threatened him, told him I would tell all his secrets." She shrugged. "Course he don't have any worth telling, but it sounded good. He was as numb as a pounded thumb. Couldn't get a word out of him," she said. "All he'd say was 'When it's right you'll know.' I told that chicken hawk *now* was right, but he wouldn't bite."

"I'm just hoping," Amy said. "If we're talking some major venture, it could mean this town would come back to life. We need something. It would improve business for everyone."

"Agreed. I keep persevering, but right now all I want to do is eat lobster, drink some beer and tell outlandish stories. How are you, Kelly?" Elizabeth squeezed her arm. "Good conference?"

"A great conference."

"Find me a date?"

Kelly laughed. "I didn't know I was supposed to."

"Course you're supposed to. I need a deep and abiding commitment to a woman." Elizabeth smirked. "Course, a little lust rush wouldn't be so bad either."

Amy gently slapped Elizabeth's arm. "Stop, you. We find you a woman and you'd be like one of those hermit crabs, pull your shell over your head and hide."

Elizabeth pretended to bristle. "Not true. In the matters of the initiation of the heart, I am cautious."

30

Kelly laughed. "As far as I'm concerned"—she hugged Elizabeth—"in the affairs of the heart, you're perfect."

"Ayuh," Elizabeth said, hugging her back.

Kelly loved the banter that flowed between the three of them and she knew even though it had been four years since Elizabeth's partner, Lois, died, Elizabeth's chatter about finding another woman was just that—all talk.

"Come on," Elizabeth said. "Just roll into the middle of all that. I know we're parked in here like a bunch of schooling sardines, but everyone seems to be having fun. And those that aren't will say they did anyway. So don't matter."

Kelly saw Maggie Beth and Terry and hugged them. She had met them through Amy and had felt an instant connection with them.

Terry was tall and blond, with an athlete's body. Maggie was smaller, her dark hair interwoven with strands of gray. They had been together for twenty-five years and Kelly admired their closeness. Being around them gave her the same comfort as slipping on a warm overcoat on a cold wintry day. They had both been real-estate agents and knew a lot about the area. The first chance, she thought, she would ask them about housing for Laurie.

"Welcome back," Maggie said. "How was the conference?"

Kelly smiled. "Are there no secrets on this island?"

Terry laughed. "No, and what we don't know, we make up."

Kelly watched as Amy also hugged their friends.

"Well, there is one secret," Elizabeth said, alluding to her current obsession. "Something's going on at the town office and I don't have a clue. I tell ya, I feel like a one-armed swimmer going against a mighty current. I just keep going 'round and 'round. You two hear anything?"

They laughed. Then Maggie said, "We don't hear a thing unless you tell us. You're the one with the information. You're like the party telephone lines you folks used to have here on the island. Remember, Terry?"

"Who wouldn't." Terry rolled her eyes.

Maggie turned back to the group. "Here we are, these two

31

women, just moved from the big city. We were here probably a month, and one night we were having dinner and across the bay from our picture window we could see a fire on the wharf over at Port Bleu. I called my neighbor because she'd lived here most of her life. I was concerned it might be someone's house or something. She didn't know, and from where her house was on the bay, she couldn't see the fire. All of a sudden some woman interrupted our telephone conversation and said that the old cat food plant was on fire. She hung up. I was dumbfounded. We didn't have anything like that in the city. I thought there'd been some kind of screwup in the telephone lines. My neighbor just howled with laughter. I asked her who the heck that was and she said that was her neighbor Mary Lou. Everyone was used to Mary Lou listening in and she didn't care who knew. Apparently she'd regularly jump right in when it suited her." Maggie laughed. "After that we watched what we said on the telephone. It was the darndest thing to get used to, thinking that some stranger might be listening in."

Elizabeth smirked. "We'd do that all the time as kids—heck, not just as kids, sometimes even as adults. I knew Mary Lou. She didn't just have her ear to the ground, it usually was right in someone else's business. When I was a kid, I got real adept at lifting the receiver off the cradle so there wouldn't be any clicking sound, like a telephone being picked up. Course never did it as an adult, wasn't right." She arched her eyebrow. "When they introduced the single-party line some of us grieved big-time, but not me," she added with a chuckle.

"I don't believe it. Knowing you, you were right in the middle of it," Amy said to her.

"No confession here. Listening in on my neighbors' telephone conversations as an adult? Well, I never." Elizabeth feigned hurt.

"Ya old salt, you probably did that and more," Maggie shot back.

"I tried to listen in but my grandmother was always chasing me away from the telephone. Told me to mind my own business and of course that made it more fun to try and sneak a listen," Amy said.

As Kelly watched the exchange, she could see Elizabeth was clearly enjoying it.

"Well, anyway"—Elizabeth surveyed the crowd of people—"I can't listen in on a party line this time."

"Driving you crazy, hon?" Maggie asked.

"Could say crazier than a poophouse rat, but since I passed crazy a week ago, now it's more like demented. I remember one time hearing this joke . . ." Elizabeth paused. "I feel like a mushroom that's been kept in the dark and fed only fertilizer. I've never seen so many tight-lipped people in that town office. They don't even let it slip when they walk out of a meeting. And believe me, I've tried to get them to talk. And I'll tell ya, their mouths move, but there ain't a thing that matters coming out."

"I expect when they're ready to talk they will," Maggie said matter-of-factly.

"What's the fun of that?" Elizabeth asked. "If you can't get the poop ahead of time, there's just nothing to the scramble. Anyway, I want you to say hi to everyone." She steered them toward a group of women.

"Hey, we're fine," Maggie Beth said. "You go do what you need to do and we'll make our way around the room."

"Thanks. I want to see how things are going in the kitchen." Elizabeth gave Maggie a quick hug. "And"—she paused dramatically—"I have a big announcement to make after we eat."

Maggie Beth frowned. "What kind of an announcement?"

"The good kind." Elizabeth winked and left.

"Wonder what that's all about?" Amy asked. It was Kelly's thought exactly.

"Can't imagine," Maggie said.

"She running for a new office or something?" Terry asked.

"I don't think so." Amy paused. "She usually can't keep that stuff a secret. Would call everyone up if she was doing that."

"Agreed." Maggie nodded reflectively. "Although that may be a possibility. But knowing Elizabeth, whatever we guess, it won't be right. So we may as well wait for the big announcement."

33

"I hate waiting," Amy groused. "I wish she hadn't told us. Now I'm going to want to wolf down my food and get everyone else to do the same so she'll tell us." They all looked toward the kitchen where Elizabeth had disappeared.

"How about something to drink?" Terry said, glancing at each of them.

"I could do with a beer, hon," Maggie answered.

"I'd like a wine," Kelly said, thinking about what Elizabeth had hinted at.

Amy said, "Me to. I'll go with you. Maybe we can squeeze something out of Elizabeth in the kitchen." She and Terry headed toward the kitchen.

"I doubt it." Maggie laughed. "You know Elizabeth. Tight as a clam when the tide's out."

Kelly watched her partner walk away. She'd worn her white jeans and teal blue top and looked oh so sexy.

"She looks so happy," Maggie said.

"I think she is. Things seem to be going well at the store."

"That's not what I meant. She's a changed woman since you've been in her life. Before you, she had a lot of relationships—most of them short-term—and it's too bad because she's bright and fun to be with and she has such energy."

"That she has," Kelly said. She could see Amy in the kitchen talking to someone half-hidden by the door.

"And you, Miss Kelly, are good for her."

"I don't know about that, but thank you." Kelly wanted to change the subject. "By the way, a friend of mine from nursing school is planning to move here. She's looking for a rental." She knew that even though Maggie had retired from the real estate market, she still had her contacts.

"Rentals are hard." Maggie frowned. "Most folks on the island own their own homes, but I think the Grange place is open. Someone said they've been spending more time on the mainland with their daughter. You want me to check?"

"Would you? I don't really know them."

"Know who?" Amy asked as she came toward them carrying

two wines and a beer. Terry followed with another beer and a plate of vegetables and dip.

"Remember Laurie? She called today, wondering if the hospital was looking for nurses. She wants to move here." Kelly turned to Terry and Maggie. "Laurie and I went to nursing school together."

"You didn't tell me," Amy said archly.

Kelly took a sip of wine. "I didn't have a chance. I only talked to her this afternoon. That's when she told me."

"Well, you could have told me first."

Maggie and Terry exchanged a glance.

Kelly looked down at her feet. How far would Amy go with this?

"If you'd told me, I'd've said call her back and tell her she can stay with us until she gets settled. Or did you do that already?" Amy's tone rang false to Kelly's ears.

"I didn't. She's going to give the hospital a month's notice. I—"

"Dinner is served," Elizabeth called from the kitchen. "Anyone too lazy to get their own plate isn't going to eat, so get on in here. Darn, I keep wanting to buy a dinner bell," she said laughingly. "Never seem to remember."

Kelly picked up a plate with a two-pound lobster on it. She spooned cucumber salad next to it. She tucked silverware and napkins under her arm. Amy was chatting on the other side of the table with Terry. She was oblivious to the discomfort Kelly now was feeling. Amy had embarrassed her in front of her friends. She felt like a child again. She remembered all the times her father had scolded her in front of company for not doing something right. She picked up a small bowl of melted butter. She was going to find a corner and eat her lobster. She needed to think.

"How are you?" Maggie's voice was soft.

They had finished with dinner and now several women were in the kitchen helping Elizabeth clean up. Amy was at the center of activity. Terry was in a corner talking with friends of theirs. Kelly

35

felt a need to take a walk outside. Spike bombarded her as soon as she stepped out on the porch. She reached down to pet his head. It was still bothering her the way Amy had reacted to Laurie's move to the island. Maggie's presence was a comfort.

"Fine, been busy at the hospital."

"By the way, congratulations on your promotion—that was really something. We're very proud of you. I didn't get a chance to call you after Amy told us."

"Well, thank you. It was unexpected. I figured I would just be doing first-line nursing, something I've always enjoyed. I wasn't going to accept it; I do like the patient interaction. Now, I mostly deal with paperwork and employee problems. A major leap."

"But one you can certainly handle."

"Handle, yes. The like part, I don't know yet." Kelly frowned. "Sometimes, I think I would like to run from reality." She stared across Elizabeth's yard at the oak trees that were staggered across her property. The sun seemed to play a selective game of light on the leaves. Some leaves were luminous and effervescent, others a dull green in the shadow of their brighter neighbors.

"You know what I think?" Maggie asked, her gaze following Kelly's as she too looked across the yard. "The only reality is that which you can keep your thumb on."

Kelly shook her head. "I don't understand."

"It doesn't matter what's out there. Or what other people perceive as your reality. The only reality for you is that which you can grab hold of, for want of a better description."

"And if I don't like that reality? Maybe want to change it?"

"Then you change what you can. And leave the rest to whatever else. If you don't like the job, then go back to what it was that made you happy. Go back onto the floor, be a nurse."

"And if they don't let me go back?"

"That's a tough one. We're pretty laid back here so I imagine they would."

"I don't know. The hospital is part of a large conglomerate. The people who run it are not from here."

"True." Maggie leaned against the porch railing. "But, Kelly,

36

there are other things you can do. We have plenty of doctors' offices. And the big hospital is right across the water—you'd no doubt be welcome there. Nurses are darn hard to get around here, I know. I served on our hospital's board of directors for years. Docs don't want to come here. They want to make money and I don't blame them. They spend a lot of time in school, spend a lot of money on tuition, and although the salary is decent here, they sure could do a lot better in a bigger city. Nurses are the same. They think working in a big city is better because they're nearer to cultural events and the arts. I don't know how much of that is true, or how much more it has to do with the isolation you find here. So many of them just can't make it in rural America. Funny, docs and nurses would rather trade the peace and safety of living Down East for the big cities where there's so much violence. Doesn't make sense to me. People here don't even lock their doors. You lose your car key, it's probably in your ignition. Anyway, I think you'd be hired in a second."

"Well, lots to think about." Kelly turned toward her. "I'm not saying I don't like my job. It's just different. I'm a nurse because I really like being a caregiver. Now the only care I give is to a bunch of forms that have to be filled out or peoples' problems."

"Is everything else all right?"

"Sure." Kelly avoided her eyes.

"Why don't I believe you?"

Kelly smiled. "You have to because I say everything is fine."

"You say it, but you lack conviction."

"I—"

"Hey, you two," Amy interrupted. "We need you inside. Elizabeth is getting ready to slice up some pies. Said she's going to make her announcement. There's also this huge cake in there. I think she's going to have a lot of dessert left over." She squeezed Kelly's arm.

"Knowing Elizabeth," Maggie said with a laugh, "we all are going to be taking huge plates of food home while at the same time trying to digest this latest thing in her life."

Inside, Elizabeth slowly cut dessert for each of her guests. Finally, when all of the plates were handed out, she put her hands on her hips, a smile playing across her face. "I wanted to share my latest adventure with my friends first."

"What's her name?" someone yelled from the back of the kitchen.

"Yeah, right," Elizabeth said. "You all know about the skydiving team that's going to be performing on the Sunday before the Fourth of July. They're from Brunswick."

"I heard something about that," Amy put in. "I guess they do some pretty neat kinds of tricks in the air." She paused. "But they're coming to perform—that's been in all the papers, on the radio, on television. So what's new about that?"

"I'm jumping with them."

"You're what?" Maggie's voice squeaked, and Kelly admitted she too was surprised.

"I'm jumping with them." A huge grin spread across Elizabeth's face. "Isn't that about the most exciting thing I've ever done?"

"You're daft," Amy said, no doubt louder than she had intended. "Look, we love you dearly," she said in a softer voice, "but this is just too crazy."

"Not crazy—safe and fun. It's something I've always wanted to do."

"How'd you team up with them?" Terry asked.

"Their advance man was in, and unlike all the other covert stuff going on at the town office, this guy was telling me about how the team lets four amateurs tandem-jump with them. Sort of a publicity stunt, but also just to get locals involved in the sport."

"Is this safe?" Kelly asked quietly, her heart pounding. This was something she'd always wanted to do too.

"As safe as crawling out of bed," Elizabeth said.

"Elizabeth Robinson, I've known you my whole life," Amy said intensely. "You're seventy-five years old and you're too damn old to be jumping out of an airplane."

"Helicopter," Elizabeth corrected. "Because our airport is too small and they might miss the drop zone, they use a helicopter. From what they tell me, they climb to ten thousand feet, open the doors, and you and your instructor are out free-falling to the earth."

"More like falling like a rock," Amy said. "I'm speechless."

"Well, not too speechless," Elizabeth shot back good-naturedly.

"I think it's a great idea," Jimmy Johnson said from the back of the room. He ran the local garage and was a friend of theirs. "What the heck, this is one of those once-in-a-lifetime things." He came over and embraced Elizabeth, whose face radiated with happiness. "You've earned the right to do whatever you want. I wish I could do it."

"You're both crazy," Amy persisted.

"Actually," Kelly said quietly. "I'd like to do it too. They have another opening?"

"You're not going to do it," Amy said emphatically.

Kelly ignored her. "They have another spot?"

"Don't know, but I can ask." Elizabeth winked at her. "I think it'd be neat if several of us could do it together." She turned toward their other friends and was instantly absorbed in the swarm of questions.

Amy pulled Kelly aside. "You're not going to jump out of a helicopter," she said between clenched teeth. "We'll talk about it later."

Kelly squirmed. Maggie and Terry were watching them.

"We'll see," Kelly murmured. "Anyone like more cake, a cup of coffee? I sure could use a cup of coffee," she said as she headed toward the kitchen.

"I could use a cup too." Maggie joined her.

Kelly could feel Amy's gaze on her as she walked away. She was going to jump, she thought. She could feel her heartbeat accelerate as she contemplated the idea. It was something she had always wanted to do and she was going to do it.

"You're not going to jump out of a helicopter." Amy stared straight ahead. Kelly could see her knuckles were white as she gripped the steering wheel.

39

"Amy, it's something I've always wanted to do."

"Well, there's hundreds of things I've always wanted to do."

"Like what?"

"I can't think of anything right now," she snapped.

Kelly could see Amy was angry, yet again. "Amy, if there's something you really want to do, I would support you."

"That's fine, but you wouldn't support me jumping off those cliffs over there." She nodded toward the granite rocks that jutted out from the bay.

"Now, that would be kinda silly." Kelly tried to keep her voice easy.

"No sillier than your jumping out of a helicopter," Amy sputtered furiously. "It's not going to happen, Kelly Burns. So put that stupid idea out of your head."

Kelly clamped her jaws shut. *Don't argue. Don't let this become yet another argument that will deplete your energy and turn a nice day into another painful memory*, she told herself.

Amy pulled into their driveway and parked next to Kelly's car. "This conversation is over," she said tartly as she put the car in park. "You're not going to jump out of some stupid helicopter."

"Why the anger?" Kelly touched Amy's arm. "Why are you so angry about this?"

"I'm not angry," Amy shrieked. She opened her car door.

"But you are." Kelly followed her toward the house. "Amy, stop. Let's talk about this. Is it because you're worried? Does the idea scare you?"

"No." Amy gaped at her. "Nothing scares me. I just think it's a stupid idea and I'm not going to be standing on the ground while you're jumping out of a helicopter. So you're not going to do it."

"Can we talk about this?"

"No, we can't talk about this. I'm going to bed." Amy slammed the screen door behind her.

Kelly brushed her hands through her hair in frustration. She'd just been berated like an imbecilic adolescent. She inhaled deeply. She quietly opened the screen door. Amy hadn't given her a chance to explain why she wanted to do it. Her eyes glittered with tears. She swallowed. It felt like a sea gull egg was stuck in her throat. *Don't cry. This is not one to cry over. Oh, hell*, she told herself, *go ahead and cry*. She knew they were tears of anger, not sadness. She turned off the lights in the kitchen. The depression she'd felt that night at the restaurant had returned. Amy had given her marching orders and she was supposed to obey. "Not this time, Amy Day," she said quietly as she slowly climbed the stairs. "Not this time."

Chapter Six

"I couldn't wait to tell you both," Elizabeth enthused over the telephone to Amy and Maggie Beth. "So that's why I used my office phone. Just love this conference call button. But I gotta be quick. They're all behind closed doors right now, but they could be out soon."

"What's going on?" Amy asked. She'd been so busy at the store she hadn't spoken with Elizabeth or Maggie since the party just over a week ago. Nor had she and Kelly talked anymore about her jumping out of a helicopter. After their argument, she'd been lovingly attentive. She tried to make it up to Kelly, but she'd been distant. Amy had decided to let her sulk. She knew she'd get over it. She always did.

"It'll be on the radio and in the newspapers. The selectmen are advertising a big meeting for next week. It'll be next Wednesday at seven o'clock. They're calling it—" Elizabeth paused. "I've got the agenda right here. It's an 'economic development meeting to talk about a new business.'"

"That's it?" Maggie asked.

"That's all they have to say."

"So what's this all about?" Amy asked, curious.

"Still don't know. Two of our local reporters have been in here, asked me all kinds of questions. They both cover the town office, so I know them well. Sometimes I can tell them things off the record, so they didn't believe me when I told them I didn't have a clue. They were in talking to Gary, but they walked out shaking their heads. I don't think he told them much."

"Why the mystery?" Amy asked.

"I can't imagine."

"Maybe it's something to do with the military? We're surrounded by ocean and we're isolated. Maybe they're going to build something down here," Amy said. "That sure would be draped in secrecy."

"That's a possibility." There was uncertainty in Elizabeth's voice.

"Amy may be right," Maggie joined in. "Remember after 9/11, how all of a sudden we had these new border patrol people in Calais? Before Ground Zero happened, when you crossed back into Maine from St. Stephen, you knew everybody on the border. They just chatted you up. I remember after nine-eleven, I had to go over for some supplies and I was coming back and *four* border inspectors were all over my car. Made me show them my driver's license. They looked in my car, opened my packages. And it seemed to just happen. There was all kinds of secrecy surrounding those border changes. They just sprung it on us."

"Happened to me too," Amy added. "I know the government said after 9/11 that our borders would be beefed up, but it just seemed to happen overnight."

"Well, I guess it's a possibility. But these guys don't look military. Hold on just a second." Elizabeth muffled the phone for a moment. "I gotta go. Meeting's breaking up."

Amy heard the click. She hung up and then dialed Kelly. "Hi, Loraine, how are you today?" she asked the receptionist at the hospital.

"Great, Amy, how are things with you?"

"Good, things have been slow at the store. How's your husband?"

"Home. Kelly probably told you he only had a mild heart attack. It's been a real lesson for him, Amy. He's on a diet and is actually exercising. The attack scared all of us."

"Actually, Kelly didn't tell me. All that confidential hospital stuff. I heard it around town. But I can understand that it scared you. He's, what, not even forty?"

"Forty-one last May. But he's got a history of heart problems in his family. So, I told him, we had to look at this as a gift. It could have been worse."

"You're right. If it means losing some weight and exercising, that's a heck of a lot better than the alternative."

"And what's funny, he sees it that way too. I thought I'd have to fight with him to lose weight, but it's been okay. In fact, I'm on the same diet and I tell you I feel better."

"That's terrific."

"You're looking for Kelly?"

"Is she in her office?"

"Don't know. I know there was some kind of staff meeting earlier today, but I'll put you through."

"Thanks, Loraine." Amy heard the click and then the ring of Kelly's telephone.

"Burns," Kelly said.

"I love it when you say that. Burns," Amy mimicked. "You sound so official. Might even scare the person on the other end."

"Well, since Burns is my last name it doesn't seem right to say anything else," Kelly said in that officious voice that just annoyed her. Yes, she thought, Kelly was still sulking. She knew the solution was to keep moving forward, unlike Kelly, who had to scrutinize and dissect every disagreement they had. She knew better than to go back over old ground. She had learned that lesson from her grandmother.

"Lighten up, hon, I was just teasing you. Look, Elizabeth

called," Amy said without missing a beat. "There's a meeting next week about that project she was talking about. I'd like to go."

"I think you should."

"I'd like you to go too."

"What night?" Kelly asked, no doubt thumbing through the planner Amy knew sat right beside her phone.

"A week from Wednesday at seven."

"I can't. There's a meeting with the hospital board of directors for that night. I won't be able to get out of that. It's our quarterly meeting."

"Heck, I really wanted you to go. Sounds like this is really important. Can't you get out of it? Better yet, tell Don to reschedule. I imagine that some members of the hospital board will want to be at the town meeting."

"Since Don called the meeting and since he *is* the hospital's chief executive officer and my boss, it doesn't seem likely that I'm going to tell him anything," Kelly said dryly.

"Well, whatever it is, according to Elizabeth, it's going to be in the papers tomorrow and all over the television and radio stations, so maybe once everyone hears about it, they'll change their plans. Maybe they'll reschedule the hospital's meeting 'cause people will want to go."

"I doubt it. It takes weeks to set these things up, coordinate everyone's schedule. Go with Elizabeth or Maggie Beth and Terry. You know Elizabeth will be there. Hang on, I've got someone on my other line." Kelly put her on hold. "Gotta go," she said as she clicked back on the line.

"Okay. But see if you can get out of that meeting next week," Amy persisted, hoping they'd be willing to reschedule.

Kelly spent the rest of the week dealing with hospital issues. The newspapers had talked about the meeting, but the journalists were short on information. A couple of reporters had speculated that a major manufacturing company might wish to expand Down

East. Another picked up on Amy's theme about a possible military connection. There was a buzz of excitement. Kelly could feel it even at the hospital. People talked about the endless possibilities and what it would mean for the island. Unfortunately, Don couldn't reschedule the board meeting at the hospital.

Kelly had shared Laurie's résumé with her boss and he had given her the go-ahead to hire her. After she called Laurie and left a message, Laurie had called her back and left a message saying she would give her notice. They kept missing each other.

Then the day would end and she would have to face going home where Amy kept pushing her to go with her to the selectmen's meeting.

In the past, she had eagerly left her day behind. But now, going home seemed less and less desirable and Kelly found herself making up reasons why she needed to stay longer at the hospital. Some of the staff groused because she had scheduled a meeting for after five o'clock. She smiled to herself. She would have to watch that. She didn't want the nurses suffering because she didn't want to go home.

She stared at her ceiling tiles and tried to count the tiny little holes. She needed something to distract her, to get her mind off Amy. She lost count and soon her brain was focused on their relationship.

Kelly sighed. She had to take control of her free-ranging thoughts. She knew they were destructive. She wasn't problem-solving, but rather reliving past hurts. She wished she could hermetically seal that part of her brain.

Since her return from the conference two weeks ago, and except for the argument about her skydiving, Amy had been affectionate and attentive to her needs. She had even suggested that if Laurie took the job, she should stay with them. Sometimes Kelly felt as if Amy just flipped a brain switch and the angry Amy disappeared. Several days went by before she had called Elizabeth and gotten the name of the advance man. She was disappointed when he said all four slots had been filled. Nights Kelly didn't work late they took walks down on the beach and sipped wine on the patio. Last Saturday they had taken the boat and gone to the mainland shopping. Sunday, they had lazed around the house doing crossword puzzles and talking. It was as if the argument had never happened.

Yet Kelly had felt off center the whole time. The argument over the skydiving and the night at the restaurant kept thundering again and again in her mind. She had been genuinely looking forward to the quixotic evening they had planned at the restaurant. They had reservations for dinner on the mainland and then home for a night of romantic splendor. Amy had put candles around the bedroom ready to be lit. She had loaded love songs on the CD player. The evening was velvety warm. They'd held hands as they drove and talked about what they would do when Kelly got home. Kelly remembered the restaurant, the soft music and the lit candle on the table. There was a vividness to their night. Then, it was as if a dirty bomb had detonated inside Amy's head and out came those words that turned their night wrong side out. It was those times when Kelly felt like she was living with a stranger.

In the past, after Amy's brutal words, they would make up. Kelly would remember that Amy loved her and she loved Amy. She used to accept Amy's outbursts as a kind of temporary craziness. This time was different; Kelly couldn't give up on the hurt. It took two weeks, but finally she realized what had made this time so different. It wasn't because she hadn't seen it coming. Most of the time when Amy went to the dark side of her brain, Kelly was unaware she was there until the words came out of Amy's mouth. What made this time different was where Kelly was in her head. She'd been absolutely immersed in the preparation of their romantic night together and then lulled into the ambiance of the moment. When Amy criticized her, it was like she had banged into an iceberg. Kelly couldn't let go of the cold that seemed to envelop her. The next day Amy seemed totally oblivious to Kelly's mood shift the night before and she still didn't understand Amy's outburst over her skydiving. It was just who Amy was. Amy shed her remarks like old skin. She cared about Amy, but this was the first time she questioned whether she loved her.

Kelly rubbed her forehead. It didn't make sense. How could she stop loving someone so fast? *What's wrong with me? What do I want?* Could she stay in a relationship where she didn't feel the love that she once felt? Or was she merely a coward? Amy loved her in her own way. Set aside the criticism, the anger. Amy did love her. *You walk, you break her heart. You walk, you break your own heart?* She'd be alone again. Kelly Burns, the thirty-six-year old homeless nurse. No one would want her. And it was so hard going through the slow waltz of a developing relationship, really almost not worth it. She stared at her computer. She could write down what she felt, she thought as her fingers shuffled across the keyboard. Keep a diary of the hurt and the pain, the things Amy said and then talk to her. *Don't be afraid of her anger. Keep telling her what's causing such pain.* They needed help, she realized. Their relationship needed help. They could see a counselor. *We've got to see a counselor*, Kelly kept repeating to herself like a chant. *We've got to try and fix this.*

That evening, Amy greeted her as soon as she opened the door. "It's an LNG plant."

Kelly smiled. "Well, that's a new way to say hello." She had promised herself before she left the hospital that she and Amy would talk about the hurtful words, but Amy was wound as tight as a corkscrew, so clearly tonight would not be the night.

"I'm serious. They want to build a liquefied natural gas terminal here on the island. Elizabeth did find out. She wouldn't say how or where she got her information. The secrecy is because of what happened in southern Maine. They wanted to tell people their way—you know, public relations propaganda—before folks got entrenched. She said the newspapers have it and it's going to be splashed all over everywhere. I wasn't really paying all that much attention when they wanted to build one in southern Maine. I know it was in the newspapers, but I just figured that it was something that wouldn't affect me. I went online today and I looked up some of the old stories."

Kelly opened the refrigerator. "I have a feeling I'm going to be listening to some really bad news. How about a glass of wine?"

"Wine isn't important. What's important is what I found out." Amy was as nervous as a long-tailed cat in a roomful of rocking chairs.

"And I want to hear," she said sincerely. "But I need a glass of wine right now to help peel away the day and prepare for what you're about to say. Now, would you like a glass?"

"Yes," Amy said impatiently. She waved some papers in front of Kelly. "But I'm not going to wait to tell you. I took a bunch of notes. Two years ago, one of those international companies wanted to put one in Harpswell. They wanted to put it in a former Navy fuel depot. After a long battle, the townsfolk said no, but surprisingly it was a pretty close vote. Then some developers wanted to put one on Sears Island. I didn't know this, but it's the largest undeveloped island in Maine. It's home to all kinds of birds, and people hike it all the time. Well, there was such an outcry from Searsport that the company slipped away in the middle of the night. Our dear governor, God love him, encouraged them to look Down East. Said it would be a 'boon' to our economy." Amy took the glass Kelly offered her and sipped. "This is not good—not the wine, but the LNG," she added quickly. "They have to shut down everything when the tankers are brought in. These ships are on the terrorist hit list and I don't mean music."

"Wow." Kelly sipped her wine, thinking about what an explosion would do to the lives of people on this small island. The pressure it would put on the hospital. That's if the hospital survived the explosion.

"Yeah, wow." Amy got up and began to pace. "In"—she frowned—"I think it was nineteen-forty, a ship blew up in Cleveland, killed more than a hundred people. The explosion took out a whole square mile of the city. These tankers are four football fields long and more than ten stories high. They're floating bombs.

49

One newspaper article said"—Amy looked down at her notes—"that if one ship exploded it would be the equivalent to fifty-five Hiroshima bombs."

Kelly shuddered, remembering the pictures of the injured people she had seen in her history books of Hiroshima and Nagasaki. "Why would anyone even agree to having something like this here?"

"Ignorance? Greed?"

"Ignorance I understand," Kelly answered. "Greed, I don't understand."

"In Harpswell the company agreed to pay the property tax for every resident for the next fifty years. Do you know what that would mean here?"

As islanders they were heavily taxed because most of them lived with the shore just at their toe tips. If some sharp company came in and waved greenbacks in some of the locals' faces and offered to pay property taxes, say for the next fifty years, they'd not only go along with it, they'd embrace it and say t'hell with what might happen. Kelly was baffled. She couldn't believe people would do that. Most people here made their money off the sea, lobstering, scallop-dragging, digging clams.

"And just think if you told those same people they wouldn't have to pay property taxes again in their lifetime." Clearly agitated, Amy sat down and picked up her glass of wine. "Greed, Kelly, I wouldn't trust my neighbors to turn it down."

Kelly blew out a breath of air. Amy had a point. "The meeting is next week, Wednesday?"

"People are all ready lining up in opposition to it. I spoke with Maggie Beth and Terry and a bunch of our other friends. Elizabeth said she was talking to others. We need to be there with questions, Kelly. Questions that make them squirm."

"But we also need to listen to what they have to say."

"Haven't you been listening?" Amy thundered. "These people are going to kill our way of life down here. Get it, Kelly? This is my home, you're a transplant, I'm going to fight it."

Kelly set her glass down, feeling defensive. Then she remembered her resolution to stay calm. "I love this place as much as you do." She tilted her head in thought. "Yes, I am a transplant, but this is my home too. So don't turn your anger at the project on me. We *do* need to listen to what they have to say, because that's where you get the ammunition to fight your battle." She pointed at the papers Amy had in front of her. "These newspaper articles are fine, but we need to formulate our own plan based on what they tell us."

"Good, so you'll be there?"

Kelly tried to lighten the moment. "Only if Don fires me."

"Then let him fire you. This is the most important battle ever to face this island."

"Amy, I'm not going to lose my job over this. You'll be there and so will our friends. I have a hospital board meeting and at this point the quarterly meeting hasn't been canceled and I don't think Don is about to try. I told you earlier, it is just too difficult to get everyone's schedules coordinated for a meeting of this magnitude."

"I know Don. I'll call him up and tell him to cancel. Even members of the board need to be at this meeting."

Sighing, Kelly sat forward in her chair. "No, you won't." She kept her tone level. "You're not going to call Don about anything." She stared directly into Amy's brown eyes. "Do you understand?"

Amy jumped up. "You just don't get it. We're fighting for our lives down here." There was fire in her eyes, her gaze steely. "We need everyone on the same page."

Kelly stood up and set her now empty glass in the sink. "This is non-negotiable, as you like to say. You're not going to talk to Don or anyone else at the hospital. Muster your troops. Get everyone there to the meeting, but leave me and the hospital out of it. There will be more meetings and I'll try to attend those." Kelly paused and looked at her. "Now if you'll excuse me I'm going for a walk."

Kelly left the room and headed for the beach. This was one of those seaside homes that each year they paid a hefty tax on. She tried to sort it all out. She tried to see both sides of the issue. She embraced Amy's fears that Bleu Island would change, but was

51

change bad? Islanders were clearly suffering. Jobs that had been part of their grandparents' lives were gone. Although tourists came to the island, the workers didn't get rich off of them. She sat down on a rock and stared at the waves. LNG was a new wrinkle in their lives, and watching Amy turn determination into passion to win, she thought, was scary.

About eight, when she returned from her walk, Amy was gone. She'd left a note and said she'd gone to the store. When Amy returned later she put on the TV. There had been a polar-cap stillness.

Now Kelly stared at her face in the bathroom mirror. She didn't like the person who was staring back. Her face looked drained, her eyes tense. She could feel the knot that had grown in her stomach lessening. Stay calm, she thought. Amy was right, this was important. *But so is your job*, she reminded herself. She reached for her toothbrush and brushed her teeth. She heard Amy turn the lights off downstairs.

She crawled into bed and closed her eyes. She heard Amy as she walked up the stairs and into the bathroom. After she brushed her teeth, she turned off the light. The bed swayed when Amy sat down on the edge. Did she want to talk? she wondered. Then she felt the bed move again as Amy lay down and turned on her side. Funny, she thought, they had agreed at the start of their relationship that regardless of the issue they would not take their anger to bed. They often did. Either out of anger or hurt. Kelly thought as she turned over for the one hundredth time that night, *When did we break that pledge?* She couldn't remember. It seemed almost a part of their lives now, when they'd had a fight. Which seemed more often, or when Amy had said something hurtful, which also seemed more often, they would not speak or touch in bed. Often they'd leave for work in the morning not talking.

Chapter Seven

Glacial was probably too caustic a word to describe the next few days in the Burns-Day household, but it was definitely deep-freeze time.

Amy, whose anger flared quickly and then dissipated just as quickly, was usually light-hearted and good-humored afterward.

Ordinarily, she would try to make it up to Kelly for losing her temper, although she never apologized. But not this time. Amy was distant and Kelly for the first time since they had fallen in love realized she didn't care that Amy was distant.

Over the next few days, Amy spent more time at the store and Kelly found she liked coming home at night to no one other than Jasper. At least Jasper didn't gnaw her head off for doing her job, she thought.

When Amy finally returned home, Kelly made it a point to be in bed, her face turned to the wall. She didn't have the energy to fight. Mornings were a standoff. Whoever got up first made the coffee. The leisurely breakfasts they usually shared did not happen because no one bothered to ask. It had been like that for days, and the night before the board meeting wasn't any different. Amy had stayed at the store late and they had not spoken when she had returned home. Now, early Wednesday morning, Amy was up early.

Kelly showered and selected a navy blue jacket to go with her tan slacks and white blouse. She hadn't heard Amy's car leave so she knew she was downstairs. And indeed she was sitting in the kitchen sipping her coffee and reading the morning newspaper.

"Good morning." Amy set her coffee cup on the table. "Any chance the board meeting was canceled and you can go with me tonight?"

"No." Kelly picked up the coffeepot and poured herself a cup. She thought about leaving for the office, but she sensed Amy wanted to talk.

"I was going to make breakfast. You hungry?"

Ahhh, Kelly thought, the hostilities were over. "No, thanks, I've been getting breakfast at the hospital."

"You just say that to make me feel bad?"

"No," Kelly murmured. "I was just telling you what I'd been doing."

"Look, get over it. I am." Amy scowled at her. "We had a disagreement. I'm disappointed you're not going tonight, but I'm over it. You're pouting again."

"No, Amy"—Kelly shot an irate glance at her—"I'm not pouting. And please don't use one word to define what's going on in my mind. I'm getting on with my life. You acted as though I chose not to go with you because I didn't care." She could feel her anger growing. "I didn't say no because I wanted to go out and play or because I wanted to sit home and watch television." She sat her cup down. The coffee tasted acrid, unpleasant. She knew it was because the juices were tumbling 'round and 'round in her stomach. "It didn't jive with what you wanted me to do and you've treated me like trash. I don't get it." Jasper rubbed against her leg. She bent to pet the cat. "I had to work, for Christ's sake. It's rare

54

that happens anymore, but it did this time. I couldn't change the meeting and you took it out on me as if I had planned it so I couldn't go."

Amy looked down at her cup and then said after a moment's reflection, "I felt it was important that you be there."

Kelly reached for her jacket and put it on. "You know . . ." She hesitated. She knew her words were going to make Amy angry. "You never take responsibility for your words, or the pain they cause. In the years we've been together, never once have you apologized and that's inexcusable."

"That's not fair," Amy snapped. "I was upset. This meeting was important to me. I felt it was important to you."

Kelly reached for the door. "It's important to me, Amy, you know that. It sounds like it's important to everyone on this island regardless of which side you're on."

"What do you mean, which side you're on?" Amy's eyes widened. "The only side is against."

"That's not true." Kelly wished she could have shoved the words back in her mouth.

"What do you mean?"

Kelly leaned against the door, her shoulders drooping, the weight of the conversation dragging on her like a grappling hook. "There's been a lot of talk at the hospital. Lunchroom scuttle. People have read about it in the newspapers or heard about it on television and radio. The media's been comparing it with similar efforts offered in communities down south that have turned it down, and I gotta tell you, Amy, not everyone here is against it. People's attitudes run the gamut from outright rejection to total acceptance. Most folks at work are taking a wait-and-see attitude. They want to learn more about it. I expect there'll be a huge turnout."

Amy's pupils grew as round as cannonballs. "I expect you've been telling those 'total acceptance' people," Amy mimicked, "to smarten up. We're talking about a way of life here that will be lost if that thing is built."

"No, I—"

"No, no?" Amy kept repeating. "Kelly, this is the most important challenge this island has ever faced. If people like you and me don't speak out against it, then who will?"

"Amy, I don't know enough about it."

"Then get informed," Amy stormed. "I've been reading about it. Elizabeth, our other friends have been reading about it. There's all kinds of stuff I've left lying around the house. All you'd had to do is pick it up and read it."

"First off, I've been reading about it." Kelly tried to choose her words carefully.

"Second, I still don't know enough about it to try to change people's minds."

"That's why you should be at the meeting tonight. To learn about what the developers want to do to our island."

Kelly put her hand back on the doorknob. "Been there, done that, Amy. I'm not going to go through that argument again. I have a hospital board meeting. Look . . ." She paused. She wanted to keep the situation from escalating into another fight. "Let's talk tonight. If you get home before me, wait up. If I get home before you, I'll wait up for you so we can talk about what these guys are planning. Agreed?"

Kelly watched as Amy got up, rinsed her cup and put it on the sink. "We'll see," she said, her smile smug. "Maybe some of us will go out afterward, kind of decompress after the weeks of tension."

"Fine, but if our friends want to decompress, bring them over here." Kelly tried to keep her voice neutral. She knew Amy was just trying to make her regret not going and she didn't want to engage in yet one more skirmish. "Tell them I'm interested and let everyone bring me up to speed."

Amy shrugged.

"I don't know what time I'll be home . . ." She paused, waiting for a response, but when there was none she added, "I'll be here as soon as the meeting's over with. I'll see you tonight." She quietly opened the door and left.

Chapter Eight

"Wow, a Power Point presentation." Amy watched contemptuously as a tall blond woman set up the computer. She was all angles with long attractive legs, slender hips and an almost androgynous chest. Elizabeth followed Amy's gaze. "They're pulling out all stops to impress us."

"And the little darlin' setting up the computer is not bad," Elizabeth whispered under her breath. "Slick as smelt swimming upstream."

Amy frowned at her. "Gory, this is not the time to get your blood pressure steaming."

"Well, I'm not changing sides, but I certainly can look. Gawd," Elizabeth said in exasperation. "Ya gotta lighten up, woman. I've not seen you this focused."

Amy ignored Elizabeth's remarks. She looked around for other friends. She waved to several of her customers. Good, she thought, they needed to be here. She watched as two men approached the blonde and spoke quietly to her. She nodded several times. Amy tried to listen but couldn't pick up any words. After a few moments, the two men walked away and the blonde resumed programming her computer.

The local reporters were out in force. Several waved to Elizabeth. She waved back. The television stations were on the side, their cameras pointed toward the front. The blonde seemed oblivious to all the activity around her, people coming in and sitting down. Amy looked around. It seemed like a good turnout. The whole front half of the building was filled with people, all her neighbors. She wondered how many were there in opposition and how many were there because they dreamed of riches. She also wondered how many fence-sitters there were. She, Elizabeth, Maggie Beth and Terry had met at her store earlier and gone over some of the questions they planned to ask. They all had copies of the questions so if someone didn't get recognized another might.

Amy felt a hand on her shoulder. "Hi hon," Maggie said as she and Terry sat down behind her. They were dressed in matching Boston Red Sox golf shirts. Maggie was wearing tan slacks. Terry, jeans.

Amy and Elizabeth turned around and greeted them.

"Good turnout." Maggie glanced around the room.

"Better than I've seen in a long time," Amy said. "And they're still coming in. I figured we'd have a good turnout. I didn't expect we'd fill the high school gymnasium, but it looks like we might."

"Check out the blonde." Elizabeth nodded toward the front.

"I saw her," Maggie said. "Acts like she's alone in the room. Now that's control. I'd be trying to figure out which one planned to stab me."

"Stop." Terry affectionately slapped at her hand.

"I picked up the handouts," Maggie said.

"We did too." Amy held up the sheets.

"Couple of people plan to record this," Elizabeth said under her breath.

"Really?" Maggie asked.

"Just so we have a permanent record. Don't want them six months from now saying they never said it even though one hundred people heard them." Elizabeth nodded knowingly.

"Good idea." Maggie stopped when one of the men stood up.

"Excuse me," he called. "Can I have your attention?" His voice carried over the din of the crowd and soon people stopped talking and turned their attention to the speaker. "It's five minutes after seven and we should get started. I'm Dean Creager, project director. This is"—he stopped and pointed at the man to his right—"Bill Leighton, our technical advisor. And the able woman handling the Power Point presentation is Susan Iogen."

Amy watched as Creager waited for more people to stop talking.

After a moment, he continued, "We thought we'd begin with a Power Point presentation. Believe me, it's not long and we're not going to bore you with a lot of facts, because right now we're only in the preliminary stages of this. We want to see if this will be a good fit for us and for you. But first, we thought we'd talk about LNG, what is it, where it comes from—" He paused and looked at the man sitting next to him. "Bill is our technical expert. He's going to talk about those issues and more. I'm more the money man. I'll talk about the safety issues and about the kinds of dollars and cents you could see pouring into this community if we decide to go ahead with the project. We'd appreciate it if you'd hold all your questions until the end. That way we can get through the presentations, which will take about thirty minutes, and then that'll leave about an hour and a half for questions."

Several people in the audience groaned.

"We will stay longer, but we figured two hours was long enough," the LNG man said. "We're going to be holding additional focus group meetings in the weeks and months ahead." He nodded to the blonde to begin.

She turned on the computer and flashed the first picture on the screen. Her voice was well modulated, even pleasant. Amy thought it would have been nice just listening to her voice if her message hadn't been so terrifying.

Chapter Nine

"Everything you wanted to know about LNG but were afraid to ask," Amy observed after the meeting. They had sat through the presentation and the question-and-answer period. But promptly at nine o'clock the developers ended the meeting. Amy, Maggie, Terry and Elizabeth were at McDonald's. They agreed they were just wound to tight to go home.

"I'm sorry Kelly couldn't join us," Elizabeth said brightly.

"Me too," Amy said soberly. "This was more important than any old hospital board meeting."

"Not if you work for the hospital," Maggie said gently. "Kelly made the right choice."

Amy shrugged. "Anyway, do you think these guys are serious about putting something that monstrous in our bay?"

"Serious as a thumbtack," Elizabeth said, leafing through the information she had picked up.

"They're talking about a six-hundred-million-dollar project. A huge pier that juts halfway across the bay and"—Terry glanced at

Maggie's handouts—"two huge tanks and two smaller ones that will hold the stuff. The two big tanks are large enough to each hold two seven-forty-seven aircraft sitting one on top of the other."

"I was absolutely overwhelmed by it all," Amy interjected. "Up until tonight I had never thought about liquefied natural gas. It's like electricity, you just turn it on and it works, you never think about where it comes from."

"What's really amazing," Elizabeth said after taking a sip of her coffee, "is that we don't even have the stuff here. We heat our houses with either propane or oil. Although, did you notice they suggested that it'll lead to construction of electric power plants here and on the mainland? But my question is, do we have enough people to offset the costs of building something like that?"

"Good question. We'll need to ask it next time." Maggie paged through some of the literature that had been handed out. "These guys are serious. They plan on bringing ships the size of four football fields into our bay, each one filled with something that could blow us all up." She nodded, wide-eyed and solemn. "Ships that will be coming from places like Algeria, Libya, Malaysia, Oman, Qatar, Trinidad—countries that hate us. Who's to say there wouldn't be some kind of terrorist activity?"

"The developers," Amy summed up. "Notice how they kept saying how safe it is. They kept repeating there've been no serious incidents or spills in the past twenty-five years. But what about before?" She frowned. "They kept insisting this place wouldn't be a target for terrorists because we don't have the population density of, say, Boston. Well, we might not have the population density, but I'll tell you we've got that long unprotected border with Canada, and a terrorist could walk right in here undetected, do his or her job and leave on the next bus. And we'd make national news—hell, we'd make international news. And it would show just how vulnerable little America is."

"Notice how they kept stressing that they're going to bring in only state-of-the-art?" Elizabeth asked, obviously frustrated. "What the hell does that mean? Hell, I'm a state-of-the-art woman, but I still got flaws."

They all laughed. Maggie leaned over and punched Elizabeth gently on the arm. "That you are, my dear. You are definitely state-of-the-art." She stared down at the handouts. "Well, they did stress the safety features a lot. They also focused on the fact that it was a cleaner energy fuel than coal or oil and that it was nontoxic."

"That tech guy said something about how you could extinguish a cigarette in it. Who'd want to?" Terry frowned.

"Well, they did have a point," Maggie said with a shrug. "Maybe there hasn't been any accident or spill in the United States, but even so that didn't make me feel any better."

"You know what, though?" Amy said lightly. "Let's assume everything they said was correct. Let's say it is safe and there wouldn't be any harm to the environment and it would be state-of-the-art like our friend here." She glanced at Elizabeth. "But that really doesn't matter. What they failed to address was destroying one of the prettiest bays in the country, or the world, for that matter. We'd look like Long Beach, California. With an ugly pier and monstrous tanks sitting around."

"I gotta kick out of the tech guy. When someone asked about the tanks he said they'd hold a contest and let local artists paint them."

Elizabeth laughed. "Yeah, I could picture a kind of Andy Warhol soup can on the side of a tank. Do they honestly believe that a bunch of murals could replace what we have to look at?"

"I expect they do, because they suggested it." Maggie Beth wrinkled her brow. "But the next step is, what do we do?"

"I thought about that." Amy was smiling. "We go see the governor."

"Just like that?" Terry asked.

"Just like that." Amy nodded, sure that her plan was a good one.

"Do we know the governor?" Maggie asked.

"No," Amy admitted.

"I do," Elizabeth said.

"You do?" the three almost said in unison.

"I gave to his campaign." Elizabeth shrugged. "I mean, it's not like he's my best friend. But he's been into the office. Met with

Gary a couple of times. We chatted. I bet I could get an audience with him. He seemed like a nice enough guy."

Amy sat upright. "Let's do it. Let's go see the governor."

"I don't think that will work, but I'll tell you, I know what would work," Maggie said. "Let's organize. We'll create a name and start peppering the company and the locals with questions and information. Then let's go see the governor. If we have a cross section of islanders who go see him, I bet he'll see us."

Amy pondered Maggie's suggestions. "Y'know, you're right. The governor could give a hoot if we want to see him or not." She looked quickly at Elizabeth. "I'm not minimizing your contacts with him," she added hastily. "I just agree with Maggie that there is power in numbers and if we organize into a group—say, fifty of the islanders—that's a pretty good cross section."

Maggie picked up her coffee and sipped it. "I got the feeling that some people liked what they had to say. 'Specially after Billy Parker asked them what was in it for us."

"That surprised me," Amy said thoughtfully. "Not the question, but the answer. Did I hear them right that they couldn't go into details because they've been negotiating with town officials, and didn't the project manager say something about it'd be similar to the agreement they had down in Harpswell? If I remember correctly, they offered that town eight million dollars a year for fifty years. It would have paid the property taxes for everyone. They almost took it. The vote was close."

"They did and he did," Terry said.

"That's going to be tough," Amy said after a moment. "That's tempting. We've got a lot of poor people in town. Just think if you didn't have to come up with, say, a thousand dollars in taxes each year."

"Thousand?" Maggie bellowed. "Try four thousand for those of us on the bay."

"No, I didn't mean those of us on the shore," Amy interjected. "Most of us have pretty decent jobs so we can afford to pay that. We don't enjoy it, but we can pay it. I meant the guy who has to spend hours bent over digging clams or picking periwinkles.

That's the one I think was listening. It's that guy or woman," she added hastily, "I think may have bought into the message."

"Not necessarily," Elizabeth said. "I talked to some of the fishermen after we all walked out and they were concerned. Giving them a thousand dollars a year ain't nothing to the fifty thousand they make taking care of their families. These guys are concerned about spills, what it could do the water and the shore. They mentioned Exxon Valdez. Funny," she mused, "I probably couldn't tell you of one other spill in this country from a ship, but you just mention those two words and everyone knows what you're talking about."

Amy nodded, remembering the huge oil spill in Alaska that occurred after Exxon's ship went aground. "So our plan of action is what?" she asked.

"Organize." Maggie set her cup on the table. "We'll begin tomorrow. Call some of those people at the meeting. Ask them where they sit on this. Those for it, don't try to change their mind. Those against it, ask them to join our group."

"Where should we meet?" Terry asked.

"I've got a room in the back of the store," Amy said. "There are some boxes sitting around, but I have a table and chairs back there too. I use it to do some of my accounting stuff. It's roomy. We could put a coffeepot back there."

"Good idea," Elizabeth enthused. "Why not make a list of those there tonight?"

"Darn." Maggie shook her head. "We should have asked for a copy of the sign-in sheet."

"I think they'd wonder why we wanted it." Amy paused. "Better we just sit here now and write down the names of those who were there. Then split the list and make the calls tomorrow."

"Anyone have any paper?" Maggie asked.

The others looked around. "I've got an idea." Terry got up and went to the counter and pulled several napkins from the holder. She walked back to the threesome. "Seems appropriate that we make our list on a napkin—'cause it's like the presentation tonight—paper thin," she said with a laugh.

Chapter Ten

Driving home, Amy thought about the conversation at McDonald's. They had been able to come up with about sixty names, people they knew or who knew them. They decided they needed more than fifty names because they'd run into the fence-sitters and the non-joiners. Several on the list were dear friends and Amy knew they'd be on their side.

She turned her car into the driveway, where Kelly's car was parked. She felt buoyed and optimistic about the group's plans and she wanted to share them. She knew she had been a bit testy of late, but she also knew it was for all the right reasons. Oh well, she thought. Kelly was no doubt pouting about the last fight. She guessed she'd have to make it up to her. Take her to dinner, or buy her something. She could see the light on in the kitchen. Good, she thought, she's probably made a pot of coffee. Like her, Kelly loved to sit in the kitchen, sip coffee and talk. Kitchens were the meeting rooms of most houses in Maine.

When she had renovated the 150-year-old Cape, she'd had a new chimney built in the kitchen. She'd also installed a cast-iron wood stove that she could cook on and use as a source of heat for the kitchen. The cookstove's firebox had a window in it, so at night it put off a romantic glow. There was a large round oak table with claw feet in the middle of the room. Oak chairs surrounded the table. There was a porcelain-covered cast iron sink with a replica of an antique faucet. She had searched high and low for that. A small hand pump, nothing more than decoration, sat on the counter next to the sink. She had caved in and bought some modern appliances, including a dishwasher, but she'd had a cupboard built around it to hide it from the rest of the kitchen.

She had planned to use as many antique appliances as possible, but she'd learned her lesson from a magazine article written by some New York guy who'd been an absolute purest when it came to antiques. He was a yard sale, junk shop and flea market addict and had gone out and bought an old toaster that looked like a silver pyramid. You flipped open the sides, put the bread in and then flipped the sides back. He'd also bought an old coffee percolator that you set on the stove and he ground his coffee beans with a hand grinder. Amy smiled. His refrigerator was the rounded version popular in the 1950s. Ultimately, he acknowledged he had to give up on the appliances. The toaster almost burned down his condo, the refrigerator died and went to Frigidaire heaven, and he had tired of hand-grinding his coffee beans.

She parked the car next to Kelly's.

Kelly heard the car door slam and looked up as soon as Amy opened the door. "How was the meeting?"

Amy kissed her on the top of the head. "Good. We're organizing an opposition group."

"Oh! That good." Kelly grinned, trying to keep the moment light. She sighed in relief. Amy seemed back to normal.

"Yeah, that good. Coffee?"

"No, I have some, thanks."

"We stopped at McDonald's afterward. I don't really need this cup of coffee. I won't sleep tonight as it is." Amy paused as she poured herself a cup. "First off, I'm sorry I've been grumpy. I know I took it out on you," she said abruptly. "But this is a bad one, Kelly. They want to put this mile-long pier out into the bay. They have to get to about four hundred feet of water and that's where it is. The ships they're going to bring in are going to make our fishing boats look like floating gnats." She sipped her coffee and sat down. "They're something like four football fields long. And on top of that they're going to build three or four storage tanks right next to the marina that are going to absolutely dwarf the town."

"You're kidding. That's huge."

Amy explained that the project would cost $600 million. "Just so the developers can pipe natural gas to Boston," she added.

"How they going to do that?"

"They're going to run miles of pipeline under the bay to the mainland at Port Bleu and tie in with that pipeline those Exxon and Mobil people built about ten years ago that starts in Nova Scotia. Then it'll be piped along Route Nine to Boston."

"Wow, they're going to absolutely decimate the bay. I can't believe people here will go along with that." Kelly could visualize the huge tanks and realized how they would harm the view of the bay. She didn't like it. The view of the bay was why many of the new people had gravitated to the island.

"Sweeten the pot and they might."

"What do you mean?"

"The guy who did most of the talking, I think he called himself the project director, said they'd been negotiating with town officials for some kind of sweet deal. Something about paying everyone's property taxes for the next fifty years. Everybody in town, that is. It's the same deal they offered down south, only those people were smart enough to say no. They didn't go into detail. We're just speculating that's what they're going to do."

"Whoa," Kelly said.

"Yeah, whoa."

"That's a tough one. A lot of poor people here, they'd see that as a darn good deal. So what's next?"

"We're organizing. Made a list of everyone at the meeting tonight."

"Were there a lot there?"

Amy's brow knitted. "I'd say way over a hundred. There's, what"—she paused—"a thousand winter and spring people, so it was a decent turnout. Course if they'd called off the hospital board meeting, there'd been another fifty people there."

Kelly frowned, hoping Amy wasn't going to resurrect that sore point. She had made up her mind that whatever mood Amy came home in she was not going to go back over that old ground.

"Just kidding," Amy added hastily. "We're going to meet in the back room at the store. I probably should order some cigars?"

"Cigars?"

"Yeah." Amy smirked. "You remember reading in history class about the back-room cigar-toting politicians who used to decide the fate of this country. Now they're Glenfiddich-guzzling politicians but doing just about the same thing, deciding the fate of this country in back rooms."

Kelly grinned. "Well, I can see the organizational meeting, *sans* the cigars."

"Agreed." Amy smiled. "I missed you and I love you."

"That's nice."

Amy got up and walked behind Kelly's chair and began to kiss the top of her head, then along the side of her neck.

"Feeling a little frisky tonight?" Kelly sighed. She wanted to talk about what had been bothering her. The one thing she and Amy shared well was their lovemaking. They could talk about the past tomorrow, she told herself as her body warmed to Amy's touch.

"All that coffee and activity. My adrenaline is pumping, love." She turned Kelly's mouth to her and kissed her. Their tongues met. Amy caressed Kelly's chest down to her breasts, cupping first one and then the other. Kelly gasped. "I'm ready. How about right here in the chair?"

"How about in the bed, so we both don't wake up with a backache tomorrow?" Kelly said against Amy's lips.

"Shucks, the spontaneity is gone." Kelly searched Amy's face wondering if she was serious, but she was smiling. "I'll turn off the lights." Amy bent down to kiss her again. "You kiss so well." She sighed.

"You're not half bad yourself, Day. Your kisses make me tingle all over."

"Good." Amy kissed the palm of Kelly's hand. "I'll turn off the lights and be right up."

Chapter Eleven

Susan Iogen parked her metallic-green Volvo in the parking lot at the motel. The LNG meeting had gone well, she thought. There were more people there than either Bill or Dean had predicted. The questions were good, even those from people who were clearly opposed to the project. Susan studied the outside of the motel. It was clean and nice, but she still hated being there. On Monday, she was moving to a rental cottage she had found advertised on television. The first few days she was in town she was first amused and then intrigued by the crawl line on TV. It wasn't that Andover didn't have something like it, but the messages posted on the Bleu Island crawl line were so quaint. She watched, fascinated. There were messages from people thanking their doctors for good medical care. Other people sold stuff. There was even one about giving kittens away. Then she'd seen the rental notice for the cottage, called the number, went to see it and instantly signed a month's lease.

She opened the door. "Honey, I'm home," she said to the empty room. She kicked her shoes off, sat down in the chair and rubbed her feet. She wished designers would make some kind of dressy running shoe, to go along with a skirt. She sighed, feeling wide awake. Meetings like that energized her. The room seemed evenly divided. There were those who obviously did not want the project regardless of what anyone said, while others seemed interested in the information. In Susan's mind it was a slam-dunk. She had researched the town. Although there were a lot of wealthy people in town, it was mostly new wealth from people who had moved to Maine from elsewhere. Jefferson County had the highest unemployment rate in the state. There were still a lot of people on the island and mainland who made their living following the tides, by digging clams or working on boats during the lobster season. Alcoholism was a problem in the county, as was domestic abuse. She sighed, again. She wasn't ready for bed and knew she wouldn't be able to concentrate on reading a book.

She unzipped her skirt and hung it on a hanger. Her half-slip she tossed on the bed. She unbuttoned her blouse and hung it next to her skirt, then pulled on her running pants and a T-shirt. She was ready for a nice long run. Funny, with all the problems she'd read about the place, the information she had gleaned also said it was one of the safest in the state. She tucked her room key in her pocket. Outside she did some stretching exercises before setting off on a nice easy pace. She turned toward the marina. It felt good running. Others turned to cocktails to unwind; she ran.

She ran past the closed shops downtown. The project would change this little community forever, she thought. When the developers had first approached her about it, she'd had her reservations. The first question she'd asked herself was would she want it in her community. Although her firm handled public relations for several companies, Susan had decided early on when she'd started her company that she would not allow money to seduce her into promoting something she did not believe in. The company she had worked for out of college took any and all clients that walked through the door. One time she'd been put on an account for a company that wanted to expand its chemical facility into a small community near Boston. The locals were enraged. And although she was only a minor player on the team, she'd hated every minute of that campaign. The senior team leader kept telling her that advertising and public relations people sold their souls to the highest bidder. That's when she'd quit and decided to start her own firm.

She'd grown up in Andover and still had lots of contacts there. Her father had been an executive in one of the large companies and her mother had worked as a teacher at a local high school. She started small, just her and a telephone. Now, ten years later, she had a part-time secretary and she could sleep at night knowing that what she was selling she also would be buying if she were on the other end of the business deal.

At forty years old she felt confident about what she had and about her life. The only thing missing was someone to cuddle up to at night. Susan frowned. *Don't go there*, she said to herself. *Don't go there.* She paused at the edge of the marina, panting from the run.

"You're out pretty late."

Susan jumped and turned toward the female voice. "So are you, I might add."

The voice stepped out of the shadow. "Sometimes, I walk my dog this time of night. She's over there somewhere. My name's Elizabeth Robinson and you're the LNG lady."

Susan laughed. "I am. You scared me. I didn't expect to find anyone down here at this time of night. It must be close to, what—"

"Eleven," Elizabeth answered. "Here, Spike." She whistled.

Susan watched as a tiny little dog ran toward them. She chuckled. "Spike? The name's bigger than the dog."

Elizabeth smiled. "You could say that." She picked the dog up. "Spike, I'd like you to meet Susan . . ." She paused.

"Iogen." Susan reached over and shook the pup's paw. "And you are the town clerk."

"How'd you know? You've not been to the town office."

"Someone mentioned it to me at the meeting." Susan extended her hand. "Nice to meet you."

"Same here." Elizabeth shook her hand. "Well, I can't really say that. I mean . . ." She sputtered in embarrassment. "I . . ."

"I understand—you're happy to meet me, not my message."

"Something like that."

"It's hard. This is a whole new concept. Something dropped on you from out of the blue. So I understand that people are concerned, but right now I think they don't have enough information to know how they feel."

"I don't agree. I think you saw some evenly divided camps there tonight. You had those who'll buy into it, regardless. Others who absolutely are opposed to it. Then that third group that wants to know more."

"I'm not going to ask you which side you're on."

"I don't have any problem telling you I'm against it. I see this messing up our landscape. I'm worried about terrorists and safety, but more importantly I'm worried about our way of life. You want to take an area that for hundreds of years has been nothing more than a beautiful fishing community and turn it into some kind of international port. Building that pier and those tanks is going to destroy one of the prettiest places on earth. I just think you haven't thought that through."

"Well, that pretty much puts it out there." Susan mentally embraced the black velvet expanse of night. Lights flickered across the bay at Port Bleu. "It's pretty down here."

"That's it?" Elizabeth demanded. "You're not going to argue with me?"

"Would it do any good?"

Elizabeth frowned. "No."

Susan laughed. "Then why debate it. Why not talk about something else. About what a pretty night it is or how wonderful the sea breeze feels?"

Elizabeth frowned. "You're good." She chuckled. "You're very good. Where you from?"

"Andover."

73

"That's a beautiful city. Why not put this thing down there?"

"No ocean." Susan spoke just loudly enough to be heard.

"I knew that. Why not put it in Portland?"

"That one I can't answer."

"That's what I thought."

"Not because I don't want to answer it, I just don't know. That question should be asked of the developer. I was hired to help—"

"Persuade people it should be here," Elizabeth finished.

Susan knew she shouldn't argue the point. "I think *persuade* is not the right word. I was hired to help the developers get their message out."

"Same difference," Elizabeth grumbled.

"You're irritated." Susan tried to lighten the moment. For some reason she was drawn to Elizabeth. She was a tiny woman, dressed in baggy running pants and a sweatshirt, but her inner strength vibrated like humming electric lines. "How long you been town clerk?"

"Forever," Elizabeth said. "More than ten years. You're right, you know."

"About?"

"I shouldn't be mad at you, you're just doing your job."

Susan shrugged. "That doesn't make you feel better."

"You're right, it doesn't." Elizabeth laughed then said softly, "You going to be here long?"

"A while."

"Where you staying?"

"At the motel, but I've rented a small cottage on the other side of the island."

"The Grange place?"

"That's it. A lovely little place. How'd you know?"

"Not much around here people don't know. We're a small town. What we don't know we make up."

Susan laughed. "Well, I'll let that be a lesson to me."

Elizabeth joined in the laughter. "You've never lived in a small town, have you?"

"No, this is a first. Although I must say I like it. You feel—"

"Safe here," Elizabeth finished, clearly a habit. "We have our crime, but mostly it's domestic stuff. Some other kinds of things, but usually it's people preying on folks they know. We've never had a murder on this island."

"Never?"

"That's what I said."

"I find that amazing."

"Life's different here than in the city. In the city you got all these people crowded together. That rat syndrome. Put a bunch of rats in a small area and they start killing each other. Something like people."

Susan shook her head, amused. "You're right."

"Here there's nothing but open spaces. You want to get away, you can. Walk on the beach. Walk in the woods. You name it there's a place to go to get away."

"Like tonight."

"Yeah, like tonight. Answer me this." Elizabeth bent over and put Spike on the ground. "Would you go out at night and run like this in Andover?"

"Nope."

"Well, after you build that LNG terminal you won't do it here either," Elizabeth said, returning to their original theme.

"Because?"

"Because this place is going to change forever. We're going to end up like those rats."

Susan turned to look at the water. "Well, on that note, I think I'll just run back to my motel."

"Look"—Elizabeth reached out and touched her arm—"I didn't mean to insult you. That's not what I do. I guess this is just a little too raw yet and I have the woman who's promoting it right here to lash out at, so I apologize. I'm not usually this rude."

"No need to apologize. This is something that's hard. Agreed, it's going to change your lifestyle here, but change isn't always bad." Susan shrugged. "Anyway, I'm not here to force this on you

75

folks. I'm here to just present a new concept. That's it. If you don't buy it then that's between you and the developers. That's not a copout. Believe me, I hear people all the time saying, look, I didn't make the law, I'm just here to enforce it, or it's not my decision, I'm just here to tell you about it." She paused. "Anyway, it's late and I do have to get back." She extended her hand again. "It was nice meeting you, Elizabeth. I hope we meet again."

"Me too." Elizabeth's voice had softened. "A word of advice?"

"Sure."

"Tell your developer friends not to rush it, give people a chance to digest this. I'm not sure how the whole town feels, but I know feelings are running pretty high against it for some of us. Tell your developers that if they can make a good case for why it should be here, people will listen. They might not go along with it, but they'll listen. Just tell them they can't cram this down our throats. I figure the selectmen are going to want to turn this over to the residents because they know it's too hot to handle. They probably are going to put it out for a vote. Let the townsfolk decide. But just take it slowly. Give us good accurate information and let us decide."

Susan appreciated her candor. "Agreed, Elizabeth. That's why I'm here. I am going to try and give you the best information I and the developers have. And I'll pass your advice on to them. Well, good night again." She turned back to the road. "And nice talking with you."

"Agreed," Elizabeth yelled. "Let's do lunch, like they do in Andover."

"You're on," Susan called over her shoulder.

I like her, she thought. She felt the pull of her muscles as she started up the hill toward her motel. Somehow, she knew Elizabeth was a no-nonsense woman.

It would be nice to have lunch with her. *I'm going to have lunch with her*, she decided. When she had left Andover she knew it would be a lonely time here because some people would hate the

76

message and would want to kill the messenger. Except for the evening conferences with the developers, she was prepared to sit alone at night in her motel room. Before she'd moved to the island she'd done her homework and knew there wasn't even a bowling alley, even though she hadn't bowled since she was in high school. The motel desk clerk suggested she go to the mainland if she was looking for some social time but warned her that the ferry stopped running at ten o'clock, so if she wanted to go to the movies, she'd better make it an early one or plan to spend the night in Port Bleu.

There was plenty to do with her job. She had set up interviews for the developers with the media, all scheduled for Friday. She would be there to make certain the interviews went smoothly. After that she would spend her time with the focus groups—fishermen, property owners, business owners—to get a feel for where the project sat with them. Then it was just a matter of churning out another press release; there would be many more to come. Then it would be dinner and back to her motel. The developers had rented a small storefront on Main Street and she had set up shop there. She was going to order some signs so that people with questions knew where to find them.

Susan sighed as she turned into the motel driveway. Not much time for a social life. She scoffed. She didn't have time for a social life. Heck, she thought, except for a few friends she hadn't had much of a social life in Andover.

She didn't even want to count how many nights she sat home alone reading a book or watching television. It had been too many years since she'd had someone to cuddle up with on the couch. Someone to share her life with. Her friends had told her she was just too driven, too focused on building her business, and admittedly she was. Then she'd been approached to handle this LNG public relations project. It was the biggest contract she'd ever accepted and if this was a success, she knew it would put her in a new league in Andover's public relations world. It would open doors to other contracts. She might even be able to hire another person to work with her. Maybe even make her secretary full-time.

After she'd started her own business, she'd determined that

nothing would distract her. Her friends had said she was too engrossed, but that was too kind. She had been downright maniacal about the success of Iogen, Inc. She opened the door to her room. "Honey, I'm home," she said again to the dark. At least, she thought as she threw her keys on the dresser, when she moved into the cottage she would feel less temporary, less transient. The project was scheduled to last at least six months, longer if needed.

As she stripped off her sweaty shirt and running pants, she thought about Elizabeth. She'd give it a couple of days and then call her, she thought. See if she was true to her word and wanted to have lunch or if she was just doing the social thing and saying she wanted to have lunch.

Chapter Twelve

"Good morning, Loraine," Kelly said as she entered the hospital. "Go to the LNG meeting last night?"

"No." Loraine looked up and smiled. "Whatever happens, happens. I can't change it so why waste my time? Besides, it doesn't really affect us. We live in town. From what I read in the newspaper, we won't ever see it from our house."

Kelly frowned. "You'll see it when you come across on the ferry."

"Aw, I'll look the other way. Here's your messages." Loraine handed her the slips.

"Thank you." Kelly headed toward her office. She was surprised by Loraine's indifference to the project. Loraine and her husband had grown up on the island. They'd gone to school together and, like Amy and Elizabeth, they should care more than anyone. She shook her head as she thought about it. She knew about the psychology of indifference. Regardless of where it was built, it would impact everyone, yet Loraine didn't care because it wasn't in her immediate back yard. Looking the other way when riding the ferry seemed downright absurd.

Kelly remembered the first time she had crossed on the ferry. When she glimpsed the tiny fishing village with its red buildings and small piers jutting out into the water, it had taken her breath away. She felt like she was looking at a picture on a calendar. And wrapped around the island was nothing but blue water. That day puffy white clouds hung like marshmallows in the sky and added to the picture.

That day she'd turned onto Main Street and followed it to the marina. There in front of her were stately granite rocks that looked like they had skirts of water around them. They stood like rock hard sentries guarding the port.

After she'd been on the island for a while she discovered that islanders had mountain goat in their blood and could hop from rock to rock until they were sitting out on the last rock with nothing but waltzing water all around them. Soon she too was hopping from rock to rock. It was the first place she and Amy had gone for a picnic. It had been a chore, balancing the picnic basket as she scrambled up the rocks, but Amy had made it seem so simple.

Kelly shuffled the messages. She saw one from Laurie and picked up the telephone. She listened to the ring and then the click of Laurie's answering machine.

"Hey, pal, I don't know if you're home or at the hospital, but I got your message and I'll be here the rest of the day. Have the switchboard page me if I'm not in my office."

The rest of the calls could wait, she thought as she turned on her computer. Within seconds the computer came to life and pictures of her and Amy began to dissolve from one to the other across the screen. The night before had been wonderful, their lovemaking intense and complete. Amy had been energized from the meeting and that energy had translated into multiple orgasms for both of them. Afterward, Amy had turned on her side and fallen asleep.

The first few times they'd made love in the early years of their relationship, their lovemaking had been very intense. With the afterglow still burning her flesh, she would crawl into Amy's arm, lay her head against her shoulder and just languish in the pleasure her lover had brought to her body. But Amy, satisfied, always turned over and went to sleep.

The first time, Kelly had tried to talk about it, to tell her of her need to just snuggle afterward, Amy had taken it as a personal slight, an insult to their night of making love. They'd had a fight. Kelly rubbed her chin. Funny, most people didn't remember their first fight. There'd been tears and painful words, but finally Amy heard her words and did try to cuddle afterward, but most often she'd forget and fall asleep.

Kelly jumped when the telephone rang. "Hello."

"Hey, lady. What are you doing?" It was Laurie.

Kelly grimaced at the thoughts she had been pondering. "Nothing really, just administration stuff. What's going on with you? You quit your job yet?"

"Done." Kelly could hear the excitement in Laurie's voice. "Gave my notice yesterday. They were great, offered me more money if I'd stay, said they were in the process of revamping things at the hospital. I just kept smiling and saying no thank you. When I told them I was going to your neck of the state, they couldn't believe it. The director of nursing kept saying, 'But they can't pay you anything.' I laughed. Told her this ain't about money."

"No, my friend, it ain't about money," Kelly repeated.

"Anyway, I gave them a month's notice. I should be up there shortly after the Fourth of July."

"Bummer."

"Why bummer?"

"That's one of our best holidays here. Everyone turns out. This little town swells to about ten thousand people. We have the biggest parade ever in Jefferson County. Bands come from all over, including Canada. It's fantastic."

"Well, I don't have to work that holiday. I may just come up and get a sampling of it all before I move."

"I think that'd be great. Look, why don't you stay with Amy and me. It'll give Amy a real chance to get to know you."

81

"Also give me time to look around for an apartment."

"Don't even think about an apartment, woman."

"Why? I need a place to live."

"We don't really have anything like that in the whole town. But friends of mine are retired real estate brokers and they know of some house rentals."

"Can I afford a whole house? We haven't even talked salary."

Kelly laughed. "You can afford it. You're coming to Bleu Island, not Siberia. Salaries are not that far off the mark. Big city hospitals just like to think they are."

"Great. That'd give me an opportunity to look around. And I'd like to get to know Amy better. What—we talked maybe once or twice the whole time you've been up there—I regret that." There was a tinge of sadness in Laurie's voice. "I've missed you. I really have. Let's not let life come between us again. Agreed?"

"Agreed. So it's settled. You come up the Friday before the long weekend. We usually have a lobster feed for all of our friends, both gay and straight. You'll get to know some really cool people and you'll be able to look around for a rental. Heck, figure on staying with us until you get moved in."

"We'll see about that. Long-term company is worse than clams left setting out in the sun."

Kelly laughed. "Agreed, but I don't think you'll ever stick around that long. In the meantime, Maggie Beth and Terry— they're the real estate agents I mentioned—are looking at places for you. I know they'll have something to show you when you get here. You're going to love them. You know"—she tilted her head in thought—"I've made some truly best friends here. In five years I've connected with some terrific people, but those two women are the best."

"I'm glad. I just wish I'd moved with you years ago instead of sticking around in a relationship that was like old milk that just got sourer and sourer. By the way, does Amy have a best friend?"

"Amy has more friends than God."

"I don't mean friends. I mean a friend." Laurie dragged the last word out.

"Oh, that kind of friend. Uh-huh. I ain't doing that matchmaking thing with you. I just get into trouble. Remember my ex's friend, Darlene?"

Laurie groaned. "Do I. She was as numb as a hake."

"I thought Robin and I were going to break up over that."

"I remember." Laurie laughed. "Darlene told her all those lousy things about me. It felt like she'd dropped a dirty bomb on my life, and of course Robin, the so-called love of your life, didn't like me to begin with so she just glommed onto all that stuff."

"I felt like I had a cauliflower ear from listening to her. Finally, she settled down and realized that it just hadn't worked for the two of you. So I ain't ever going there again. You're on your own. Besides, I thought you'd given up women."

"Well, that was before, today is different. Any prospects?"

"Would you stop? You just broke up with someone and already you're hot to trot."

"Hey, lady, I ain't getting any younger and I don't want these supple lips of mine to chap." Laurie laughed.

Kelly thought about those supple lips. Lips that looked like two cushions in a distinctive face accented by terra-cotta brown eyes and raven hair. Laurie was about Kelly's height but stockier. Laurie called it her "athletic frame." They were both thirty-six, so Laurie's argument that she was getting older didn't wash with Kelly. She said, "Slow it down, pal. You're here to work and then search. Remember, work and then search."

"I'm just yanking you. Right now I don't need another woman in my life. I need to get over this latest mental bruising. So not to worry, I'm coming there to work, but if I just happen to find something warm and cuddly I probably won't look the other way."

"You're bad, really bad, Laurie Stocking."

"I know, but y'know—" There was a pause, then Laurie said seriously, "I'm really looking forward to working with you again. I know it's different this time, you're not on the floor with me, but you're still going to be there and that gives me a lot of comfort."

"Actually, I'm glad you're back in my life. I've missed our talks, our . . ." Kelly paused, searching for the right word. "Our history together. We've pulled each other out of a lot of broken hearts."

"Speaking of hearts, how is your main squeeze?"

"Amy? She's fine."

"She's got to be great. Anyone who can turn my best friend's head is someone I want to know."

Kelly laughed. "Well, you'll have that chance when you come house-hunting. See if you can arrange your schedule so you can spend a couple of days with us. I'm not concerned about finding you a place to live. Heck, we'll do that as soon as you get here. After that let's play. I don't work any kind of swing shift; I'm eight to five Monday through Friday so we could spend some time together. Go out on the boat. And speaking of boats, probably better to go out now than after they build an LNG terminal down here."

"You're kidding. Have they got your island in their sights?"

"'Fraid so."

"Wow, we went through that here. Not right here in Portland, but I followed it first in Harpswell and then Sears Island. People were hopping mad about it. Really put up a fight. The company tucked its tail between its legs and left."

"Well, I don't know that much about it. They had an information meeting last night, but I had a hospital meeting and couldn't go. From what Amy said we're talking huge. Something that will really dominate the bay."

"How are people reacting?"

"Don't know, except Amy said people seemed divided." Kelly frowned as she recalled the initial fight she'd had with Amy over the board meeting. "I suspect something like this is going to have to go to the town for a vote. I don't believe our selectmen are going to make a unilateral decision. People would chop them up and smoke them like they used to do herring around here."

"Is Amy upset?"

"She's going to be leading the charge. She's a self-propelled torpedo when she sets her mind to something. She knows a lot of people. Her friend Elizabeth is the town clerk and she's in the thick of it. Other friends are rallying in opposition. Amy's going to have her first organizational meeting sometime this week. Knowing her, they'll come up with a great name and an aggressive information campaign of their own."

"Well, you can count me in. Like I said, I followed it closely down here and I didn't like anything that I read. I know the argument that we have to have some kind of stopgap energy program, but I'm not sure this is it."

"Amy will appreciate the help, I know."

"Hey, I can march on a picket line with the best of them."

Kelly laughed. "Ah, there's my other line. Gotta go. So I can count on you for the Fourth of July?"

"Absolutely, looking forward to it."

That evening, Kelly picked Jasper up as soon as she opened the door. "Hey, I'm home."

"I'm upstairs."

Kelly carried Jasper up with her. Amy was in the bedroom putting clothes from the dryer away.

"Hi." Kelly kissed the top of her head.

"You can do better than that!" Amy put her arms around her and gave her a smoldering kiss.

"You're right." Kelly kissed her back. "I can do better than that." She dropped Jasper on the bed and pulled Amy against her. "Got some good news."

"What's that?"

"I invited Laurie to stay with us for the Fourth, and she accepted."

Amy stepped back. "You're kidding. You invited her without asking me?"

"Well, yeah, we were talking on the telephone and she's handed in her resignation. At the party you said she could stay with us. You said it again later." Her tone was slightly defensive.

"Well, yes. I just thought you'd ask me first before inviting her."

"Why are you getting so upset? I told you we were talking about it and she said she had the long weekend off, so I asked her."

"You know, Kelly Burns, you seem to forget two people live in this house."

"What's the big deal?"

"The big deal is I'll have someone underfoot when I'm getting ready for the party."

"What am I, chopped liver? I'll help get us ready for the party. It's not just you."

"I just wish you'd ask."

"Fine, I'll call her and tell her not to come. Tell her that I need to ask you first." Kelly could hear the sarcasm in her voice and stopped. She didn't want another fight.

"So you can embarrass me? I don't think so." Amy stuffed the last of the clothes in the dresser. "Just forget about it, but in the future I would appreciate it if you'd ask." She turned and walked out of the bedroom.

Kelly stared after her open-mouthed. How the hell did that happen? She'd just invited Laurie for a few days. She hadn't asked her to stay with them for a year. She followed Amy downstairs. "What's going on?"

"Nothing."

"Amy, something's going on."

"I said nothing is going on. I'm getting ready to fix dinner. Why don't you start the grill."

"I'm not going anywhere until we talk this out."

"All right." Amy's face was tense with anger. "I don't like surprises. I don't like them dumped on me. I have a lot of stress preparing for the party and I just don't think it's fair that you would ask someone who is a veritable stranger to me into my house."

"Our house, Amy."

86

"Whatever."

"Our house," Kelly said quietly.

"All right, our house. Don't change the subject. You could have called me at work, said it had come up in conversation. You could have called her back and invited her after we had talked about it."

"It was spontaneous. I didn't plan to ask her. It just happened."

"Well, I hope it won't happen in the future."

"It won't, Amy, believe me. You're right, this is your house. I moved in with you."

"Now, don't be like that."

"Like what? You just reminded me this is your house."

"I didn't mean it the way it sounded."

"How did you mean it?"

"Just forget about it, go start the grill."

Exasperated, Kelly stared at Amy. "Living with you is like walking on eggs. I never know when one is going to break and set you off."

"That's not fair, Kelly."

"Maybe not, but it's true." Kelly opened the door. "I'll start the grill."

Chapter Thirteen

On Friday evening after she'd closed the shop, Amy went into the back room and filled the coffeepot with water. From a Ziploc baggie she dumped the coffee she had ground at home into the filter. It was nearly six. She'd had just enough time to change her clothes and eat the sandwich she had brought from home. Kelly was still at the hospital. She knew Kelly was still upset about her reaction to Laurie's visit and God only knew what else. So what if she'd said invite her. She still expected her to discuss it before doing so. Kelly was wrong this time, and Amy was going to wait her out until she admitted she was wrong. This wasn't her fault. She had more important things to think about.

After their meeting at McDonald's the group had spent two days working the phones. Although there had been disappointments from people Amy thought would join, they still had commitments from at least thirty people willing to put together a group opposed to LNG. Tonight was their first strategy meeting.

Amy opened the box from Dunkin' Donuts and put it next to the coffeepot. She set napkins and plastic spoons next to the sugar bowl and milk pitcher. She looked up when the door opened.

"Hey, love." She walked over to greet Elizabeth. "Somehow I knew you'd be the first to arrive." She kissed her on the cheek.

Elizabeth gave her a big hug. "Where's Kelly?"

Amy frowned. "Working."

"I expect there's lots going on at the hospital." Elizabeth held up a bag. "I brought cranberry bread," she said as she put a loaf pan and serrated knife on the table. "Is everything okay?" She put her hand on Amy's arm.

"I don't know. We've seemed . . ." Amy let the words trail off. "You know something funny." She rushed on, not expecting an answer, "I was thinking about you and Lois tonight."

"In what way?"

"I was remembering the first time I was with the two of you. I was in high school, and you'd invited a bunch of us over to your house for a cookout on Earth Day. I remember how much fun we had, but honestly, before that you were always around, but I'd never really thought much about you." Amy tilted her head back in thought. "I thought you were just old, like my teachers. Although I thought you were pretty neat, because you had your own lobstering boat and used to go out all by yourself. Then those times you trudged into the woods and carried truckload after truckload of wood you'd cut yourself."

"I had more energy back then and heck, we're *so* old." Elizabeth laughed tepidly. "But when you're in high school everyone seems old." She paused. Amy could sense her clicking back to those days. "Each year Lois and I would invite the junior class for a cookout and a walk on the beach. She loved kids and she loved sharing what she knew about the ecosystem—the plants, the tiny periwinkles. It was like having a front-row seat with Mother Nature." She sighed.

"That was a wonderful day."

"Happiness boomerangs. We got as much out of it as the kids."

"Y'know, that was the first time I saw you two together as a couple. Oh, I'd seen you around town, but I never thought about it. Then that beautiful warm Saturday I knew . . . not that you did anything—I don't know." She blushed, remembering that moment of realization that Elizabeth, her mentor, was gay. "I could see the warmth in your eyes when you looked at her. Somehow I sensed, even at that awkward self-absorbed age, that you loved each other. You know, I'd known for a long time that there was something different about me. I knew that my crush on Jenny Beston was more than just a high-school friendship, but I didn't know who to talk to and people from time to time made mention of the two of you."

"Really?"

"You're surprised."

"I guess I am. We'd been together for probably twenty-five years at that point. I just figured people didn't care."

"Actually"—Amy smiled at the memory—"they didn't. People would make mention of the two of you, but not in a mean sort of way. Just that you were a couple. Funny, it wasn't until I was in my twenties and involved with my first girlfriend—except of course for a little necking in the woods with Jenny—" Amy laughed. "That I realized how brave you and Lois were. Here you were living not just in a small town, but on an island. You had a high-profile job as a lobsterwoman, and, I might add, the only woman in the bay who did that job, and Lois had a high-profile job working as the postmaster, and no one seemed to care." It was true. They lived their lives quietly, never forcing their status as a couple on anyone, and people accepted it. Hell, they embraced it. "You two had so many friends—have so many friends," she corrected herself.

"I remember when you came to our house." Elizabeth's brow knitted. "You fidgeted."

"I never fidget. But I did hang back after everyone left." Amy frowned as she remembered that day. "And you guys comforted me."

"Lois was the one who sensed you wanted to talk. She just had this wonderful sensitivity for people. Me, I just blithely skim along the top of life loving everyone and everything."

90

Amy laughed. "She did sense why I was there. I don't know, we were talking about general things and then the next thing I knew, I was crying my eyes out and there she was with her arm around me, holding me close and comforting me. I'd broken up with Jenny. God, that was so painful."

"I loved the reason you gave for the tears—you'd gotten a C on some exam."

Amy pondered that. "I know, I just couldn't tell you two about Jenny. I was scared out of my mind, worried that I was a lesbian, worried that you guys weren't and I was wrong. I won't say young lesbians have it easier now, but at least there are counselors and people they can talk to. Me, I just stayed buried in the closet."

"Cut yourself some slack, love. You were maybe sixteen?"

"A painful sixteen. Love is so damn hard."

"It always is."

"But not for you. Lois was your first love."

"No." Elizabeth looked Amy in the eyes. "She wasn't, but she was my only love."

"Did you ever think about straying? In all those years, you weren't tempted to get involved with someone else?"

Elizabeth said after a moment's reflection, "Never. Infidelity is an indication of a serious problem in the relationship, otherwise it can't happen. When things are perfect, there isn't room in your heart for anyone else. I was never tempted. We had a lot of friends, both single and in couples, and I guess it could have been a problem, but it never was," she said confidently.

"Never?"

"We knew a few couples over the years where one ended up cheating on the other. The partner that strayed usually persuaded herself that she was desperately in love with the new person. Sometimes it worked, often it didn't. In the end you had three people with broken hearts. Sometimes the original couple could fix it. In fact, Lois and I knew this one couple; they ended up getting back together. I always said the cuckolded partner had a merciful heart. But more often it got messy, especially when the cheated-on

91

partner found out. Lois and I decided it was more about passion than about love. Those who strayed never agreed. They claimed they couldn't help themselves because they'd fallen in love. It was never like that with us. Lois was everything to me—my mother, my lover and my best friend. How can there be room for anyone else? We just loved each other."

"I believe you," Amy said thoughtfully. "You probably don't remember this. I was already in my twenties, but one time I was with this girlfriend of mine—heck, it doesn't matter which girlfriend I was with. We were in your car. You were driving." She looked past Elizabeth. "We were laughing and talking and Lois said something and you reached over picked up her hand and gently kissed her fingers. It was such a loving gesture. I always remembered that."

Elizabeth looked down at her fingers. "I did that a lot."

"I know." Amy studied her friend. "The affection between the two of you was always so palpable, even when you weren't touching. I've never loved a woman that way. Ever."

"Problems between you and Kelly? Is there someone else in your or Kelly's life?"

"Yes, no, maybe. Not someone else, just some problems right now. I know Kelly and she wouldn't cheat on me with anyone." Amy forced herself to smile.

"I agree, but what kinds of problems?"

"I don't know. Kelly's wonderful. I—" Amy poured coffee into two cups and handed one to Elizabeth. "I don't know, sometimes I think there's something wrong with me. I'm not a touchy-feely person."

"Have you two thought about—" Elizabeth stopped when the door opened.

Jim Bows hugged both of them. "Glad you set this up," he said. "Have you been reading anything about the exclusions zone that goes along with these terminals?"

"Have I?" Amy threw a helpless look at Elizabeth. She wondered what Elizabeth had been going to ask before Jim came in. "It's almost an armed camp. The Coast Guard shuts everything down a few miles in front of the ship and at least a mile in back. Then there's this zone on either side. Everything stops, including fishing. In Boston, they supposedly close the Tobin Bridge, and I guess planes don't fly into Logan."

"That would pretty much ruin my sailing business." Jim, a longtime sea captain, who owned two fishing and two sailing boats, shrugged. "Can you imagine me telling tourists, 'I'm sorry we can't go out today because a floating bomb is nearby.' One of the trips that I take people on would go right past that proposed pier. I'm just sick about it."

"You and a lot of people. That's one of the points we're going to fight them on. I invited a bunch of lobstermen," Amy said as she picked up the coffeepot. "How about some coffee?"

"No, thanks. I'm already wired. What are the selectmen saying?" He turned to Elizabeth.

"Nothing, not a damned word, at least publicly. Usually they'll say something to me on the side, but not this time. It's been strange—heck, *strange* is too easy a word—it's been downright weird." Elizabeth picked up a doughnut. "I know they're going to turn this one over to the town. It's a political horror and they're not about to get into the middle of it. You talk to them, they say they're taking a wait-and-see attitude. I don't buy it. Of the five, I'd say they're split between those who see it as an economic boon to those who hate it. One is probably a fence-sitter, something like the town. 'Course they're not talking to me because I've made my thoughts known."

"Has that created problems for you at work?" Amy asked, concerned.

"Nope. They put up with my shenanigans."

"Well, it's going to be our job to change the fence-sitters, and the proponents' minds. That's why—"Amy stopped when she heard the door open. She smiled and gave Maggie Beth and Terry each a hug. "So glad you're here."

"I hope we're not the only ones showing up for this." Maggie surveyed the small group.

"Heavens, no. I had promises from at least ten people that they'd be here tonight," Elizabeth said. "It's early."

"Well, Terry's been online and pulled a bunch of stuff off various Web sites." Maggie grinned as she set a small box of papers on the table. "Elizabeth let me make some copies on the town office copy machine."

"Shh," Elizabeth said with a smirk. "You'll get me in trouble. Using town equipment to foment a revolution."

"Are you serious? Would you get into trouble?" Terry asked.

"I'd say not. Wouldn't matter. I know the selectmen regularly use the copy machine for things other than making copies for the town. God, that little we did doesn't even have me worried."

"That's a good point though," Amy said. "We're going to need access to a copier and other equipment. Probably wouldn't be a bad idea to bring in a computer and set it up here in the office. All I have is a small laptop."

"I've got an extra computer I can loan you," Jim said.

"Look, here come some more folks," Elizabeth said. They all looked toward the shop window.

"Good," Amy said as she began to move some chairs from around the room. "How about you guys help me set up some chairs. Damn, I didn't think about extra chairs." She ran a hand through her hair. "I should have asked people to bring some of their lawn chairs to sit on."

"We'll be fine," Elizabeth said. "Those who want to sit will. Others can plop down on the floor. Those who don't want to sit will lean against the wall. This really is just an organizational meeting. I don't expect it's going to take all night."

"So what do we do first?" Amy asked after everyone was seated. A few more stragglers had arrived.

"Let's make a list," Maggie Beth offered. "I'll take notes."

"Our strategy?"

"We need a name," Jim said.

"Suggestions?" Amy asked.

"I have one," Elizabeth said, tentatively raising her hand. "I thought we'd play on LNG. I came up with Let's Not Give our Bay Away."

"I like that," Terry said.

"So do I," Bill Boyd said. He owned the car dealership. His house was right next to where the developers planned to build the facility.

"Okay. What else?"

"Well, we're going to need a media spokesperson," Maggie Beth said. "I think you'd be great at that, Amy."

"Me?"

"I agree," Elizabeth added.

"What about you, Elizabeth?" she asked good-naturedly.

"Nope. I don't do well with all those television cameras staring at me."

"Okay." Amy sighed. "No one else wants the job?" She waited. "Thanks a heap. What else?" At one time she'd been on the town's holiday planning committee, and she'd handled the media before talking about the Fourth of July Festival, but never for something this big. After she'd started her store, she dropped a lot of her community service jobs. She was just too busy. She was still too busy, she thought, but LNG was too important.

"I'll help write press releases," Maggie Beth offered.

"Good. Now that you've volunteered me to handle the press, that's the least you can do." Amused, she winked at Maggie.

"Now that we've got that settled," Jim said, "we need a strategy. How are we going to fight this?"

The meeting seemed to take on an energy of its own, Amy noted. They made a list of state and federal officials they needed to talk to. They also listed item after item of information they needed to gather and people they needed to talk to. They had heard about the focus groups the developers planned to hold and agreed they would take turns attending them. Jim agreed to attend those that dealt with the fishermen.

After more than two hours, Amy rubbed the back of her neck. Everyone had left except Elizabeth. "That was good, but the

95

turnout was disappointing. Well, I guess all in all it was a good first meeting."

"Twelve people isn't a bad start."

"I don't know. I had a commitment from ten people myself and of those ten only four showed up."

"People get cold feet," Elizabeth said. "You know folks around here, they like to grumble a lot among themselves, but they're not given to really organizing and protesting."

"You'd wonder how we won the Revolutionary War. You know it was the ancestors of some of these very same people who threw the tea in Boston Harbor. Today they'd probably drink it."

Elizabeth laughed. "Don't be too hard on them, hon."

"I just don't get it." Amy could hear the frustration in her voice. "These developers come in here, tell us to trust them. If this thing goes through it's going to change forever not only the landscape, but us. If it's true that it's going to lead to a hundred new jobs with salaries that begin at one hundred thousand dollars, that's going to bring in a lot of new money along with new problems."

"Well, they did say they would give preference to local people first." Elizabeth was washing out the coffee cups.

"Here, let me help you," Amy said, putting the dried cups on a shelf next to the coffeepot. "True, and a lot of local people are going to take those jobs, once they're trained, of course. But what about the technical jobs? Are they going to delay opening this place while they train engineers and other techies? I don't think so. And for the less technical jobs, it means that places like the grocery store and the car dealership are going to lose valuable employees, because those people are going to be the ones who'll take the jobs. It'll be people who already have full-time jobs. And you know as well as I do that there will always be a segment of the population that doesn't work. I love it when a new company comes in." She threw the empty Dunkin' Donuts box in the trash. She put Elizabeth's empty cake pan in her bag. "You hear the same shit from the town leaders. Send us the jobs. We have a workforce just waiting to work." She wiped off the table. "Well, that's just not true because there's also that workforce out there not waiting to work. So at some point we're going to have to bring in people to fill some of those service positions. That means more people looking for housing and we just ain't that big."

"I hadn't thought about that. You're right of course. Every time something new opens more often than not it's a familiar face that's in the job."

Amy shook her head. "It's going to be a real battle, Elizabeth."

"I know," Elizabeth said softly.

"We can't lose this one, it's too important. Putting aside safety and the environment, just the aesthetics of it is going to so impact this little village. But I'm afraid once the developer starts waving money under everyone's nose a lot of people are going to say t'hell with the view and glom onto the money." She turned off the lights in the back room.

"Some, not all."

"You look tired," Amy said, searching Elizabeth's face.

"I am, but I'm glad I helped you clean up," Elizabeth said as she put on her jacket. "By the way, I got a call from the public relations woman."

"Oh?" Amy said as she picked up her jacket.

"I'm having lunch with her next week."

Amy turned to Elizabeth, who was standing at the door. "Lunch? You're kidding."

"I forgot to tell you, I ran into her after the public meeting."

"Where?"

Elizabeth laughed. "I was walking Spike down by the marina. Usually, it's just Spike and me. Imagine my surprise when this figure comes running down the hill. We chatted."

"About?"

Elizabeth frowned. "Not much, really. Mostly I told her to not push it, give people a chance to digest the information."

"Why'd you tell her that?" Amy could feel her irritation well up.

"Because it was the right thing to do. They shouldn't push it.

97

They should give us time to digest their proposal. Think about it, ask questions."

"Elizabeth." Amy tried to keep the exasperation out of her voice. "We are not here to help the enemy. We shouldn't offer them any advice. Let them make their mistakes."

"Easy, sport," Elizabeth said after a moment. "I didn't really see it as helping the enemy. I saw it as kindly advice. Amy, we don't have all of the information. We know what we've been reading on the Internet, other places. But I don't want us to be listening only to the choir. I want to make sure we get all the information. I've thought about it and I know I plan to attend some of those focus group meetings," she said, picking up on their earlier discussion. "I'm opposed to this, but it's for a lot of selfish reasons. I don't want to see my little island change. I don't want to see something ugly sitting on the horizon, but I also want people to have jobs. I want people to be able to work here. I want to stop exporting our children because we just don't have enough jobs here for them."

"I agree, we need jobs, but not at the cost of our history and culture." Her temper rising, Amy paused and pretended to busy herself with sorting through the pages of the strategy paper. This was Elizabeth. She didn't want to lose her temper. "Look," she said more quietly, "those are valid points, but it also means this will change us. I just think we have to think about that, jobs aside."

"I think we have to fight it," Elizabeth said cautiously. "But we also have to listen."

"So you're going to have lunch with her."

"I am. Besides, I got the feeling she's kinda lonely." Elizabeth cocked her eyebrow.

Amy smiled. "That's my Elizabeth. You'll pick up any stray." Amy was relieved the tension had been released.

"Well, she seems to be a very nice stray." Elizabeth smiled. "You know, I have this big mouth that sounds like I'm on the prowl for any woman who comes along the path, but you know I'm not. Lois was my one true love and there is no other. It's just a lot of bravado."

Amy searched her face. "I know." She rubbed a hand over her tired brow. "In that fifty-one years, you never thought about straying? Never thought about maybe having an affair with another woman?" she asked, returning to their earlier conversation.

Elizabeth pursed her lips. "Never. We were soul mates. When you truly love someone, whether it's for five years or fifty, they fill up your life. They're your life and you don't need anyone else. No, I never even thought about it."

Amy turned away; she'd never asked Elizabeth about something as personal as that in her life. She had seen the tears of remembrance in Elizabeth's eyes. "So, when you having lunch?" she said to change the subject.

"On Monday." Elizabeth cleared her throat.

Amy picked up some of the papers she had brought to the meeting. She opened the door. "Just be careful. I would hate to think she's just having lunch to use you. To pick your brain, figure out a way to sell this. Remember, she's being paid the big bucks to convince us this is the best thing since candy apples."

"I know. Funny, I just didn't get that feeling. I think she's looking for a friend."

"Well, if you want to be sure about that, just tell her that you won't talk about the project," Amy said as she locked the door behind them.

"I will." Elizabeth hugged Amy.

"You take care and no LNG!" Amy watched as Elizabeth got into her car.

"I know, I know and it's not a date." Elizabeth's eyes sparkled. "It's a humanitarian mission. That lady is lonely."

Chapter Fourteen

Susan picked up her keys and locked the office door. She smiled; she was really looking forward to having lunch with Elizabeth. They had agreed to meet at the SeaBleu Restaurant at one o'clock. Susan decided to walk the four blocks. It was the end of June and she was feeling good about the project. The meetings with the reporters had gone very well. The developers were pleased with the resulting stories. There had been more meetings with the selectmen. She'd set up several focus group meetings with the fishermen, the business community, and even church leaders for the first week after the Fourth of July holiday. The participants had all agreed to the dates and times. The developers had gone back to Boston for meetings there and were due to return on the Tuesday after the Fourth. Susan had planned to go home to Andover, but she'd heard about the festivities the town had planned and decided to stay. She wanted to see the town wearing all of its faces, plus in two days she was going to move into her cottage. Although she'd enjoyed the motel, it wasn't homey. She was glad she was finally moving into her own space. She opened the door to the restaurant and spotted Elizabeth in one of the back booths. She felt all eyes on her as she walked in. She smiled to herself. Small town, she thought. She often wondered how tourists felt when they entered a restaurant frequented by locals and everyone turned to look.

"Hi," she said as she slid into the booth.

"What a gorgeous day." Elizabeth smiled at her.

Susan liked her. There was something just absolutely guileless about her. "No question about it."

"Well . . ." Elizabeth cleared her throat. "Ground rules, no LNG."

Susan said teasingly. "No LNG. Frankly, I'm tired of talking about it. How about talking about that getting-to-know-each-other stuff."

"Agreed."

"So . . ." they both said together.

Susan laughed. "Go ahead."

"I heard around the office you're from Andover?"

"My whole life. Grew up there."

"Family?"

"A brother. He lives in Los Angeles. My mother is still alive, but my father passed away several years ago." Susan's father had died at age fifty-five from heart problems that a doctor failed to correctly identify. She still felt angry.

"Sorry."

"It's okay. Still hurts, but it's okay. You?"

"Born and raised here. Will die here." Elizabeth offered a sheepish grin.

"Hi, Elizabeth," the waitress said, setting a cup in front of her. She poured the coffee. "Would you like some?" she asked Susan holding out a second cup.

"Yes, please." Susan noted that her nametag read *Carrie*.

"Your usual?" she asked Elizabeth after she poured Susan's coffee.

"Sure."

"What's the usual?" Susan asked, surveying the menu.

"Their large salad with grilled chicken. I love it. I usually have it with blue cheese dressing."

Susan set the menu in the holder next to the salt and pepper shakers. "I'll have the usual also." She waited until Carrie left. "Family?" she asked, picking up on the theme.

Elizabeth studied her. "Not anymore. I was an only child. I'm seventy-five. My mother and father are long gone. My partner of fifty-one years died a few years ago."

"I'm sorry. Fifty-one years, that absolutely takes my breath away. Today, people are lucky to make it a year."

"Heck, I've seen young folks here marry and get divorced the next month."

Susan smiled mischievously. "Well, I guess marriage is like everything else, just part of our disposable society."

"Probably, but it's a shame. Lois and I had our share of problems, but we never stopped loving each other."

Susan put her cup down, relieved at how easily Elizabeth had revealed who her lover was. When she'd said her partner of fifty-one years, Susan had wondered if she meant a man or woman. Would she herself be so nonchalant about it with a stranger? If she'd had a partner, of course. Funny, she never talked about her personal life to anyone but friends. In Andover she was out to those who mattered. She marveled at the ease with which Elizabeth had discussed that important part of her life.

"Something wrong?" Elizabeth was studying her.

"Sorry." Susan toyed with her cup. She had to organize her thoughts. "Actually, I was thinking about what you said and wondering how I would react in the same situation." She frowned.

"About Lois? I don't understand."

"I'm a lesbian, but I don't think I've ever just sat down and told a stranger that. Not on the first conversation and especially not in the business world. In the business world we all pretend we're asexual."

"I'm sorry—"

"Don't apologize," Susan added hastily. "I find it refreshing."

Elizabeth grinned. "Well, no one's ever described what I say that way. I don't know. I just guess because everyone around here knows it, and she was so much a part of my life I talk about her a lot. At least that's what my friends tell me."

"Well, think about it," Susan said gently. "You spent more time with her than anyone else in your life. So why not talk about her?"

"You're right. So are you in a relationship?"

"No. I'm building my business."

"Seems a shame. You can't cuddle a business."

Susan put her head back and laughed. "You're right. Are you always this blunt?"

Elizabeth scratched her ear. "Well, I guess."

Susan noticed the blush. *How charming*, she thought.

Just then Carrie arrived with the salads. "Anything else I can get you?"

"No, this is fine, hon," Elizabeth said as she poured blue cheese onto her salad. "Anyway, now what do we talk about? Now that we have the important stuff behind us."

"That's it, no more personal questions?"

"Oh, I have lots of personal questions. My friends tell me I'm a busybody and I am," Elizabeth said matter-of-factly. "So, you been in a relationship?"

"Ten years. We broke up shortly before I started my business."

"What happened?"

"Stresses of my job, her job. She was an engineer for a large company in Andover. One day we were madly in love, the next we were strangers, fighting." She quashed the emotional response that was whirling inside her. She didn't like to think about her ex.

"I'm sorry." Elizabeth put her fork down and gave her a quizzical look. "You been looking?"

"Honestly? No."

"Now that is too bad."

"I'm married to my business, but you're right though, you can't cuddle it." Susan wanted to ease the seriousness of their conversation.

"You two still friends?"

"Yes, no, I don't know. We're civil. But friends, I'd say no."

"Too bad. You shared ten years of your life with a woman—she probably knows more about you than anyone, including your family. Seems to me there's a solid foundation there for friendship."

"I hadn't thought about it like that." Susan lapsed into thought. "You're right."

"Course I'm right."

"And you, are you looking for someone new?"

"No. Oh, I josh about it a lot. Ask all my friends to be on the lookout for a new squeeze for me. That's what the young ones call it, a new squeeze. Truth be told, there isn't anyone out there for me."

"Don't kid yourself. I've seen not a lot, but some new couples in their sixties and seventies in Andover. It's downright charming. Kind of an inspiration for those of us in our thirties and forties, who think life and love ends at fifty."

"Oh, it doesn't, I grant you that. I'm just not looking. Anyway"—Elizabeth took a bite of chicken—"you going to be around for the Fourth weekend."

"I am. I'm moving into a cottage over on Baring Cove on Wednesday, so I decided to spend the weekend."

"Good. Some friends of mine, Kelly and Amy, have a lobster feed every year and I want you to join us."

"I'd love to, but shouldn't you ask them?"

"Heck, no. We're all family here. They'll have more food than a White House banquet. They'll love it."

Susan frowned. "Remember who I am? The enemy. You sure they'll want an LNG advocate at their party?"

"They'll accept whomever I bring. Don't worry about it. And remember, we're not talking about LNG."

Susan smiled. "So what should we talk about?"

"You." Elizabeth smiled too. "So tell me more about yourself. I know you were raised in Andover, I know you've been out of a relationship a while, but what else about you?"

"Gosh, I don't know. I don't really have any hobbies, although I love boating and hiking, and I play tennis and golf—"

"Golf?" Elizabeth interrupted. "Now you're a woman after my own heart. I'm the world's worst duffer. Didn't take the sport up until I was sixty, but I love it. Lois just used to shake her head as I headed off to the golf course over in Port Bleu. Friends talked me into it one day, next thing you know I was hooked."

Susan smiled as Elizabeth talked on and on about her game. She liked this woman. She may be on the other side of the LNG fence, but she truly liked Elizabeth.

"Anyway," Elizabeth said, pushing her now empty salad bowl aside, "I sometimes just ramble on and on."

"Don't apologize."

"So you'll join me on the Fourth at Kelly and Amy's for lobster?"

"Well, sure, if it's all right with your friends. I know you said that they wouldn't mind, but I think you need to ask."

"I'll mention it, but you're my guest. By the way, I also want to invite you out to the airport on Sunday."

"Sure. What's happening on Sunday?"

"I'm jumping out of a helicopter."

Susan stared at her. "You're kidding." She couldn't picture this wrinkled old woman with a parachute.

"Nope, I'm as serious as a flat tire."

"You skydive too?"

"Not likely. This'll be my first time."

"Don't leave me hanging, woman. Tell me about this."

Elizabeth pursed her lips as she pondered her words. "Well, when I was with Lois, life was wonderful. But I had to think like a couple, be careful like a couple. I don't know . . . I guess that's changed. Now I want a little adventure before I die. On Sunday, the Brunswick Skydiving Team will be performing—we tried to get them for the next day, on the Fourth, either before or after the parade, but they had a prior commitment—so they're coming here on Sunday. Going to put on a show at the airport in the morning."

"Okay, but that still doesn't tell me how you teamed up with them. You didn't used to skydive and you don't skydive now."

"Simple, their advance man come into the town office a few months ago to talk with the town manager about setting things up. We were just kidding and I said for him to save a parachute for me, that I was going to jump with him. He just turned real serious and said, 'You want to jump you can.' Well this little old heart of mine started to race faster than a Nascar stock car at super speed."

"You're jumping with them?"

"Tandem, but it's still jumping."

"Well, yes." Susan sat back, impressed. "You're quite a woman."

"Not really." Elizabeth's smile was radiant. "It's something I always wanted to do, but I was in a relationship and when you're a couple you gotta consider the other person. Lois wouldn't have set still for it. And I wouldn't have wanted to give her even one moment of anxiety or worry."

"I'm excited for you. Aren't you scared?"

"Not really. Heck, I figure if George Bush Senior can do it, I can. Course, he wasn't as considerate as me. 'Cause I'm sure Barbara bit her nails to the cuticle until he was safely on the ground."

"So do they train you?"

"No, he just said for me to be at the airport an hour earlier. They have room for three other people. I understand two of our local reporters have signed on. I don't know if the fourth slot is open or not." Elizabeth paused. "Come to think of it, Kelly mentioned she wanted to jump, I must ask her if she signed up."

"So you're going up in an airplane. I'm almost afraid to ask how high?"

"Actually, we're going up in a helicopter. He explained that because our airport is so small they might miss the jump zone, land us in the ocean. We're jumping at ten thousand feet."

"Ten thousand feet?" Susan exclaimed, shocked.

"Pretty high." Elizabeth's smile was smug.

"I'd say."

"He brought in a videotape, showed me and the town manager some of the tricks they do. Pretty spectacular."

"Don't tell me you're going to be doing tricks."

"No, we're just going to do their practice jump with them. After that they do the show. There's something like fifteen of them. I gotta tell ya, you're not going to want to miss the show. It's going to be wicked good. Why don't you come out with me on Sunday morning. You can be my second." Elizabeth's grin was mischievous and Susan smiled. "Y'know, like in dueling. If I can't do it, you'll stand in for me."

"I'd love to be there, but I'll pass being your second." Susan mused aloud, "Somehow, I think the developers wouldn't be pleased if their PR woman was jumping out of helicopters."

"Oh, I don't know. It might add more of a human face to all of you."

"Well, let's just say I'll wait until I'm seventy." Susan smirked.

"But you'll come out to the airport and on Monday, you'll go over to Kelly and Amy's with me."

Susan paused. "I will, but only if you promise me that you'll ask them first. Like I said, I'm not the most popular woman in town right now."

"They'll be fine. Amy's against it. Kelly, I don't know. I haven't talked with her. You actually saw Amy—she was the one sitting next to me at that first meeting you held."

"That night was a blur. There were so many people there all I saw was a sea of jackets and men wearing baseball caps."

"Well, that part is true. Men and women here wear a lot of baseball caps. It's part of our Down East culture. In fact, you can usually tell if someone's from away, because usually they're bareheaded."

"Away?"

"That's what we call you flatlanders. There are three classes of people here. Those born here and stayed; those born here, then left and then came back; and those people from away."

"Does this class society impact how people treat one another?"

107

"No, but it's something to rib folks about."

"So what does Amy do?"

"She owns the local gallery and frame shop. Have you been in there?"

"I've seen it. In fact, I walked past it today on my way here. She has some beautiful pieces in the window. I've been tempted to go in, just haven't had the time. But I will."

"Amy's talented. She has an eye for artwork. You should see her house. Well, you will see her house, come to think of it, at the lobster feed. Kelly's a nurse. She's from away. She's a wonderful woman; I just love her to pieces. They've been together about five years. In fact, I introduced them," Elizabeth said proudly. "There'll be other folks there. Some gay, some straight. Nice people, people you should get to know."

Susan scratched her neck. "I don't know. Again, I'm not so sure people are going to welcome me with such open arms. Maybe if I was here for different reasons, but I know this issue is going to be divisive. I have no illusions about that. I know it's going to pit family members against family members and friends against friends. It did down south. Some folks wanted it for all the right reasons, but more folks didn't, also for all of the right reasons."

Elizabeth held up her hand. "Now hold on just a minute. First off, we agreed not to talk about LNG. I think we ought to hold to that pledge. I don't want to feel like you're selling me something, and I don't want you to feel like I'm judging you because of what you do. So we're just going to set that part aside. I like you, and people I like I include in my life, and my friends love my friends. So if I say you're going to a party with me, my friends will accept it and they'll embrace you. You know, young lady, you're more than your job. You remember that and we'll be fine."

Susan pondered that. "You're right. I forget sometimes, but I am more than my job. Okay, forget about caution. I'll go to the lobster feed and agree to no LNG discussion. And I most certainly will be there on Sunday to watch you jump out of a helicopter, although I'll be the one woman on the ground holding her breath. So I hope they jump quickly."

108

"You and the rest of my friends. I've invited a whole pack of people out there to watch. What the heck, this is probably one of the more fun things I'll be doing this time around."

"Undoubtedly." Susan paused as Carrie came up to the table with their checks.

"I know you're not having dessert, Elizabeth," Carrie said. "But can I get you something?" she asked Susan.

"Just the checks, thanks, and I'll take both, please." She reached for them.

"You don't have to do that."

"Ah, but I want to. I'm having lunch with a famous person, or at least someone who will be once she jumps out of that helicopter." Susan reached for her wallet.

"It's true, Elizabeth? You're really jumping out of a helicopter?" Carrie asked.

"It's true."

"I always knew you was crazy."

"More teched than anything." Elizabeth laughed.

"Well, it's all over town, and everyone's talking about it."

Elizabeth shook her head. "Undoubtedly. I guess then they aren't talking about someone else. You ever want to do that, Carrie?"

"No way. I'll just keep both feet on the ground, thank you very much. You know, I've never even been in an airplane and I have no desire to do so. God didn't intend for people to fly around in sardine cans."

Susan and Elizabeth laughed. "Well, that pretty much says it all," Susan said as she handed her credit card to Carrie. "Anyway," she said after Carrie left, "this was fun. I'm glad you asked me to lunch." She looked down at her hands and frowned. "I have to confess, I thought you had an ulterior motive."

"How so?"

"Well, you're the town clerk and all. I just figured you wanted to pump me about some of the details of the project. I know you've been excluded from the negotiations. Sorry." Susan laughed, embarrassed at her confession.

"Well, truth be told, I would like to pump you and I would like to know the details of the negotiations. But that stuff will come out eventually. It has to because people have a right to know." Elizabeth paused. "I don't know. It was funny that night we talked at the marina. You seemed so alone, I felt sorry for you."

"Well, I'm glad you did, Elizabeth, because this is one of the most enjoyable days I've had here on the island. I'd like to do it again. Once I get moved into my cottage, I'd like to invite you for dinner."

"And I'll accept. I'd invite you for dinner, but Lois was the gourmet cook in our family. About all I can do is cook lobster and steak on the grill. But you wouldn't starve."

"Well, you invite me, I'll be there."

"And I'm glad you found a place to live. Motels aren't homes and the Grange place is something nice. They are nice folks and if they're renting something, you can bet it's quality."

"I was lucky. A vacancy came up and I was able to rent it for the rest of the summer. I understand the owners may be back in October. I don't really know. I've been dealing with the caretaker."

"Sam? He's a good man. You plan to be here that long?"

"The developers said for as long as it takes."

"Hmm."

"Why hmm?"

"Don't know. I just figured we'd kick it around for a couple of weeks and then vote on it."

"It's not that simple." Susan paused, thinking about all the paperwork and meetings facing them. "Well, here we are talking about the very thing we agreed not to talk about."

"You're right. Sorry."

"It's okay. It's a major deal down here."

"More than that," Elizabeth said softly. "It means it will change our way of life forever. This isn't some manufacturing plant coming in that plans to make widgets. This is something that will change not only our town, but for a part of the island the horizon. This is not just big, it's monstrous."

110

"True," Susan admitted. She stopped when Carrie handed her a pen and the credit card slip. Susan filled in the tip and signed her name.

"Well." Elizabeth cleared her throat. "Thank you for lunch."

"Thank you, Elizabeth, this was very special. And I'm going to take you up on your offer. I'll be there Sunday for the jump and Monday, I'd love to join you at the lobster feed. How about if I call you for the address? And I promise, at no time will I discuss LNG, regardless of what anyone says or what questions they ask."

"No address, this is the country, call and I will give you directions. And don't forget the parade on Monday morning. It's the biggest one ever Down East. We have bands coming in from as far away as Saint John and Moncton, New Brunswick. Our U.S. senator sees to it we get a ship in port. That's fun. We've had destroyers and one time we even had a small aircraft carrier in port. Now that was something to see. They usually open it for tours Saturday through Monday. Then all those young men and women in their white uniforms march in our parade. It's really a sight. I've never seen so many ironed young people."

"Well, I definitely will be there. Billy, the manager at the motel where I'm staying, first convinced me I should stay for the Fourth."

"I'm glad he did. It's something everyone should see."

"Elizabeth, this has been fun. Again, thank you." Susan eased out of the booth.

"My pleasure. I've enjoyed getting to know you," Elizabeth said, getting up and standing next to her. "You mentioned you walked over here. You want a ride back?"

"No, I really enjoyed the walk."

"Well, I should do more of that, but just too darn lazy. I keep telling myself I should watch my diet and get more exercise, then I figure what the heck. I love to eat and I love to sit."

Susan chuckled. She held the door open for Elizabeth. "Thank you for a fun lunch."

Elizabeth hugged her. "I had fun too. Anyway, if I don't talk to

111

you before Sunday, be at the airport at nine a.m. I have to be there at eight, but we're not jumping until nine."

"I'm up early. I might just come out at eight o'clock and watch you train. It should be interesting."

"Good, see you then."

Susan watched as Elizabeth headed toward the parking lot. She noticed a slight limp, but other than that Susan marveled at the energy of her walk. She really liked this woman. *You're lucky, Susan Iogen. Your whole life you've met some very interesting people.* She thought about their conversation, how open and inviting Elizabeth had been. She would have liked to have known her and Lois as a couple. She noticed the sign for Day Gallery. She peered in the window. There was the shadow of a woman walking around at the back of the store. She started toward the door and then stopped. Elizabeth's words echoed in her mind. The woman who owned the gallery was against the project. *Don't push it, Susan,* she thought. *You had a wonderful lunch with an exceptional woman, but this one might not be so inviting.* Susan turned back up the street and started walking toward the developer's office.

Chapter Fifteen

Amy was reluctant to close the store Friday evening. She knew she would have to go home and deal with Kelly and this stranger who would be sharing her house. It wasn't as though she didn't like company. She did. She just didn't like surprises. Kelly was being her usual huffy self. How many times over the past five years had they talked about that? she wondered.

She loved Kelly with all of her being, but she didn't understand her. People exploded, people had tempers and people said things that didn't come out right, but rather than get over it like she did, Kelly steeped in it for days. And she knew Kelly replayed conversations over and over in her head because when she would talk about it later, she'd repeat the exact words she said had hurt her. Then she'd get mad all over again. Amy was growing weary of having to defend what she said. Most of the time she didn't even remember. It was usually spontaneous and triggered by whatever situation had upset her.

Try as she might to explain how she reacted to things, Kelly just didn't get it. She remembered one time they'd had an argument over something—things had not been going well at the store and she'd lost it—instead of Kelly telling her to take her anger out on whomever had upset her at the store, she just stood there silently taking it.

Kelly just didn't understand her. And how many times after an argument had she made it up to Kelly, bought her a gift or taken her to dinner.

Amy began to fume inside as she thought about their relationship. Kelly wasn't without fault in this. Kelly sometimes got upset and on occasion had lost her temper. She wasn't a saint, although at times Amy thought Kelly took on the role of the martyr. Many times Kelly did things that upset the household, like inviting Laurie without first discussing it with her.

As Amy got into her car, she looked at the gallery window and noticed she hadn't turned the *Closed* sign. She got back out of her car and went inside and turned the sign. They needed some groceries, she thought once she was settled again in the car. She'd run over to the market. Kelly no doubt had forgotten to pick up dessert for their dinner with Laurie.

And what about Laurie? she thought as she drove toward the market. She was supposed to be Kelly's best friend and yet in the five years they'd been together, she'd met Kelly only once for dinner halfway between Portland and Bleu Island. Amy remembered the visit had been a disaster. She sensed that Laurie and Heather had had some kind of fight and Heather spent the evening sullen and withdrawn. After that Laurie rarely called. Kelly explained it away by saying that when Laurie was in love it was like she'd been hit with a stun gun. What kind of love was that? Amy wondered. When you loved someone you wanted to share them with your friends, show them off. She had certainly done that with Kelly. She remembered the party she threw after they knew they were in love. She'd invited all of her friends because she wanted her friends to meet the new love of her life.

114

At the grocery store, she bought a dozen biscuits and two quarts of strawberries. She picked up a can of whipped cream in the dairy section.

"Well, how are you?"

Amy turned when she heard Elizabeth behind her. "Wonderful, love. Just picking up some last-minute goodies. Kelly's friend Laurie gets here tomorrow for the long weekend."

"That's great."

Amy noticed that Elizabeth had her arms full of groceries. "Where's your basket?"

Elizabeth chortled. "I just came in to get one or two things." Amy again looked at Elizabeth's overflowing arms. "What'dya think, I overdid it a bit?"

"Here, put it in my cart," Amy said, pushing her items aside. "I get a cart for three things and you look like you're a clown in a juggling act. You're something else, Elizabeth Robinson."

"True, true, but we love me."

Amy laughed. "That we do."

"I'm so glad Kelly's friend is coming. It'll be great, her having someone from her past in her present." Elizabeth paused. "You're okay with it?"

"Absolutely. I think it's wonderful. You're right—most of Kelly's friends are my friends, so her having Laurie here will be nice for her. They can do a girls' night out." Amy could hear the sarcasm in her own voice. She wasn't jealous of Laurie, she was certain of that. She just didn't want someone cluttering up their life. She hoped Laurie wasn't the type who felt like she had to hang around all the time. Amy liked her quiet time.

"That won't happen if I know Kelly." Elizabeth hadn't seemed to notice the sarcasm. "Anyway, invite her to the jump on Sunday."

"You're not still doing that."

"What would change?"

"I thought common sense."

"Common sense went out the door when Lois died. Now it's daredevil and more daredevil."

"Don't remind me." Amy groaned. "How did lunch go with the LNG lady?" She had promised herself that when she saw Elizabeth she wouldn't ask. She was going to pretend the lunch meant nothing. *Well, so much for that resolve.*

"Good. She didn't talk about LNG and neither did I. But I did invite her to come watch me jump."

"You're kidding." Amy stopped in the aisle.

"Nope."

"You sure she didn't pump you over lunch?"

"Not even a mention. Except how it'd help build her business if they won."

"Well, that's a pretty important *mention*," Amy mimicked.

"Well, what'd you expect?"

"Did you say anything?"

"Nope, mostly listened."

"What did you talk about then?"

Elizabeth shrugged. "Nothing that important. I did invite her to your party."

"Now you're really kidding."

"Nope."

"Why, for God's sake?"

"She's lonely."

"She's the enemy. You don't invite your enemy to a party."

"She's lonely," Elizabeth insisted.

"She's the enemy." Fuming, Amy was just as insistent.

"She's lonely," Elizabeth repeated more assertively.

Amy took a deep breath. "I think you should have asked me before you invited her to my party." She wondered if the whole world was going a bit nuts. First Kelly invites a stranger to her house for an overnight and now Elizabeth had strayed into uncharted grounds by inviting an opponent.

"I've invited other folks in years past, and you never said a word about it."

"That was different."

"How so?"

"She works for the other side. Remember them, Elizabeth, the people who are here to destroy our island?" Amy tried to keep the frustration out of her voice.

"No, she's not." Elizabeth started toward the checkout aisle.

Amy followed her with the basket. "You should have asked me," she said quietly.

"Well, if you feel that way, I'm asking. Can she come?"

Amy felt flustered, uncertain how to answer.

"That's what I thought. Look, Amy, get mad at me, whatever. But I invited her. She's my new friend and I ain't going to say she comes or else, but I'm saying she's my guest. It's up to you."

"I guess I have to accept it."

"You do," Elizabeth said as she unloaded her section of the basket. "Hi, Sammy," she said to the checkout clerk.

"Afternoon, Elizabeth. Heard about your jump," the young clerk said.

"Well, mighty fine. I didn't know it was all over the island."

"Everyone's talking about it."

"Don't encourage her, Sammy." The teasing helped relieve the tension she'd felt with Elizabeth. "I've tried to tell her she's nuts."

"Nuts is okay in my book. I think it's great. You being older and all."

Elizabeth laughed. "Well, not quite ready for the rocking chair, young fella," she offered agreeably.

Sammy blushed a deep red and stammered. "I didn't mean . . ."

"I'm just joshing you."

"That'll be eight dollars and fifty-six cents," he said to Elizabeth.

"See, not everyone thinks I'm daft." Elizabeth paused to look mischievously at Amy. She handed Sammy the money. "Why don't you come out Sunday and watch?"

"Wish I could, but I gotta work."

Amy shook her head. The whole world was going crazy. She set her three items on the counter, fished out a ten-dollar bill and handed the money to Sammy, who handed her her change.

"You take care now, Elizabeth. Hope you have a gentle landing," he said.

"I plan on it."

In silence, Amy walked Elizabeth to her car and helped her put her groceries inside.

"I'll see you Sunday morning?" Elizabeth asked.

"I should say no, but I'll be there," Amy said reluctantly. She could open the store at ten instead of nine.

"Good. I know Kelly will be there and so will Susan. So bring Laurie. It'll be fun. By the way, did Kelly get ahold of the advance man? Is she jumping?"

"Not on your life."

Elizabeth hugged her. "Lighten up, love."

As Elizabeth drove off, Amy put her package on the front seat and started the car. She and Kelly needed to talk, she decided as she drove home. Things had to return to normal in the house because she didn't want Laurie to sense that they were having problems. If she'd learned one thing from her grandmother, it was that you put on a good face for guests and friends. Amy had always followed those rules.

She also wanted to talk to Kelly about Elizabeth. She was worried about her. Lately, Elizabeth was doing weird stuff and it was unsettling. Jumping out of a helicopter, inviting not just a stranger but someone who could harm the island to her party. She knew she couldn't talk to their friends. All her friends thought Elizabeth was a curmudgeon. They'd just make up excuses and say Elizabeth was getting somewhat eccentric. They would tell her not to worry. But Amy was worried. She knew life defied categorization, but lately life seemed to be the conundrum of her being. She hated it when she wasn't in control. She turned into the driveway, where Kelly's car was already parked.

Chapter Sixteen

"We need to talk," Kelly murmured.

"Agreed." Amy had handed her the bag of groceries and Kelly put the strawberries and whipped cream in the refrigerator. Laurie had called and confirmed she was coming the next day, Saturday, so Kelly had taken the afternoon off to clean the house and get things ready for her visit. The night before, she had rolled around in bed trying to decide if she should talk to Amy or not. Plus she had to tell her the advance man had called the day before. She was the fourth jumper. She'd been so excited after he called, she'd picked up the telephone to call Amy, but had stopped. It was already the Arctic Circle at their house. She didn't want to tell her over the phone. So it had been another sleepless night. The armed standoff was unmistakable between them and she knew it couldn't go on. All night she kept telling herself she had to confront the issue or start screaming in frustration. When she finally woke up, Amy had already left.

"We're living together like roommates."

Amy agreed. "I've missed our mornings together. Funny, often we don't even talk, but I miss just sitting here reading the newspaper together."

"Me too." Kelly put the biscuits on the counter, then poured two glasses of wine. She gave one to Amy.

"I know I've been too preoccupied lately with all the meetings we've been holding and all the developers' meetings I've been going to. I've been about as driven as a drill bit going after oil. And I saw Elizabeth at the store and she just informed me she invited that LNG woman to our party. I was flabbergasted. She promised there'd be no discussion of LNG." Amy gulped some wine. "I don't believe her. I'm really upset."

"It shouldn't surprise you. You know Elizabeth and strangers." Kelly smiled and then said seriously, "Elizabeth is Elizabeth."

"You're not upset?"

"Not really," Kelly sipped her wine. "It's just a party, not a political campaign."

"That's what I'm afraid of. That it will turn into a pro-LNG public relations party."

"I trust Elizabeth. If she says no LNG, I believe her."

"I trust Elizabeth, it's that LNG bimbo I don't trust."

Kelly winced, she hated that word. "Well, there's nothing we can do. She's been invited. I'd rather stay focused on us and our problems." She returned to the barb that had been pricking her.

"The problem. The problem!" Amy's voice flared with contempt. "That's all you want to talk about."

"Amy, I love you. I just don't like the way you treat me sometimes. This thing with Laurie was just so blown out of proportion. The thing with the helicopter jump was so blown out of proportion." Kelly didn't bother to mask the frustration in her voice.

"That's the point, all of this distraction has made me focus on everything but us, and I just got upset because we hadn't talked about either of those things."

"All this distraction has made you tense and at times very angry, and instead of directing that anger at the source, you turn it on me. I feel like life is a minefield around you. I don't like that. I've been spending more time at the hospital, driving all my nurses crazy, rather than coming into this house."

Amy reached over and took her hand. "That's my point, it's this LNG thing."

Kelly laced her fingers through Amy's. "Then what was it before that and the time before that?" she asked gently.

Amy pulled away. "Are we going to repeat that age-old argument that I say things that upset you?" She ran her hands through her hair in a gesture Kelly recognized as frustration. "Okay, maybe I do say things that I shouldn't. But most the time I'm just kidding or I might say things when I'm upset that do hurt. But I love you and if you trust my love you know that."

Kelly stared at the floor. "Everyone says things that are from time to time unkind or hurtful. Everyone says things they wish they could take back. But when you get upset you lash out at me. I've become your verbal punching bag. Your words can be absolutely crippling. There's no other way to describe it."

"But I get over it, Kelly, and so should you."

"It doesn't work like that. Sometimes it goes beyond hurt and I feel cut to the core. Amy, I've thought long and hard about this. I love you, I'm in love with you, but I think we need to seek counseling."

"Counseling?" Amy stood up so fast she knocked the chair down.

"Yes, counseling," Kelly said wearily.

"I don't want to do that." Amy set the chair upright and sat down again. "I think we can talk this out ourselves. We've done it before."

Kelly smiled sadly. "I know and it just hasn't worked for us. You say something, I get hurt or angry, and you just think I'm being supersensitive."

"Well, in some ways I think you are."

"In most ways I think I'm not. I think we're too close to the problem. We need someone else to look at it and tell us what we're doing wrong."

"I don't know, I just hate the idea of going to a shrink."

"A family counselor."

"Whatever." Amy waved her hand in dismissal.

"Look, I'm not perfect either. You say something and instead of handing it right back to you, I internalize it, chew on it until it boils over in my brain."

"That's what I mean by your being supersensitive. If you'd just say to me, look, you screwed up, don't take it out on me, we wouldn't need a counselor."

"That's why we do."

"Why don't you just do that?" Amy's tone was accusatory, which made Kelly feel disheartened.

"Fear."

"Fear?"

"Yeah, fear. Fear. I've tried to do that." Kelly could feel herself slipping backward into her morass. "I've tried to say to you it's wrong. To point out how your words hurt. I've done that and the fight has escalated. So fear that it will make things so bad that we won't ever get over it. Just plain old fear." She willed herself to shrug off the melancholy. "So I stay quiet."

"Pouting."

"Amy—" Kelly stopped. "Don't denigrate what's going on inside of me. I don't do it to you and I would appreciate it if you wouldn't do it to me. We have some problems and I sense that we're headed for another fight." She took a deep breath. *Stop this now*, she thought. *Don't even go in the direction of how much her criticisms hurt.* "Would you at least consider seeing a counselor? A third party, someone who doesn't know us and who could maybe teach us how to deal with these problems."

Amy picked up her now empty wineglass and set it back down.

"Would you like more wine?" Kelly started to get up.

"No, not really. I think it's just old habit. I remember one time a dear friend of my grandfather's used to fiddle with his pipe—you know, tamping the tobacco and then lighting it. He told me years later it was a communication stopper. Gave him time to think about what the other person said before he answered. Maybe we should start smoking pipes." Amy grinned.

Kelly could picture the two of them with pipes. She smiled. "Well, except for the risk of cancer that might be an idea."

"It's nice to see that smile again."

"Leave it up to you to find something funny even in this." Kelly held up her hand to stop the onslaught of protest. "That's not a criticism. It does help lighten the load at times."

"Well, I'm glad I'm good at something." Amy reached over and took Kelly's hand again. "I love you, Kelly Burns. I'm in love with you. I don't want this to happen to us. Most times things are really good in our lives. I know I've been distracted with this LNG stuff. I'll try to cool it. I can't stop though. It's just too important for me to stop, but at least I can temper it. Spend more time here rather than at the store. But I need for you to be here also."

"I can do that, Amy, but we can't ignore the problems between us."

"I'm not trying to overlook them, I just think we can handle them. Like now we've talked and things are good between us, aren't they?"

"But we haven't solved the problem," Kelly persisted.

"That's the point—if we keep talking about it we will solve the problems. When I get that way, you need to stop me. You need to say something. Tell me I'm acting badly. I'm sure I can put the brakes on."

Kelly felt like her nerves were humming like a power line. Amy had not heard her. "So you don't want to see a counselor?"

"No, I don't. I hate the idea of telling someone else about me, about us. It's just too intrusive."

"What if it means a lot to me? What if I feel that it's about the only thing that will save our relationship?" Kelly waited for the explosion.

Amy started to pull her hand away and then stopped. "It means

123

that much to you. You don't think we can do this alone, maybe work this through, just each of us trying a little harder?"

"No, I don't." Kelly said it so softly it almost wasn't heard. "I don't," she said louder.

"Well . . ." Amy cleared her throat. "Are you talking about breaking up?"

"No! God, Amy, don't even start down that path. All I'm saying is that it means a lot to me that we fix the problem. I think the only way we're going to do it is for us to see someone who can, for want of a better cliché, shine a light on our problems. We need to see ourselves and our relationship through someone else's eyes."

"Look, your friend Laurie will be here tomorrow. We've got a big weekend planned. Sunday we have to go watch Elizabeth jump out of a helicopter." Amy shook her head. "I don't even want to think about that. And let's not forget our dear friend inviting that LNG woman to our party." Kelly sensed that this time Amy was trying to keep a tight rein on her anger.

"It's okay," Kelly said soothingly.

"It's not okay. There's just nothing I can do about it. But what really irritates me, she didn't call me, she didn't ask me ahead of time. This seems to be a pattern."

Kelly ignored Amy's dig. She knew Amy was talking about her desire to skydive. She shifted in her chair uncomfortably. She should tell her she was to be the fourth jumper. *Tell her*, she ordered herself. *Tell her!* "It's all right. We've made it a policy to include anyone and everyone—heck, we've had people here we didn't even know. At least we know something about this woman."

"Yeah, that she's a wolf in Park Avenue sheep's clothing."

"Well, knowing Elizabeth, she had her reasons."

"She felt sorry for her."

"As I said, knowing Elizabeth," Kelly repeated, "I'd believe it."

"You're not upset?"

"Not really."

"She's probably here to spy on us."

"What's there to spy on?"

"Our group, our strategy."

"I doubt she'll learn much over lobster. Tell everyone no LNG discussion."

"You know, Kelly, I thought you'd back me on this one. Help me."

"Do what?"

"Tell Elizabeth that woman's not welcome."

Kelly paused. "And possibly lose Elizabeth's friendship? Somehow I feel that if she doesn't come, Elizabeth won't either. I'm not willing to risk that. I like her too much."

Judging by her sneer, Amy was disgusted. "You don't care how I feel about this."

"I think we can handle this," Kelly said quietly. "Just make certain everyone knows who she is. Tell our friends not to discuss LNG and it'll be fine. In the grand scheme of all the problems we have, I see this one as minor."

"You're not going to harp on that counselor thing again are you?"

"Why the reluctance at seeing a counselor? It's all confidential." Kelly was relieved they had turned away from the discussion of Elizabeth and back to what she knew was important to their lives.

"I don't know, it just sounds so mental. We're adults here. I think we can solve the problems between us just the way it should be solved." Amy added emphatically, "Between us."

"But we've tried that," Kelly persisted. "How many times in the last five years have we had this conversation?"

"Not that many times. Really, Kelly, I think you're overstating it."

"You just don't get it. Having this conversation more than once means we're unable to fix the problem."

"I hear you, Kelly. I know what you're saying to me. You want me—"

"To stop lashing out at me when you're angry or frustrated or upset," Kelly finished for her.

"That's unfair, Kelly. Lashing out? I don't lash out."

125

Kelly frowned. "What would you call it?"

Amy stood up and carried her glass to the sink. "I don't know, but lashing out is too mean-spirited."

"Ah." Kelly also stood up. "Then what would you call it?" she repeated.

"Getting upset. Getting angry. But you just miss such an important part of all of this. When I do get angry and I say something to you, you need to just turn it back on me. Say something like, 'Hey you're angry at such and such, don't take it out on me.'"

"So you make fixing your bad behavior my responsibility?"

"Foul, Kelly."

"Well, how else am I to interpret it? You say something nasty to me or you get angry at something and it's my job to fix the problem."

"Well, not fix the problem, no one can fix the problem, but you certainly could defuse the situation."

Kelly turned her back on Amy. *Don't say it*, she told herself. *Don't go there, because this is going to escalate into a huge fight. Don't talk about all the criticism she levels at you and how it hurts.* She said, "Amy, I really want us to see a counselor."

"I don't know." Amy came up behind her and put a hand on her shoulder. "I just hate the idea of airing our laundry in public. I do."

"It's not public. We don't even have to see someone here on the island," Kelly said hopefully. "We could go over to the mainland. No one would have to know."

"Can I think about it?"

"Of course," Kelly said, heartened. "And—"

"I love you, Kelly Burns. You're the best thing that's ever happened to me. There isn't a thing you wouldn't do for me. You're devoted, caring, loving. The best lover I've ever had. I'd be crazy to lose you," Amy said with a smile. "And speaking of the best lover."

"Don't even go there. We need to—"

"Why not?" Amy said, kissing Kelly's fingertips. She drew her tongue in circles across the palm of Kelly's hand. Kelly shuddered.

126

It felt so good. "The best part of fighting is making up. Think about it." she said as she kissed her way up Kelly's bare arm. Her tongue trailed a line along Kelly's neck. Then Kelly turned to her and their tongues did a familiar dance. Amy pulled Kelly's hips against hers. "I love you, Kelly Burns," she said again. "And I am going to make love to you right here on the kitchen floor."

It had been a long time since they had made love most of the night. In the morning they shared a leisurely breakfast. There was no more discussion about Elizabeth or the LNG woman, although Amy knew the idea was still unsettling.

Now in her car, she thought about the passion they had shared. She was continually amazed at the spark that still ignited both of them. Kelly was such a sensitive lover that when they were making love it was as if Kelly was listening to her body. And even though there was a familiarity to their lovemaking after all these years, there was always something different. Amy smiled to herself. In the past she'd had relationships that after a year or two reminded her of football—one, two, three, kick. It was so predictable it became downright boring, but Kelly's lovemaking was spectacular. Amy shuddered as she thought about it. *Keep your eyes on the road*, she said to herself.

The issue of seeing a counselor had not come up again. Amy frowned at the road. She hated the idea of seeing one. She always believed her friends were her counselors. Whenever she'd had a problem she could go to Elizabeth or Maggie Beth and Terry. They'd listen, give advice. They were better than a counselor because she knew they loved her. She would talk to Elizabeth, she decided.

Amy turned into the driveway next to the store. She thought about all the things she had to get done. The shop had been busy and she knew today wouldn't be any different. She loved Fourth of July on the island. There was such an air of festivity. It was the only time of the year that she needed help at the shop. Not even the

Christmas rush could compare. The little town just exploded with all the tourists and the many family members who came home for the long weekend, and the town office even closed on the Friday before a long holiday weekend. In years past she would hire one of the high school students to help, but she usually ended up frustrated because they just didn't relate to her older clientele. Then she had hired Elizabeth, which had been a battle because she complained she couldn't learn everything there was to run a store, but Amy had persevered and after the first year, Elizabeth loved it. It was just 8:30 when Amy unlocked the door and began to set up for the day. Ten minutes later she saw Elizabeth at the door.

"Wow," Elizabeth said as she came in. "I think there're more people in town today than ever before."

"It does seem busier, and thank God Mother Nature cooperated. It's going to be a wonderful holiday." Amy could hear the enthusiasm in her own voice. "You know, it doesn't even bother me that I work like a dog these few days."

"Listen, you going to be all right Sunday morning? I won't be able to get here until after the jump."

"It'll be fine. I'm not going to open up until ten. I'll put a sign on the door that says *gone to watch a crazy woman jump out of a helicopter.*" She placed her hand against her chest as if to emphasize the seriousness of her words. "You're not going to go through with that, are you?"

"Absolutely." Elizabeth's eyes were shimmering with excitement. "I talked to the advance man just yesterday. The group will be here today. They're staying at the motel. The town is having a reception for them at the Community Building tonight. I'm going to be there. He said he thought it'd be nice if the four of us got to meet the people we're jumping with."

"Four?"

"Yeah. Me, two reporters and someone else. I was so excited talking with him, I forgot to ask who the fourth person was."

"It won't be Kelly. We had a long discussion about that. So it's

128

obviously someone as crazy as you. I can't talk you out of this?" Amy asked her hands on her hips.

"No." Elizabeth smiled. "It's like I'm going through my second adolescence. You know when you're in a relationship you want to build your life around that person, so you put things you'd like to do on hold. When I turned forty I fantasized about jumping out of an airplane, but I didn't do it because I knew Lois would have a fit—or at least some very anxious moments. Funny, in retrospect I know she wouldn't have stopped me, but I just didn't want her to even have to worry for a minute. So I didn't do it. Now I don't owe my life or time to anyone, so I can do whatever I please. I'm seventy-five years old. I could die tomorrow of a stroke or heart attack, but it seems to me it'd be more fun to die jumping out of a helicopter or dangling from a bungee cord."

"Bungee cord? Elizabeth Robinson, I don't even want to think of you doing something like that. My God, people get killed."

"Really." Elizabeth raised her eyebrow. "How many people have been killed in the last year jumping off a cliff with a bungee cord?"

"I don't know. We live on an island, we probably don't hear about it," Amy said in exasperation.

"And how many people die in a car crash or in bed."

"I don't know."

"Well"—Elizabeth looked up at the clock and then turned the sign on the door from closed to open—"read the obituary column like I do. There isn't a one that says Joe Blow died because his bungee cord broke. But a lot of them say, 'In lieu of flowers please make a donation to the American Heart Association or the American Cancer Society.' So what does that tell you?"

"It tells me there's no Bungee Cord Society," Amy said with a laugh.

Elizabeth laughed too. "By the way, you okay with that other issue?"

Amy shrugged, knowing the reference was to Susan, the LNG woman. "Just okay."

"Because I've thought long and hard—" Elizabeth stopped when the door opened and in walked Maggie Beth and Terry. "You two are out early."

"What brings you two to the shop?"

Terry said, "We were in town and decided to stop by. Listen, got a call from a friend of ours who's coming up for the weekend. It was totally unexpected. Anyway, could we bring her to the party on Monday?"

"Of course, the more the merrier. Kelly's friend Laurie gets in sometime today and Elizabeth has a surprise for you." Amy tried to add lightness to her tone.

"I invited someone too."

"Who'd you invite?" Maggie Beth asked.

"Susan."

"Susan? Do we know her?" Maggie looked confused.

"The LNG lady," Elizabeth said hesitantly.

"She invited the LNG woman to my party!" Amy said indignantly. She repressed the flash of anger she had felt when Elizabeth first told her.

"A woman who is, I might add, a very nice person." She turned to Maggie Beth and Terry. "We had lunch a few days ago. I really like Susan. I told her I don't like what she's doing here, but I also know I can separate the two."

"We don't have a problem," Maggie said with a shrug, looking at Amy.

"Well, I do," Amy said more loudly than she intended. She inhaled deeply. "I do," she said more quietly. "You should have told me sooner."

"I told you yesterday at the store. Honestly," she said to Maggie Beth and Terry, "I didn't think it was a problem so I didn't even think to bring it up. I guess I could have called you. But why? You've got this open-door policy. So why would you shut it on her, a complete stranger in town?"

"So springing it on me makes more sense."

"I didn't spring it on you," Elizabeth said somewhat defensively.

130

"If I was going to spring it on you, I would have shown up with her. Now, that is springing something on someone." She looked at Maggie Beth and Terry. "Did that make sense?"

They nodded in agreement.

"I can't believe this." Amy turned her back to them. *Get control*, she said to herself. *Get control.* "Like I said yesterday, Elizabeth, I don't think you thought this through."

"Actually, you're right. We had lunch and on an impulse I invited her. Then I didn't think another thing about it, really. Amy, you're the one who's said anyone and everyone is welcome at your parties. I took you at your word."

"Not our enemy."

"She's not the enemy," Elizabeth shot back.

"Look," Maggie said kindly, "you two work this out. Terry and I have more errands to run." She gave Elizabeth a peck on the cheek. "See you tomorrow. Harnessed and ready to jump."

"You bet." Elizabeth hugged Terry.

"Nothing we can say to get you to change your mind?" Maggie asked.

"Nope."

"I thought so."

Amy knew she had to say something. The awkwardness hung in the air like the stench of a dead right whale. She tried to lighten her tone. "You guys go ahead. Elizabeth may or may not be jumping tomorrow. I may kill her today," she added with a laugh. She watched as Maggie Beth and Terry quickly departed. "Getting back to your friend Susan. You should have told me, Elizabeth."

"I know, but I also knew you'd react this way."

"Afraid to confront me?"

"No, I just didn't feel I needed to. I'm bringing a friend to your party." Elizabeth shrugged. "A friend, I might add, who is lonely and you've got to just accept that. In the past, I've brought friends. Heck, remember the time Lois's family dropped in. There were four of them. We just showed up and you were all hugs. What makes this any different?"

131

"She's part of the plan to kill our island. That's what makes this different. It's like sleeping with the enemy."

"Amy, she's not the enemy. I don't want LNG here either. She's the hired gun."

"The hired gun that could seduce people into wanting this."

"That's her job. On a personal level, she's nice. I like her a lot."

"You're not . . ." Amy raised an eyebrow.

"Interested? Not likely. She's just a baby."

"Then what?"

"I feel sorry for her—she's all alone here. The developers have gone back to Boston for a few days. She was going to go home to Andover, but she was able to move into her cottage this week, so she decided to stay here to get settled in. If I hadn't invited her, she'd be spending the weekend alone, and you know what? That's just not right."

Amy sniffed. "Hang out with her today."

"Well, that's a thought, but I agreed to help you, remember? I invited her to come to the airport tomorrow."

"You're kidding." She could hardly keep the disgust out of her voice.

"Now, what's the harm in that?"

"Just that all of your friends will be there, me included, to support this crazy-ass scheme of yours."

"Great, the more the merrier. Bring Kelly's friend along, maybe the two of them will hit it off."

"Don't tell me she's a lesbian?" Amy could just imagine Laurie and Susan hitting it off.

"Bingo."

Amy groaned. "A lesbian and a turncoat all in one package."

"And an attractive package," Elizabeth said, clearly trying to lighten the tone.

"You're sure you don't have a thing for her?" Amy asked suspiciously.

"No," Elizabeth said quietly. "I do feel sorry for her. If she'd come into this town under any other circumstance and you'd met her you'd have welcomed her with open arms. We can do battle with her and the company she represents, but let's not minimize her value as a very nice person."

"I—" Amy stopped when the door opened. "We're not done talking about this," she said between clenched teeth.

"I think we are," Elizabeth said as she walked forward to help the customers.

Chapter Seventeen

"Heya, woman," Laurie said as she got out of the car.

Kelly had watched her drive up. It was just after eleven o'clock on Saturday morning. She was out the door before Laurie had her car door open. She grabbed Laurie and hugged her. "God, I've missed you," she said, giving her a second bear hug.

"Me you," Laurie said, returning the hug. "You look great."

"So do you. A few more wrinkles, maybe." Kelly stepped back and surveyed her. "Some extra grays around the edges." She shrugged.

"Stop," Laurie said, laughing. "What, you've become a beauty expert now?"

"Naw, come on. Where's your suitcase?"

"No suitcase, just my backpack," Laurie said, reaching into the back of her car. "Where's Amy?"

"At the store. This is her busiest weekend. So she and another friend of ours, Elizabeth—I can't wait for you to meet her, she's a delight—they'll be at the store until six o'clock. Then we're going to have a quiet dinner here at the house. Tomorrow we're going to the airport. A skydiving team from Brunswick is going to be doing some practice jumps. Some locals are jumping with them."

"How cool is that?"

"Well it gets even cooler," Kelly said confidentially as she held the screen door open for Laurie. "I'm tandem-jumping with one of them. No one knows—it's going to be a big surprise for everyone."

"You're nuts!" Laurie exclaimed.

"Well, we've always known that. Sit down. Do you want to use the facilities? I'll show you to your room." Kelly stopped and inhaled deeply. *Slow down*, she said to herself. She was nervous. She still hadn't told Amy about the jump because she'd rationalized they'd just gotten over another fight and they needed quiet time in their relationship, at least for a short time. Plus, she didn't want to give Amy any more ammunition. It was pure cowardice, she knew. She'd been going to tell her after they made love but was afraid. How strange was that? she thought.

"Now, let me get this straight." Laurie eyed her, and Kelly knew that her face was flushed. "You're going to jump out of a perfectly good airplane."

"Helicopter."

"Helicopter, airplane, what does it matter. They all go very high. How high, by the way?"

Kelly shrugged. "They said ten thousand feet."

"Ten thousand feet?" Laurie croaked. "How does Amy feel about this?"

"Well, I haven't exactly told her."

Laurie laughed. "You don't have to worry about jumping out of a helicopter tomorrow because she's going to kill you."

How right you are, Kelly thought. "Naw, she'll be fine with it once she gets used to the idea."

"Hell, I'd kill you if you were mine. What, you got a death wish?"

"It's safe," Kelly said defensively. "Besides, I thought you'd be happy for me. This is one of those once-in-a-lifetime things you get to do. I just couldn't pass it up."

"I'm amazed, really."

"Amazed why?"

"Of the two of us, you've never been the daredevil. Remember that time we went snowmobiling? It was a first for both of us."

"I remember." Kelly laughed, relieved that Laurie had changed the subject. They'd just graduated from nursing school and a bunch of them decided to have one last fling before settling down to work. Laurie was out there with the best of them zooming across the environs at more than fifty miles an hour. "I was riding the snowmobile—" She couldn't stop laughing.

"Help me out here." Laurie giggled. "You were riding it how?"

"Slower."

"Like your great-great-grandmother's Model T Ford. You were going so slow even the chickadee was outdistancing you."

"It wasn't that bad," Kelly said happily. "I just didn't want to go fast, that's all. I was there to see the countryside, not join in that snowmobile subculture called speed."

"And jumping out of a helicopter, you're not going to be able to put the brakes on and slowly float to the ground while you look at the countryside," Laurie mimicked.

"Well, that's not true. Once the chute opens you're supposed to just float to the ground. Then you can see the countryside."

"And what are you doing before that?"

"Well, kinda falling through the air." Kelly laughed. For some reason the idea didn't scare her.

"Bingo. Just my point. And what kind of speeds are you dropping at?"

"I didn't really want to know," Kelly said with raised eyebrows.

"For as much of a daredevil as I am, and I'm a heck of a lot more of one than you are, I'm not sure I'd jump out of one of those things."

"Well, I don't agree. Somehow I think if you'd had the opportunity you'd be going up there with me."

136

"I'd have to think about that."

"Come on, I'll show you to your room." Kelly picked up Laurie's backpack. "By the way, good news. Maggie Beth and Terry did find you some digs. On the other side of the island, there's a large property. There's a cottage and a carriage house and the owners have turned the top of the carriage house into an apartment. We tried to get you the cottage, because it's bigger, but that's been rented by someone else. The carriage house is only one room, but Terry said it's really nice. We have an appointment to look at it this afternoon."

"Great. Want to go now?"

"We have an appointment to meet with the caretaker at three." Kelly looked at her watch. "Hungry?"

"A little. I grabbed a doughnut and coffee this morning. Haven't had much else."

Kelly opened the door to Laurie's room. "It's small, but then all of the rooms are small. The house is more than one hundred and fifty years old."

"I love the way it's been decorated. It feels comfortable."

"That's Amy's doing. This was her grandparents' house. After she inherited it, she had it completely renovated. So all of the touches are hers."

"I'm really looking forward to getting to know her. We just wasted so many years." There was a wistfulness in Laurie's voice.

"Years we can make up for, now that you're here." Kelly set the backpack on the bed. "I'm so glad you're back in my life. It's like having a piece of my past. Not that I don't love it here. I've made some wonderful friends, friends that I'll keep for life, but you're just like an old shoe."

"Thanks." Laurie laughed. "Some smelly old sneaker, no doubt."

"You know what I mean."

"I do," Laurie said quietly. "I've missed us, Kelly. I got into that relationship and I just let all the important things slip away. I was really worried I'd done some damage to our friendship. Before, there were partners in our lives and we were still best buds, but oh well. It's hard to explain. I'm just glad I'm here."

"Me too. Now let's turn off this walk down memory lane and go get a bite to eat. I'll meet you downstairs." Kelly gave her another hug. "I'm going to take you to one of our local hangouts. Thought we'd stop at the gallery first so you can see Amy. I also want you to meet Elizabeth. She's a great friend—seventy-five years old and a poster child for growing old with gusto."

"This the same woman you mentioned a few minutes ago. She's jumping out of the helicopter?"

"Absolutely. She's something else. I just love her to death."

Laurie faked a cringe. "Please don't use that word."

Kelly gently punched her in the arm. "Do you know that jumping out of a helicopter is safer than walking across a street in Portland?"

"Why doesn't that comfort me?"

"Freshen up. I can't wait to take you over to the gallery," Kelly said enthusiastically.

"That," Kelly said, pointing out the side window, "is the road to the marina. They have these gigantic rocks that jut out of the water. That's where a lot of people go to have picnics. You have to have some billy goat in you in order to get from one rock to the other, but everyone around here does it. And this"—she waved her arm in the air—"is downtown Bleu Island."

"I like it. And I especially love the decorations."

Kelly looked around at the flags hanging from the street lamps. Flower baskets with red, white and blue flowers had been hung below each flag. She was so used to seeing them that she had actually stopped seeing them. "I hope so, because this is your new home."

"I was up here years ago."

"After I first moved up here."

"No, as a kid. My parents brought my brother and me up here.

I can't even remember why. I remember thinking it was small. Y'know, I think it must have been the Fourth of July. We went to this parade and I remember afterward eating hot dogs down at the marina. I'm not sure why we came up here. Day trip, I guess." Laurie shrugged. "It was probably my dad's idea. He used to love to pile us all into a car and go for a Sunday drive. Sometimes that Sunday drive went on for hours."

"That's neat." Kelly looked out the car window. "Here we are." She pointed toward a vacant parking spot. "Park there. The gallery is right over there." She gestured across the road. "Come on, Amy is anxious to meet you." They headed toward the gallery. "Ah, by the way, it's mum on the jump. I'm going to surprise everyone."

"I think 'surprise' is putting it mildly. Try shocked."

"Well, just a mild shock," Kelly said as she opened the door. "Hi, there. Look at the straggler I found hanging around our doorstep. Laurie, you know Amy, and this is Elizabeth."

"Nice to meet you," Laurie said, extending her hand.

"Put that hand away. Everyone gets a hug that comes into our lives," Amy said, reaching out to embrace Laurie.

"Well, I like that tradition." Laurie seemed uncertain if she should also hug Elizabeth.

"Me too," Elizabeth said. Kelly noticed how dwarfed Elizabeth was next to Laurie, whose burnt umber eyes danced with pleasure as she looked first at Amy and then Elizabeth.

Kelly said, "She hasn't eaten, so I thought we'd go to the SeaBleu for a bite of lunch."

"Not too big a bite," Amy said. "I have a big meal planned for tonight. Elizabeth is going to join us."

"Great." Kelly smiled at Laurie. "Elizabeth will no doubt regale us with stories about the good old days."

"Not so old, Kelly Burns. I'm not even thirty years ahead of you."

"Ah, but so much has happened in those thirty years," Kelly teased. "We moved from horse and buggy to the automobile. You watched as they replaced gaslights with electricity—"

"You keep that up and I'm going to really bore you with all those sad stories about how we used to have to walk to school in the snow and how, back when we were growing up, the snow used to be up higher than an elephant's eye. Course, what everyone forgets"—Elizabeth put her hands on her hips—"elephants were a lot shorter back then." She laughed at her own joke.

"Well, you can regale us with any story you'd like," Laurie said joining in the fun. "Don't let this bag of bones think that I'm not interested."

"Bag of bones, I don't think so." Kelly feigned hurt.

"Well, compared to this sturdy stock, you are, my friend." Laurie said, laughing. "By the way, Amy, you got yourself a piece of work here, you know that, don't you. Now, if you want to hear some stories, I can fill your ears about some of the shenanigans our friend here used to get into in nursing school. Why, I can even tell you about the time—"

"Stop." Kelly held up her hands. "What happened in nursing school stays in nursing school. No tall tales out of school."

"Well, maybe, maybe not," Laurie said, clearly trying to keep the smirk off her face. "It depends upon whether you can bribe me or not."

Amy laughed. "I would love to hear some stories. This woman is just so closed-mouthed when it comes to talking about herself. It's worse than prying open a scallop shell."

Laurie laughed. "Now, that's a new one. I doubt it's a willing scallop."

"My point exactly." Amy was laughing too.

Kelly looked from Laurie to Amy. She could see that Amy was enjoying herself. Good, she thought. She knew that once Amy got to know Laurie she would adore her. "Anyway, I'll take Laurie over and feed her, then we're going to see that place Maggie and Terry found."

"Isn't that terrific." Amy turned to Elizabeth. "The old Grange place. They've gone over to the mainland to be with their children. So they're renting the cottage and they've renovated the upstairs above the carriage house and turned that into a small apartment. Someone's renting the cottage, but the carriage house is still vacant. I haven't seen it, but I know anything that family does is first-rate."

"Uh-huh," Elizabeth said, frowning.

"What's 'uh-huh'?" Amy demanded.

"I know who's renting the cottage."

"Don't tell me the LNG lady," Amy said.

"Bingo."

Amy groaned. "Can't we get her out of our lives?"

"I don't understand." Laurie looked from Amy to Kelly.

"It's okay. Amy's just having a serious gas attack." Elizabeth laughed.

When the others realized Elizabeth's pun, they also laughed, even Amy.

Laurie said, "Kelly told me you're getting ready to do battle on this LNG thing. Anything I can do, just ask, from carrying petitions around to painting placards."

"Well, I'm glad to hear that. Better than your friend here," Amy said lightly. "She's so busy at the hospital, I can't get her to a meeting."

Laurie nodded. "Well, we'll change that. Don't you worry. She was like that in school. Everyone else would be sitting around relaxing and having a glass of wine and Kelly would have her head buried in a book."

"By the way, our friend here," Amy said, pointing at Elizabeth, "has invited the LNG woman to our party."

"Susan. Her name is Susan, not LNG," Elizabeth said.

"Whatever."

Kelly looked at Elizabeth, who looked away. That must have been an interesting conversation, Kelly thought, between Elizabeth and Amy. She wondered at how much of a verbal beating Elizabeth had taken. "I told Amy I thought it was fine. She's alone here and we've always had a policy of inviting anyone who didn't have a place to go on the Fourth." She turned to Laurie. "We've

141

always had an interesting mix of people. We've even had people there we've never seen again." She scratched her cheek. "Don't know if it was the company or the food."

"Neither." Elizabeth laughed. "Mostly it's been people who've come to the island and then left. They can't stand the isolation here. Kelly and Amy always open their house to any stray that lands here. I think that's pretty darn nice. So when I found out Susan was going to be alone here I invited her, and I invited her to the airport tomorrow."

Amy shook her head. "Another crazy thing you're doing. You've been on a roll this week, Elizabeth."

"Just buying into some fun of what's left of my short life."

"Kelly told me you're jumping out of a helicopter," Laurie said. "I must say you're the first skydiver I've ever met. I've seen it on television, so you're sort of a celebrity."

"Well, that's nice of you to say."

"Yeah, right," Amy joined in the banter. "Just think, everyone's going to want your autograph."

"Well, I might just give it to them," Elizabeth replied. "Heck, I might even charge them for it. I might even write a book. Include it in one of those lesbian romance novels you young lesbians like to read. Why, I think we should take out a full-page ad in the local newspaper, 'Famous Skydiver and Author to Perform Sunday.'"

They all laughed. "I think it's going to your head." Amy looked at her affectionately. "But I'm going to tell you one thing right now, Elizabeth Robinson, you kill yourself and you can bet I'll never speak to you again."

"Interesting thought." Elizabeth frowned as if pondering Amy's threat. "But if I'm killed, I doubt I'd even want you to speak to me again. I can just imagine it. As I'm headed for the afterlife you'd be saying, 'Elizabeth Robinson you are one dumb clam. You got yourself killed jumping out of a helicopter,'" she mimicked. "'Why, all I can say is you went out with a big splat.'"

"Stop it." Amy was laughing. She said to Kelly, "Take your friend to lunch. Take her with you." She nodded to Elizabeth.

"Would you like to join us, Elizabeth?" Kelly asked, also laughing.

"I would to get away from all this abuse, but I'll stay here. You never know, it's quiet now, but in a few minutes that door could open and an entire busload of people come trotting in with little greenbacks clutched tightly in their hands."

"It's okay," Amy said. "If you'd like to get some lunch, go ahead."

"Not to worry, love. I brought my lunch with me. I'll grab a bite between customers. Speaking of customers—" Elizabeth nodded toward the door.

"Listen, I'll catch you later at the house," Kelly murmured. She squeezed Amy's hand.

Amy smiled at her. "Okay, and good luck on the carriage house," she said to Laurie.

"I'm excited," Laurie said enthusiastically. "I figured I'd be stuck in a motel until I found something more permanent."

"Well, first off," Amy said matter-of-factly, "you wouldn't have been stuck in a motel room, you'd stay with us." Kelly noticed Amy didn't even look at her as she said it.

"And I appreciate the offer," Laurie said with a smile. "But you know that saying about guests and day-old fish. Well, let's just say I'm glad there's something to rent. In fact"—she turned to Kelly—"I would have trusted your judgment. As far as I'm concerned you could have said yes."

"Wasn't necessary. You have first dibs on it."

"I just love the idea of living in a carriage house, it sounds so Victorian. I have a feeling I'll take it regardless."

"Well, that's probably not a bad idea," Elizabeth said, "since there really isn't much else around here. Nice meeting you, Laurie. I'll see you tomorrow."

Chapter Eighteen

"Well, here it is," Kelly said, turning into the driveway. They'd had lunch and now were ready to see the carriage house.

"Wow, look at that house. This is an estate!" Laurie exclaimed as she gaped at the main structure, a formidable three-story captain's house painted yellow with brown trim. Next to it sat a cottage that Kelly knew had at one time belonged to the gardener. Across the driveway was a two-story stable where the original owners had kept their horses. Above the carriage house was an apartment.

"It was." Kelly also admired it. "The man who built the first sardine plant on the island used to live here. I understand from what folks say around here that there used to be some pretty lavish parties on the island. This place used to be humming."

"What happened?"

"The sardine factories went down the drain and along with it a lot of the spin-off businesses that had supported them. According

144

to Amy, for a long time this place would have put some of those Western ghost towns to shame. She said people just left. You couldn't sell a house here, because there was no one to buy."

"When did that change?"

"Oh, I don't know." Kelly got out of the car. Laurie followed. "At first New Yorkers and folks from Massachusetts bought land dirt-cheap here on the ocean. They were speculators and for a time, as properties turned over and over, people would buy whatever. Then there was a second wave that wanted to get out of the city. They'd made a bundle working there and decided to look farther north. They're the ones who began to buy up the properties and live here year-round. A lot of the places were fixed up and this was one of them. A man and his wife from New York bought it. Lived here a long while. I understand they have some sort of health problems now and are on the mainland. They always rented out the cottage, but never the carriage house. But, I guess they changed their minds because according to Maggie Beth and Terry, now they're renting it."

"Are we going to be able to get in?"

"Maggie Beth and Terry got the key from the caretaker." Kelly stopped when she heard a car. "That should be them now." She frowned as she looked at the Volvo coming toward them. "Well, maybe not. I don't recognize that car."

"Hi," a blond woman said as she opened her door. She had parked next to Kelly's car. "I'm Susan Iogen. Are you family of the owners?"

"No." Kelly stared at her. "I'm . . ." She paused. Amy hadn't mentioned how beautiful Susan was. "Let me start that again," she said with a laugh. "I'm Kelly Burns and this is my friend Laurie Stocking. Laurie is thinking of renting the carriage house. The owners have an apartment above the former stables."

Susan's smile radiated toward them. "Good, we'll be neighbors," she said, shaking Laurie's hand. Kelly noticed Laurie for the first time. She was speechless as she stood staring at Susan.

"Nice . . . to . . . meet . . . you," Laurie stuttered stupidly.

145

"I understand you're coming to my party Monday," Kelly said, having recovered her composure. The sun created an almost halo effect around Susan's blond hair. Her eyes reminded Kelly of the emerald waters she had seen in Key West.

"Ah, you and Amy, right?"

"Right."

"Look—" Susan paused. "I met Elizabeth, and God love her, she's so open and warm and inviting. She insisted I join her. I felt funny, given my reasons for being here on the island."

"Not to worry," Kelly said. "People will be fine with it. Some will think we're sleeping with the enemy, but most folks will accept you for who you are."

"Well, that's nice to hear. So, have you seen the carriage house yet?" Susan asked Laurie.

"No. I just got here." Laurie looked like a street sweeper had flattened her. Kelly suppressed a smile.

"It's wonderful. I saw it before. In fact, I was going to rent it, but when they showed me the cottage, I fell in love with it." Susan turned toward the door of the cottage. "Come in. You two will be my first guests." She opened the door and stood back to let them in. Kelly noticed her smile was absolutely provocative. She felt a soft shudder move up her spine. There was something utterly beguiling about her. Kelly stopped. What was that about? she thought. Just a brain burp. She focused again on what Susan was saying. "It's small but wonderful. Look at this living room." Her voice was tinged with excitement. "It reminds me of a dollhouse. The furniture just seems to fit perfectly into every little nook and cranny. The kitchen is small, but I just love this floor plan. My kitchen, living room and dining room are all right here," she said, waving her arm.

"It's neat," Kelly said as she walked around the room. Susan was right. It did remind her of a dollhouse, yet it felt so comfortable.

"And look at this." Susan slid two doors back to reveal a small bedroom. There was a canopied bed with a matching dresser and end tables. "This is perfect. As a child I always wanted a canopied

bed never got one. My mother said my bed was just fine. And"—
she opened another door—"this is the bathroom. Look at that
great shower stall." She pointed at the glass blocks that served as
the shower door.

"I love it," Kelly said. "What a great idea. No shower curtain,
no door, just a half-wall of glass blocks."

"That's what I thought. Whoever designed this had a wonderful sense of what this place needed."

"I'm envious," Laurie said. "I hope the carriage house is this
nice."

"It is. I just liked this place more. I don't know, it just seemed to
suit me."

"It does," Kelly said, looking around the house. "Sorry." She
smiled to cover her embarrassment. "I don't even know you, but
somehow I can see you here."

"Maybe after I move out, you can rent it," Susan said to Laurie.

"You're not staying?" There was disappointment in Laurie's
voice.

"No, I'm just here for however long it takes for people to
decide if they want my bosses here."

"Oh, right, LNG." Kelly could see Laurie was still flustered.

"LNG." Susan smiled. "Right now not the most popular folks
in this town."

"Well, people have to—" Kelly stopped when she heard a car
outside. "Here's Maggie Beth and Terry," she said, walking out
onto the porch. She smiled when she saw them. "Come here," she
called to Laurie and Susan, who were still standing in the living
room. "I want you both to meet two of the nicest women in
America." She hugged first Maggie and then Terry.

"How are you, hon?" Maggie said.

"Great. I want you to meet my best pal." Kelly nodded at
Laurie. "Laurie Stocking." Laurie extended her hand.

"I'm Maggie Beth or Maggie, I answer to both and we hug new
and old friends," she said with a laugh as she embraced Laurie.
Terry also hugged her.

147

"And this is Susan—"

"We know, the LNG lady," Maggie finished the sentence.

"Guilty," Susan said self-consciously as Terry and Maggie hugged her.

"You're not the enemy," Maggie said, surveying her. "Your bosses are, but you're just doing your job. I can only hope you don't do it too well," she added with a laugh.

"Susan's coming to our party," Kelly said to cover the awkwardness.

"We know," Maggie said. "We stopped by the gallery."

"Then you know Elizabeth invited me," Susan said quietly, looking first at Maggie and then Terry.

"That doesn't surprise me. We know you had lunch with her, but when'd you meet Elizabeth?" Terry asked.

"After the first meeting. I went for a run; Elizabeth was walking her dog at the marina. She's someone you just know you've met in other lives."

"She's our capricious curmudgeon," Maggie said affectionately. "We love her to death. Anyway"—she turned to Laurie—"we have the key." She held it up. "And I expect you'd like to see where you're going to be living for a while."

"I would. Why don't you join us?" Laurie said to Susan. Kelly could sense Laurie was already on the prowl.

"Sure."

"Well, come on then," Maggie said, walking across the parking area to the carriage house. "They renovated this about four years ago. Visiting family members have mostly used it so there's not been a lot of wear and tear." She opened the door. "As you can see, it's just one big room with a small bathroom over here," she said, gesturing.

Kelly looked around. There was a small twin bed and end table in one corner, a round table and chairs nearby that seemed to spill over into a small living area. A counter that served as a working island separated the kitchen from the rest of the apartment. She tried to gauge Laurie's reaction.

"I'll take it," Laurie said quickly.

"You haven't even seen the bathroom," Kelly said.

"I don't have to." Laurie shot Susan a smile. "I'll take it," she repeated.

"Great, I'll call the caretaker and tell him," Maggie said. "Kelly told you about the rent and the fact that they want a one-year lease on this."

"She did. I'm fine with the details. How soon can I move in?"

"Immediately," Terry said. "But I thought you planned to spend some time with Kelly and Amy."

"You won't mind if I move in immediately, would you?" she said to Kelly.

Kelly chuckled to herself. *Oh yeah*, she thought, *Laurie was definitely smitten.* "Have at it," she said. "We can get your backpack later."

"Since I'm going to be living here, how about we go to the party together?" Laurie suggested to Susan.

"That would be nice, but I did promise to go with Elizabeth. I'm sure she wouldn't mind if you joined us. I'm driving over to the airport early tomorrow so I can watch her skydive."

"Great, I'm going over to support this crazy friend of mine—" Laurie stopped.

"You're not jumping too?" Maggie was clearly surprised.

"Well, I am." Kelly looked pointedly at Laurie.

"I'm sorry. It just popped out." Laurie smiled at Maggie Beth and Terry. "Please don't say anything."

"To whom?" Maggie demanded. "Uh oh. You haven't told Amy."

"Not yet, I didn't want to upset her."

"And you're getting to the airport and then telling her will, what, not upset her?" Maggie asked with a raised brow.

"Well." Kelly felt uncomfortable with the way the conversation was going. How could she tell Amy's best friends that she hadn't mentioned it because she was a coward and wanted to avoid yet another fight after the upset over Laurie's arrival. She'd finally decided to tell Amy at the airport in front of their friends. That way she knew Amy's anger would be mitigated. *You really are a coward*, she chided herself. Hiding behind her friends. She knew she'd have to listen to Amy afterward, but afterward was a long ways away. "I just didn't want her to worry," she said lamely. "Are you going to tell her?" She looked from Terry to Maggie.

"No, it's not our place, but you should tell her. Waiting until she gets to the airport is not the place to tell her," Terry said.

"Sorry, pal. I didn't mean to broadcast it to the world, it just slipped out," Laurie muttered, clearly uncomfortable.

"I know, it's fine."

"Look, this seems like a family matter," Susan said. "I think I'll just go back over to my place and leave you all here to discuss this."

"I'll join you," Laurie said, following her out. Kelly smiled when Laurie threw a look that said, "What can I do?"

"You need to tell her," Maggie said quietly after Susan and Laurie had left.

"I know. Honest, I just learned I was selected two days ago. Someone else backed out. The advance man called me and told me I was going to jump." Kelly looked down at her feet. "I had to decide if I really wanted to do it. I decided that yesterday. I know that's no excuse. I wish I could say I didn't have a chance to tell her, but that'd be a lie."

"I know it'll be hard," Terry said. "I know Amy will get upset, but Maggie's right—to let her find out the day of the jump, that would be unfair."

"I know, I know," Kelly said miserably. She couldn't tell them that she dreaded telling Amy because Amy's anger would run over her like stampeding horses.

"It seems like you're going to have plenty of opportunity," Maggie said with a glance at the door. "I think your friend is smitten."

"I think you're right," Kelly said, relieved that the conversation moved to more solid ground. "*Smitten* is probably too nice a word. I'd say more like lobster hot on the trail of bait. Just crawl into the trap and not even look back."

"Well, that wouldn't be such a bad trap." Terry blushed. "Sorry, I didn't mean that the way it sounded."

Maggie smiled at Terry. "Sometimes you can't help but notice the packaging. We may be married, but we ain't dead."

"Agreed." Kelly nodded. "Actually, I'm glad Elizabeth invited her. You know we all have this open-door policy about inviting new people into our lives. I know she's here to do a job, but she seems nice."

"And your friend there is definitely after nice." Maggie added, "Is she family?"

"Don't know. I haven't had a chance to ask either Elizabeth or Amy. My gaydar went off, but heck, I'm most often wrong, not right. The first time I moved to the island, I thought I'd moved to Provincetown. Half the women looked gay to me. Come to find out, they just look that way 'cause so many of them have had such a hard life. They're not into primping. Hell, they're not gay, they're just sturdy. They all have this kind of soft butch look, pardon my stereotyping," Kelly said with a laugh.

"You're right," Maggie agreed. "We had the same impression. Thought the same thing. Women just don't have a lot of time to be femme and frilly here. When we met Amy, we had a dickens of a time. She's so feminine looking. Missed completely that she was gay. I thought she was married with children until I found out she was living with a woman." She paused. "I shouldn't bring that up."

"Don't worry about it," Kelly said. "Amy wasn't just sitting around waiting for me to land on this island. She's talked about the women in her past, as I have with her. We're fine with it. It's the past. We're the present."

"Well, as I've said before, I haven't seen Amy this happy in years. To your credit. Now don't turn that into something else— you tell her. She deserves to know and yes, she'll probably fuss and fume, but she'll understand."

"I don't understand it," Terry said, heading toward the door. "Jumping out of a airplane, helicopter or whatever just isn't my idea of fun. I can't even understand why you'd want to do it, but you're our friend, Elizabeth is our friend and we'll be out there."

"Good, because I want you there," Kelly said, following them out.

"We can assume that Laurie's going to take the apartment then?" Terry asked, standing beside her car.

"Most definitely, but I'll double-check. She wasn't really focused on the space, if you know what I mean." Kelly opened the screen door to the cottage, where Susan and Laurie were sitting on the couch talking. "Excuse me," she said.

"Come in," Susan said, getting up. "Laurie and I were just chatting."

"Maggie and Terry are ready to leave. They want to make sure you want to rent the carriage house."

"I do," Laurie said. "Susan and I were just talking about how much fun it's going to be being neighbors."

"Do you want to look at it one more time before they lock up?"

"Nope." Laurie glanced at Susan. "It's just fine. I just need to know who I pay my first month's rent to."

"Well, why don't we ask?" Kelly and Laurie went outside to get the details from Maggie Beth and Terry.

Ten minutes later, after hugs all around, Maggie and Terry left.

"Well," Kelly said, "that was unpleasant."

"Kelly, I'm really sorry." Laurie touched Kelly's arm. "I wish I had a good excuse for blurting that out, but I don't. It just came out. I'm embarrassed. I don't know. I met Susan and I just got rattled. I'm really sorry."

Kelly shrugged. "It's not your fault." She sighed. "I should have told Amy."

"Is everything all right between you two?" Laurie asked.

"Of course," Kelly said lightly. "Look, we do need to get back. Let's tell Susan good-bye and get going. It looks like you've got some new digs."

"I'm sorry about that too." Laurie shook her head. "I met Susan and for some reason, my brain just started to come apart."

"Is she—?"

"Oh, yeah. That's what we were talking about when you came

in. She's been out of a relationship several years. Very driven by her public relations business."

"God, you two covered a lot of ground in a short period of time."

"We did, but come on. She's probably thinking we're some of the rudest people she's ever met." Laurie softly knocked on the cottage door.

"Come in," Susan said.

"Sorry about that," Kelly said to Susan. "I know it must look kinda strange me not telling my partner I'm jumping out of a helicopter."

"You don't have to explain it," Susan said. "I understand. If I were in your shoes I'd probably do the same thing to keep her from stressing out."

"Well, something like that," Kelly mumbled. She didn't want to discuss Amy with Susan or Laurie.

"Look, I also know that I was dumped on you and Amy. I can certainly find an excuse not to go and not to go to the airport to watch Elizabeth jump."

"No!" Kelly and Laurie said at the same time.

"I mean—" Kelly thought for a moment. "Look, there are some folks who believe you're Typhoid Mary. Heck, I live with the woman who's spearheading the opposition group, but that aside, Elizabeth is our dearest friend. She's right when she said we have a policy of inviting new people to our lobster feed. She invited you and that's it." She paused and then said more softly, "We'd really like you to come."

"Thank you."

"Besides, who's going to keep me company?" Laurie said with a wink. "Here my best friend is going to be jumping out of a helicopter and I'm on the ground all by myself. Worrying."

"Oh, God," Kelly said, rolling her eyes. "Pretty soon we'll have to drag out the crying towels."

"Alone." Laurie hung her head. "No one to talk to. No one to hold my hand while my best friend is busy trying to kill herself, and the next day I'm going to be at a party where I won't know a soul. All alone, standing in a corner somewhere, watching all of the fun and frivolity." She faked a sob.

Kelly shook her head. "Just give up," she said to Susan. "This gal is on a tear and unless you say yes, we'll have to stand here and listen to all of this hogwash."

"Okay, okay." Susan laughingly held her hands up in surrender. "I'll be there tomorrow and I'll be at your party on Monday."

"Good." Kelly smiled. "Come on, Helen Hunt. Your performance was absolutely B-rated."

"Unfair, I thought it was quite convincing. Susan did after all agree to join us." Laurie smirked triumphantly.

Susan and Kelly laughed. "That I did," Susan said. She held out her hand. "Thank you. I would enjoy spending the Fourth of July weekend with some pretty neat women."

"Good, now let's get going," Kelly said to Laurie. "I've got things to do. We have to get you in touch with the caretaker to pay the rent. When do you want to move in?"

"Tonight," Laurie stole a look at Susan. "That's of course if it's all right with you and Amy," she said to Kelly. "That way you won't have me underfoot while you're trying to get ready for your party."

"That's fine." Kelly sighed inwardly. Her friend was a goner, no question about it.

Chapter Nineteen

When Amy arrived home from work that evening. Kelly told her about the carriage house and detected a note of relief on Amy's face when she mentioned Laurie's plan to move that night. She omitted Laurie's reaction to Susan but did tell her Laurie was at that moment paying her first month's rent and would be back for dinner.

"Elizabeth canceled," Amy said, setting some groceries on the counter.

"Why?" Kelly said as she opened the refrigerator to put the tomatoes and lettuce away. She took out the wine and poured a glass for her and Amy and set them on the counter.

"Said she was tired. I think it has more to do with that damn helicopter." Amy pulled bread and wine out of one of the grocery bags.

Kelly stopped. "Speaking of helicopters." She pushed her hands in her jean pockets. "I got something to tell you." She shifted from one foot to the other. "This only came up two days ago and I haven't had a chance to tell you. It's something I've always wanted to—"

"You're jumping out of that damn helicopter."

"How'd you know?"

"You don't fidget unless you have to tell me something you don't want to."

Kelly looked down at the table. *I'm a coward*, she kept saying over and over to herself. If she told Amy now, she reasoned, once Laurie returned her presence would stop it from turning into a full-blown fight. "I'll have to watch my fidgets." She tried to keep her tone light.

"Does Elizabeth know?"

"Heavens, no. Elizabeth gave me the guy's name. We haven't talked about it again. You know Elizabeth. She's preoccupied with her own jump. Anyway, at first he told me they were full up. Like I said, he just called me and said he had an opening. It just popped out of my mouth." She didn't know what to say to cover the awkwardness she felt. "I volunteered."

"And you planned on telling me when?"

"I honestly don't know. I just kept putting it off. I'm telling you now."

"You coward," Amy spat. "If you loved me you wouldn't even think about doing this. You're not going to jump." She poured both glasses of wine into the sink. "This isn't going to mellow us out."

Kelly could feel the rumble of Amy's anger. She knew there was going to be an explosion. There would be no turning back this time. No placating her with soothing words. "Amy, I am. This is something I've always wanted to do, now I have this opportunity to do it and I'm taking it."

"Well, expect to sleep elsewhere tonight." Anger seethed in Amy's voice. She almost shouted the words. "Because I'm not standing on the ground like some pilot's wife waiting for you to return."

"Okay then," Kelly said softly. "Look, Laurie is due back here, so maybe we could not fight about this?"

"Where is she?"

"I told you she went over to pay the caretaker her first month's rent and sign a lease. She can move in tonight. As I said, she's anxious to get her own digs." Kelly smiled to herself. Get her own digs so she can begin her pursuit of Susan. Kelly liked Susan. There was a soothing earnestness about her that was extremely attractive. She also liked the way she looked you in the eye when she talked. Kelly sighed. She hoped Laurie wasn't going to end up with yet another broken heart. Laurie was impulsive and loved to think about things after she was in the middle of them. "Anyway, I promised her dinner when she gets back. I have steaks for the grill and baked potatoes and I've already made a salad. Do you think we could get through dinner. She doesn't have to know we're fighting."

"I can play that game as well as anyone, Kelly. That's why you told me now. It's a control thing on your part. I won't explode." Amy's eyes snapped and crackled anger. "You don't want your friend to know we're fighting. She won't know. But we're not through with this conversation." She stopped. A car had pulled into the driveway. "You're damn lucky she's here."

"Hi, all," Laurie said as she slammed the screen door behind her.

"So," Amy said, an accusatory tone in her voice, "what do you think about our friend here jumping out of a helicopter?"

"Really? Are you nuts?"

Kelly was immediately relieved. She hadn't thought to tell Laurie to pretend surprise if Amy brought it up.

"You crazy woman you." Laurie gently punched her in the arm. "God, do they have an extra slot? I'd love to do it."

"You're both crazy." Amy stormed out of the room. "I've got to change my clothes," she called over her shoulder.

"Thank you." Kelly mouthed the words.

Laurie nodded in agreement.

"So," Kelly said, picking up the steaks, "why don't you join me out on the patio? I'll get the fire started. By the way, how'd it go with the caretaker?"

"Good." Laurie followed her outside. "Papers are signed. He gave me a key and I have a home tonight. The place is completely furnished, even down to clean sheets on the bed. You don't mind my bailing out on you, do you?" There was a touch of anxiety in her voice.

"No." Kelly laughed. "Although"—she frowned at the door and lowered her voice—"if I'm dead in the morning, it's going to be all your fault."

"You're kidding, right?"

"Of course. Amy's mad but she'll get over it." Kelly didn't want to tell Laurie about the ultimatum to sleep somewhere else. Laurie may be having her first guest.

"Why didn't you tell her before?"

"It's a long story. I don't want to bore you with it right now. I knew it would upset her and I was too big a chicken to confront her."

"Well, she's upset now," Laurie murmured.

"I'm glad you pretended you didn't know. I think that would have upset her more."

"Well, after what happened earlier today with your friends, I figured feigned ignorance was best."

"You figured right," Kelly said. She heard Amy moving around in the kitchen. Kelly put the steaks on the fire. "Okay if I microwave the potatoes?"

"What did we ever do before we had microwaves? I know I love to cook, but I use that little microwave like every other American," Laurie said, following her into the kitchen.

"Truce?" Amy asked.

"Truce," Kelly said, relieved. Amy was right, Laurie's being there helped defuse the anger. Hell, she thought as she got the tongs out of the drawer, maybe they needed to start a commune to help their relationship.

"I'm still mad at her," Amy said to Laurie. "But I can't stay angry at her all night. You understand what a shock it is to hear that the woman you love thinks she's superwoman and wants to jump out of a helicopter at how many feet?"

"Well, pretty high up," Kelly said sheepishly. She wished people would stop talking about the altitude. She just wanted to think about floating like a bird.

"You just don't want to talk about it," Amy said. "Well, at however many feet." She opened the refrigerator and set three bottles of dressings on the table then brought over the salad Kelly had made. She put placemats on the table and gently nudged Jasper off a chair. He jumped to the floor and licked the fur she had touched before he sauntered off. "Anyway, I'm pleased you found a place to rent." The controlled hostility in Amy's voice was evident.

"Me too, and that Susan Iogen is one interesting woman." Laurie glanced sheepishly at Kelly.

"Ahh." Amy raised an eyebrow. Kelly could tell Amy was thinking about something as she put plates and silverware on the table.

"She's really a wow," Laurie said, her enthusiasm now bubbling over.

"My friend here doesn't want to admit it, but she threw our warm hospitality over for a chance to start a romance."

"Kelly you do like to pick on me." Laurie was joining in the teasing.

"Well, you took panting to a new high." Kelly chuckled.

"I did not," Laurie said with mock seriousness. "She's nice and is absolutely gorgeous, but that's not why I decided to move into the carriage house tonight. I didn't want to be a burden on you guys. You know, having to deal with the poor brokenhearted lesbian."

"Hardly brokenhearted. What's it been now, two or three months since you and Heather broke up?" Kelly scoffed. "You're not brokenhearted, my friend, I'd say more like on the prowl."

"I for one don't trust her," Amy interrupted them. "I think she's LNG twenty-four-seven and I'd prefer not to discuss it around her. She might pick up on our strategy. Hell, who's to say she

159

didn't go down to the marina that night looking for Elizabeth and then pretending she'd bumped into her."

"I don't think she did," Kelly said. "I think she was out for a run, bumped into Elizabeth and they hit it off. You know Elizabeth, she's taken in more stray dogs and cats than an animal shelter. I think she just naturally gravitated toward her."

"Well, I'm not as trusting."

"How about I check her out?" Laurie said eagerly.

"How about you just be careful," Kelly quipped. "You're supposed to be here to work."

"Work, yes. Dry up like a raisin? No way."

"Well, you're hardly going to dry up." Kelly put the potatoes in the microwave and hit the timer.

"I think you can probably help us a lot," Amy said prudently.

"How so?" Laurie turned toward her.

"If she's sniffing out our strategy, you can certainly zero in on hers. Find out what the company is offering the town. Find out what she's—"

"Hold on." Kelly looked sternly at Amy. "Laurie is not CIA or FBI."

"Agreed." Laurie laughed. "I'm HTT."

"HTT?" Kelly asked.

"Hot to trot."

Kelly noticed Amy's frown. She obviously was tiring of their banter.

Kelly groaned. "I should have known," she said as she took the potatoes out of the microwave and set one on each plate. "I'll get the steaks."

"Well, that's the best news I've had all evening," Amy was saying as Kelly came back inside.

"What best news?" she asked, setting a steak on each plate.

"Laurie said she told you she'd help in our fight against LNG. You didn't tell me."

"I honestly forgot," Kelly said. She gestured toward the vacant chair. "Sit, sit. Let's eat."

"This is wonderful," Laurie said as she chewed a piece of steak. "Anything I can do to help I will. But I don't know how good I'll be at questioning Susan."

"Well, people say things. Just keep an ear open. We have another meeting this Wednesday and anything you learn over the next few days we could share with the group. Kelly could bring you with her." She said to Kelly, "Unless of course you have another meeting at the hospital." Her words were embroidered with sarcasm.

"I don't think I do," Kelly said.

"I'll try and ask her some questions. I don't know how good I'll be," Laurie repeated. "Anyway, I'm more interested in your store, Amy. How long have you had it? I didn't get a chance to look around, but maybe I could stop in tomorrow?"

"That'd be nice." Amy started to tell Laurie about the store.

Kelly inhaled deeply, glad the topic had turned away from LNG. Laurie had bailed her out yet again tonight, she thought.

"I like her," Amy said as they were preparing for bed.

Kelly was relieved. Laurie had left just a few minutes earlier. Amy seemed to be over her anger. There was no reference to her sleeping somewhere else. Amy had not even brought up the helicopter jump, and once they had stopped talking about LNG, she seemed to relax and enjoy Laurie's company. "I'm glad. She's really good people."

"Of course, if she starts dating that LNG woman, she's not going to help us any, and you realize that that LNG woman can't be part of our group. I'll not have her spying on us. I wouldn't trust her."

"Amy, let's just let it rest." Kelly sat down on the edge of the bed. "Laurie always acts like she's hot to trot, but really it's an act. If she's attracted to Susan, great. She deserves to be in a good relationship."

"Regardless, she isn't going to be a part of our group if she gets involved with that woman," Amy insisted.

"Whatever." Kelly rubbed a finger against her brow to push away the tension in her head.

"And I'm still angry you didn't tell me about the jump." Amy stood in front of her her, hands akimbo. "I don't understand. Why?"

"Simple. I wanted to avoid this." Kelly gestured as if to draw a circle around Amy's anger. "I just didn't want to fight about it. I know it's dangerous, but so is driving a car. So is walking across an icy sidewalk. Amy, it's something I've wanted to do."

"You know, that's the second time I've heard that. Elizabeth said the very same thing. But you know what the difference is?"

"No, I don't."

"Elizabeth said it was something she always wanted to do, but she didn't even think about it as long as Lois was alive. Because she loved Lois so much she didn't want her to have a moment's stress. Now, what's wrong with this picture?"

"Nothing. If you're suggesting that my jumping out of a helicopter means I don't love you, it's not true. I do love you, Amy, and I didn't intend for this to cause you stress. I don't know." Kelly shrugged. "It seems a lot safer than other things we do every day. I asked that question of the advance man and he said the club has been around for more than twenty years and they've never had a mishap. I felt comfortable with that."

"Well, what did you expect him to say? They regularly lose jumpers? I don't think so."

"How many jumping accidents have you heard about? Contrast that with the number of snowmobile and boating accidents we see in the emergency room each year. Or the number of people who are in automobile accidents, even right here in our little town."

"I think I feel more violated than anything else."

Kelly groaned inside. Amy had turned the argument in a new direction. "Violated? What the hell does that mean?"

"You didn't trust me enough to tell me you were doing it."

Kelly broke eye contact and turned away. "Look, I'm sorry I didn't tell you. But I just wanted to avoid this."

"We're not fighting."

"Isn't that where we're heading?"

Amy went to her side of the bed and sat down, her back to Kelly. "I would like you to withdraw your name, not go through with this." Her voice was a whisper.

"I can't, Amy." Kelly stared at her back. "I won't do it. It's something I've always wanted to do. I'd probably never go to Brunswick to join the club. But it's here in our backyard. Our best friend, who I might mention is seventy-five years old, is jumping with me. If she can do it, I can too."

"I won't be there tomorrow."

"That's up to you," Kelly said softly. "I want you there. I know you've got the store covered because you were going to be there when Elizabeth jumped, so that isn't an excuse. So if you decide not to come, it's because you don't want to be there. I'm not going to try and change your mind." Hurt, Kelly pulled the sheet back. "Right now I'm going to bed. You do what you want."

"I'm too upset to sleep," Amy said, getting up.

Kelly turned on her side. She heard Amy pick up her book and walk out of the room. Kelly tried to sleep. She pondered how anxious she felt. Not about Amy and the fight, but a new anxiousness. She smiled at the dark. She was nervous. Downright petrified. She closed her eyes. *Sleep*, she willed herself. *Just sleep.*

Chapter Twenty

"You look tired," Elizabeth said. When Kelly had gotten up Amy was already gone. She had tossed and turned all night. At some point during one of her many bouts with trying to sleep, she realized she was *really* nervous about the jump. How strange was that? she wondered. She'd been so preoccupied with not telling and then telling Amy, she hadn't thought about having a man on her back and dangling from a harness at ten thousand feet. The advance man had told her about being strapped to a jumpmaster. When she wasn't thinking or dreaming about the jump, she was thinking about Amy. She had not returned to bed. Kelly suspected she had slept in the guestroom and left early for work, despite the fact that she had planned to be at the airport. She knew she wasn't going to open the store until ten o'clock.

"Actually, I'm fine. I slept pretty well last night. How about you?"

"Like a baby." Elizabeth rubbed her hands together.

Kelly picked her up at eight o'clock after phoning to say she was the fourth person. Elizabeth was thrilled. They were now waiting for the advance man. They could see the team jumpers; some were on the ground stretching their muscles, others were setting out the gear.

"I wonder where the other two jumpers are?" Elizabeth looked around.

"Don't know. Maybe they chickened out."

"Maybe. Boy, will I give those two reporters what for," Elizabeth joshed then turned serious. "I'm really glad you're jumping with me, Kelly, although I suspect Amy's not happy."

"She's not—"

"Good morning, ladies."

"Frank, hi." Elizabeth shook his hand. "Have you two met?"

"Only by telephone." Kelly shook his hand.

"Well, let me introduce you to the guys." He started toward the tarmac. "Elizabeth, you're going to be jumping with Randy Burger and Kelly, you're going to be jumping with Brian Leavitt. They're both jumpmasters and they're the best."

"That's comforting," Kelly said as they approached the helicopter.

He introduced them to the group and then handed her and Elizabeth black jumpsuits with red trim and a set of goggles. "Put the jumpsuit on over your clothes then Randy and Brian will talk you through the jump."

"I thought two reporters were going to be joining us," Elizabeth said.

"One called yesterday and canceled, the other begged off this morning, tied up on some story today."

"I can't wait until Tuesday. I'm going to give them both what for." Elizabeth grinned as she struggled into the jumpsuit and zipped it up.

"Anyway," Frank said with a smile, "you two are here and you're both in for the time of your lives."

"I can't wait," Elizabeth enthused. "Should I put these on now?" She held up the goggles.

"The jumpmaster will help you with those during the briefing. After you've been briefed, I have some forms you'll need to sign. Liability. If you want to read them ahead of time, there's time."

"Not me," Elizabeth said. "I know those forms. They give them to you in the hospital. If the doctor kills you, you promise not to sue. Like you'd care once you were dead. Does anyone read those forms?" The question was directed to Kelly.

"You're asking me?" She thought for a moment. "I haven't really considered it. Some people do, I guess. Most people probably don't."

"My point exactly. So," she said to Frank, "don't bother going over them, just bring them on and let us sign them."

"Okay." He laughed.

Kelly listened closely to everything her jumpmaster told her. He then strapped her into a harness that ran across her chest and between her legs. It felt like a corset. Now as she was holding her goggles, she wondered if she would remember it all. Funny, she thought, she could remember everything there was on a patient's chart, but today she'd asked Brian to repeat himself several times. Although she felt calm on the outside, she knew there were jitters on the inside. She wasn't scared, just excited.

"What'd you think?" Elizabeth asked her. The jumpmasters had rejoined their group and were checking their gear one last time.

"I think everything's fine."

"You know what I asked him?"

"I can only imagine," Kelly said with a laugh.

"I asked him if he got a good night's sleep and if he'd packed his own chute. I figure if he packed it, it'd be right."

"What'd he say?"

"Yup, packed his own chute and was in bed at nine o'clock last night."

"Well, that sounds good to me."

"What'd you ask your guy?"

"To repeat himself." Kelly laughed to cover her embarrassment.

"Repeat?"

"I must be more nervous than I thought, because his instructions to keep my knees bent, arch my back and hold my arms out were just too complicated for my little brain to absorb."

"This is going to be just fine," Elizabeth reassured her.

"I know. Aren't you just a wee bit nervous?"

Elizabeth chewed on her bottom lip. "Honestly, no. Look, isn't that Susan there with Laurie?"

Kelly looked to where Elizabeth was pointing. "It is," she said, relieved to think about something other than the jump. "I haven't had a chance to tell you Laurie checked out that carriage house and loved it. Moved in last night."

Elizabeth cocked her head. "Romance?"

"Definitely some attraction on Laurie's part. I don't know about Susan."

"Well, good. I like Susan. If Laurie can help her have some fun, then more power to her." Elizabeth stopped when Susan and Laurie came within earshot.

"We decided to ride out here together," Laurie said. She hugged Kelly and then Elizabeth. "The crazy duo." She was laughing. "You're a legend around here," she said to Elizabeth. "Susan told me all about it last night. Lobstering until you were way past sixty. Then instead of retiring, getting elected town clerk. Now jumping out of helicopters. I'd say you're one classy lady."

"How'd you know about the lobstering?" Elizabeth put her arms around Susan. "Let me give you a hug too."

Susan laughed and embraced her. "Well, like you said, there aren't any secrets here on the island. People told me all kinds of things about you. We're glad to be here."

"You won't be alone," Elizabeth said. "Maggie and Terry are coming. I invited a few others. Look, there's some more folks now."

167

"A few?" Kelly said as she stared at the line of cars driving into the airport parking lot.

"Well, you know me. I had to ask the town manager. Then I couldn't leave out the selectmen. After that I just called a few friends. Everyone seemed to want to be here."

Kelly groaned. If she had thought about backing out, she couldn't do it now. Elizabeth had apparently invited half the town.

"You two ready?" Frank said as he approached them. "Wow, look at all these people. They here for you?"

"Elizabeth." Kelly nodded toward her friend who was now greeting more people. "She knows everyone in this town."

"Where's Amy?" Elizabeth asked as she greeted yet one more person.

"Emergency at the store. She won't be able to get away." Kelly noticed Elizabeth's questioning look.

Kelly turned when she heard the rotor on the helicopter begin to spin, relieved she didn't have to explain anymore to Elizabeth. She swallowed. *Well, it's now or never,* she thought. *You've always wanted to do this and now you're going to get your chance.* As the blades started to rotate faster she saw the absolute joy in Elizabeth's face and for just a hair of a second she saw a young Elizabeth, her youthful delight flowing from her face.

"I'm ready," Elizabeth said over the noise.

"Me too." Kelly started toward the helicopter. Brian was standing next to the open door, she could see Randy standing on the other side. Two other men were nearby. Assistants, she figured.

"I'm going to strap myself in first," Brian said over the noise. "Then I want you to sit between my legs and Tom will fix your seatbelt."

Kelly nodded and watched as Brian shimmied up into the back of the helicopter. She turned and looked at the pilot, who winked at her. She smiled. Once Brian was cinched in she crawled between his legs. Elizabeth was already seated in front of Randy while an assistant tied a strap over her legs. Tom did the same thing to Kelly's legs. Just then a guy wearing a helmet embedded with a camera crawled in and sat facing them. He casually saluted Kelly and Elizabeth.

"This is Jerry Hurst. He's going to be filming us," Brian yelled over the noise.

After Jerry was cinched in, Tom slammed the door shut on the helicopter. Kelly heard the door slam on Elizabeth's side. She looked over at her friend, who was all smiles. Elizabeth gave her the thumbs up. Kelly rested her back against Brian as the helicopter lifted off, its nose pointed toward the ground. It turned and followed the length of the runway and then slowing began to climb. The loud whirring of the rotors made conversation almost impossible. Kelly watched the people on the ground grow tinier and tinier until they disappeared.

"We're at a thousand feet," Brian said in her ear.

Kelly looked out the window. *Wow*, she thought, at a thousand feet the ground seemed a long ways away. They still had another nine thousand feet to climb.

"You okay?" Brian asked as he checked his altimeter.

Kelly nodded. She kept thinking about Amy. She had kept watching the cars, hoping Amy had changed her mind and would be there to support her, but by the time they were ready to take off, she hadn't appeared.

Kelly had seen the look in Elizabeth's eyes. It was clear she knew there'd been a fight. *You should have told Amy sooner*, she scolded herself. Why had she put off telling her? She'd known there'd still be words. There'd be a fight. *If she'd done the same to you, you'd have been furious.* This one was her own fault, definitely her own fault. Now, if she was killed, she wouldn't be able to apologize. *Don't think about getting killed.* Kelly swallowed.

"We're at five thousand feet," the jumpmaster announced, interrupting her thoughts. "This is where I hook on to you." He yanked at her harness, first one shoulder and then the other. She felt the snap shackles being hooked to her sides. Brian then grabbed ahold of her harness and pulled two straps. *Oh yeah*, she thought as her breath whooshed out of her. *Definitely a corset.* "At nine thousand feet, Jerry is going to open the doors. Now remember what I told you. He's going to jump first. Then we're going to move to the side of the helicopter and I'm going to count to three and we're going to jump. You ready?"

"Absolutely," Kelly yelled. Elizabeth's partner was also shouting in her ear. Kelly reached over and squeezed her hand. Elizabeth's smile was radiant. She couldn't remember the last time she'd looked this excited.

"Ready?" Brian asked again, and she nodded.

Jerry pushed the door open. He winked at Kelly and then dove head first out the door with the grace of an Olympic diver. Kelly swallowed. A rush of cold air pelted her. Brian had told her she would notice the cold once they were at ten thousand feet.

"It's minus three degrees," he yelled over the wind.

Kelly thought fleetingly about Amy and the deep freeze she was going to get when she got home.

"Okay, we're ready," Brian yelled. "Now, I'm going to just scoot to the side. I want you to hook your thumbs under your harness. Just like I told you on the ground."

Kelly nodded. Brian inched them toward the door. She looked at the ground, which seemed a million miles, not ten thousand feet, away. The airport had disappeared, but the deep blue of the bay was mesmerizing. The other islands that surrounded Bleu Island that looked large from the ground were tiny dots. The whole world looked like microscopic dots, except for the ocean. Fearlessly, she smiled.

"Okay, we're ready. One, two, three—"

A rush of air assaulted her face and then she was looking at the ground. Then she was looking at the sky. *We're tumbling*, she thought. *He didn't brief me on tumbling.* Then their bodies righted themselves and she was again looking down. Her arms were out, her fingertips inches away from Brian's. Jerry appeared for what seemed like a second in her view, smiled and then disappeared. She wondered what she'd look like on his videotape of the jump. Her back was arched and she was flying. The only thing she felt was the

170

rush of air in her ears. *I'm flying, just like a bird.* She looked around. The ground was moving closer, but it didn't even feel like she was moving. She loved it. She felt the tap on her shoulder and then heard the whoosh of the chute opening. Just like in the movies, her feet flew up in the air as the parachute pulled them upward. Kelly looked up at the white canopy with the red chrysanthemum on it and smiled. Now they were floating. Below, people looked like gnats.

"Pull left," Brian yelled as they drifted over the airplane hangars.

Kelly pulled on the canopy's strap and they started to veer left, away from the hangars.

"If you want to have some fun, pull left and then right and see what happens."

Kelly did and they floated to the right, back over the hangars. She pulled on the left strap again and they floated toward the runway.

"Okay, when I say ready, lift your legs. We're about ready to land."

The ground drew closer and closer.

"Ready."

Kelly lifted up her legs and felt the slight jerk as Brian's feet hit the ground. A ground crew member grabbed them and began to unhitch Kelly's straps. Now Jerry was on the ground. He was still filming them. Where'd he come from? she wondered. He smiled and gave her a thumbs up. She smiled back.

"I love it," Kelly exclaimed. "I love it." When the last snap-shackle was unhooked she turned and hugged Brian. "Thank you, my man. I loved it." She looked around. "Where's Elizabeth?" she asked the ground crewman. He pointed upward. Elizabeth and Randy were hovering just slightly over their heads. Just then Elizabeth lifted her legs and the two set down. The ground crew-man ran over to unhook them. Elizabeth was grinning from ear to ear.

Kelly was going to give Elizabeth a hug when she felt a tap on her shoulder.

"Glad you're on the ground," Amy said.

"Me too." Kelly hugged her tightly. "But I'm glad you're here. I love you," she whispered in her ear.

"I'm still mad at you, but I couldn't stay away," Amy said gently.

"Well, I hope not too mad." Kelly stepped back and searched her face. Thank God Amy was smiling. "I—"

Laurie suddenly grabbed her and pulled her into a huge bear hug. "Damn, you did it. It was unbelievable. I had this huge lump in my throat the whole time. My heart was racing—gosh, I was more excited watching you than if I'd been doing it myself."

Kelly laughed. She noticed Elizabeth also being hugged by Maggie and Terry, who were laughing and asking her questions.

"That was great." Susan shyly hugged her.

"Thank you."

"Well, sport, we did it," Elizabeth yelled across to her.

"That we did, old sport," Kelly yelled back. Everyone was kissing and hugging everyone else.

Jerry tapped her shoulder.

"Hey, Jerry."

"We'll send you a tape of the jump."

"Great. Hey, Elizabeth, they're going to give us a tape of the jump."

"All right."

Amy slipped her hand into hers. It felt warm and comforting. She was glad she had both feet planted firmly on the ground, but she knew she'd jump again. She looked over to where the helicopter was parked on the tarmac. The jump crew was storing gear inside. She saw Brian and waved. He waved back. Definitely her best day, she thought.

Afterward, Amy had gone to work and Kelly had later gone home to get things ready for the party the next day. When Amy got home later she saw the look in her dark liquid eyes. There was a sensuous invitation to what lay ahead. Somehow they moved quickly from their hello kiss to making love. It was as exciting as the first time. They'd skipped dinner.

Now, lying in bed the next morning, Kelly remembered how her body and soul tingled afterward. She definitely had to jump out of more helicopters. There had been a fire and intensity to their lovemaking that had sent sparks up and down her spine. And even now every nerve in her body was singing. Amy had pulled herself out of bed. Kelly knew, for the first time in a long time, she didn't want to go to work. Amy had kissed her deeply, promising more excitement after the party. She picked up the telephone on the first ring. It was Amy. "I miss you too." She swallowed. "I'll see you at noon."

Kelly showered and went downstairs. She squeezed hamburger into patties for those who didn't eat lobster. She sct paper plates, napkins and silverware on the table. Soon the table would be filled with dishes brought by friends and filled with wonderful salads and Elizabeth's famous beans. Maggie Beth had promised to bring three of her celebrated apple pies. She heard the car and headed for the door.

"I love you," Amy gushed and took her in her arms. She kissed her deeply.

"I love you."

Amy handed her a bottle. "This is for us after the party."

"Champagne?"

"Champagne."

"How were things at the store?" She followed Amy inside.

"Busy, as usual I'm losing lots of money. I know it's silly to close a half a day on this holiday, what with all the tourists in town. Oh, well!" Amy turned and embraced her again. "But you know this is the only real holiday I take off and this year I just don't care. And Elizabeth was still jazzed. All she talked about was the jump. Y'know I was thrilled for her. Anyway, we both kept watching the clock and waiting for noon"—Amy paused—"I wish we had time . . ." Her voice trailed off.

"Me too, but we both know Elizabeth will be the first one here.

You said three," Kelly looked at the clock. "That means she'll be here in about ninety minutes."

"How about a shower together?" Amy grinned, the cat that swallowed the canary. She touched Kelly's cheek. "I love you and I want to capture last night. That was the most incredible night I've had ever."

"It was pretty incredible." She felt herself teetering on the edge. They might have time for a shower together.

Amy was closest to the ringing telephone. "Elizabeth. Hi." Amy rolled her eyes at Kelly. "Great. See you in ten minutes." She took Kelly in her arms. "You heard." Kelly could hear the disappointment in her voice. "Laurie and Susan are coming together, so Elizabeth's coming now to help."

Kelly kissed her lightly on the nose. "Go take your shower. Just think what we have to look forward to tonight."

"Well, I'd prefer now," she said softly as she kissed Kelly again. "But you're right. I'll be right down."

Within minutes Elizabeth arrived and helped Kelly set up the lobster boiler in the yard. They chatted about the jump. Kelly could see Elizabeth was still thrilled. How sad, she thought. Her adrenaline had dissipated somewhat during the hours she and Amy had made love, Elizabeth's excitement was still very real and palpable. Kelly hadn't thought about what it must be like to experience one of the biggest thrills of your life and not have someone there to share it. Friends, yes, but friends couldn't replace a lover's embrace. For the first time since she'd met the woman, she felt sad. Elizabeth couldn't share her moment with Lois.

"Hi, my two loves." Amy kissed Elizabeth.

"Hi, sweets." Elizabeth put her arm around Amy's shoulder. "My beans are on the counter. I plugged them in so they'd stay warm."

"I saw them, thank you. They are always a hit."

"Speaking of hits, I was just telling Kelly, Laurie and Susan seem to have hit it off. She'd asked me yesterday if I knew a good picnic spot and I told her Boot Cove. Susan called me this morning and said they'd spent the rest of the day there. They had a wonderful time with their impromptu picnic. That's when I begged off driving over with them. I told her I had to be here early to help out. She sounded disappointed, but truth be told, I think she's enjoying Laurie."

"I think that's great." Kelly turned on the propane tank under the burner. A blue and yellow flame jumped to life. She stood back and watched. The pot on top was huge and it would take a while before the water started to boil. She'd already filled the grill with charcoal. She would start it in a bit.

"Well, I for one will be civil to them, but that's it," Amy said. "And if I hear anyone from our group talking LNG with her, I'm going to politely interrupt."

"Not to worry. I decided this morning since I invited her I'll be on LNG patrol."

"LNG patrol?" Kelly asked.

"Yup." Kelly could hear the lightness in Elizabeth's voice. "I left my gun at home. But I hear anyone talking LNG, I'm going to throttle them. Better yet, threaten them with having to listen to me talk about every second of my jump."

Amy laughed.

Kelly was grateful. Elizabeth's teasing had helped relieve the tension.

"Here come Maggie Beth and Terry." Amy headed toward their car.

Kelly watched as Amy offered hugs all around. It felt like a comfortable mantle had settled over her. Amy was sparkling. Occasionally, she would glance over at her and Kelly could see the bold passionate fervor in her eyes. It was definitely going to be a good night, she decided. She felt a quiver inside.

"Look, here come Laurie and Susan," Elizabeth said. They all looked to the entrance to the driveway. It looked like a parade of cars. "Jim's right behind her and look, there's Max and Jenny. Did I tell you, Max is thinking about selling his clothing store?" Max's store was next to Amy's.

"That would be a shame. I love that store," Maggie Beth said. "New owners like to change things."

"It's not confirmed, but I plan to ask him today," Elizabeth said matter-of-factly. She stopped as Laurie and Susan came toward them. They each had a dish in hand.

Everyone greeted one another. Kelly noticed that Amy was restrained as she embraced first Laurie and then Susan. Neither woman seemed to notice.

Soon everyone was there and Kelly lost track of time. Laurie helped her get the lobsters in the pot. They threw the shucked corn on top. Although there were many hands in the kitchen, she knew Amy would need her help. When they weren't fighting they worked well together. She noticed Elizabeth was outside talking with Laurie and Susan. The way her hands were moving, Kelly knew she was telling them about the jump. Both women were grinning.

Once dinner was ready, Kelly felt her nerves relax. People lined up at the lobster pot. Using tongs she dropped a pound-and-a-half lobster on everyone's proffered plate. Elizabeth was at the grill. Those non-lobster lovers were grabbing up juicy hamburgers.

"You okay?" Amy was at her side.

"I am. You?"

"I'm terrific." Amy kissed her cheek. "I love you," she whispered.

"And I love you. Have you eaten, yet?"

"Not yet, been busy making sure everything was going well in the kitchen. You?"

"Not yet."

"I'll be right back." Amy returned carrying their plates. "Elizabeth, you get your butt over here. I bet you haven't eaten either. You want lobster or a hamburger or both?" Amy gave her a plate.

"Hamburger. I've had way too much lobster this summer already." Elizabeth was laughing, clearly enjoying herself.

"That's right, you guys eat. I'll watch the grill," Maggie Beth said, wiping her mouth on a napkin.

"You haven't finished," Kelly insisted.

"I have and I will take care of this. Now you guys eat." She pushed them toward the kitchen. "There's still plenty of food in there. If you want, come back out here and keep me company, but get some food, women." Maggie Beth paused to look mischievously at Amy. "Any arguments, young lady?"

"No." Kelly could see the sparkle in Amy's eyes. Her heart did a two-step. Amy was definitely having fun. For the first time in weeks, LNG wasn't the first thing out of her mouth. She was also relieved that Laurie and Susan seemed to have found a place in the corner of the room. Kelly noticed they were deep in conversation. She smiled. Her best pal had definitely crossed over some kind of Rubicon and Kelly suspected there was no turning back. Laurie seemed to sense she was watching her and looked up. She waved. Kelly waved back. She motioned her to come over.

"Come on, I've set some lawn chairs up next to Maggie Beth so we can talk." Amy was at her elbow.

Kelly shrugged and winked at Laurie. Yes, Laurie definitely had her hands full. Kelly looked around. People were eating and laughing. This was definitely one of their best Fourth of July parties yet.

Chapter Twenty-one

At last, things had settled down at home. Weeks had gone by since the jump and Amy still was involved with LNG. She had organized a speakers' group and was spending even more time out of town. There were tons of calls from the media. She was sought after by the Bangor and Portland television stations and had even done a small segment on CNN. Her picture had been in the paper and now she was the official spokeswoman for the group. She seemed to handle it all with aplomb.

The group's strategy was to get as many communities as possible involved, even though they might not be directly affected by the LNG facility. People on the mainland had joined the fight after they'd learned that lights from the terminal would shine across the bay into their homes and that the new mile-long pier would stretch across a portion of their channel, blocking a section of the entrance to their fishing grounds.

On the nights Kelly wasn't exhausted from work, she would

attend the meetings and help. At the last one a week ago, the group had decided to go to Augusta to brainstorm with other environmental groups for a major strategy initiative. Amy, of course, was the point person. When Kelly had declined to go along, she had expected a battery of artillery fire, but instead Amy seemed fine with it. Truth be told, she thought, she rather looked forward to a weekend alone.

She hadn't seen Laurie except at work but knew she was getting more entangled with Susan. Laurie was definitely captivated, and the few times they were able to talk in her office, Laurie talked about nothing else.

Kelly also knew Susan was busy with the project. That's all Amy talked about, the developers' strategy. They had borrowed a page from the opponents' book and were bombarding the same communities with their information.

By Thursday morning, Kelly was looking forward to her "bachelor weekend," as she thought of it. The mid-August morning was beautiful, with clear skies and temperatures that demanded light cottons and sandals.

"Good morning, Loraine."

"Hi, Kelly," Loraine said, handing her a few messages. "Been quiet of late. I'm waiting for the other shoe to fall. September's coming, cold and flu season."

Kelly groaned. "Don't say that. The last time you used those words we had a flu epidemic, every bed in the hospital full."

"I remember." Loraine laughed. "But you can't blame me for that one. All I said was it had been too quiet lately."

"That's the point," Kelly said. "You put a jinx on everything."

Loraine put her head back and laughed. "Laurie stopped by a couple of times wondering when you might get in."

"She on duty?"

"Let me check." Loraine looked at the schedule on her desk. "She's on night duty. I think she said she'd be in the cafeteria."

"Thanks. I'll stop there first." Kelly pushed open the double doors that led to the administrative offices. "Do me a favor and hold all calls for about two hours. I have a mound of paperwork on my desk."

"Sure will."

Kelly said good morning to several people as she made her way to the cafeteria. Laurie was sitting at a corner table reading the newspaper.

"You're here early," Kelly said, pulling out the chair across from her. It was just after eight o'clock. "Something wrong?"

"I've got to go back to Portland."

"For good?"

"No." Laurie laughed. "Sorry, that didn't come out right. My ex needs me." She grimaced.

"Does she want to get back together?" Kelly shot her a sideways glance.

Laurie laughed again. "No, not in the least. It has to do with our house. She's been trying to sell it and she has a possible buyer."

"That's good, right?"

"Well, yes and no. She's being a real jerk about it. We split the cost when we bought it, but she now wants a little more of the profit because she says she's been the one who's had to do all the work."

"Are you selling it privately?"

"Hell, no. A realtor is handling it."

"Then what extra work is she doing?"

"That's the question I've been asking, but so far she hasn't given me a very good answer. I'm nervous about it. She may be putting the screws to me and I don't know it."

"You don't think this is some kind of ruse to get you back?"

"Absolutely not."

"Do you need some time off?"

"Actually, no, I'm off this weekend, so I hope to leave after my shift tonight and come back Monday." She paused, and Kelly sensed a problem. "Then there's "Susan.""

"You don't plan to take her to Portland, I hope. It seems to me

180

if Heather's causing problems now, wait until you show up with Susan."

"Heavens, no." Laurie sat back and laughed. "You want some coffee?" she asked. "I need a cup."

"No, thanks. I'm coffeed out."

Laurie went to the urn and poured herself a coffee. The kitchen staff was busy setting out the morning breakfast. The room smelled of scrambled eggs and bacon.

"You want something to eat?" Laurie asked, looking at the Danish.

"No, thanks."

Laurie picked up a cheese Danish and her coffee, put two dollars on the counter and came back to the table. "I need your and Amy's help."

"What can we do for you?" Kelly eyed the Danish, it was tempting.

"Well, I promised to take Susan to dinner and a play on the mainland on Saturday night. Anyway, I can't and I was wondering, if I can find an extra ticket for Amy would the two of you go with her? I'll pay for it."

Kelly frowned. "Amy's going to Augusta tomorrow. She and some of the other members of the group have a strategy meeting with several environmental groups. I think they're trying to rally statewide support for the cause. They've also got an appointment with the governor."

"You know, I promised Amy I'd go to some of the meetings." Laurie's grin was sheepish. "I've been rather busy lately."

"It's just as well. You'd probably just make everyone uncomfortable, hobnobbing with the opponent."

"How could I forget." Laurie picked up her Danish and bit into it. "You know, we don't even talk about LNG when we're together. Believe me, that's the last thing I've been thinking about."

"So how are things?"

"Moving slowly. She doesn't want to get into anything serious

181

right now. We have fun when we're together, but this is good, right?"

"Not getting too involved? I don't know."

"No, that Amy's going to be gone, so you can go to the play with Susan."

Kelly groaned. "Laurie, don't ask me to do that. I was really looking forward to a quiet weekend alone. You know, just Jasper and me. Remember, alone time?"

"Please? This is really important to me. I haven't told her yet that I won't be here, but if I can say that my best friend is going to step in and go with her, well . . ." Laurie paused. "It'd mean a lot to me."

"I hate you," Kelly said, her eyebrow cocked.

"No, you don't. You love me. You just hate the idea that I'm asking you to give up a boring Saturday night alone with a cat. When you can be with the most enchanting, exciting woman I've ever met."

"Oh, well, when you put it that way, foolish me. Of course I'd want to be with 'the most enchanting, exciting woman' you've ever met," Kelly mimicked.

"So you'll do it." Laurie was clearly excited.

"No."

"No?"

"No."

"What can I do to change your mind?" Laurie sat back, clearly disappointed.

"Nothing."

Laurie reached into her shirt pocket and pulled out the tickets. "They're orchestra seats for *Sweet Charity*."

"No."

"I've made reservations at the best restaurant on the mainland, the Emerald Lagoon."

"No."

"I'll do whatever you want me to do here or for you at home."

"No."

"Kelly," she said dejectedly. "Please? I beg you to do this. For me and I seem to recall a time when I helped a friend pack up and move." Laurie glanced sideways at her.

Kelly forced a tight smile. "That's blackmail." She inhaled deeply. "You're going to owe me big-time."

"Good, then you'll do it. I knew you would." Laurie giggled. "The dinner reservations are for five and the play starts at seven. That will give you time to have a nice leisurely dinner. I'll pop for dinner too."

"And what do I talk about for two hours with a woman I've barely met. At our party, it seems to me you had her sequestered off in a corner, talking your heads off."

Laurie laughed. "She's really easy to talk to. You won't have any problems. Talk about me. Tell her what a sterling character I am. Tell her I'm the world's best catch, that she should value me. Tell her I'm just about the easiest thing in the world to love. Tell her I'm like the tides, I'm consistent, I just keep rolling in. Hell, tell her I'm like the tides of passion."

Baffled, Kelly stared at her. "What does that mean?"

"I don't know, but it sure sounded good. I like the rhythm of the tides. I just threw in passion for old time's sake." Laurie grinned impishly.

"I will not. You want an advertising manager, hire one." Kelly shook her head. "I have a feeling I'm going to regret this."

"No, you won't," Laurie said. "She really is special."

"Have you fallen in love?"

"I think I have. I know I think about her every waking and sleeping moment. I so look forward to being with her. And y'know what's ironic? We haven't even so much as kissed."

Kelly sat back, stunned. "Now, that's a first for you, Miss Wine, Dine and Bed Them."

"I know. This is really spooky. But it's been kinda nice." Laurie took a sip of her coffee. "Maybe that's what the problem has been in the past. I've always rushed into the physical part, never taking time to think about the other parts of a relationship. Heck, when all that passion wears off, a lot of times you don't have anything to talk about. With Susan it's been really different. I don't think there's a topic we haven't touched on."

Kelly sighed. "Look, I'll do it, but I have to talk it over with Amy. If Amy says no, then it's no. So don't tell Susan anything until I've spoken with her, agreed?"

"I hate it because you could tell Amy to say no so you wouldn't have to do it."

"I promise I won't do that, but Amy has a say over this."

"Agreed. Let's go call her right now."

"No, I'm not going to call her right now, but I will do this for you. I'll call and ask her to lunch."

"That's good. She gets all comfy and full of food, she won't say no."

"God, you're pathetic," Kelly said affectionately.

"I am, aren't I."

"I hate to say it, Laurie, but you've gone down the drain over this woman."

"I can't believe it myself. When Heather called, I tried everything to reschedule our appointment with the buyer for next weekend. Can you imagine I was willing to throw away a hefty profit on—what? Love? What do you call this?"

"I don't know, but I assume Heather said no."

"Oh, very loud and very clear. It's a control thing on her part. She loves that driver's seat role." Laurie picked up her cup. "Let's go call Amy."

"Hold on. I'm going to call Amy," Kelly said, getting up. "I'll let you know what she says this afternoon. Where will you be?"

"Outside your office waiting."

"God, Laurie, would you relax? I told you I'll talk with her, and knowing her she'll be fine with it, but you're not going to sit outside my office while I'm having lunch with her. You're going to go home and I'll call you when I get back."

"I'll call you on your cell phone."

Kelly shook her head in amazement. "No, you're not going to

184

call me on my cell phone. If lunch is delayed, I'm not going to be placating you while I'm trying to have lunch with Amy."

"Okay, okay," Laurie said as the two started to walk back to the floor. "You're the best friend a person could ever have."

"You bet your sweet bippy, and you're damn lucky to have me in your life," Kelly said fondly. "Go home," she said ruffling her hair. "And I don't want to hear from you. I promise I'll call you."

A few hours later, Kelly finished up the last few pieces of paperwork. She looked at the clock; she had ten minutes to make it to the shop. Amy had seemed genuinely pleased at the invitation.

Kelly pulled up in front of the store and Amy hurried out the door.

"You find someone to cover for you?"

"Elizabeth's covering the store for me. She said she could sneak away from the town office for an hour. So I'm free for a while." Amy settled herself in the car. "This is nice. You know when we first got together we did this a lot."

"I know." Kelly smiled at the memory of that.

"I'm anxious about our meetings in Augusta tomorrow. I haven't thought about much else. If we can gather the support of some of the other environmental groups, it could help. They have clout, and if they start fundraising for us, it could help, especially if we have to take this to court."

"And you're going to see governor."

"Absolutely. In the beginning, he was all push push to have it built. Later he said he'd support any community that wanted one. Well, we don't want one."

"But he doesn't really know that. He knows the group doesn't want it, but he doesn't know what people on the island are thinking."

"Well, he will. We plan to circulate a petition, once we get back and once we collect all the signatures we'll force a vote. It's just too big an issue for the selectmen to decide. Although I think those

185

that favor it want to push for a selectmen's vote. I don't think they will. Elizabeth says they haven't signed the LNG contract even though the town's lawyer helped draw up that hundred-page document."

"Have you seen the contract?"

"No, they keep hiding behind the state law; say because it's in negotiations they don't have to talk about it in open session. That's one of the things we want to talk about in Augusta. Those environmental folks down there have done battle before, so they should be pretty good at advising us."

Kelly pulled in front of the restaurant and parked. "Well, I know they're going to help," she said as she held the door to the restaurant open for Amy. They walked to a table in back.

"Gosh, this is nice," Amy said, as she seated herself. "We just don't do this enough." She paused, "This LNG thing, Kelly, I know it's been consuming, but it's so important."

"I know." Kelly picked up the menu and looked at it.

"I already know what I want," Amy said staring at the blackboard behind Kelly. "Today's special."

They ordered the Yankee pot roast specials with mashed potatoes and salad.

The waitress, Carrie, ripped off the order. "By the way, Amy, me and my family support your efforts one hundred percent."

"That's good to hear, thank you."

"Mind you I don't know a lot about it. They're promising eighty jobs with big pay and it'll bring new businesses to town, which would mean even more jobs, but turning our little community into Massachusetts just isn't worth it." With that Carrie disappeared into the kitchen.

"So," Amy said, "getting back to our having lunch together. This is very nice. I do wish you'd consider coming down to Augusta with us. Any chance you've changed your mind?"

"No, I really am looking forward to some quiet time at home. It's been busy at the hospital." She told her what Loraine had said about how quiet it had been and how last year all hell had broken loose with wave after wave of flu patients. "I told Loraine to bite her tongue."

Amy laughed. "She'd better be careful or people will start saying she's psychic."

Kelly laughed too, then they spent time discussing business at the shop.

"Once Christmas is over, it would give you more time to focus on this protest," Kelly suggested.

"I'm hoping that'll be long gone by November." Amy leaned forward and said quietly, "We're thinking of pushing for a vote way before Thanksgiving, sooner if possible. It'll give us time to muster our troops, although they're not sparing any expense with all these focus groups and experts they've brought in. They've had engineers, marine biologists and economic development specialists here. They're spending some big bucks on this. I'm getting a little worried. Some people seem to be buying their message."

"Then it makes sense to move the vote up. Hold it sooner," Kelly agreed.

Amy asked about the hospital and Kelly gave her the scuttlebutt. "Mavis Breton announced she plans to retire," she added. "She's a good nurse. Old school, but it works. I wish I had fifty of her. She doesn't grumble about a thing."

"Oh, she grumbles. You just don't hear it."

Kelly cocked her head. "How do you know?"

"Everybody grumbles about their job, Kelly. Sometimes you can be a little dense."

Kelly sat back as Carrie put the salads in front of them. *She just had to get that zing in*, she thought. *Don't engage. Just ignore it. Don't ruin lunch with a fight.*

"We haven't seen much of Laurie," Amy said, clearly unaware of the insult she'd hurled.

"I saw her today," Kelly said, pushing her salad around with her fork. "In fact, she's asked me to do her a favor, a huge favor. I said I wouldn't do it without your consent." Kelly told her about Laurie's trip to Portland, the sale of her house and how Heather had been acting. She also mentioned the tickets for the play and Laurie's invitation to take Susan on Saturday night. "She invited you too, but I told her you'd be in Augusta."

"You did?" Amy bristled. "What if she tells Susan?"

Kelly sighed. "Amy, people on the island know you're going to Augusta. They're talking about it at the hospital. It's no secret. So telling Laurie wasn't a big deal."

"Well, even so . . ." Amy picked at her salad.

"Frankly, I'd been looking forward to a whole weekend of just relaxing. Nothing to think about but a good book."

"Tell her no."

"Well, that's the hard part. I did tell her no and she insisted I go. Besides . . ." Kelly studied her. "When I left Portland, Laurie was there to help me. I owe her one."

"You owe her nothing. You're a grown woman and her boss, I might add. Tell her you won't do it."

"She's also my best friend."

"I thought I was your best friend."

Kelly put her fork down. She bit back a retort. She promised herself this wouldn't turn into a fight. "I misspoke, she's my oldest best friend. Anyway, I told her I would talk it over with you. It's *Sweet Charity*."

"Frankly, I wasn't crazy that Laurie was going out with her. I don't think she can be trusted. What if she pumps you, tries to get you to talk about our strategy."

"Amy, I deal with these types of issues every day. Do you hear me coming home and violating patient confidentiality? Or sensitive issues for the hospital?"

"You rarely talk about your work."

"Right. Now, if I can keep those issues secret, I can handle cross-examination about LNG. Besides, I barely know what you're doing."

"And whose fault is that?"

"Amy, I'm not here to pick a fight with you." Kelly looked at her intently. "We're here talking about taking someone to dinner and a play."

"I don't care really, Kelly. I think it'd be okay as long as you promise not to talk about LNG."

"That's an easy one, I rarely talk about LNG with anyone but you."

"Well, you should. In fact, I was hoping that's what you wanted to have lunch about. Oh, well, dream for a wish." When Kelly, confused, glanced at her she went on. "Something we used to say when we were kids. If you dreamed hard enough about your wish, it'd come true."

"And did they?"

"Surprisingly, sometimes yes. More times than not, no. Funny, how when you look back you only remember the good things. I remember the dreams for wishes that came true. I can't even remember the ones that didn't. Anyway, if you promise not to talk LNG, I don't mind."

Relief washed over her. When Laurie first asked her she was irritated, but after she thought about it she actually was looking forward to dinner and the theater with Susan. She liked her and hoped they could be friends. At the party she'd been so preoccupied with cooking she hadn't had time to even visit with Susan and she'd felt guilty. But despite the blur of the party she seemed to recall that Laurie looked really happy and for that she was grateful.

Carrie arrived and set the pot roast dinners in front of them. "Mmm that smells good," Amy said to Carrie, who peppered their meat and then left.

"I'm almost envious, I'd thought about our going. But I've just been too darn busy," Amy said of the play. "Oh, well, there'll be plenty of plays to attend once LNG is behind us."

"We're going to the Emerald Lagoon for dinner. Should be nice."

"Good choice. Laurie's quite taken with her, I guess. Dinner and theater. It sounds downright romantic—for Laurie, not you." Amy was ready to tease her. Good.

189

"I've got my hands full with you," Kelly said affectionately.

"You bet, and don't you forget it."

They finished their meal in comfortable silence, then ordered coffee.

"You know, Laurie's had several romances. She's just this wonderful woman, but she has the worst luck when it comes to choosing a partner. I think she wants me to sound her out, see where Susan is in their relationship."

"So it's a fact-finding date." There was a hesitancy in Amy's voice. "I like Laurie, although she seems a little irresponsible. First she's going to stay with us, then the next thing you know she's living in a carriage house. We don't really hear from her and now she wants you to take the love of her life out."

Kelly laughed. "Well, when you put it that way, I'm sorry I let her talk me into this. She sounds downright irresponsible." She paused. "Of course, she's one of our best nurses, no question about it. Maybe it does appear that Laurie's just running through life knocking anything and everything out of her way—she's a high-energy person—but she's also compassionate, loving and understanding. Three qualities that makes for a damn good nurse. The other nurses seem to like her. That's important."

"Well, I think it's good that you can do her this favor. I've heard the play's been sold out for weeks."

"She was going to find an extra ticket but with your going out of town . . ." Kelly shrugged. Somehow she could not picture Amy spending an evening with Susan. During the Fourth of July party, Amy had been cordial but definitely on the other side of the room. Come to think of it, Laurie didn't seem to care if Amy went to the play or not. She'd noticed how Amy had treated Susan at the party, although Laurie never said a word.

"Just promise me," Amy said, interrupting Kelly's woolgathering, "no discussion about LNG, about my group, about me, about—"

"I promise, Amy."

❦

Back at the hospital, Kelly picked up her phone. "The answer is yes."

"Yahoo!" Laurie screamed. "So Amy was all right with it?"

"She was. I've been ordered not to talk about LNG."

"Don't worry, Susan really keeps that separate from her private life. LNG has not been a hot topic." She went on, "I really appreciate this. I like her a lot and I didn't want to disappoint her. I could have killed Heather, but if we have a real live buyer I need to be there to sign papers and also make some decisions about the furniture—some of it's mine, hers and ours. Plus, I know I'm going to have to do battle with her over how we split the profits."

"Do you think she's going to give you any problems?"

"I don't think so. If she does, I'll just mention my attorney, and I know that should be enough to cool her jets. She's afraid of spending money. God forbid there'd be lawyer's fees. She's cheap. I've always been in relationships where we just pooled our money and lived together as a couple. There was never a balance sheet. Not with Heather. She had it down to the penny what she spent and by God if she spent two cents more for food or whatever, I had to fork over that penny."

Kelly winced at the idea. "But she's a psychologist?"

"Yeah, and she makes twice as much money as I do. Not that I wanted to live off of her, don't get me wrong." Laurie paused. "Anyway, let's not talk about her. All it does is give me acid reflux. I'd rather talk about Susan."

"Have you told her I'm your substitute?" Kelly groaned. "Why do I feel like I'm going to a duel? I'm your second."

"You're my friend and I really appreciate your doing this. I could have called and canceled, but we both were so looking forward to seeing it. I've had the tickets for months."

"Well, it worked out. Amy will be out of town."

Laurie chuckled. "Funny thing, I think Amy and Susan would like each other. It's just this LNG crap. Susan would probably be all right with it, I just don't think Amy would be. I saw how she acted at the Fourth of July party, like Susan and I had chicken pox."

"Sorry about that." Kelly grimaced. "I figured you'd noticed. Was Susan offended?"

"She hasn't even mentioned it. She is one classy lady, I gotta tell you."

"Have you thought about the possibility she might not want to go with me? She might not appreciate this substitute thing?"

"Not to worry, I have a handle on that. Why don't you pick her up before four. Give you ample time to catch the ferry. The play is over at nine and the last ferry is at ten so you can even go out for a cup of coffee or drink afterward if you like. Everything is set at the restaurant, and dinner's on me."

"That's not necessary, Laurie, I certainly can buy dinner."

"No, I want it this way, my treat. Hey, you're my stand-in. I want things to be just perfect. And by the way—"

"By the way?" Kelly interjected.

"Well, if you did say some nice things about me, it wouldn't hurt."

"You're impossible. Look, I've got to go. Believe it or not I do work here and there are some hospital things I have to take care of."

"Kelly, thanks. I was really on pins and needles until you called. And tell Amy thanks also. I do appreciate her letting you do this."

"Well, like you said, you're going to owe me big-time."

Laurie laughed. "You got it."

Chapter Twenty-two

After Amy had checked to make certain that her newly trained clerk was at the shop, she left around nine Saturday morning and Kelly found herself enjoying the peace and quiet of the house. Jasper was curled up on the window ledge, the sun dancing on his fur. The telephone was quiet. She hadn't bothered to get out of her pajamas, something she never did when Amy was home because there was usually some project that had to be done or something that had to be fixed.

She'd gotten up early with Amy, made her breakfast then carried her small backpack to the car and kissed her good-bye. Afterward she stacked the dishes in the sink and stretched out on the couch to read a novel she'd started months earlier. It was now two o'clock and she hadn't moved.

With the book open on her stomach she looked out the window at the bay. There were dishes to do and a shower to take.

Now she wished she hadn't agreed to go to dinner and the theater with Susan. All she wanted to do was curl up and take a nap. She hadn't been this relaxed in years. Blast Laurie for asking her, she thought.

When she'd first met Laurie they became instant friends. When she and Robin broke up, Laurie was there to hold her hand, help her move.

Then she'd moved to Bleu Island and met Amy. Looking back, she was glad she and Laurie had remained just friends. There was never that stress of romance on their relationship and Laurie often rolled into a mess and looked to Kelly to pull her out. Over the years Laurie had asked her to do a lot of strange things, and taking Susan out was right up there.

Kelly thought about the time Laurie was dating two women simultaneously and had dragged Kelly into the middle of it. Laurie had told them she loved them both, and knowing Laurie, she had. But Portland's lesbian community was so small, the two eventually found out about each other. One night both women showed up at the apartment demanding that Laurie make a choice. She kept yelling at Kelly, "Help me out here." In the end both women dumped Laurie, but within weeks she was dating someone new.

Funny, she thought, her best friend and her partner were not only high-energy, but high-maintenance too.

Amy could be positively frenetic, her body sucking up all of the adrenaline it could produce, and Laurie was the same way, but after an adrenaline rush tended to become downright catatonic. Amy's crashes often turned to anger. It was those times Kelly dreaded because that's when she'd become the object of Amy's moody ire. Kelly could do nothing right and Amy would just pick and pick at her until it either turned into a full-blown fight or Amy criticized her so severely that Kelly would shut down.

She looked at the clock and groaned. Where had the day gone? She had a little over an hour to stack the dishes in the dishwasher, shower and get ready for her "date." Yeah, right, she thought. More like a long night of trying to figure out what to talk about. Hours after she'd agreed to go with Susan, she'd mentally kicked herself—and Laurie for asking. Then she'd put it out of her mind.

An hour later, Kelly turned into the driveway in front of the cottage where Susan was waiting at the door. She was dressed in navy blue slacks and a white silk blouse. She had a light jacket thrown over her arm. Kelly was struck by how beautiful she was. No wonder Laurie was all thumbs when it came to her.

"Hi," Susan said as she closed the car door.

"Hi, back." Kelly slipped the car into gear. "Well—"

"Look, I told Laurie that she could just cancel, that she didn't have to send in the reserve team."

Kelly laughed. "You know?"

"Well, it wasn't too hard to figure out. Believe me, she tried her best to convince me that you volunteered to go with me tonight."

"Well—" Kelly cringed. "That's not exactly true."

"Of course it isn't. I'm sorry. Look, if this is uncomfortable for you, we can just turn around and you can drop me off and go do what you'd rather do tonight. We can both tell Laurie that we went. It'll be our little secret."

"It's okay." Kelly turned toward the marina. "Let's just put it behind us and enjoy the rest of the evening. Agreed?"

Kelly could feel Susan's gaze on her. "Agreed." She hesitated. "I assume that Amy is fine with this."

"She is, although I'm not allowed to talk about LNG."

"And I don't want to." Susan chuckled. "That's a self-imposed order. I deal with it all week and I'm just not up to making it my evening conversation."

"Well, good," Kelly said as she eased in line behind other cars waiting for the ferry. "Looks like others are going over to the play."

"I'd say. I haven't seen this many cars since the big Fourth of July weekend. I thought I'd do a little shopping that weekend but I turned around and went back home after I sat in line for the ferry."

"Rule of thumb, you never ever try to get to Port Bleu on a holiday weekend. You either go before or after or you stay put."

"By the way, thank you for including me in your party. I really enjoyed myself." They traded glances.

"Forgive me for not spending more time with you. It just seems like I do nothing but cook on that day, but we love it."

"Well, you looked pretty busy. The best part, I got to spend more time with Elizabeth. She is special and I just love those eyes of hers. They're downright sexy. I bet she was quite the looker in her day, and she still is. I couldn't believe it when she told me how long she'd been in a relationship. They were like pioneers living together on this little island."

"She's quite something. Lois passed away before I moved here, but from what everyone's told me they had a unique bond. Rare that you find that in relationships today."

"Agreed. We've had lunch and dinner several times since then. She's been a wonderful friend. And, by the way, we also don't talk about LNG."

Kelly laughed. "It must be hard. You're here working on this major project and yet it's like you're the Black Death. No one wants to be around you." She eased her car down across the ramp and onto the ferry, then turned off the ignition.

"Let's get out and watch," Susan said as she opened the door. "If we're lucky we'll get to see porpoises playing, maybe even a minke whale."

The sun crept behind some clouds. Kelly loved living at the easternmost point of the continental United States but hated the fact that the sun came up early and went to bed early.

"I understand you and Laurie have been friends for a long time."

"We were best friends in nursing school and afterward. We shared an apartment for a while. Now is this the part where I'm supposed to tell you what a wonderful woman she is, list all of her attributes?" Kelly teased.

"You don't have to. I know how special she is. We've had some good times this summer. I'm grateful she was here or it would have been one long summer. Work, even lots of work, doesn't fill in

196

those times when it's just nice to walk on the beach or picnic on the rocks with a friend."

Kelly heard the loneliness in Susan's voice and said, "Well, I know she's enjoyed those times also, so it's good you two found each other."

"It is, but I'd like to hear more about you. I've heard some things from Laurie."

"There's not much to tell really. I was born in Lewiston and grew up there. Still have family there. My mother's alive, my father's gone. I have a sister and brother who live out of state. I liked to play doctor as a kid and ended up a nurse." Kelly laughed. "That's not really true. I went to nursing school in Portland because that's what I really wanted to do. That's where I met Laurie. After a while I really got tired of city nursing so I looked around for a slot in a rural area. Hadn't planned to come this far north. I'd thought maybe I'd accept a position nearer to Lewiston. After I came up here and interviewed for the job, they called the next day with the offer. It's funny, I really didn't think about it. I just took it."

"You met Amy here?"

"Through Elizabeth. She has a knack for picking up strays. Stray dogs, stray cats and stray people." Kelly pointed at herself. "Anyway, I met Amy through her and well"—she gestured non-chalantly—"the rest is history."

"You're right about her picking up strays." Susan laughed. "I gravitated to her the minute I met her."

People started to move toward their cars as the ferry reached the landing. She and Susan talked while they walked to Kelly's car. "I always thought Amy had more friends than God, but Elizabeth has her beat. I don't think she has a single enemy." Kelly got in the car and started the engine. "So tell me about you."

"I grew up in Andover, went to college in Boston. I got a job with a public relations firm right out of college. I liked the work, not the job. After a few years of working for them, I took all the money I'd saved and opened my own business. I didn't want to compete in the Boston market—too many established firms. Through my family and job I'd made some contacts in Andover so I decided to hang my shingle out there. Starved for a lot of years." Susan laughed. "I couldn't afford a secretary, so I had a friend put a message on my answering machine so it sounded like I had one. It was silly, I know, but I didn't want people to think I was a fly-by-night operation."

"It must have worked—you're still in business. So do you have a secretary and associates now?"

"A part-time secretary, no associates yet." Susan looked as if she wanted to say more but didn't.

"Here we are," Kelly said, turning into the parking lot of the restaurant.

"I haven't been here."

"They have great food. I've yet to have a bad meal here. Most islanders come here to celebrate birthdays, special occasions. As you noticed we don't have much in the way of ambiance on the island. Our restaurants are long on stick-to-your-rib food and short on elegance."

"Agreed, but I've had some good meals there."

"No question, food's good but it comes with paper napkins," Kelly said as she opened the door.

The play was a delight and dinner superb. Now, driving Susan back home, Kelly could see why Laurie was so taken with her. She was fun and interesting. She liked how when Susan was pondering something she bit gently on her bottom lip. It was both charming and somewhat sexy, she thought. Uh-huh, sexy wasn't a good choice. *You're in a relationship, Kelly Burns. You don't think sexy about another woman.* But it was sexy, and *sexy* could be an abstract word also, she argued with herself. Kelly sighed. It was too bad.

If Susan had arrived on the island under different circumstances she would have quickly been folded into the group.

"I want to thank you," Susan said.

"No, thank you. I really had fun."

"I was going to say a penny for your thoughts, but I thought maybe it'd be a little too personal."

"You can save your penny. I was thinking about how if you'd come here under different circumstances you'd have been included in our circle of friends. It's too bad, because people do like you. They're just afraid of what you're bringing with you."

"Is it that bad?"

"I'll admit I'm not as informed as Amy and her group, but I have thought about it. Yeah, it will bring jobs and, heavens, we need them. It'll pour money into this broken economy of ours, no question about it. But it'll also turn our world as we know it upside down. If this goes through, it's going to change this place forever. This isn't like some company that comes in here, hires maybe fifty people and sits quietly in a corner of the island somewhere producing widgets. We'll have huge tanker ships in the port. And whether LNG is safe or not, it's going to cut our landscape in two. Sorry, we agreed not to talk about this." Kelly was surprised at how passionate she felt against it.

"You know, I'm a little frustrated also. Natural gas is the cleanest and most environmentally friendly form of energy in the world. It's been used in this country safely for more than sixty years. People talk about Exxon Valdez and I don't think there's anyone in this country who doesn't remember those struggling birds, their feathers bathed in oil. But LNG isn't like that. God, gasoline is more frightening than natural gas. You talk about blowing up, I'd rather live next to an LNG terminal than a gasoline farm or oil refinery." Susan clearly was frustrated, yet Kelly couldn't feel sorry for her. "Sorry, I sound like my PowerPoint presentation."

"I understand," Kelly said, turning into Susan's driveway. "Let's say if everything you say is true—"

"It is true," Susan snapped.

"I'm not arguing that," Kelly said quietly. "Say everything is true, I don't think that gets to the nut of the issue, and that is what's it going to do to our way of life. That's what people are weighing."

"But change is good. If it wasn't, you'd be walking or getting around the island on a horse."

"Well, frankly, I wouldn't think that was so bad," Kelly mused. "I know we've seen change and the change that's come here has impacted the island, but the difference is that change has happened gradually. Sure, we may have cars, but those cars were introduced onto the island very slowly, just like in the rest of America. Cars were parked next to horses and buggies. But this is different; this is going to smack us right in the face. If the islanders agree to this, you're going to come in here with thousands of people and build it. Where are we going to put thousands of people? Then you're going to bring in these enormous ships and park them right outside our door. And on top of it you're going to build two or three tanks that'll make us look like New Jersey instead of Bleu Island, Maine. That's what people are afraid of."

"True, but people adapt. It's called progress."

It was a snide comment and Kelly snapped. "Some people call it rape," she thundered. Susan's jaw dropped, but Kelly didn't care because it was her island. "For hundreds of years—" She inhaled deeply and began again in a more modulated tone. "We've built plants all across America without even thinking about what they might be doing to the environment. And they've sat there spewing out their crap. Some toxic, some not. But we didn't give any thought to the chemical companies and the kinds of things they were dumping in our streams. We didn't give a hoot about the Rust Belt states and what they might be belching into the air. We were caught up in the Industrial Revolution and if it worked, it got built. That's not what we want here. I'm a transplant and I love this place. Hell, I don't just love it, I'm passionate about it. So don't expect people like me to embrace you folks because you're going to give us jobs or you're going to put money in our pockets. Some things just are not for sale, and our landscape is one of them."

"You know, I figured you of all people would understand this," Susan said, her hand on the door handle. "Because you didn't seem to be as involved as Amy, I figured you were taking a wait-and-see attitude until you understood all the facts and then you'd make an informed decision, but I was wrong." She opened the door.

"You were wrong. I've made a decision based strictly on emotions. I don't want you folks to screw with my view." Kelly inhaled. Why was she so angry? Why was she taking it out on Susan?

"Good night," Susan said. "Thank you for a lovely evening." She quietly closed the car door.

Kelly watched her walk into the cottage. Why were they beating up on each other? Why the anger? She put the car in gear, pointed it toward home. *You're a jerk.* How many times had she told herself that lately? *You're angry at the message, so you shoot the messenger.* She was surprised at her reaction. Before when she listened to Amy talk about LNG, she had felt Amy's passion but hadn't been drawn into it. Now, saying out loud how she felt, she understood the depth of her feelings. She pulled to the side of the road. Still, why take it out on Susan? She made a U-turn. Back in Susan's driveway, she could see a light on in the living room. Oh, well, she thought. She'd apologize and Susan would either accept it or slam the door in her face. The door opened as Kelly raised her hand to knock.

"I'm sorry," they said at the same time.

Susan laughed. "I'm sorry. It really was my fault. Would you like a cup of tea or a glass of wine? I was just making some herbal tea for myself. I realized that I wasn't going to sleep with all that adrenaline pumping inside of me."

"Sure, a cup of tea would be nice."

"Come into the kitchen. It's my favorite place to sit."

"Welcome to the island," Kelly said lightly. "Most people spend their lives in the kitchen. When I lived in Portland, life was cooking dinner, putting it on a TV tray and sitting in front of the television set. Not now. I don't care what time of day or night or what the meal or snack might be, I'm right there in the kitchen. It's wonderful."

"It is," Susan said, taking another mug out of the cupboard and putting a tea bag in it. "Can we call a truce?"

"We can, but really, I got to tell you this rule about not talking about LNG is silly. You're here to sell us something, we should be willing to listen. I'm not saying I'm going to agree with you, but where is the harm in words?"

"I don't know. It's just something that's happened. When Laurie and I spend time together we never talk about it. I hang out with Elizabeth and we talk about everything but that. I go to dinner and a play with you and I'm yelling about LNG. Now, that one I can't figure out." Susan laughed, her cheeks flushed with embarrassment.

"It must be hard to be focused one hundred and ten percent on something, yet not be able to talk about it in general conversation. We all talk about our jobs, but no one wants to talk about your job. You've got to feel frustrated."

Susan cocked her head. "I do, I just never say it. Well, is there anything else I can beat up on you about?"

Kelly could hear the playful tone in Susan's voice. She was glad she'd come back.

Susan handed her a cup. "Milk? Sugar?"

"Straight, thank you."

"I've got some cookies around here," she said, opening cupboards.

"No, thanks, really. The tea is just fine."

"Can I tell you something? Something you won't repeat?"

"Of course."

Susan looked at her quizzically. "This is really an important opportunity for me and my company." She stirred sugar into her tea. "I'm small, and when the developers approached me with this offer I could see big things happening for my company. I've been absolutely consumed by that. When I was working for that firm in Boston, this chemical company wanted to put a plant in a small community near Boston and I've got to tell you, even though I was being paid, my heart wasn't in it. But this is different. LNG is not bad. I know everyone wants to believe it is, but it really isn't. I wouldn't be able to sell it if I didn't believe in it. And tonight I realized selling it has been consuming me because I know it's important for my company." She shrugged. "But that's wrong. What's important here is the LNG message. Kelly, it would turn this little community around economically—that's the message I need to get out."

Kelly eyed her. "Please accept this for what it is. If this is right and people want it, then it will happen. If it's wrong, it's for us to decide. Get your message out, but give people a chance to digest it."

"And if they turn it down?"

"Then you go away. Which I hope won't happen."

"Really?"

Kelly could feel Susan's gaze on her and she felt a warmth inside that she hadn't felt in a long time. "Yeah! Besides, you'd break my best friend's heart." She wanted to keep it light. Why had she said she didn't want Susan to leave? "Remember, I'm supposed to tell you about all her good points."

Susan smiled. "I like her. She's been a breath of fresh air in an otherwise restricted environment. I'm enjoying her friendship."

"She's special, all right."

"Is she always so high-energy?"

"Oh, yeah, Laurie doesn't do anything in low. She's all revved up and ready to go. I love her dearly, she's my best friend, my best oldest friend," Kelly corrected herself. *Now why had she said that? Amy*, she thought. *Those were Amy's words. Funny, she hadn't thought about Amy until now.* "She's my best friend. I've known her longer than any other friend in my life. And we've always been there for each other."

"I have friends like that in Andover," Susan said wistfully.

"It must be lonely, being in a place like this where everyone has known each other for years and you're the outsider."

"It is." Susan sipped her tea and looked directly at her. "Can I ask you something?"

"Sure." Kelly felt that flush of warmth again under Susan's gaze.

"Would you like to go on a picnic tomorrow?"

203

Kelly smiled. "That'd be nice."

"If Amy's back, I'd love for her to join us," Susan hastily added.

"She won't be. So what do we talk about?" Kelly teased.

"Whatever we want. You're right, I've been frustrated because I can't talk about my job in a non-Power Point way. I'm glad you came back."

The warmth continued growing inside of her. *What the hell was that all about?* she pondered. "Me too and, Susan, it's okay for us to disagree on this. It really is. And I want to thank you. I've been skimming along the top of this, not really paying all that much attention to details. I figured there was time for me to make up my mind. And I don't know why really. It's an important issue. I've just not gotten involved." She stopped. Why hadn't she gotten involved? This was important, not just to the island but to its residents. What had stopped her? "Amy's been consumed by it." She smiled tepidly. "Maybe that's enough passion for one family. Anyway, I've picked up bits and pieces listening to her, but our conversation tonight—"

"Argument?" Susan offered.

Kelly smiled. "Our conversation helped crystallize my thoughts. I kept saying I was going to wait until I had more information, but now I realize that for me it's strictly gut level. I don't want this thing in my backyard and as selfish as that may be, with all of the unemployed people on this island, then so be it. I really don't want it here or anywhere near here, and I didn't realize until tonight how passionate I felt about it."

"Well." Susan laughed. "I must be pretty good at my job then. It's my job to persuade and I persuaded you right over to the other side."

"You did, but that's not bad. Because there are a whole lot of other people on this island, and you've persuaded them to your side. I hear people talk at the hospital and although a lot of them are concerned about what this would do to our environment, there are a whole bunch more who say, 'What's the alternative?' You're the best dance to come into town in a long time and they figure they might as well join in the fun." Kelly finished her tea and got up. "I've got to go. My God, look at the time. It's one o'clock."

"So I'll see you tomorrow? Or have I completely scared you away?"

"What time?"

"Noon? I'll bring the lunch. You won't have to do a thing."

"Let me bring part of it."

"My treat." Susan walked her to the door. "I'm glad you came back."

"Me too." Kelly could feel that warmth stirring inside her again under Susan's gaze. *This is silly*, she thought. *You're a married woman. You don't feel warmth inside when a woman looks at you.*

"I can meet you here, or we can meet at your house."

"How about I pick you up?"

"Great."

Suddenly, Susan's hand was on her arm. "Can I give you a thank-you hug?"

"Of course." Kelly turned and encircled her in her arms. Just a hint of Susan's perfume lingered in her hair. She loved the smell of Red perfume. She thought about Amy. She never wore it, said it was too sweet-smelling for her tastes. The quick hug she usually gave her friends lingered just a moment. Warmth? Hell, she was burning up inside. She stepped back. "Well, good night." She almost swallowed the words.

"Good night." Kelly could hear the huskiness in Susan's voice.

Chapter Twenty-three

Susan put the cups in the sink and turned off the kitchen lights. She felt energized, awake. In the bathroom she looked in the mirror and saw that her cheeks were flushed. She brushed her teeth and creamed her face. She thought about Kelly. She had had such a good time with her. She'd hated it when dinner ended and they had to leave for the play. They just seemed to talk and talk over dinner. She sensed Kelly had felt the same way about leaving. Then they'd had the argument over LNG on the way home, and when Kelly left the first time she remembered thinking how sad she felt. She'd felt lonely. When she returned she resisted a desire to crush her in her arms, tell her how glad she was that she came back.

What was that about? she scolded herself. Kelly was in a relationship and a happy one at that. Why'd she invite her on a picnic? If she was that lonely she could invite Elizabeth, who'd no doubt be more than happy to accept. But she didn't want Elizabeth, she thought. It had been an impulse. The words had just popped out of her mouth. She'd asked her because she wanted to see her again. Not in a group of people, but alone.

Susan thought about the evening and how she had bathed in the comfort of their conversation. The restaurant had been perfect. The waitress had seated them away from everyone else, off in a corner where they could talk quietly. There was a candle on the table and soft music playing in the background. She'd been absolutely captivated by the way the candlelight intensified Kelly's blue eyes and how animated her face became when she talked about nursing. How passionately she talked about those years when she had worked as a nurse.

And she liked the way Kelly listened intently when Susan talked about her job. She'd asked good questions and really seemed interested in what she had to say. What a contrast with her friend, she thought. Laurie loved to talk and regaled her with funny stories about things that happened in a hospital that the public never heard about. She enjoyed Laurie's company. She loved her energy and the way she seemed to push through life. She knew Laurie had taken their relationship to the next step in her mind and was attracted to her, and she knew she was going to have to deal with that. She liked her, but it stopped short of attraction. Kelly, however, was another story. In the restaurant and sitting next to her at the play, she had wanted to reach over and hold her hand.

Put a lid on it, she scolded herself. Kelly was clearly a one-woman woman. Letting her fantasy run amok was only going to cause pain. She snapped off the light and went into her bedroom. She pulled back the covers on the bed and sat down. What she wanted to do was go for a run, but not at one o'clock in the morning. If any of her neighbors were looking out the window, they'd think she was crazy. Some already thought she was crazy because of the people she represented. Funny, she thought, if she were in Andover she wouldn't even think about going out on the streets at that hour of the morning, but here she felt safe.

She pulled off her blouse and threw it on the chair. She

unhooked her bra, balled it up and threw it on top of the blouse. She stood up and pulled her slacks and panties off. She slid under the covers. If only she was here for some other reason, she thought. Was Kelly right? Would an LNG terminal change the social fabric of this community? Would that be so bad? She had done her homework and gotten information from the State Planning Office. Jefferson County was the poorest in Maine. Unemployment was in the double digits compared with the rest of the state. Bleu Island was growing, but the people coming in were retirees and offered little in the way of new jobs. What the island needed was jobs. Right now its major export was its youth. They left the island soon after graduation from high school in search of work.

As much as she tried to concentrate on her job her mind kept circling back to Kelly. What would it feel like if Kelly were in bed with her? she wondered. Their naked bodies would be touching, first gently and then passionately. She willed herself to think about Jefferson County, think about the poverty and think about LNG.

She thought about lying on top of Kelly, kissing first her mouth and then her neck. Then feasting on those breasts. Several times at the restaurant she had glanced at those breasts. She rubbed her hand against her own breast. What it would be like to have Kelly's touching hers?

She rolled onto her stomach. *Go to sleep, woman,* she ordered herself. *Dream about tankers and terminals and money. Think about your company. Don't think about a woman who is in a relationship.* She'd call her first thing in the morning and cancel. She'd come up with an excuse. *I fell while running and hurt myself.* That was stupid. She was a nurse and would be over here in five seconds to check it out.

The developers called—that was a good excuse, she thought. They'd scheduled an emergency meeting at eight o'clock and she'd have to be there even though it was Sunday. That was a good one. She'd call her and tell her that. It was perfect. She yawned and closed her eyes. Her mind drifted back to Kelly's body. *You're bad,* she said to herself. She stretched her fingers out on the sheet. *I want to kiss that body.* She wanted to get her job done and get the hell out of there, the other side of her brain argued.

She had to decide. She felt herself slipping into that first level just before sleep. No more alone time with Kelly Burns. She had to stay focused. She told herself that over and over again like the repeat chorus of a song. *You have to stay focused.*

Susan rolled over and reached for the telephone. Who the hell would be calling at this hour? she thought as she glanced at the clock. It was eight o'clock.

"Good morning," Laurie said. "I have a feeling I woke you."

"You did, but I should be up anyway." Susan turned on her side.

"How was dinner? Did you enjoy the play?"

"It was a delight, thank you. And the fact that you coerced your dear friend into taking me was very nice of you."

"Isn't she a peach, but did she tell you that I coerced her?"

"Absolutely not, but I just knew it was not something she had suggested."

"Guilty as charged. But I've already talked with her. She said you two had fun, said you were going on a picnic today. I think that's wonderful."

Susan remembered the thoughts she had had about Kelly just before she fell asleep and shivered. "Well, it was one of those impulse things. I asked her and she said yes."

"She is one special lady and I'm so glad you're getting a chance to know her. You know, Kelly has a heart as big as one of those tankers you're pushing. But more importantly, she would do anything for her friends. I feel so lucky to have her in my life and I'm so glad she's becoming a part of your life," Laurie gushed.

"So how is your trip going?" Susan changed the subject.

"Good. We met yesterday with the buyer and the realtor. Actually, I'm disappointed. I'd hoped to get back there tonight for a celebration dinner, but we're going to sign papers tomorrow. I

209

tried for today, but the buyer wanted to think about it one more day. I wanted to kick him in the butt and tell him it's a good deal—hell, it's a great deal and get on with it so I can get on with my life. But I couldn't. So it looks like I won't be back until tomorrow."

Susan noted the disappointment in Laurie's voice and felt for her. "I have a meeting every night this week. But what about the weekend? Hey, it's Labor Day weekend, let's have dinner."

"I can't," Laurie said miserably. "I start my twelve-hour shifts seven to seven on Friday."

"Let's have dinner after seven o'clock."

"It'd be an awfully early dinner since the shift, starts at seven, at night. I'm on evenings for four days, then I'm off for four days. How about a celebration dinner after that?"

"You're on."

"Good." Laurie's voice was gentle. "I'm looking forward to getting back."

"I'm glad, and I'm looking forward to our dinner."

They rang off and Susan hung up the telephone. She stretched. She had to call Kelly and cancel the picnic. Laurie had already called her, so she was up. She wondered if she'd told Laurie about the fight or that they'd been up talking until one o'clock in the morning. Had Laurie sensed that she was attracted to her? She wondered if—Susan picked up the telephone on the first ring.

"Did you get your wake-up call?" Kelly's voice sounded sexy and sleepy.

"I did."

"That's my pal, an absolute ball of energy at eight o'clock on a Sunday, no less. Although I doubt she was up as late as we were."

"Probably not."

"I just called to tell you I'm really looking forward to the picnic. I want to take you to a favorite place of mine here on the island. It's in a remote spot and really breathtaking. I thought I'd pick you up around noon. We have to hike a ways."

I have to tell her I have a meeting, she thought. "I'd like that."

"Good, so I'll see you then."

"Oh, Kelly, do you have any dietary restrictions? I don't even know what you like."

Kelly chuckled. "Olives. I hate olives—green olives, black olives, big olives, little olives."

Susan laughed. "Stop, I get the picture. So if I happened to have olive loaf sandwiches you would what?"

"Toss you to the sharks."

"Whoa, that's harsh. Couldn't you just toss the olive loaf sandwiches to the sharks?"

"They'd spit them out. Sharks hate olives."

Susan loved the teasing note in Kelly's voice. She closed her eyes and imagined Kelly's naked breasts again, then she opened her eyes and swallowed. "Okay, no olives. Any other restrictions?"

"Liver, I hate liver."

"Well, who doesn't? Is that it?"

"That's it," Kelly exclaimed. "Don't worry about bringing something to drink. I have a bottle of wine chilling even as we speak."

"Good."

"So, I'll see you in a couple of hours."

"Looking forward to it."

"Me too."

Chapter Twenty-four

Kelly rolled over, hung up the phone and closed her eyes. She thought about Susan and the way her gaze had captured Kelly's and held it in the most intimate look. She loved the way she ran her fingers through her hair or delicately held a fork like a baton in the hands of an orchestra conductor. She liked how her voice softened when she talked about her family and became animated when she talked about her work.

She thought about those long legs that seemed to go on forever and ever and her small breasts that—Kelly stopped. *Don't think about breasts and long legs.* Think about a really nice woman who is fun to be with.

Susan had talked about the people who were close to her, her mother and friends. She hinted at her last relationship, saying that they'd been together ten years, but work and goals had interrupted their lives. Kelly had wanted to ask her hundreds of questions. Had she loved the woman? Had the woman delighted in her body when they made love? Kelly rolled on her side. *Don't go there*, she told herself. *Don't go there.*

Kelly got up and made some coffee. She'd planned to work in the gardens today, but somehow that didn't seem important anymore. It had been such an unusual summer. The things she and Amy usually got done in the past had been put on hold. Last year, they had spent weekends cutting grass and planting flowers. This year, Amy had hired a high-school student. They hadn't talked about it. Amy had just done it. Last year, they had cleaned the garage and held a huge yard sale. This year they'd spent their summer with Amy mostly attending meetings. Now it was almost the end of August and Amy was in Augusta and she was getting ready to go on a picnic with the most enchanting woman she'd met in years.

Maybe next weekend she and Amy could take a day and work in the gardens, she thought as she crawled back into bed. She liked the daydreams she was having. There was no harm in going on a picnic today with someone she enjoyed. This attraction she felt for Susan was simply that, an attraction. It was something that she could hold at bay like the flu. Not a good thought, since she was one who usually caught the flu. She and Amy had problems, but she loved Amy even though at times she didn't like her.

That night Amy had told her she lacked class was the first time she wondered how Amy could love her and yet say those things to her. Rather than confront her and talk about it and start yet another fight, Kelly had swallowed her remarks, yet again. Someday, she decided, she was going to choke rather than swallow. She contemplated their relationship. Funny, she thought, it had been a good July and August because they hadn't seen much of each other. She thought about that. In the past, the occasions they'd been apart—conferences for Kelly or buying trips for Amy—seemed to be the best moments she'd had at the house. She sighed. *Don't be silly*, she thought. *You're overstating the past. Work on the future. With a little patience on your part you can convince Amy to see a counselor, someone who can help you work through the problems.* She was positive a counselor could help them.

Kelly knew she also was at fault. She had analyzed their relationship enough times to know that she brought to it her own insecurities. The bad habits she had learned from her parents' screwed-up marriage had skewed her relationship with Amy. As an adult she had promised herself she would not relive her mother's marriage. In her teens she'd been addicted to happy-ending stories and believed if she pointed her heart in the right direction, life would follow. She didn't realize that she'd chosen a rocky path, like her mother. She recalled the thousands of times her father lost his temper and her mother told her and her sister and brother to say nothing to upset him and it would go away. So everyone tiptoed around the house waiting for the storm to pass. That was how she had dealt with Amy's temper, by tiptoeing around. It scared her to think she had become involved with the female version of her father. They both had charisma to burn and dynamite tempers. They would blow and then afterward, they were cheery and happy. She didn't want her mother's life.

She'd left home when she was seventeen and never looked back. Her sister and brother had done the same. Only they had put a greater distance between them; Caroline had moved to California, her brother, Steve, to Texas.

After she'd left home, Kelly moved into an apartment with friends, found a job at McDonald's, got several scholarships and started nursing school. She'd met Robin and they moved in together.

Her father had died while she was in nursing school. Kelly found a counselor. She learned that she did not have to be like her father. She could talk through her problems, not yell. Kelly scratched her head. Memories were like trickled thoughts, they just seemed to creep to the foreground. How many times had she buried those growing-up years? Tucked them away in the part of her brain she had labeled *Do Not Open*. Now, with Amy, she found herself falling back into those old insecurities. That portion of her brain was *Open for Business*. She looked at the clock. She had to get out of bed and get ready for the picnic.

She was about to step into the shower when the telephone rang. *It must be Amy*, she thought as she went back into the bedroom.

"Good morning."

"Kelly," Elizabeth said, "I was thinking it'd be fun if we did something today."

"I can't." Kelly thought about Susan. "I'm tied up. I thought you were going to Augusta with Amy and the others?"

"I was, but I backed out. I can't take all that running up and down the road followed by long meetings and stuff. I'm just too old, so I begged off. Let them handle it. I'm holding down the fort."

"Gosh, I feel terrible. If I'd known you were going to be around I would have called you."

"They all thought I was going and I really thought I was going, then at the last minute I called Amy and told her I just can't do it anymore. But how was the dinner and play with Susan? Isn't she terrific."

"Wonderful. The food was great and the play was just outstanding. I think she enjoyed herself."

"I'm glad you went with her. She's really one lone soul here. She's been over here several times and we've had dinner at her house. She's a great cook. I try to include her as much as possible in my life."

"I know. Amy just can't get past what she does so everyone is sort of juggling, trying to make Susan feel included, but still holding her apart. It's hard."

"Agreed. Hopefully Amy will reconcile that. But I'm sorry you can't spend the day with me. I thought we'd go out on the boat, maybe have a picnic."

"I can't." Kelly stared down at the floor. *Tell her*, she thought. *Invite her to join you. What's stopping you?* "But I'd love a raincheck."

"Of course. Maybe next weekend. Amy's back, so maybe we can do something then."

"You're on."

Kelly walked back into the bathroom and opened the door. The

215

steam from the shower washed over her face. Why hadn't she invited Elizabeth to join them? She picked up a washcloth and stepped into the shower. She hadn't invited Elizabeth because she wanted to be alone with Susan. *You're attracted to her*, she scolded herself. She hadn't invited Elizabeth because she didn't want any competition. She wanted to bathe in her attention, soak in those eyes. She couldn't be attracted to her, she reasoned. She was in a committed relationship. She could call Elizabeth back and invite her. But that would be silly. It would seem like an afterthought, like she hadn't wanted Elizabeth there. No, she couldn't do that. It would hurt Elizabeth's feelings. Sure, she wanted to be alone with Susan, but could she keep that attraction for her locked in a box? She and Amy had problems, but they were working them out. She lathered her hair. She had so enjoyed the night before she just wanted one more day to get to know her, to talk about those things that two people talk about when they're at the beginning of a friendship. Friendship, that's what it is. She rinsed the soap out of her hair. Yes, there was an attraction, but she wanted to embrace Susan as a friend, and what about Amy? She should call her and ask how things were going, how the meeting went with the governor. She should tell her about how nice it was to have dinner with Susan and that they were going on a picnic today. She grabbed a towel, stepped out of the shower and dried herself off.

Downstairs, dressed in her hiking clothes, she poured herself a glass of cranberry juice and cut an English muffin in half and put it in the toaster. Jasper was rubbing against her leg.

"Hungry, sport?" she asked. He was wound around her legs. As she opened a can of Fancy Feast, he anxiously jumped up onto the counter. Kelly lifted him and the bowl onto the floor. "Not up here, buddy boy."

She set some butter, jam and peanut butter on the table and plopped the English muffin on a plate. She felt comfortable with the silence. It might make more sense, she thought, to call Amy tonight. More than likely she'd be strategizing right now and wouldn't appreciate being interrupted. That made sense, because if Amy hadn't been busy she'd have called her. She'd wait a few more minutes to see if Amy called. She looked up at the clock. Eleven. She'd give her two more minutes to call, then she'd leave. She had to pick Susan up at noon. She watched the second hand sweep around the face of the clock.

"You're on your own, little buddy," she said to Jasper. "If you're mom calls, tell her I had to leave and I'm sorry I missed her call." She reached down and stroked the cat. "If only you could talk . . . or maybe not."

Chapter Twenty-five

"You're going to love this place," Kelly said as she turned her Ford Explorer onto the Cutler Road. "It's magnificent." Susan had been waiting for her when she arrived at her house. They had loaded two large backpacks into the back of Kelly's car. She had joked that there was enough food to feed the two of them and half the seagulls in Maine.

"Do you come here often?"

"Not as often as in the beginning. Funny, when I first moved here Elizabeth knew I loved hiking and told me about this place."

"Has Amy hiked it with you?"

"Once or twice. She likes to hike shorter trails." Kelly shut off the engine. "It's a ten-mile loop. We can do it all or we can do that part where we just hike in and have our picnic and hike out."

"Let's do whatever moves us. I'm up for a ten-mile hike."

"I bet you are. You're a runner—you could probably run the ten miles and not even break a sweat."

218

"Thanks for the vote of confidence, but I'm not the runner I once was. Funny how you just get so distracted by everything else that you don't take time for the important things, like good healthy exercise."

"You're right. A few years ago a friend of mine e-mailed me this piece by Erma Bombeck."

"I remember her. She was sort of today's Mark Twain when it came to sage advice. Her column was in our newspaper."

"Anyway, I can't remember the title, but she wrote it after she found out she was dying of cancer. It was a list suggesting you focus on what's important and not on life's distractions, like you should drink that bottle of wine you bought for that special occasion instead of saving it." She laughed to herself as she thought about it. "Robin—my ex—and I had gone to California on vacation and we had found this wonderful winery and bought a very expensive bottle of mead. She was a history buff and liked the idea of drinking one of the oldest wines in the world. When we got home we promised ourselves we'd open it on a special occasion. It would be our celebratory wine, so we put it in the wine rack and never drank it."

"Why?"

"Well, for some reason that special occasion never came along, even though we had several wonderful things happen and then it was too late."

"You broke up?"

"We did. But before we broke up her dog, Buster, one night was running around the kitchen and he accidentally bumped into the wine rack. The bottle broke. We had mead all over the floor, but it was ironic. There were six other bottles in the wine rack and that's the only one that broke."

"How strange."

"Months later we broke up." Kelly turned onto a dirt road. "Not because of what the dog did, but because we'd been having problems. But I look back at that moment and think how serendipitous. Here we'd had many wonderful moments, including celebrating our fifth anniversary, but we kept putting off opening it. We kept looking for that next really big special occasion and it never happened. Now I'd drink the mead, regardless of why. That's what struck me about that Erma Bombeck piece. Her advice was to seize every minute, stop sweating the small stuff. Don't look for tomorrow's special occasion when every day should be a special occasion."

"Are you able to do that?"

Kelly turned down a second dirt road. "Not as much as I should, even though I have what she wrote on my bulletin board to remind me."

"Me neither. I've put off doing so many things that I really want to do."

"Like what?"

"A trip to Scotland. I want to golf in Scotland."

"You're a golfer?"

"I play at it. How about you?"

"Amy loves golf. I learned the game about two years ago. I'm the world's worst golfer, but I have fun. Maybe the four of us—including Elizabeth—could play a round on the mainland."

"I'd love to."

"So why haven't you gone to Scotland?"

"Because I keep saying I'll do it next year."

"Go to Scotland."

"I will. How about—"

"Here we are," Kelly said pulling into a small parking lot. She opened her door. "Getting here was the easy part, now we begin the hike." She reached into the back of the car and grabbed both backpacks. She picked up her small cooler.

"Here, I can carry some of that," Susan said sliding one of the packs onto her back.

"Come on, I want to show you this wonderful place."

Susan followed her along a small path that wound around under an immense canopy of maple and white birch trees. A bird fluttered overhead. They stopped.

220

"Listen," Kelly said softly as the chickadee peeped. "You can hear all kinds of birds in here. I wish I had time to take some bird-watching classes." She paused. "Ahh, another Erma Bombeck moment."

"It's funny," Susan said, "if I knew I had another forty years, I'd probably spend the next twenty focused on building my business and reaching all those financial goals I've set for myself and then spend the next twenty years doing the things I really want to do. But what if I only have another twenty years, or ten years or one year? I'll never get to do those other things, like going to Scotland or on a safari trip to Kenya."

"That's one of the reasons I jumped out of the helicopter. I remembered the column and decided I had better do it, not wait." Kelly laughed. "You're the only one I've told this to, but I called it my Erma Bombeck jump. I grabbed hold of the moment and I'm so glad I did. Otherwise, I would have said, well, I'll do it another time. It would have been another one of those shoulda woulda coulda moments that I would have blown."

"When I worked for that public relations firm in Boston, I set up a number of what we used to call feel-good seminars with motivational speakers who said much the same thing. Fill today with things you want to do, don't wish the day away on what you plan to do in the future. I set those seminars up and was there to make certain everything went smoothly. I even listened, and I always promised myself someday I would take their advice."

"I know I've been guilty of that so many times."

"So how do you fix that?" Susan asked as they climbed a small hill.

"You stop and look around," Kelly said as she stopped on the trail. Susan almost bumped into her. "I'm doing it again. I'm so eager to get us to that special spot where I love to sit and dream—and look what we're missing." She nodded toward the moss on either side of the trail and the small mushrooms that had punched through. "Have you ever seen a red mushroom before?" She pointed at a tiny mushroom buried in green moss.

"Never." Susan bent over to look at it. "It's beautiful. It's so delicate."

Kelly nodded. "And you'll see them all up and down this trail, red, yellow and orange mushrooms. They don't last long, but while they're here they're beautiful. Look," Kelly said as she moved a few feet up the path. "There's a cluster of yellow ones."

"They're perfect."

"Wouldn't it be nice if we had this thing in our brain that said 'stop, this is an Erma Bombeck moment.'" Kelly leaned over and studied the delicate, albeit inedible, mushrooms. "Or better yet, wouldn't it be nice if we did that for our friends? If I won the lottery I'd give all of my friends their Erma moment. I'd ask them what it was they've always wanted to do in life and then, if money could make it happen I'd give it to them as a gift."

"I like that." Susan looked at Kelly.

Kelly moved silently up the path. "Listen." She held up her hand.

"Surf?"

"And lots of it," she said as she rounded the bend and stepped back for Susan to see.

"Oh, wow, Kelly, you're right, this is breathtaking." They were standing on a tall cliff that seemed to just burst forth from the ground. The terrain was rugged. Sea grass and tiny purple flowers snaked between fissures in the rocks. The foamy ocean water washed in and around the rocks while tiny waves that looked like diamonds sparkled on the distant water.

"That's Grand Manan," Kelly said, pointing at the long expanse of rock that dominated the horizon and sat just miles away in Canada. "You can't see it from the other side of the island."

"Have you been there?"

"A few times. This side of Grand Manan is all cliffs, no development. People live on the other side."

"Is this where we're going to picnic?"

"Farther up on the trail. Come on." They climbed farther and farther up the trail. She found the spot and stepped off the path into a thicket of trees. She held a branch up for Susan to walk under. "There's a wonderful rock backrest near here. I can sit there for hours." She stepped upon a small outcropping of rocks. She held out her hand and pulled Susan up next to her. "Listen."

Susan frowned. "Rushing water?"

"Exactly."

Susan followed her around a bend. "Oh, double wow," she said as she looked at the water cascading off the rocks and flowing into the ocean. "It's like a tiny waterfall. I love the intimacy of this." She set her backpack down.

The rocks reminded Kelly of a giant amphitheater. "It's a stream and in the spring and fall it just expands into this waterfall. In the summer, there isn't even a trickle of water, but by the end of August it's running well. By October, it's gushing. And," she said as she stepped down onto the rocks, "this depression here gives you the illusion that you're standing below sea level."

"You're right." Susan glanced around. "Kelly, this is wonderful."

"I knew you'd like it." She looked intently into Susan's eyes and swallowed.

"Well . . ." They said together. They laughed.

"We've hiked about five miles," she said, looking at her watch. It was three o'clock. "How about lunch?" Kelly said to lessen the tension. She pointed at the backpacks. "If I'd have packed lunch, it would have all fit into a tiny little knapsack. Ham sandwiches, pickles and potato chips. Somehow, I get the feeling that there's a lot more inside there."

"Just a bit more." Susan smiled. "I love to cook." She unpacked the first backpack. "Madam, if you choose, you may select any seat in the house." She affected a maitre d's voice.

"Thank you." Kelly bowed ceremoniously. "By the way, I have wine," She held up a bottle of Riesling from the cooler. "May I decant this for you, madam?"

"Please."

"Would you like to savor the aroma for just a moment?" Kelly held the now opened bottle for her to smell.

Susan laughed and waved the bottle away. "I will accept that the aroma is perfect."

"Grand," Kelly said. She handed Susan a glass and took her own glass from the cooler and sat down.

"We begin," Susan said, opening one of the containers, "with watermelon cocktail." She spooned it into two cocktail glasses she'd wrapped in tea towels.

"I don't believe it. You brought along cocktail glasses?"

"Absolutely," she said handing her a spoon and a cocktail glass. "I was so amazed my cottage is equipped with everything, even fancy dishes."

"This is wonderful," Kelly said after the first bite. "I'm not going to ask you for the recipe because my cooking consists of putting it on the grill and not burning it."

"Well, that's important in and of itself. How many times have people put stuff on the grill and burned it?"

Kelly smirked. "Not many, but thank you for trying to make me feel better. It's funny, cooking is not something I enjoy. I love to eat, God knows, but looking through recipe books or trying to figure out a complicated recipe is a chore." The watermelon was heavenly. "Now Laurie, she is one heck of a cook. When we roomed together, she did all of the cooking. She could make tuna casserole taste like a gourmet meal."

"Actually, she's cooked a meal or two since she's been in the carriage house and you're right, she's a great cook."

Kelly shifted uncomfortably. Was that a flash of jealousy? It couldn't have been. Why would she be jealous of her best friend doing what her best friend does so well—cooking? "Have you cooked for her?"

"A few times." Susan paused and looked out over the bay. "This is truly beautiful. Thank you for bringing me here."

"You're welcome, but I have to thank you. If the rest of the meal is like this watermelon cocktail, I'm in for a wonderful treat."

"Well, you are." Susan smiled impishly. From a large Thermos she poured Maine seafood chowder into two bowls. "This is supposed to have stayed hot, so this is the test," she said.

"I don't believe it. If this were me you'd be eating out of Styrofoam bowls."

"Hmm, this is nicer," she said. "Maine seafood chowder with just a hint of Iogen spices, handed down from generation to generation." She handed Kelly a spoon.

"Really?"

"No." Susan laughed. "But it sounds so good when you say it."

"I was impressed." Kelly tasted the chowder. "Oh, funkalishish."

Susan smiled. "You certainly have a way of expressing yourself."

"Oh, double funkalishish," Kelly said again after she put another spoonful in her mouth. "When did you have time to prepare this?"

"Actually, I'd made the chowder ahead for the weekend—I planned on eating it myself. Now I get to share it." Susan opened a plastic container lined with another tea towel and handed it to her. "Warm rolls and"—she opened another container—"butter."

"Now, if you told me you got up this morning and made these rolls I am definitely going to freak out."

"Although that would be tempting, I have to confess that I cheated on these. They were in my freezer and I simply thawed them and cooked them."

"But what a nice touch. Lightly browned rolls and seafood chowder. Susan, this is to die for." Kelly raised her voice. "To die for!"

Susan laughed. "I'm glad you like it. Funny, of all the things I miss most about a relationship, it's days like this."

"I know." Kelly added seriously, "I can imagine how lonely you must be here."

"Not all the time," Susan said just as seriously. "The weeks just fly by. I'm usually either hosting or attending some meeting or writing press releases, answering questions from the media. If I'm not in a meeting, I'm with the developers. It's the weekends that are the hardest. That's why I've so enjoyed Laurie, who's funny and fun . . ." She shrugged. "I just like her."

Kelly felt that little green monster whip its tail ever so gently around her heart. "I think that's wonderful." *Focus*, she thought. "I'm lucky to have her in my life. Laurie's special."

"I've noticed that." Susan stared across the bay, "She's been the difference between sanity and insanity this summer. She pops in all the time."

"Well, I hope she's not becoming too much of a pest." Why did she say that? It was none of her business if she popped in all the time. It was none of her business if the two of them were sleeping together. She wondered if they were sleeping together. *Stop it*, she ordered her wild thoughts.

"No, I didn't mean that," Susan said quickly. "We just seem to have fun together. It's funny the kinds of things you talk about when you're cooking together."

"What kinds of things?" Kelly wanted to slap the words back into her mouth.

"Oh, I don't know." Susan seemed unconcerned about the pointed questions. "Life, love, relationships. We just seem to talk on and on. Just before she left we were at my house and all of a sudden we started talking about what we want most in a relationship."

"What do you want most in a relationship?" Kelly asked quietly. She put her spoon back in the bowl.

"To be cherished."

"Not loved?"

"That's assumed. But beyond love. You get together because you love each other. I think—" Susan stared out at the bay as if trying to collect her thoughts. "For me at least, it's that rung above love. I want someone who will cherish me. Someone who will after whatever kind of hour or day they've had look at me and see me as the one place where they can feel safe, and I want the same. I remember a dear friend of mine saying you know you're truly cherished when you reach out for comfort in the darkness of the night and your lover, in her sleep, covers your hand with hers and holds it close. I don't want someone in my life who takes their frustration or anger out on me because they're mad at themselves or the world. I had that once and I never want to go back there."

Kelly sat forward as if the rock behind her had burned her back. "Have you?"

"It wasn't a long relationship, but it wasn't a healthy one either." Susan continued, "Funny, I loved her. I just didn't love how she treated me, but out of that relationship, spooky as it may seem, came some good. It helped me crystallize what I wanted from a relationship, and I'm unwilling to compromise that." She put down her bowl. "That's probably why I'm not in a relationship now, but that's okay because I now know what I want. I want someone to be sensitive to my needs and wants, just as I'm sensitive to hers. I want tenderness and a soft voice, not just when we're making love, but in the daytime too. This is not a Pollyannaish thing. I know we'll have problems and frustrations and I know there'll be times when it will be difficult because that's how it is when you marry the heart, mind and soul of two people. But I also know that there's everything else in between. My parents had it and I want it. I remember—" She stopped and smiled. "I remember one time when my parents shared a tea bag."

Kelly waited, mesmerized by Susan's words.

"People do that all the time, so you probably think I'm being silly, but let me tell you the story." Susan's voice softened as she thought about it. "We were at the kitchen table. I was in high school." She frowned. "We were talking, about what I can't remember, and my parents always shared a tea bag—it's what frugal people do." She laughed. "My dad was talking about something and without missing a beat, he took his spoon and lifted the tea bag out of his cup and reached across the table and put it in my mother's cup. But do you know what I saw?" She paused. "I saw the love in his eyes. I saw the way he looked at her. They'd been married twenty years or longer, I can't remember, but that tenderness was still there, and in that moment I saw how much he cherished her, and that's what I want. I want someone who thinks I'm more important than life itself. Is that such a tall order?" She looked directly at Kelly.

"No, I think that's what everyone should have in their relationship." The sadness that had enveloped her would not go away. She looked out at the water, Susan's words replaying in her mind.

"I'm sorry. I've been rambling on and on. Please believe that what I said was not some kind of litmus test for my love life. It's just what I know I want. Now, let's stop being so serious. Would you like more chowder?"

"No, thanks, that was delicious." Kelly finished off her last two spoonfuls. "Don't apologize. I think if we don't articulate what we want in a relationship we might miss it when the right one comes along." She tried to hold the smile. She stared at a tiny leaf poking through one of the rock crevices. How ironic, she thought. Sometimes she felt like that leaf. Alone, pushing through fissures of life. In search of what? *Stop this melancholy*, she ordered. *Soon you'll be whining about your life with Amy.* "So what else do you have in those backpacks?" She forced a light-hearted tone.

"Now, for my crowning moment." Susan was watching her, no doubt trying to gauge her mood. Out came more dishes from the backpack. One dish was tucked inside a small cloth sack. "This is called peach slump." She pulled out a can of whipped cream. "Some people call it peach cobbler, but I call it peach slump because the peaches are all slumped down under this blanket of crust." She handed her a bowl.

"Oh, wow," Kelly said after she tasted it. "I am amazingly non-verbal when it comes to your cooking. You sure know a way to a woman's heart."

"Well, if not her heart, at least her stomach." Susan's tone was light.

After they'd finished eating, they stacked the dirty dishes in the backpacks and started off on their hike. It was more a leisurely walk now that the trail had smoothed out.

"Sixpence for your thoughts." Susan smiled warmly. After hiking about two miles, they had stopped to look at the lighthouse off in the distance.

"I don't know," Kelly turned back to her. "I think when people talk about what they want in a relationship, it makes all of us think about relationships."

"What do you want in a relationship?"

"Easily captured in one word—ditto. Anyway." Kelly smiled.

228

"That lighthouse has an interesting history. Amy told me about it. Up until—" She stopped. "I think she said it was about ten years ago the lighthouse had a keeper. Of course it'd always had a keeper, but this couple was the last of the lighthouse keepers and apparently they were two of the nicest people you ever wanted to meet. They didn't have any children, so every year they made cookies for every kid on the island and delivered them the day before Christmas."

"How caring. What happened to them?"

"He retired from the Coast Guard after the government, in its infinite wisdom, automated the lighthouses all across the country and they were out of a job. Anyway, they moved back somewhere in Massachusetts. People still talk about them. They left their mark on this little island." Kelly looked at her watch. "Look at the time. I guess eating took a little longer than I'd expected. We've got to get back or we're going to become a news story."

"Why?" Susan glanced at her watch. "It's only five-thirty."

"We have a few more miles to go and we're going to lose our light. I didn't think to bring a flashlight, sorry."

"Why would we become a news story?"

"It's happened. You noticed at the head of the trail I put our names and the time we went in and the time I thought we'd be out?"

"I did, but I didn't think much about it. I thought it was like signing a guest registry."

"Uh-huh, it's a lifeline in case someone gets hurt on the trail and can't get out. The game wardens check at night, especially if there's a car in the parking lot. People who come in to camp so note on the form. I just wrote that we would be out at sunset, so if my car is still there after sunset, they'll come looking. Once they start looking for us, the reporters will hear it on the scanner and if it's a slow news day, they'll come out and write about it. I can see the headline now." Kelly laughed. "'Nurse and LNG Woman Lost on Trail.'"

"That would not be my idea of a good time. I guess we'll have to get back." Susan turned to Kelly. "I've really enjoyed this, thanks," she said softly. She quickly looked away.

How strange, Kelly thought. Last night they'd hugged each other. She'd have given a friend a hug but she knew if she hugged Susan now she'd want more. She'd want to feel her body against hers. She'd want to touch her lips to Susan's. She'd want to—*Stop*, she yelled at herself. Susan hesitated and then turn back toward the trail. "We'd better get going," Kelly said.

Chapter Twenty-six

"It was a spectacular trip to Augusta. By the way, I did call you a couple of times on Sunday," Amy said. Kelly started to explain why she wasn't home but Amy clearly wasn't about to miss a beat in her story. "We were a little upset we didn't get a face-to-face with the governor, but we met with his chief of staff."

"How'd that go?" They were having dinner together. Amy had gotten home Monday afternoon. She had called Kelly at the hospital absolutely jazzed that things had gone so well in Augusta. Amy hadn't asked her how she had spent her Sunday, she was so busy talking about her trip to Augusta. Kelly thought about her Sunday, a lot. Hours after she had gotten back she wanted to call Susan, tell her how much fun she had, but she stopped herself. She was trying not to think about how she kept thinking about Susan in a most provocative way. Tossing and turning last night she had vowed there would be no more alone time with Susan. She'd read about people who seemed to be attracted to more than one person.

She had never understood that and didn't have a frame of reference for it. Her friends had nicknamed her Loyal Kelly. She had stuck with Robin until the relationship imploded and burned. Loyalty had been her life then and it was now with Amy.

"Good. Of course the governor's position has been in all the newspapers—he's for it as long as the community wants it."

"And we don't know if the community wants it because the selectmen haven't called for a vote." Kelly knew they'd been over this ground before, but said nothing.

"Exactly, so one of the things we talked about with the chief of staff is forcing a vote."

"What did he say?"

"Do it." Amy stirred her spoon around in her soup, not having even put a spoonful to her mouth. "We've already written the petition and plan to present it at the next selectmen's meeting. We have enough people to take them around and I know we're going to have more than enough signatures. We're having our usual meeting Wednesday. One of the agencies we went to see was the Maine Municipal Association; Elizabeth set that up for us. They told us a lot of stuff and even suggested how we should word the petition. They said they would work with us. That'll help a lot."

"That sounds terrific."

"But I have something more important than that on my mind." Amy sipped her wine. "I really missed your being with us. This is so important I want you to be more a part of our group." She held up her hand to stop Kelly's response. "Now, before you start with being too busy at the hospital, I think it's important we spend more time together and I also think we need someone from the hospital to be a part of our group."

Kelly was silent. How could she tell Amy that she really enjoyed the alone time at the house? "I hadn't thought about it. I just figured you have a lot of volunteers already. I've attended some of the meetings with you."

"You have and I've appreciated that. But you really haven't been a part of the group. This way we could spend more time together and, honestly, we need a representative from the hospital with us. The hospital is our biggest employer."

"I don't know, Amy, I attend so many meetings at the hospital. It's kinda nice not to have yet one more to go to."

"Kelly, this is important," Amy repeated, urgency in her voice.

"Well, I'm not certain what the hospital's position is on this. They prefer their employees remain apolitical, not that they've ever said anything. Look, I'm going to have to clear it with Don."

"He can't keep you from doing your civic duty after hours. The hospital always has been behind the community. Whenever we have any kind of fundraiser, whether it's the Polar Bear Dip or a charity basketball game, the hospital always fields a team and they participate. So I can't believe when we have something this important, the hospital wouldn't be foursquare behind it."

"I don't know, Amy." Kelly got up and got the bottle of wine. She held it out to Amy, who shook her head no. "This is pretty political. The hospital board is loathe for its staff to become politically involved as representatives of the hospital."

"So we won't say Kelly Burns, Director of Nursing. They can't keep you from personally getting involved. But everyone on the island knows who you are, so it suggests that the hospital is involved. There's something else."

"What something else?"

"I've been thinking a lot about us," Amy said ethereally. "I think it would be good if we spent more time together. I think that's been part of the problem. I've been preoccupied with this project for weeks and you've been preoccupied with the hospital and I just think that that's been some of the problem between us," she repeated.

Kelly sighed inwardly. That was not the problem. It was the separation that was making the relationship work. How could they each have come to conclusions about the problems in their relationship and yet ended up on opposite ends of the spectrum? She didn't want to get into an argument with Amy before bed. After she had dropped Susan off at her house, she'd gone home and

233

thought a lot about her and Amy's relationship. After a day with Susan she knew she was attracted to her, but she also knew that five years with Amy was an investment in her life and she was not about to throw it away on a five-minute attraction. She had decided that she was going to talk with Amy, convince her that a counselor was the only solution. Hadn't Amy promised to think about it? She was determined to beg, plead, do whatever to get Amy to go with her.

"You don't seem very enthusiastic about my suggestion."

"It just surprised me, that's all. I've been thinking a lot about our relationship too and I guess I just figured out a different solution."

"What's that?" Amy pushed her half-eaten bowl of soup away. "Oh, that counselor thing."

"I really want to go see one, Amy. You said you'd think about it. I think—"

"It's a stupid idea," Amy flared. "There's nothing wrong with our relationship except maybe we're just spending too much time apart. I was thinking about how much fun it would have been if you'd been in Augusta with us. I was bummed out about Elizabeth backing out too—she can jump out of a helicopter, but she can't go with us to Augusta. I didn't understand that one."

"She called here yesterday, said that traveling that distance and then sitting through marathon meetings was just too much for her. Think about it, Amy. She's seventy-five years old. There has to be a point where she feels as though she's reached her limit."

"I guess, but it sure didn't make the folks at the Maine Municipal happy. They were expecting a town official so they could cover their tail about not giving information to the public. Not because they're hiding anything, but because they'd be inundated with calls from every Tom, Dick and Mary. It would just be too much."

"Well, they kept their appointment with you even though Elizabeth wasn't there."

"They did, and I must say we walked away with all of our questions answered." Amy paused. "Kelly, I think our relationship is fine. Heck, it's better than fine, it's downright wonderful. I do think that you've been a little too preoccupied with this counselor thing, I gave it a lot of thought too."

234

"How so?"

"You're in the medical field. I think that you look to experts coming in to solve problems. I agree with that. I just don't think it fits us in this case. I think that we need to fix the problem, but the problem started when we spent just way too much time apart."

I can't do it now. I can't get in a big fight with her just before we go to bed, I can't do, Kelly thought. "Why don't we talk about this tomorrow. We both have to go to bed and I just don't think it's something we should get into right now."

"There's nothing to get into." Amy stood up and snapped, "You're so selfish. I'm not asking you to do anything more than get involved with a group of people, most of whom you know, to try and save this damn island. In addition, it would give us a chance to be together. What's so wrong with that?" She dumped her bowl of soup in the garbage and rinsed out the bowl, drank the last of her wine and rinsed her glass.

"Amy, I don't want to get into a fight about this. Can't we just put this on hold until tomorrow, give us both time to sleep on it. I think what's important here . . ." Kelly turned and looked at her. "What's important is that we both realize that there's a problem. We just came to the fix-it part from two different perspectives. I don't want to fight about it," she repeated.

"We're not fighting."

Kelly could hear the rawness in Amy's voice. *Bite your tongue, or this will lead to a fight.* "Telling me I'm selfish, telling me I don't want to get involved. It amazes me that you can be as rude as you want, say things that absolutely hurt and I'm just supposed to take it." *Well, so much for biting your tongue.*

"I didn't mean it that way. I just meant that we have important issues facing this island right now and I think that is where we need to keep our focus."

"And solving our problems, where is that on the priority list, Amy?"

"Don't turn this around. I told you I was thinking about it all weekend and I told you what I thought the solution would be. You obviously won't agree and so we're at some sort of impasse. It seems

235

to me that we should be working at solving the problem, although I don't really see it as that much of a problem. I think it's more a symptom of the pressures I've been under lately. Those of us who are doing battle have had to make sacrifices. I have at the store. I've been pulled and pushed trying to keep it going during the summer and still working on this. Others who are on the team have had problems. A lot of them have convinced their husband or wives to join."

"And what about our problem?"

"Our problem will be solved by spending more time together, I think that's a workable solution. I think we should try it."

"Can we compromise?" Kelly lowered her voice. She wanted to keep their disagreement from blowing into a major storm. "How about if I become part of the group and we also go see a counselor. Amy, I'm willing to do whatever to make this work."

"All right, all right. Why don't you research it, find someone we both like and we'll go see her. It has to be a her. I'm not telling my problems to a man."

"I've done that. The one who came highly recommended is a man, but I'm sure there's a woman counselor out there who's equally qualified."

"Fine." Amy waved her hand as if dismissing the topic.

"You really mean that?" Kelly could feel the excitement. "You'll go see a counselor with me?"

"I said fine, didn't I?" Amy said testily. "But more importantly can you come to the meeting Wednesday night?"

"I don't think I have anything on my calendar for that night so I'll be there. If there's something on my schedule, I'm sure I can change it." Kelly reached out to embrace Amy. "I love you and I know that spending more time together and seeing a counselor will only mean good things for us."

Amy gave her a perfunctory hug and stepped back. "Well, I'm not so certain about the counselor, but I know spending more time together will help us both."

Chapter Twenty-seven

On Tuesday morning, Susan picked up her papers, stuffed them into her briefcase and headed to her car. Her meeting yesterday with the developers had gone well. They had finished the last of the strategy sessions in anticipation of the big town meeting the Wednesday after Labor Day. She knew the selectmen were on board with the project, especially after the developers had put an annual payment of fifteen million dollars, adjusted for inflation, on the table. If accepted, it meant islanders would not have to pay property taxes ever again and would get an annual stipend. A damn good deal, she thought. The plan was to present the information at the public meeting and once the islanders heard about the generous payment they would push the selectmen to vote to approve the project. Her public relations campaign had been going well. They had found pockets of support among members of the community, including some high-profile business people. She frowned at the windshield. Although the developers felt confident of the outcome, she had warned that the opponents had been quiet of late and that should concern them. But they had dismissed her concerns and labeled the opponents a minor irritation. Susan wasn't certain how minor the opposition really was.

She pulled into the hospital parking lot. It had taken her weeks to set up a meeting with the hospital board, but they had finally agreed to a sit down today. Some of the business leaders who favored the project were also on the hospital's board of directors and she had worked through them to get the meeting. She looked at her watch as she parked in the visitor's section; she had fifteen minutes until the meeting. She wondered if Kelly was in her office. She thought back to their Sunday hike. It had been a perfect day and she had felt an attraction for her. In fact, that was all she had thought about since Sunday, to the point of frustration. Kelly was in a five-year relationship. Susan had never ever gotten involved with a woman who was in a relationship and she was too old to start now. She had even put Kelly out of her mind for several minutes at a time, then she would think about her face and the way she smiled or the way she held her head when she was deep in thought, and Susan's fantasies would run amok.

She had gotten up and gone for her morning run to try and burn off the frustration that had built up since then, but instead of feeling the usual calm she got after a run, she felt even more hyper. *You've got to stop this*, she thought as she opened the door to the hospital. *You've got to quietly sit in a chair and wait for your meeting. You are not going to ask to see if Kelly is in.*

"Good morning," she said to the receptionist. "I'm Susan Iogen. I'm early for my meeting with the board of directors. Is Kelly Burns in?" How did that get out? She chastised herself.

"Let me check." The receptionist dialed Kelly's extension. "Hi, Kelly, I have a Susan Iogen here to see you? Good, I'll send her down. Go through those double doors there." She pointed. "Kelly's office is the fourth on the right. The sign says *Director of Nursing*."

"Thank you." Susan could feel the excitement building in her.

238

Good one, Iogen, she thought. She was supposed to just sit and wait for the start of the meeting, but instead the first words out of her asked to see Kelly. Susan walked through the double doors. She simply wanted to thank her for a great weekend, nothing more. "Good morning."

"Susan, I'm so glad you stopped by." Kelly was effusive in her greeting.

"I wanted to thank you, I can't remember the last time a picnic was that much fun."

"Me either. In fact, I kept thinking about that wonderful meal you prepared."

"That was nothing compared with the beauty of that place. Kelly, that was so extraordinary."

"Well, I'm glad you enjoyed it." Kelly pointed at a chair. "Please sit down."

"I can't. I have a meeting with the hospital board of directors in a few minutes. That's why I'm here. That and to thank you, of course." Susan felt shy all of a sudden.

"I enjoyed the day, really."

Susan could feel the awkwardness between them; she shouldn't have come. "Would you like to have lunch today?" she blurted out.

"Sure, I'd love to."

Susan inhaled deeply. Now, where the hell did that come from? She had not planned to ask Kelly to lunch. *You're losing your mind.* "My meeting is supposed to be over at noon. Would you like to have lunch here at the hospital or somewhere else?"

"Somewhere else." Kelly laughed. "Don't get me wrong, the food here is pretty good, I just get to eat here a lot. Why don't you stop by my office after the meeting and we can decide where we want to go."

"Okay, I will. By the way, Laurie got back."

"I figured. I haven't heard from her. How did things go?"

"Good. She seemed downright thrilled that the sale of the house went so well. Said the sale meant she now had cut all ties to Portland."

"That's my Laurie, extremes to the max. She has dear friends there, so the sale did not cut ties to Portland. I suspect it meant it cut ties to her ex."

"I'd gathered that. I'm happy for her. It's as though she feels life here can begin."

"It's hard when you do leave entanglements behind—it's like you have a foot in both places."

"Well, I agree," Susan said reflectively. "Anyway"—she looked at her watch—"I have a meeting to attend. I'll see you afterward." She picked up her briefcase and left.

Susan could feel the excitement inside, not about the meeting but lunch with Kelly. Where the hell was she going with this? She chided herself. Nothing good would come of her pursuing a relationship with someone who was obviously in a committed relationship. Kelly was definitely a one-woman woman and she, Susan, was doing nothing more than playing with her own heartstrings by pursuing this. She wasn't chasing anything, she argued with herself. She was just going to have lunch with someone she liked. What was so bad about that? Everyone had levels of attraction to people. It didn't mean she wanted to hop in bed with them. Except she did want to go to bed with her, that was the problem. *No, I don't. I just want a friend*, she thought, trying to beat down the negative side of her brain.

"I'm ready to meet with the board of directors," she said to the receptionist.

"They said to send you right in. The boardroom is on the other side of the hospital." She gave her directions. "The others are already there."

"Thank you," Susan said as she went down the hall. Calm down, she told herself. She was ready to meet with some pretty important people, people who could help her efforts, so she'd stay focused on that. She could hear voices as she headed toward the room. She paused outside the door, put on her best smile and walked in.

"Oh, here she is," Dean Creager, the LNG project director,

said. "Susan, this is the hospital CEO, Don Allen." A tall good-looking man offered her his hand.

"Nice to meet you," she said, shaking it.

"I'm going to let him introduce you to everyone else," Dean added. Susan shook hands with the twelve people in the room.

Once everyone was seated she said, "I want to thank you for allowing us to meet with you this morning. I understand that none of you were able to attend the first public presentation we had, so we want to bring that to you right now. Rather than make you sit through a thirty-minute presentation"—she reached into her briefcase—"I put together information packets that you can take home. If you have any follow-up questions the information will be at your fingertips. Or you can reach any of us by phone. I've put our cell phone numbers on the fact sheet." She handed the packets to each person. "At the present time, our company is working with town officials to site a six-hundred-million-dollar facility here on the island. Please remember we're really in the preliminary stages of development. Over the next year and a half numerous studies will be conducted, including engineering studies as well as environmental studies. At each step, the facility will be given the green light to move forward or the red light to stop as it goes through numerous state and federal permit requirements. Now, let's talk about what liquefied natural gas is. It has been used in this country for the past sixty years. It is one of the cleanest and most environmentally friendly forms of energy known today. This is the stuff that someday will replace oil and coal as a primary form of energy. Right now there are four such facilities in the continental United States and one in Alaska. It arrives in large ships in liquid form from such places as Algeria and Australia, then it is off-loaded and piped to holding tanks where it's turned into natural gas and piped into people's homes."

She watched each of the faces react to her monologue. Some were browsing the packet she'd given them, and others were staring straight at her. Right now it was too early to judge who was for the project and who was against it. She'd be able to tell by the kinds of questions they asked. It was a game she played whenever making a presentation to a group. In the end their questions often presented a picture of what they believed.

She had practiced her presentation so much she now had it down to a solid fifteen minutes. In her experience, anything beyond that, without pictures, cost you your audience. "Anyway," she said at the end, "do you have any questions for me or for Dean or Bill? Bill Leighton, our technical advisor, is putting the package together." She glanced at the clock. She had asked for a two-hour meeting, so there was about ninety minutes to answer questions. She stepped to the side of the room. Although she was as knowledgable about the project as the developer, she knew that the questions would be directed to Dean or Bill. After all, she thought, she was just public relations. She followed the question-and-answer period with interest. So far no ringers, nothing the developers couldn't answer. Her mind drifted. She wondered what Kelly was doing right now. She wondered if she was thinking about her. Frigging idiot, she chided herself, thinking about a woman who was happily in a relationship. *Focus*, she thought, *focus on where you are*.

"I have a question for Susan," one of the two women board members said.

Susan stepped forward. "Yes?"

"Would you want this in your backyard?"

Susan had answered this question many times before. "I would not have a problem having this in my backyard," she said. "In fact, of all the commercial properties that could be developed, this is one of the best. It brings in new jobs to a depressed area, which from all the state numbers we've been able to gather, this is. It's clean, so we're not going to bring something in that pollutes the environment and, contrary to what some people have said, it's safe." Susan noted that the woman was probably in her sixties.

"But what about the aesthetics. Right now, Susan," the woman persisted, "I get to look out at one of the most pristine places in the world. My view is open ocean, a quaint harbor, and the biggest boat to pass in front of my window is the ferryboat going to and from the mainland. So why would I want to exchange that for tanks large enough to park two seven-forty-sevens and ships that are four football fields long? Why would I want to exchange what I have for that?"

"Jobs," Bill Leighton said. "Right now we're offering upward of eighty jobs with an entry-level salary of one hundred thousand dollars a year. We're offering this island a future. We've also decided after earlier meetings to hold a contest. The tanks can be painted in such a way that they'll be made to blend in with the environment or possibly have large attractive murals on them that tell a story about the area."

"You're not the one I was asking," the woman said tartly. She looked at Susan.

"Jobs," Susan said quietly. She cringed inwardly. She had tried to argue the developers out of recommending murals on the tanks. It was an insult to the islanders. Susan believed approval would come based on what the project could do for the community. The tanks were secondary. If people approved it, islanders wouldn't care if the tanks had murals on them or were painted Navy gray. "But also these gentlemen are offering you something else, a future for your children. Right now your greatest export is your children. The fishing industry, although it's thriving, is not keeping them here. Those that leave to get a college education have no place to come back to." She looked directly at the woman. "Yes, you will be giving up a lot in exchange, but you have to weigh what you'll be getting, a chance to keep your children here. A chance to build this island into something it once was, a thriving place. The spinoffs from this are unlimited. Many of the businesses you used to have right here on this island more than likely will come back. Instead of people moving away, they'll be moving back. Right now, you're attracting mostly retired people who've sold a home somewhere else. They're buying up your land and building homes, and although they are contributing to the tax base of the island, they are not contributing to the future of the island."

243

"Well, I happen to be one of those people who sold their home somewhere else and moved here because of the beauty and serenity of the area," she persisted.

"Then I'm not going to try and persuade you that anything else is going to make you happy," Susan said kindly.

"Well, I applaud your honesty," the woman said just as calmly. "I'm not saying I'm against this, I'm just wondering about the why of it. I can understand jobs and keeping our children here, but I also wonder about the trade-offs we may be making," she said to the rest of the board members. "And is that trade-off worth jobs. I know that our economy is suffering. I also know that we don't have anything here to keep young people on the island, but I also know that if we approve this project, then we have to be willing to say that our lives and boundaries will be changed forever and we must accept that."

"I don't agree," a middle-aged man said. He was sitting across from the woman. "I grew up here, can trace my family back to one of the earliest on the island. They were always able to make a living here, something I was unable to do when I came of age. I'm one of those who had to go away. Granted, I came back, but I never ever was happy away. I was one of the lucky ones. I said the day I left that I would be back. Little did I know it would take me forty-five years." He directed his statement to the woman. "I too love this area, but by my leaving, I also lost something even more important, a chance for my children to grow up here. Now, they have lives away from here and although they love to visit, there's nothing here to keep them. This"—he held up the brochure Susan had handed out—"could change that. My son is an engineer, which could mean he'd be able to come home. Raise my grandchildren right here. I don't think it's such a bad deal. It's not as if the facility is going to take up the whole island—they're talking about fifty acres. Fifty acres out of how many thousands? No, I don't consider that such a bad deal at all," he repeated.

"But at what price?" the woman insisted. "At what price, John?"

"I don't think we should site just anything here, but this isn't going to hurt the environment one bit," he replied.

"But what about safety?" Another board member directed the

question to the developers. "I know you said it was safe, but are we totally safe from terrorist attacks? Could you guarantee us that someone might not sneak across that huge border we share with Canada and drop a rocket in the middle of one of those tanks? I wasn't able to read all of the information in here, but the resulting thermal fire would wipe out two thirds of this island."

"First of all, I believe your name is Sam?" Dean continued after the man nodded in agreement. "That's one of the reasons the federal government favors siting a facility in remote areas. If you looked at the places where they currently are we're talking major metropolitan areas. I'm not going to lie to you, the mayor of Boston would like to have the one near his city gone. That's because once a week a gigantic tanker floats through the inner harbor past downtown Boston. Now, if a terrorist wanted to make a statement all they'd have to do is drop a rocket in the center of one of those ships. They'd take out most of Boston. That's a more attractive target than one here on the island."

"That doesn't make me feel any better. Dead is dead," the woman who had asked the first question said. "I don't agree with you. If I was a terrorist, I would select a target just like this one to prove that rural America is as vulnerable as New York City or the Pentagon. I think they'd be making a bigger statement by wiping us out."

"But the same safety features that are a part of Boston would be a part of this project. The difference is, a terrorist wouldn't be able to move about the island as easily as in a place like Boston, which is a giant melting pot."

"Unless they found a blue-eyed terrorist," another board member quipped.

"What about Timothy McVeigh, the guy who killed all of those children in Oklahoma, he was a blue-eyed terrorist," the woman went on.

"I still say that what this offers us in terms of a future is a heck of a lot better than what we have on the island now," the male board member insisted. "I think we have to look at the long-term benefits to the island, not just what may happen."

"Well—" The CEO looked at the clock. "As you can see my board probably represents a cross section of how most people here on the island think. However, our time is up and many of us have to get back to our jobs. I want to thank you for attending," he said as he shook hands with each of the developers and then Susan. "I want to wish you luck on your project."

"On behalf of all of us, we want to thank you for your time," Dean said.

Standing outside the hospital, Susan could tell that Dean was not happy. He said, "That was going very well until the end. I think that woman scored points."

"I think what the CEO said is true—his board is a microcosm of what's going on on the island," Susan said thoughtfully. "And I think when we meet the Wednesday after next with the public we have to address those issues."

"How do we address what she said? It's true, we can't guarantee there won't be a terrorist attack. We can't alter the fact that it's going to forever change the aesthetics."

"Then that's what we say. We tell them the truth. Yes, it will change your social fabric, but in exchange for what? The future of the island. Yes, terrorist attacks are a real possibility, but the protective measures we and the state and federal governments have put in place will deter any possibility. And we've got to keep hammering on the fact that they need to weigh eighty guaranteed high-paying jobs with something that may never happen."

"Do me a favor," Dean said. "Between now and that meeting, I want you to run more focus groups. Let's invite some of those opponents. I want to know what people are thinking so that when we go to that public hearing, we'll have all of the answers. Skip Labor Day—most folks will be away for the last screech of summer. Afterward I want focus groups leading up to Wednesday's meeting."

"Done." She'd schedule them for a week from today, the day after Labor Day. The town meeting was the next day.

Bill looked at his watch. "You two want to grab a quick bite?"

"I can't. I'm having lunch with one of the staff here," Susan hoped he wouldn't ask any more questions about her luncheon date.

"Good idea. Ask questions, see what other kinds of things are going on that we should know about before the public hearing. Come on," he said to Dean, "let's grab lunch. Susan, we'll meet you back at the office in, say, two hours."

"I'll be there." Susan turned back to the hospital.

"Look who I found lurking in the hallway just as we were ready to go to lunch," Kelly said, pointing at Laurie. "I can't get away from her for a minute."

"Susan. Hi." Laurie gave her a big hug. "I just stopped by to bring Kelly up to speed on my Portland trip and she said the two of you were having lunch. She kept twisting my arm until I agreed to join you," she said with a laugh.

"Now, that is an exaggeration. I told her we were having lunch and she insisted she join us." Kelly joined in the laughter.

"Great," Susan said, returning the hug.

Kelly couldn't read Susan's face. Was she happy or sad that Laurie was joining them? Susan looked slightly let down, as if she'd wanted to talk with Kelly alone.

"Let's take my car," Laurie said as she held the door open. "And lunch is on me; I feel quite wealthy right now."

"Not on your life," Kelly said with a smile. "Every time you buy lunch I end up owing you more."

"Foul play." Laurie got in her car. "Well, not so foul. As a matter of fact, I do have a favor to ask."

Kelly groaned. "Let me ride in the backseat," she said, opening the car door. "That way if she asks me a favor I don't like, I won't pop her one."

"You're so bad," Laurie said, glancing at her in the rearview mirror. "Actually, it's not that big a favor. I was wondering if I could store my furniture in your garage. Miss Prissy is being just

247

that and even though I did everything she asked so that we'd get that property sold, she informed me this morning she doesn't want anything of mine around. On top of that she said if I wanted it, I had to move it immediately or she'd call a junk dealer and give it away free."

"She really is jerking your chain." Kelly shook her head. "Of course you can store your furniture in my garage. That's not such a big favor."

"Well, as a matter of fact, there's just a bit more," Laurie said, quickly looking at Kelly again in the rearview mirror.

"How much of a 'bit more'?" Kelly asked suspiciously.

"I have to move it this Labor Day weekend," Laurie said.

"So? If you want my help, you know I'll help you."

"Well, if it only was that easy. I work this weekend."

Kelly groaned. "I can't change the schedule for you."

"I wouldn't ask."

"How about switching with someone else?"

"I've tried, but it's Labor Day weekend and a lot of the nurses already have plans."

"So you want me to do what?"

"Well, go down there and move me." Laurie hesitated.

"You're kidding." Kelly sat forward.

"I wish I were. Look, I've already got it lined up. Friends in Portland will be there to stick everything in the U-Haul, so all I need is for you to drive it back up here. I didn't feel right asking anyone in Portland to drive it all the way here. Once here, I know we can get a bunch of people to unload it."

"And what am I going to do with my car?"

"I've arranged for a hitch."

"Couldn't you just ask Heather for more time?"

"I did, but she's got me bulldozed to the ground and buried and enjoying every minute."

"God, breakups are so lousy. Why can't they be civilized?" Kelly heard the frustration in her own voice.

"Look, I'm off that weekend," Susan offered. "How about if I

248

drive down with you," she said to Kelly. "You can drive your car back and I can drive the U-Haul."

"Would you do that?" Laurie asked, clearly grateful.

"Sure. That way Kelly won't have to go down by herself and she won't have to hook her car onto a towbar."

"Well," Laurie said thoughtfully, "that's a solution."

"No, it's not," Kelly said peevishly. "It's not fair to ask Susan to give up her Labor Day weekend. Look, let me talk it over with Amy and see if she can go with me."

"You'd do that? Amy would do that?"

"Of course, or I'll never hear the end of it. How in your hour of need, I wasn't there to help you."

If Kelly wasn't mistaken, Susan seemed disappointed. "Well, again, if one or both of you can't do it, I'm more than happy to help."

"Heck, if Amy can't go then you two should go together," Laurie suggested. "Be nice if you two could really get to know each other. Check with Amy." She said enthusiastically, "Wow, this is better than I thought. Lunch is definitely on me."

Kelly greeted several people as she entered the SeaBleu. "This table all right?"

"Fantastic," Kelly sensed Laurie's euphoria. "Lunch is on me," she said again as she looked at the menu board behind Kelly. "Susan, sit here," Laurie said as she slid over on the seat.

"Hi, Kelly." Carrie handed them menus.

"Carrie, I'd like to introduce you to Susan Iogen, the PR woman for the LNG project, and this is Laurie Stocking, a nurse at the hospital. This is the SeaBleu's star waitress, Carrie Perkins."

Carrie laughed. "The only waitress most lunch hours. Nice to meet you. I've seen you in here," she said to Susan. "I remember you've been with some men, but you've also been with Elizabeth."

"Very good memory. The men are the LNG developers. Elizabeth is definitely a lot more fun."

"What's good today?" Kelly asked.

"Definitely the haddock dinner. Fish is fresh off the boat."

249

"I'll have the haddock dinner." Kelly handed her the menu.

"Make that two."

"Make that three." Laurie was clearly enjoying herself.

"And bring three iced teas," Kelly said. "I know you two will enjoy it. It's sun tea."

"So." Laurie sat back in the seat. "Let's talk about anything but Heather."

Kelly chuckled. "Well, that'll ruin my day. Just kidding."

There was a long silence. How strange, Kelly thought. Dinner with Laurie was usually a marathon talkfest, the same with Susan. Now, together at lunch, they needed to find a common topic. They couldn't talk about LNG. If they talked about the hospital that would exclude Susan from the conversation. Politics, even if it was George W. Bush, also didn't seem appropriate.

Kelly sensed Laurie was feeling the same way.

"How about we talk about life. Wasn't that the magazine that went belly up like my life?" Laurie's laugh had a nervous undertone to it.

Susan smiled at Laurie's bad joke. "Have you seen Elizabeth?" she asked Kelly.

"Not since the party. She's called a few times and we've talked. You know what's so special about her? She really makes an effort to include people in her life. I betcha she's on the phone more than anyone in this town. She just takes the time to say hi. I like that. And she seems to still get her work done at the town office."

"She does. She's called me. Just to see how I'm doing," Susan said. "I feel guilty, though. I'm running so fast through life, I don't take the time to call her."

"I don't think she minds."

They fell silent again.

"Did I ever tell you the time J. Edgar Hoover's wife stopped by the ER in Portland?" Laurie smiled impishly.

"I didn't realize he was married." Kelly looked at her quizzically.

"He wasn't. God love her. She was probably eighty. Harmless as all get out. She'd stop by the ER late at night. Drop off doughnuts, whatever. She'd walk up to the receptionist and pull out this business card and slap it down on the desk. 'Gena Edgar Hoover' she'd announce in a voice loud enough so that everyone in the ER waiting room could hear. After a while, she did it so often it didn't even cause most people to look up from their month-old magazine. 'Here to investigate some goings-on in this hospital,' she'd say. At first, the staff would turn her away. Then it just seemed right to help her live out her fantasy. I think it was Jeanne—she's a nurse and friend of ours," she told Susan. "Anyway, it was really slow one night in the ER, so Jeanne escorted her around the hospital. One night she spent hours digging through the trash cans in the ER."

"For what?"

"Who knows. It was just part of her fantasy. You'd ask her what she was looking for. She'd say, 'If I told ya, I'd have to shoot ya.'"

Laurie and Susan laughed.

"I don't remember her." Kelly sipped the tea Carrie had put in front of her.

"I think she started showing up in the ER about a year after you left. You know she actually saved a guy's life one night?"

"How so?" Kelly asked.

"Like I said, she'd walk around late at night. Thank God it was Portland and not Boston. Anyway, there was this bad accident. Single car. Guy was drunk, ran into a bridge abutment. She applied pressure to his wound until the EMTs arrived. No question about it, she saved his life. But the EMTs told us afterward that she'd told them she'd caught a Russian spy. Said she could tell cause she'd smelled vodka on him. Said he was here to steal secrets from the city offices. She wanted to ride in the ambulance with him. When they told her she couldn't she'd tucked a business card in his pocket. Wrote a note on the back, said she'd be back to arrest him the next day. I often wondered if that bugger found the card and kept looking over his shoulder."

"I just love your stories." Susan laughed. "I told Laurie funny things just don't happen in the PR world."

"Three haddock dinners," Carrie said, setting the steaming dishes in front of them.

"Ohh, that smells good." Laurie sniffed.

For the rest of the lunch, Laurie regaled them with more ER stories. She then paid the bill and drove them back to the hospital parking lot. "So, you're going to talk to Amy," she said, returning to their earlier discussion about the trip to Portland.

"I said I would and I will." Kelly had enjoyed lunch after the first few awkward moments. Now, back at the hospital, the reality of what Laurie had asked her to do was back and she knew Amy would not be happy about the trip to Portland.

"Again, if Amy can't get away, I'll be more than happy to help." Kelly could see the bashfulness in Susan's eyes.

"I think that's great," Laurie said putting an arm around each of them. "My oldest friend and my newest friend getting to know each other, I love it. When can you let Susan and me know?"

"I'll talk to Amy tonight. I'll call you tomorrow. Thanks for lunch. Nice seeing you, Susan."

"I'll walk you to your car," Laurie told Susan.

Chapter Twenty-eight

"Well, she's not really asking that much of us," Kelly said. She and Amy were driving home from the Wednesday night LNG meeting.

"Driving all the way to Portland on Labor Day weekend? I think she's asking a lot of both of us, and besides, this weekend is our last strategy session before the big town meeting."

Kelly thought the meeting had gone well and the group seemed pleased with how well the petition drive was going. She'd enjoyed the give-and-take of the discussion. It was clear that although the group was diverse, they shared one common belief— they didn't want an LNG facility in their backyard. In fact, Kelly had been surprised at some of the people who were there. Some, she knew, weren't joiners, people who more often than not sat in the background, never taking a public stand, but not this time.

"You do whatever you have to do, but right now I know where my priorities lie."

Kelly could hear the anger in Amy's voice, so she said, "Why not schedule the strategy meeting for Monday, that way we could drive down on Saturday, load up, spend the night and drive back early Sunday. Heck, you could even schedule the meeting for Sunday afternoon. I guarantee we'd be back in time. If you don't want to spend the night, we could load up and drive Saturday night. That way you'd have all of Sunday and Monday."

"How about you tell her to get some of her Portland friends to drive her furniture up here and leave us out of it."

"Come on, Amy, I'm her oldest friend. She'd do the same for me in a heartbeat."

"I just can't understand this. You know how important these meetings are to me. I can't be waltzing around the countryside when I need to be focused on every aspect of the project. We're trying to anticipate everything they may throw at us on Wednesday night."

Kelly sighed. "Amy, try as hard as you like, you won't be able to anticipate everything. There may be surprises. Then you'll have to regroup and go from there."

"That's the point of all of this planning. I don't want any surprises. For everything they bring up we're going to have to have a response and that response needs to be that night. You let a suggestion simmer in people's minds and soon they think it's a great idea. I don't want that to happen."

"*I*, Amy? I thought it was a group thing."

"It is a group thing. Just because I used the personal *I* doesn't mean I'm thinking for the group. You saw us tonight. We're all in this. We're a team. In fact, I've never seen anything that has so inflamed this island. There were people there tonight that I never thought would join us. There are always the few activists, but never the fence-sitters."

"I thought the very same thing," Kelly said softly. "I was impressed. You've done a terrific job, and win or lose you can be proud of that."

"Lose is not an option," Amy said fiercely.

"But it's something you have to be prepared for."

"It's not an option. Tomorrow, we collect the rest of the signatures. We need three hundred to put this before voters, and I suspect we'll have those numbers and more. Look at how many we've collected already. We're planning to present the petition at the meeting on Wednesday night. It won't catch them off guard, but it will make them squirm."

"Don't be too sure, Amy. They have their own supporters. I suspect they're just as prepared for what you'll throw at them as you are them."

"So, no big deal," Amy said, turning into their driveway and parking her car.

"But what about Saturday?"

"There's no way—" Amy turned and looked at her. "Look, she's your friend. If you want to go off on this ridiculous trip, do it, but don't ask me to be a part of it. I know what's important here and I would hope you felt the same way."

Kelly inhaled deeply. "My priorities are here on the island—I'm not going to have that discussion again—but a friend has asked me for help. I told you before, when I moved from Portland she stepped up to the plate to help me."

"Why don't you just change the schedule? Give her off this weekend and she can do her own damn moving."

"I won't do that. Everyone at the hospital knows Laurie and I were classmates and friends, so if I changed the schedule for her I might as well hang up my director's job. Besides, it's not something I would do."

"Why don't you work her shift?"

"It would be setting a precedent. Again, do I work for Cathy or Barb when they need a weekend off? I can't do that."

"Well, I just think it's damn unreasonable of her to ask this favor of you, especially since she knows you're now involved with the LNG strategy meetings, which by the way—" Amy said accusatorily. "She said she was going to help, so where the heck is she?"

"Well, she's gotten rather distracted."

"I heard." Amy opened the car door. "She's involved with that PR woman. It's all over the island."

"She's not involved." Kelly shot her an irate glance. "She and Susan are just friends."

"That's not what I heard. The caretaker told one of our members that they're always at each other's houses. Just real cozy."

"So, Laurie is single and so is Susan. What does it matter if they're seeing each other?"

"Just that it doesn't look right. Everyone knows Laurie's your best friend, our friend."

"She's not sleeping with the enemy." Kelly could feel her anger bristle. Why the jealousy? she thought. So what if Laurie and Susan were sleeping together? It was none of her business, and it seemed like she'd told herself that before.

"Well, it doesn't matter to me if they're rolling in the hay like a couple of hot bunnies on an August night," Amy admonished, opening the door. "What matters to me is the next few days, so if you want to go to Portland, go. I'm going to be right here doing what's important."

"Okay," Kelly said, turning on the lights in the kitchen. "I'll go."

"Whatever," Amy said forcefully.

Kelly knew Amy was boiling. *Don't pursue this, just go to bed*, she said to herself. *Don't talk, don't breath, just go to bed.*

It had been another frosty night in the Burns-Day household. Amy had gotten up early Thursday morning and left. They had not spoken.

"Well, Jasper, it's a good thing you can't understand what's going on," Kelly said to the cat. "Although sometimes I get the feeling you can feel the tension in the house."

The cat rubbed against her hand. Amy had already fed him and he had interrupted his bath to lick Kelly's hand.

256

She rubbed his head as she picked up the telephone. "I hope I woke you," Kelly said sarcastically.

"As a matter of fact you didn't. I was just getting in the shower," Laurie said. "I hope this telephone call is a good one."

"Well, good if you consider that I'm driving to Portland this weekend," Kelly said grumpily.

"That's great!" Laurie said enthusiastically. "I'll call Susan and tell her."

"I can do this myself. We don't need to bother Susan," Kelly insisted.

"Hey, she wants to do it."

"I don't need any help. How about you drive me over to the mainland and I catch the bus to Portland—that way I won't have a vehicle and we won't have to bother Susan," Kelly said again.

"Can't, she really has her heart set on helping me. I think . . ." Laurie said conspiratorially. "I think our relationship has moved to the next level."

"Really?"

"Really. We haven't done anything. She's in no hurry and neither am I—" Laurie chuckled. "Well, that's not really true. I just have a feeling that this is kind of a—" She paused. "*Commitment* is too strong a word, but just a thing that says she's thinking more about me than just as a friend."

"Laurie, I love you dearly, but just because a friend offers to help you doesn't necessarily mean she's ready for marriage."

"I'm not saying that." There was a hesitancy in her friend's voice. "I just think it means she cares about me. I know I care about her a lot."

"Laurie, you've just walked away from a relationship. I know we've had this discussion before, so just be careful."

"I am, otherwise I would have been in bed with her. No, this one's different, Kelly. She's one special woman."

"I've heard you say that about Heather and before that Claudia and before that I can't remembers all of their names."

"Well, maybe so," Laurie grumbled. "But this time is different.

I can feel it. With the others it was sort of like go to bed and then fall in love. I'm falling in love with this woman and whether we go to bed or not is secondary to how I feel about her."

Kelly swallowed. How could she give Laurie advice? "I think if you're in love with her that's great. I just don't want you to break your heart. Okay?"

"Okay. Anyway, Susan's going with you. I suggested you leave here early Saturday morning. Get into Portland around eleven, load up. I have people ready to help. I've already made hotel reservations for you at the Holiday Inn. Notice I don't spare any expense for my friends. You can get an early start and be back here Sunday. I don't start work until seven."

"We don't need a motel. We'll load up and drive back Saturday night. But I am glad you're off Sunday during the day to help unload."

"It's going to take a while to load the U-haul."

"How much furniture are we talking about?"

"Well . . ."

"How much, Laurie?"

"Let's just say I rented the largest U-haul they have."

Kelly groaned. "You couldn't sell some of that stuff?"

"Right now the carriage house is furnished. That's only a temporary fix. Eventually I want to buy a house and I'll want my own furniture."

"So you ended up with all the furniture. Wasn't some of it Heather's?"

"She didn't want it."

"That's generous."

"Not really. That's why she got a little more out of the sale of the house, but that's okay."

"Look, I still say I can do this myself," Kelly insisted. "Susan can enjoy her Labor Day weekend here. Heck, there's a big parade on the mainland, she and Elizabeth could have a weekend of fun."

"Nope, she said it was something she wanted to do for me."

"All right." She was just too tired to argue. "I'll pick her up. We'll take my car." Somehow Kelly felt apprehensive about how things were going. "Right now we need to get your furniture and once that's done your life in Portland is behind you."

"Thanks, Kell, that's just how I feel about it. Somehow, I feel like a part of me is still down there and I don't want that. I need for me to be whole and it's not so much the furniture. I could have sold it all, but you know my whole life I've left relationships with just the clothes on my back, a suitcase in hand. This time was different. I want that furniture. It's not that my life is tied up in things. I just feel like I need an anchor to my life. So when Heather said she didn't want any of it, I decided I did. Does that sound downright silly?"

"No, I understand." Kelly thought about her own situation. After she and Amy had gotten together she had moved into Amy's family home. All of the furniture belonged to Amy. At first they had talked about including some of Kelly's furniture, but days turned into months and finally, the next thing she knew, Amy had talked her into holding a huge yard sale. So the furniture had come out of storage and been sold pennies to the dollar. At the time it hadn't mattered, it was just stuff that could easily be replaced. She loved Amy and was content living with her and her furniture. But now, if they broke up, she would leave with just the clothes on her back and a suitcase in her hand. Why was she thinking about breaking up? She hadn't even had a chance to tell Amy she had found a woman counselor on the mainland who specialized in family counseling. She had scheduled a meeting with her for next Thursday night. She had planned to tell Amy, but the discussion about getting the furniture from Portland had caused her to hesitate. Now, she would have to tell her today, it would be unfair to wait until she got back from Portland.

"Kelly, you're wonderful, you know that."

"Yeah, I do. You're damn lucky to have me as your friend," Kelly groused.

"Believe me, I know that and will always remember that," Laurie said softly. "Anyway, enough of that mushy stuff. I love you."

"I love you too," Kelly said less enthusiastically.

"You do, you know." Laurie laughed before hanging up.

259

Chapter Twenty-nine

"Look, I can't deal with this right now." Amy slammed the dresser drawer. "I had a long day at work followed by an even longer night talking about LNG and now you want me to agree to go see a counselor next Thursday? It's not going to happen, Kelly, not now, not in this lifetime."

"Why are you so angry?" Kelly sat on the edge of the bed. "I just did what you had agreed to. I found an excellent woman counselor and she agreed to a meeting with us next week. That's all I did." She had gone right from the hospital to the Friday night meeting and was pleased to see how well everything had come together. The petitioners had collected more than four hundred signatures. There was energy within the group that was infectious and Kelly was glad she'd become an active member. Amy was animated after the meeting. They had sat in their kitchen afterward rehashing the night, and Amy's eyes were radiant as she talked confidently about defeating the proponents. Kelly sensed this was a good time to bring up the appointment with the counselor.

"When I agreed to see this person, it was in the future. A . . . long . . . ways . . . away." Amy dragged out the words. "I have a battle to win here and I don't have time to fool around with some woman who wants to poke around in my brain."

"She's not going to poke around in your brain. She's going to ask us to talk about our problems. Bring an outsider's perspective to them."

"I don't need some outsider telling me what she thinks my problems may be. If you feel you need that, Kelly, you go for it. Airing my dirty laundry in front of some stranger is not even on the table."

"But you agreed," Kelly said desperately.

"I agreed in order to get you off my back," Amy stormed. "Look, I think it's fine if you want to go see her. It's obviously something you need. You've got this fixation with your father and how he treated you and you seem to transfer that fixation to me. I get a little testy or upset about something or offer mild criticism about something you did wrong, and you dig into this well of emotions conjuring up all this crap you lived through with your father. Frankly, Kelly, I'm tired of it. Don't hang your problems with your father on me."

Kelly could barely catch her breath. She swallowed and then quietly got up off the bed. "First of all, the problems I had with my father are not being transferred to you. Secondly, you're right I've been conditioned to accept abuse and so I'm slow to react when you become verbally abusive. Silently, I just take it. I walk away hurt or bruised, but I take it."

"Verbally abusive! Labels! Everyone likes to attach labels to everything. It's so easy to compartmentalize with labels, isn't it. Stick me in a box and identify that box as verbally abusive. How about truth! Stick me in a box that says I tell you the truth about yourself and you can't take it. Verbally abusive? How dare you!"

Kelly had never seen Amy so angry. Her face was red and she was panting as if she'd just lifted a two-hundred-pound weight.

"Verbally abusive," Kelly said even more quietly. She refused to engage in a shouting match with her. Funny, she thought. She

261

finally had said out loud those two words that had been rolling around in her head. The two words she was afraid to put in the air. "You are, Amy. You don't even know the depth of abuse your words reach. You are absolutely mean-spirited at times and what's really sad, you know what you're saying. It's not as if the words come out by mistake. You mean every word you say. You've said things that have embarrassed me in front of our friends, and you know I won't say anything back. You feel you can put me down and I'm supposed to roll over like Jasper and take it. You're selfish and self-centered and when you're bitchy I'm supposed to sit quietly by until it passes. You criticize me, but if I suggest for even a second that something you've done is wrong you go ballistic."

"That's such crap." There was fury in Amy's eyes.

"Is it? I remember that time you went to your physician and his nurse screwed up a test or something. Instead of getting mad at her and blaming her for the screw-up, do you remember what you said?"

"How the hell can I remember something that was a few years ago. I've been to the doctor several times since then. Do you expect me to remember that one incident?"

"I do."

"The only reason you remember is because you compartmentalize everything. You stew over it, you frigging pout. That's why you remember."

"No, Amy, I remember because you turned your anger at the nurse on me."

"That's ridiculous."

"You did," Kelly said softly. "You said you'd decided that all nurses were incompetent."

"And you took that personally."

"I'm a nurse. How would you expect me to take it?"

"Just as I meant it, that at times nurses are incompetent."

"One nurse screwed up, so why condemn all of us?"

"I wasn't doing that."

"You were, Amy, because you had to get mad at someone and

you wouldn't confront the nurse who made the mistake, so you had to attack me and my profession."

"You know what, Kelly Burns?"

"Tell me, Amy Day."

"You do need to see a counselor, because you're one screwed-up woman."

"You're probably right, but if you want to make this relationship work, you'd better make a commitment to go with me. Otherwise, this is not going to work."

"Is that a threat?" Amy was facing her; Kelly could see her fists clenched hard against her side.

"No, Amy, I'm telling you we've got some serious problems and unless we work through them together, they're not going to go away."

"The only problem we have is your preoccupation with something I might say when I'm upset. The problem is, you just take everything so personally. Shine it on, Kelly, for God's sake, shine it on. I don't mean anything by it."

"You know what I want from you?"

"No, Kelly, I really don't."

"I want you to treat me like you treat your friends. You'd never say the things you've said to me to Elizabeth, or Maggie Beth or Terry, never. You'd never allow them to see that side of you and do you know why?"

"I'm sure you're going to tell me."

"Because you're scared. You know that if you allowed that side of Amy to come out among your friends, you wouldn't have any. So it'll never happen. But you don't care if your partner sees that side of you. It's as if—and I'm not sure I'm going to explain this well—it's like you want to test my love. Because I love you you can do anything you want to me, so you keep pushing the boundaries of verbal abuse and if I keep loving you, then you push it some more. It's some kind of weird test." Kelly paused. "I know I'm not explaining this well."

"You sure as hell aren't. Look, I've had enough of this conversation. I'm going to bed. Go to Portland tomorrow and when you get back, well—"

"Well?"

"Just well, I'm not going to say anymore. Look, I can't sleep with you tonight. I don't want to be with you tonight. Just leave me alone."

She watched as Amy picked up her nightshirt and walked out of the room. She waited. She could hear Amy moving around in the guest room. They needed to resolve this, Kelly thought. *Go in there. Make her understand that we need to talk this out.*

She knew their relationship was hanging precariously like a single-clawed lobster holding on to the side of a bucket. God, her head was pounding. She lay down on the bed. She'd just stretch out for a minute, let her heart rhythms return to normal. She closed her eyes.

Kelly reached over and slapped at the alarm clock, but it kept ringing. She opened her eyes and reached for the telephone. It was morning, already.

"Rise and shine, my friend. It's time for you and Susan to hit the road."

"What are you, some kind of motel clerk?"

Laurie chuckled. "No, but I figured you wouldn't be moving. Remember, you two are going to catch the early ferry so you can be in Portland by eleven o'clock."

"What time is it?"

"Seven."

"Seven?" The ferry left at eight. "It takes me fifteen minutes max to get up and moving. You've given me a whole hour."

"Good, you can have a good breakfast. Start you out right this morning."

Kelly groaned.

"How'd Amy take it?"

Kelly thought back to the night before and inwardly shuddered

264

at the anger they both had felt. She'd been so exhausted, she'd fallen asleep fully dressed. "She's fine. She's all tied up with LNG."

"Well, I'm glad you're doing this for me. Anyway, get up, get your shower, put on your traveling duds and Susan will be waiting. I told her you wanted to take your car."

"Good. I'll be at her house in about forty-five minutes. Tell her we can grab doughnuts and coffee on the way."

"Love you, pal."

"I know, otherwise I wouldn't be doing this."

"I know that better than anyone."

Kelly sat on the side of the bed. She rubbed her hands across her eyes and then stood up. She grabbed clean underwear from the drawer and went into the bathroom. The door to Amy's room was shut.

She closed her eyes as the hot water cascaded across her body. She ducked her head under the stream and let the water massage the back of her neck. She was tired. She'd slept but hadn't rested. She turned off the faucet and toweled off. As she dressed, she wondered if she should talk to her before she left? She grabbed her backpack out of the closet and stuck an extra pair of underwear and socks inside. She rolled up a pair of jeans and a shirt and put them on top. Her toiletry kit she stuck in the front pocket. She zipped the bag shut and threw it over her shoulder. She walked up to the closed door and listened. She knew the telephone had awoken Amy. She raised her hand to knock. Something made her stop. She dropped her hand and turned toward the stairs. *If Amy opens the door, I'll hug her. Tell her how sorry I am for last night. Make her see that five years is just too important to throw away, ask her to put all of our words on hold until I get back. Make her see that I do love her and I am willing to make this work. Get her to agree to see a counselor, but take it step by step.* Kelly went slowly down the stairs. She waited at the bottom landing. The door didn't open. Kelly turned toward the kitchen, opened the door and walked out into the morning air.

Chapter Thirty

Laurie was waiting for her as soon as she pulled in front of Susan's house.

"Good morning." She opened the door for Kelly.

"No one should be that happy so early in the morning. Didn't you just come off the night shift?" Kelly grumbled.

"I did. I feel wonderful. Susan's already packed. I tried to get her to eat some breakfast, but she said she wasn't up to it, so here—" Laurie reached in her pocket and pulled out some money. "Take her to Dunkin' Donuts."

"Put that away." Kelly knew that her tone sounded harsher than she meant. "Put your money away. We'll be fine," she said more gently. "I told you we'd stop at Dunkin' Donuts either here or on the mainland."

"You look beat."

"Didn't sleep well last night, just a bout of insomnia."

"Kell, I'm sorry. Maybe Susan could drive and you could catch a few winks." Laurie's voice suggested concern.

"I'm fine." Kelly looked up as the door opened.

"Good morning," Susan said, carrying a small suitcase.

"Good morning."

Laurie took the suitcase from her and put it in the back of Kelly's car. "Well, I wish I could be going with you, but I just know this is going to be for the best. I spoke with Jeanne and she's got a bunch of folks lined up. She's that nurse friend of Kelly's and mine from the hospital that I mentioned," she said to Susan. "Here"—she reached in her pocket and handed a piece of paper to Kelly—"are the directions for the rental truck shop. It's about a half a mile from the house. The guys will meet you at the house and this"—she pointed at the telephone number below the directions—"is Jeanne's cell phone number, so if you have any problems give her a call. She and the gang stand ready to do whatever they have to, to come rescue you or whatever. I'm gonna be on pins and needles—"

"Stop," Susan interrupted. "She's been like this for two days," she said to Kelly. "Everything is going to be fine. Kelly and I are going to be fine. We'll make all of the deadlines. You concentrate on what it is that you have to do here."

Laurie inhaled deeply. "You're right, for some reason I'm just hyper about this whole thing. I know that everything will be fine because my oldest and my newest best friends are doing this for me."

"That's right, so put that adrenaline on hold. We're going to need it when we get back tomorrow and have to unload the truck," Kelly said. "Now let's just say our good-byes so we don't start off by missing the ferry." She reached over and gave Laurie a hug.

"I sure appreciate this, my friend," Laurie said to her. "And I appreciate the fact that Amy didn't mind. I've got to spend more time getting to know her."

"When we get back."

Kelly watched as Laurie hugged Susan. Instead of the huge bear hug she had given Kelly, Laurie's hug was slower and softer. She held Susan close, one hand caressing Susan's back. Embarrassed, Kelly looked away.

"You're pretty quiet this morning," Susan said after they were on the ferry. The ocean breeze felt luxurious.

"I've had a couple of insomnia nights."

"I'm sorry. Would you like me to drive? Give you a chance to nap?" She studied Kelly's face, looking for lines of exhaustion.

"No, I'm fine really. I guess my face gives me away."

"I suspect your face gives you away a lot."

Kelly laughed. "It has and it does. Not at a professional level, I'm able to maintain that stoic stone face as a nurse, although at times over the years it's been hard because of things I have had to tell family members."

"I doubt stoic stone face. Somehow I have a feeling there's real compassion in your face."

"Hmm, well, I hope compassion, but you can't break down and cry with the family when you have to give them bad news. Although at times I wanted to, especially with patients you get close to."

"Does that happen in a hospital?"

"More than you realize. It's like in life. Why is it that we can know someone for years and never feel really close to them, and then we meet someone for five minutes and we connect with them like we've known them a lifetime?"

"Like us? I hope?"

They'd been leaning against the railing looking out at the water.

Kelly raised an eyebrow. The suggestion clearly jarred her. "Like us," she said agreeably, as if tasting the words for the first time.

"I would appreciate it if everyone would head to their cars. Land's just minutes away. That way we can get you folks off and the next batch on," the deckhand yelled.

Susan turned toward the car. *Why did you get so personal?* she chided herself. She'd promised herself she was going to keep it light and cheery all weekend. No declarations of attraction, no statements of what if. *Come on, stick to the plan. Keep it light and cheery*, she ordered that practical side of her brain.

"Does that happen often?" Susan said, resuming their earlier discussion now that they were in the car. She was glad Kelly was driving.

"What?"

"Telling family members the bad news."

"Not so much in a small hospital, but in the larger ones it's happened. The family members couldn't get ahold of the doctor. Sometimes you get doctors who just don't want to tell family members and they push it off on the nursing staff. Other times the doctor just isn't around, he may be simply going from one surgery to the next. And now in this day of specialists, a lot of times the nurse is the only one family members feel comfortable with. We're there with them day in and day out at the hospital, so it happens, not a lot but it happens."

"Rough."

"It is, but at the island hospital it really isn't like that. The family docs have been with the same person for years, so they have that connection and if there's bad news to tell it's the doctor who does it, but it isn't any easier for them, believe me. Everyone is family, and I've watched some of those doctors give the family the bad news and walk away with tears in their eyes. I've seen doctors cry."

"As an outsider, you just don't think about those things. My dad had a heart attack and died en route to the hospital. I still remember my mother—ah, the pain. They wouldn't let her ride in the ambulance. My aunt drove her to the hospital. When she got there they gave her the bad news. I was in Boston, but I didn't think she was ever going to get over that. It took a long time."

"I'm so sorry, Susan, that must have been devastating. From what you described it sounds like your folks had one of those enviable relationships."

"Well . . ." Susan sighed. "I've never had anyone describe it like that, but I guess they did. In the summer, while a lot of my friends' parents were wrapped around television sets after work, my parents were taking a walk together. It was their quiet time."

"Have you had that in any of your relationships?" Kelly grimaced as if she wanted to swallow the words. "I'm sorry, that was really out of line."

"No, it wasn't. You can ask me anything you want. I don't have a thing to hide. I've only been in two what I guess you would call long-term relationships. I lived with a woman while I was in college—that lasted about three years—and then the one I told you about over dinner. We were together ten years. It always started out that way, but y'know —and I've thought a lot about this, especially after Jesse and I broke up because unlike a lot of people I had a perfect model—I don't know why it went wrong."

"Really?"

"Really." Susan thought about those weeks and months after she and Jesse had broken up. She had even talked with a psychologist friend of hers who suggested maybe she'd set her expectations too high. "A friend of mine, who by the way is a family counselor for straights and gays, suggested that I'm looking for my father in a relationship and no one will ever measure up."

"Is that it?"

"Kelly, I honestly don't know. I hope not because if that's true I need to see a family counselor full time because no one is going to measure up to my father, and when you add on the fact that I've idealized him since his death, who could measure up?"

"I guess we all idealize the people we love. I did it with my mother. Unlike your family mine was screwed up."

"How so?"

"I don't want to bore you with the details, but there was both verbal and physical abuse. It's funny, I've idealized my mother and villanized my father. It was tough growing up in that house, but now I remember only the bad things about my father, yet he wasn't all bad. When things were good and he wasn't ranting and raving or screaming about something, he was a good father. Never a loving father, but a good father. He fed us. Saw to it that we had whatever we needed and more if money could buy it. And I guess, truth be told, he never had a chance. His mother died when he was eighteen months old. Two crazy aunts raised him. Then my grandfather married the proverbial Cinderella stepmother and he had a really hard life. That doesn't make what he did to me and my sister and brother right, but now as an adult, I can see where it began."

"I'm sorry, it must be difficult when you listen to someone like me who waxes on and on about how wonderful their life was with their parents."

"It really doesn't bother me. I'm happy for you and I'm happy for those kids who grow up in a normal home. I don't see a lot of that around here."

"You don't," Susan said with emphasis. "Remember, I'm the one who ran the numbers for this county. Boy, you have a lot of single-parent households and a lot of abuse. Did you know your statistics for domestic abuse in this county lead the rest of the state?" It still appalled her.

"I can believe it. We have a lot of poverty and poverty is ripe for everything else."

"How did we ever get on this topic? I can't think of anything more depressing to talk about than that, and look at this beautiful day."

"It is a beautiful day, and look at where we are—Freeport. Just a few more miles and we'll be in Portland."

Susan picked up the paper that Kelly had put on the seat. "Our pal has this all worked out," she said.

"She does, and if all goes well, we can drive back tonight."

"Good idea." Susan could feel her disappointment. She didn't want to drive back tonight. She wanted to ask Kelly why her face looked so sad. She wanted to know what had happened that turned those usual dancing eyes into a dead woman's walk. "Can I ask you a question?"

"Of course." Kelly took the Congress Street exit off the freeway and stopped at the light at the bottom of the ramp.

271

"Is everything all right?"

"Yes, just Amy and I had a disagreement last night."

"About the trip?"

"The trip and some problems we've been having. See, we don't exactly have the type of relationship that you described with your parents, but we're working it out. It's just that I haven't gotten much sleep thinking about it all. Sorry."

"Don't apologize. I'm sorry, I'm going on and on about my life and you're feeling sad. Do you want to talk about it?"

"Yes, no. I don't know. It doesn't feel right talking about it. I think that—we have a whole bunch of people waiting for us."

Susan looked to where Kelly was looking. "My goodness, look at all those people," she exclaimed. "That's our friend—talk about overkill. There are enough people here to move ten houses. Do we know any of these people?"

"Some. Jeanne Black's heading up the group. I see her right there."

Susan saw a tall woman with frizzy red hair coming toward them.

Kelly pulled in behind another car. "Jeanne," she said as she opened the door.

"God, look at you, you never change, Kelly Burns," Jeanne said.

"I do. Your eyesight is just going." Kelly hugged her. "Jeanne, this is Susan Iogen."

"Susan, welcome. Well—" Jeanne turned to the group and introduced the two women to them. "We got a major problem," she said after the introductions.

Kelly groaned. "And that is?"

"We can't get in. The plan was for us to have most of the stuff packed up before you got here."

"I thought that was all done," Kelly said.

"Heavens, no. I have a ton of boxes in the back of my van as do the rest. We got here early to pack dishes, clothes, you name it."

"Have you called Laurie?"

"She's not at home. I even tried her cell phone."

"That's not going to help."

"Why not?"

Kelly said, "We have only two towers in all of Jefferson County. Most of the time you can't get a signal. If she's not right near the harbor she's out of range."

Jeanne groaned. "I don't know what to do."

"What was the plan?"

"Heather was supposed to leave the key under the mat. We looked but it isn't there. I was hoping Laurie gave you her key."

"She didn't. I don't think she even thought about it, really. What about breaking in?"

"We thought about that also, but it's a damned fortress. Scott— you met him, he's the one in the white shorts—even went looking for a ladder. Thought possibly an upstairs window might be open, but we couldn't find one. The garage is locked."

"Did you call Heather?"

"First thing, I know her cell phone is working, but she's just not answering. I think she's just jacking Laurie around."

"But it's not Laurie, it's us."

"So tell me." Jeanne leaned against Kelly's car. "When are these breakups ever amicable?"

Kelly rolled her eyes. "Don't ask me that one, Jeanne. I am not an expert on relationships."

"How about a locksmith?" Susan asked.

"We thought about that, but we figured we'd have to show some kind of proof that we're supposed to be here, otherwise anyone could appear at a house with a moving van, load up and drive away. The only hope is Heather or Laurie."

"Do you have your phone?"

"I do." Jeanne reached in her pocket and handed it to Kelly.

"I'm going to call Elizabeth—maybe she knows where Laurie is," Kelly said to Susan. "Elizabeth is a dear friend of mine and if anyone knows what's going on on the island, it's her," she explained to Jeanne. "Elizabeth. Hi." Kelly paused. "We're in Portland and we're locked out of Laurie's house. Susan and I came down here to help move her furniture. Have you heard from her?" She cupped her hand over the mouthpiece and said to Susan and Jeanne, "Elizabeth hasn't seen or heard from her either. She said she'll call around and see if anyone knows where she is." Kelly listened again. "No, no, I haven't talked to Amy this morning." Susan watched her while she gave Elizabeth her cell phone number. "She says if she can track her down, she'll have her call us." She handed the cell phone to Jeanne. "You heard."

"Gone to the mainland?" Jeanne said. "As in car ferry and long trip."

"Not so long, but again, depending upon where you are, your cell phone works or not."

"So what do we do?"

"I don't know." Kelly looked at her watch. "Look, why don't I get the truck then we all take a breather and get some lunch. Maybe Heather will be back by then."

"We were just talking about that," Jeanne said. "We decided rather than leave because her royal highness might come back, someone would make a Subway run. Is that all right with you?"

"Fine with me," Susan said.

"Me too," Kelly added.

"Hey, guys," Jeanne called to the rest who were lounging against their cars or sitting on the front porch. "Let's get some sandwiches and then we can regroup and figure out what we're going to do. Kelly is going to get the truck."

"How about we hang her from that tree over there," Scott yelled. The rest laughed. "No court of law would convict us."

"Tempting, but I think what we need to focus on are sandwiches and drinks." Jeanne laughed. "I never was much for hanging people on an empty stomach. You understand," she said to Susan. "we're all Laurie's friends, and not too many of us care about Heather."

"I can understand why." Susan surveyed the group. "Is it possible Heather may be at work?"

"We thought about that too, called there, no answer. It's

Saturday, it's Labor Day weekend, and no one's around." Jeanne stopped. "Look, we have to eat anyway. Let's just hope we connect with either her or Laurie in the next hour."

"Well, I don't know how Laurie can help us from two and a half hours away," Kelly said. "Gosh, I never even thought to ask her for the key."

"Don't beat yourself up, Kell. I figured she might have given a key to someone in case she locked herself out," Jeanne said.

"Possible. But I don't know who." Kelly shook her head. "Why don't you do the sandwich run. Susan and I will get the moving van and when we all get back we can sort this out."

"Agreed." Jeanne turned to the group. "All right, let's get a list of what everyone wants, and no hangings until I get back."

An hour later, they all lounged around on the porch or grass while they ate their lunch. Susan enjoyed talking with Jeanne, who regaled her with Laurie and Kelly stories. The more Kelly protested, the more stories Jeanne told. After they'd finished eating they again tried to call Laurie and Heather, with still no answer. Scott had suggested they break a window in the back, crawl through and open the front door. The rest had rejected that idea for fear a neighbor would call the cops.

"Funny," Kelly said to no one in particular, "if we were on the island we'd have help from someone. Heck, on the island all we would have had to do was tell someone what we were doing and they'd have helped us break in. Just so different here. I don't really miss it."

"In Andover the neighbors would have called the cops by now. Heck, in Andover the cops would have carted us off to jail by now," Susan added.

"It must be—" Jeanne stopped. "Well, well, look what the rat just dragged in," she said to the others. They all looked toward the road. Heather was driving toward them. "I can't wait to hear her excuse."

Susan looked to where Jeanne was looking. The woman exiting the car had brown hair. She was taller than Laurie, billy club thin, with a raw-boned face. She was a lot older than Laurie and dressed conservatively in brown slacks and a brown blouse. If it had been the sixties, Heather would have had a polyester look about her. In contrast, Susan knew that on this warm September day, Laurie would have been in cut-off shorts and a top, her energy like static electricity. Heather looked like her power was a proverbial brownout. Heather was not at all what she had expected. Susan thought she hadn't really thought about what Laurie's partner might look like. Strange, she pondered the idea. If she'd been interested in Laurie she would have cared.

"Hi, guys. What are you waiting for?"

"A key." Controlled anger flooded Jeanne's voice.

"It's under the mat." Heather waved toward the porch. "Kelly, hi." She hugged Kelly. Susan noticed that Kelly's hug was restrained, about as warm as embracing a dead fish.

"It's not. We looked," Jeanne said.

"Oh, dear." Heather dug around in her pockets as Susan looked on. "I must have forgotten to leave it. Sorry." She handed the key to Kelly. Susan noticed Heather didn't even look at Jeanne. "Well, if you don't need me I'll be on my way. The new owners will be here tomorrow. I told them you'd leave the key under the mat so do it so they can get in. 'Bye, all," Heather said as she walked away.

"Where's that rope?" Jeanne threatened.

Kelly put her hand on Jeanne's arm. "She's gone. She had her moment of drama and she's gone. Let's get this place packed."

"I'm beat," Susan said as she put her suitcase on the bed. It had taken them longer to pack than expected. If they had left Portland they wouldn't have gotten to Port Bleu until one o'clock in the morning. They would have had to stay in a motel there because they'd missed the last ferry to the island. They'd agreed they were just too tired to drive and had finally gotten ahold of Laurie, who threatened to kill Heather. Kelly had settled her down and told Laurie to focus on her hospital work. She had assured her they'd

276

have everything packed and would be back on the island on Sunday. Afterward, they had all gone out for pizza and now she and Susan were at the Holiday Inn. Susan looked at the clock—it was just nine o'clock.

"Me too, but this sure is pretty," Kelly said, looking out at the bay. "The best motel in town when it comes to the view. I just wish I wasn't so tired. I would be able to enjoy it more. Would you like to do something? Go to the bar and have a drink?"

"Take a bath and go to bed."

"Me to, but a shower, not a bath. Go ahead, I can wait."

"Actually, why don't you grab your shower. I'm going to soak in the tub for a while."

"Sure." Kelly opened her backpack. She dug around inside.

Susan noticed she was searching for something. "Something wrong?"

"No, not at all," she said as she took her Boston Red Sox shirt and toiletry bag and went in the bathroom.

"How about some wine?" Susan called through the closed door.

"Sounds good."

"Good, I'm going to call down for a bottle and some glasses. Anything else?"

"If they have a cheese plate that would be nice. I could do with a few munchies before I go to sleep."

"I'll check," Susan said through the closed bathroom door.

Susan called the dining room and ordered. She could hear the shower. She knew that if she stretched out on her bed she would be asleep. She sat down on the chair and looked out at the bay. She looked at Kelly's bag sitting on her bed. Kelly had not called Amy all day. Something definitely had happened. She thought about Amy and how driven she was about the project. Susan thought about her own role. She was determined to win, but not passionate about it. Funny, she thought, she never had that sense of devotion to one place. Maybe if she'd grown up on an island, she would feel just as passionately. She knew the opponents were holding marathon meetings over the weekend. She also knew they probably were aware that the developers planned to offer them money to put the project in their backyard. She had heard about the petition and the demand to put the issue before the voters. She'd told the developers the petition was a go. None of the obstacles raised by the opponents seemed to even bother the developers. They had come in with a strategy and they were sticking to it. Susan had suggested on occasion tweaking it, which at times they did, but for the most part she agreed with them. Their strategy was to educate those who were reachable and ignore those who were adamantly opposed to it. No amount of information would change their mind. What was at issue was whether there were more who were on the fence than opposed. The developers seemed to think there were.

"Oh, that feels better," Kelly said as she opened the door. She had on a T-shirt that said Boston Red Sox. It hung down past her thighs. Susan swallowed. *Don't even think about those thighs*, she said to herself. "Heck, I'll even be able to stay awake for that glass of wine."

"Well, maybe I'll just shower," Susan said as she picked up her pajamas and her overnight bag. She closed the bathroom door. *God, she's gorgeous.* Susan thought resting her head against the door. *Don't think about it. Just get through this night and go home.* She hung her pajamas on the back of the door. She put her overnight bag on the sink and turned on the shower.

"The wine's here," Kelly said through the door.

"Great, I'll be out soon." Susan stripped off her sweaty clothes and stepped into the shower. She'd decided to forego the bath; she just wanted to get clean and go to bed. She let the water run down across her body. She put her head under the water and lathered her hair. With her back to the shower she let the water wash the soap out of her hair and run down her body. She moved her back around so that the water hit at first down low and then higher up. She wished the motel had a masseuse; she could have used a back rub. They had carried ten rooms of furniture out of Laurie's house. After the first go-around with Heather, they had not seen her the rest of the day. Although Kelly didn't say a thing about Heather, Jeanne had given her an earload while they were packing the kitchen. Nope, Susan thought. Heather was definitely not going to be part of Jeanne's inner circle.

She turned off the water and toweled herself off. She looked at her hastily gathered pajamas, a deep blue shirt and white shorts. She liked sleeping in the nude so after she had volunteered to help Kelly, she had gone to Wal-Mart in search of something to wear. The women's pajamas had left her cold. She'd found the shirt in the men's section. It was oversize, but she was looking for comfort, not style. She had found the shorts in the women's section. She pulled the price tags off. She looked at herself in the mirror. She looked like Little Orphan Annie. She ran her hands through her wet hair. She turned on the hotel hairdryer and blew warm air over her hair.

"Hi." Kelly was stretched out on her bed, a glass of wine nearby. She had turned off all the lights except between the beds.

"Are you as beat as I am?" Susan glanced at Kelly and then down at the floor. *Don't look at those legs*, Susan ordered herself. Kelly swung her legs to the side of the bed and stood up. *Look at the floor*, she said to herself.

"I am." Kelly handed her a glass of wine. She picked up hers and held it out for a toast. "Well, to a good finish." She clinked her glass against Susan's.

"To a very good finish." Susan sipped the wine. *Oh, God, I want her so bad*. She inhaled deeply.

As if reading her mind, Kelly reached out and took Susan's glass, their fingers touched and Susan felt a tingle reach down to her toes. Kelly set the glass down and looked at her. She knew Kelly had felt the same tingle.

"I don't know what's happening, and I know we're going to regret this in the morning, but I have this desire to kiss you." Kelly stepped toward her. "I know I should ignore it, but I can't. You look so gosh darn inviting in that blue shirt, your eyes are down-right sultry, your . . ."

279

Susan swallowed deeply. Her arms went around Kelly's neck and she pulled her to her. She traced her tongue over Kelly's lips, which were open and inviting. *I don't care about tomorrow,* she thought. *I don't care about tomorrow or the next day.* She had to taste her, she thought as she pulled Kelly's mouth to hers. "I've fantasized about this," she said against her lips.

"Me too." Kelly's arms encircled Susan's waist. "Fantasized and dreamed about this."

With one fluid motion, Susan eased her onto the bed. She buried her mouth against Kelly's neck. "I'm not going to be able to stop."

"Don't stop," Kelly pleaded. "Don't stop."

Susan pulled Kelly to her and kissed her deeply. Their tongues at first were a gentle ripple, then a ferocious swell as they locked around each other in an ardent wave of pleasure. They took power from their kiss.

Susan lifted Kelly's shirt. Never had the Boston Red Sox been so inviting, she thought. With her other hand she pulled Kelly's hips to her.

She felt Kelly tug at her shirt and she raised up so she could pull it over her head. "I want to feel you against me," Kelly said against her neck.

Susan felt Kelly's intake of breath as she lay naked along the length of her body. She heard Kelly moan as she caressed her skin. She kissed Kelly's shoulder, her lips following that same slow path down to the soft place between Kelly's breasts.

She imagined her hair felt like a feather on Kelly's skin as her lips and then her tongue did a slow circle around Kelly's nipple and finally drew it into her mouth. Susan reveled in the taste of Kelly's nipple. She kissed up Kelly's chest to her neck, tilted Kelly's head back and kissed her mouth with an intensity that demanded a response. She touched Kelly between her legs and felt a small quiver.

Kelly began stroking her back first at her shoulders and slowly moving downward. Kelly rolled her on her back. Kelly's tongue traveled down and under Susan's breast, tracing a warm path to her belly where she stopped at the top of her white shorts.

"I want to make love to you," Susan said through clenched teeth.

"I want to taste you first, everywhere." Kelly's voice smoked with desire. She slowly pulled the shorts down over Susan's hips. Her tongue followed the slow movement of pulling the shorts down. She stroked the skin just above the coarse, curly hair, then kissed her way back up Susan's belly, to her breasts. She sucked first one and then the other. Her hand snaked downward, and Susan arched her back and opened her legs.

Kelly massaged her with the heel of her hand and Susan matched the rhythm. Suddenly, Susan felt the first wave of orgasm, and she lay back panting, her eyes closed. "That was nice." She smiled. She opened her eyes and looked directly at Kelly, her eyes fiery and inviting more. "How did that happen? I started to make love to you and then you were making love to me."

"There's no first, I wanted us both to be first and I've just started," Kelly said, again kissing the skin just above the curly hair. Kelly's breast felt hot against Susan's legs, her tongue now darting across and behind Susan's knees in a circular pattern. Susan bit her bottom lip in anticipation of the climb upward to the spot where all her happiness seemed to be concentrated.

Susan arched as she felt Kelly's tongue on and in her. Kelly traced a large circle around Susan's wonder spot, momentarily touching it and then pulling back to continue the circular motion. Susan reached forward and grabbed Kelly's hands as they gripped her thigh. "Don't tease, just do it, please do it."

Kelly returned to that magical spot between Susan's legs and focused her attention on those tiny nerves.

"Oh, God, yes." Susan gasped between clenched teeth.

Kelly lifted Susan's hips, her tongue and lips sucking in Susan's passion. Susan's body began to react, and suddenly she felt that tightness inside.

"Oh, God, yes," she cried.

281

As she began to relax, Kelly slipped inside her. She could not believe how hot those fingers felt as Kelly caressed her. As Kelly's motion intensified, Susan's body began to match the rhythm of Kelly's hand.

The rhythm intensified. Kelly's hand moved faster and Susan met each of her thrusts. Then she knew she couldn't take it anymore. She pushed down and stopped as the climax shuddered through her.

She pulled Kelly to her. "That was magnificent," she said against Kelly's mouth. "That was absolutely celestial."

Kelly looked at her. "Would you like some wine?"

"No, just you." Then Susan began her own slow, passionate exploration.

Chapter Thirty-one

Kelly opened her eyes and looked at the clock. They were not going to make it back to the island by noon; it already was noon. She closed her eyes. She wished it was still night. Somehow the night offered so few complications. Susan was spooned against her. She could smell their lovemaking on her skin.

"You're awake?" Susan said quietly.

"Yes."

"Are we going to regret this?" Her voice was hesitant. Kelly sensed fear.

"Yes, we're going to regret it, and no, we're not going to regret it."

Susan turned over. "I don't understand."

Kelly rolled over onto her back, Susan still lying on her arm. "Of course we're going to have regrets because we've complicated our lives a lot, but I'm not going to pretend it didn't happen. It was the most beautiful night I've ever spent."

"For me too." Susan touched a finger to Kelly's cheek. "You don't have to respond to this, but I want to say it now before I lose my nerve. Somewhere between the hike in the woods and last night I fell in love with you. I know you're in a relationship and I'm not going to ask anything of you, but I fell in love with you. For me, this is more than a one-night stand." She paused. "Back on the island, I know what the complications are. We don't ever have to be alone again and we don't ever have to do this again."

"Life is a complication." Kelly sighed. She didn't want to say Amy's name. "A major complication, and if things had been right in my life, last night never would have happened. We'd had a major fight right before I left."

"I suspected something was wrong when you picked me up. Was this some kind of—"

"Don't say it." Kelly put her hand over Susan's lips. "Don't say it." She murmured, "This was nothing more than two women who love each other making love. That's all."

"You love me."

"I do. Somewhere between the hike and last night, I realized that too." Kelly rubbed her hand against her brow.

"It wasn't just a passionate moment?"

"No. It was passion, but it was not just a moment. I know that, Susan. I don't know how to fix this mess, but I know what happened last night." She kissed Susan's fingertips. "Amy and I have been having a lot of problems lately. I've blamed LNG and her obsession with it, but the problems were there before. I'm not going to talk about those problems, because it doesn't feel right. Weeks ago I asked her to go see a counselor with me. Someone to help us work through our problems. She agreed. I think she agreed just to get me to stop talking about it, although at the time I thought she was really interested in making our relationship work. I brought it up the night before we left. She got angry. Felt I was pressuring her. I wasn't. I was just telling her I had found a woman counselor."

"What if she's changed her mind, wants to go see that counselor?"

"I don't know."

"She might. If we were having problems, I'd want to do anything and everything I could to make my relationship with you work," Susan said kindly.

"That's the problem. Amy doesn't think we have one. She thinks I have a problem, but she doesn't think we do."

Susan rolled away from Kelly.

"Don't go away."

"I have an unbelievable knack for screwing up my life when it comes to relationships." Susan sat up. "Kelly, I'm not going to apologize for last night. I'm not going to say I'm sorry it happened, because I'm not. But I'm going to say we need to shower, get dressed and go back to the island where two different people live. We've got to go back to our lives. Last night was a fantasy come true, so let's end it there."

"And if we can't?"

"Let's end it there."

Sadness weighed on her like a bag full of books on her back. "I don't—"

"Let's leave it there."

Susan used the time she had traveling behind the rental to think about what had happened. She knew that any hope of staying on the island was gone. Even if voters approved the LNG facility, she would have to turn down any other contracts with the developers. She just couldn't be near Kelly and not be able to touch her. She thought about the night before. It had been spontaneous lovemaking and it had been fantastic. Kelly was a gentle and thoughtful lover and she seemed so attuned to Susan's body.

When they got to the ferry landing they had to wait. They were in line with several other cars, their drivers lounging around waiting. She sat with Kelly in the rental truck waiting.

"I want to see you again," Kelly said, staring out at the water.

"Kelly, we're going to see each other a lot. We live on an island."

"I didn't mean that."

"I know. I'm sorry. I just don't know how to handle this. I've never done this before. I hope you believe that."

"I do. I've never done it before either and I hope you believe that," Kelly said in a faint voice.

"You have a life to go back to. My life is less complicated. No one's waiting for me."

"But there is—"

"Laurie?"

"Laurie."

"I've not made a commitment to Laurie."

"No, but she has to you, at least in her own mind. She's falling in love with you."

Susan blew out some air. "I think *love* is too strong a word."

"It's love. I know her. Funny, I was jealous of her." Kelly was staring straight ahead as the ferryman lowered the ramp and cars began to inch forward.

"I gotta go," Susan said, reaching for the handle on the truck door. "People behind me will be upset if your car remains parked on the ramp." She opened the door and ran back to Kelly's car. She waved to the car behind her. She watched as Kelly put the rental truck in gear and inched forward onto the ramp and then onto the ferry. She followed behind her. *If only the ferry would just sail around and around the bay, never landing. Never taking them back to their problems*, she thought.

Just then, Kelly got out of the truck and walked back to the car. "We've got to keep talking, you know," Kelly said as she got in and closed the door. "We've got to solve this. I don't want to lose you."

"Are you going to tell Amy about what happened?"

"I have to. I just don't know when yet. Are you going to tell Laurie?"

"No, I'm not in a relationship with Laurie. So what goes on in my private life is really no one's business. I love her, but not in that way. I suspected that there was more going on in her head than in mine, but I never led her on. I never even hinted that we would have anything other than a friendship. In fact, I've told her over and over what a great friend she is, how much I enjoy her company."

"I suspected as much, but Laurie wears her emotions like a nametag. She lets it hang out there for everyone to see."

"I know. Are you going to tell her?"

"She's my best friend, but no. Like you said, she's not your partner, so it's not any of her business."

"Sounds right in the abstract."

"It does." Kelly was staring at the water, a sadness in her eyes. Susan thought about how tangled their lives had become.

People began to move toward their cars. How could the ferry ride be over that quickly? Ordinarily, when she was going to the mainland it seemed like the ferry ride took forever.

"I want to see you again, alone."

Kelly's words jarred her and she blurted out, "That's suicidal." She bit her tongue. "Look, without bringing up the devil in your backyard, LNG, the major public meeting is Wednesday. The developers know there's going to be a petition and a demand that the question be put before the voters. They're going to agree and even push for a quick vote. By the end of September or mid-October the issue should be resolved. For me it's not going to matter if it's up or down. My job ends with the vote. I leave the island."

"Really?"

"I'm contracted until the matter either is approved by the selectmen or the voters."

"If it's approved, there will be more public relations work." Kelly sounded awfully confident.

"Agreed, and more than likely they'll offer me another contract. Until then my end date's certain and I doubt I'll accept any more contracts."

"Why?"

"Kelly, I can't come back here. I've fallen in love with you. Distance is the only thing that's going to help me. And believe me, I'm not going to sneak around behind Amy's back."

"I'm not asking you to." Kelly was clearly frustrated and she looked everywhere but at Susan.

"So we have to avoid each other. We have to get through the next few weeks and then I quietly leave the island."

"I don't want that."

"Nor do I, but I'm not going to be the other woman in a triangle. I've seen it happen and it's nothing but messy. I'm not going to do it," she said more to herself than Kelly. She ran both hands through her hair. How could she screw up her life like this? She loved Kelly, was desperately in love with her, and yet she was sitting here talking to her as if she was some stranger and they were talking about the weather. Only hours earlier they'd been passionately making love.

Kelly's head snapped up. "Damn, I've got to go. He's waving me to the truck. Please, let's just talk for five minutes."

"How can we? Look at the time. Laurie's waiting for us. We were supposed to be here hours ago."

"So another five minutes. Please."

"Where?"

"When we get off the ferry just follow me."

"All right, but I think it's nuts. What can we say in five minutes?"

"Please." Kelly's eyes were begging.

Susan nodded in agreement.

"Just follow me," Kelly said as she slammed the door.

Susan followed closely behind the rental truck after they left the ferry landing, turning off the main road and onto one of the side roads. They went past the landfill. Susan didn't know where the heck they were. Kelly turned into a gravel pit.

Susan stared at it. Great, she thought, Tony Bennett lost his heart in San Francisco, I lost mine at a gravel pit. If the situation wasn't so damn sad, she decided, she'd start laughing.

"Sorry, I couldn't think of any other place where I knew we wouldn't be bothered. I found this place one time when I got lost looking for a hiking trail that's around here."

"A gravel pit."

"Hey, we can tell our grandchildren about it someday."

Susan shot her a look.

"Susan, I'm not going to promise you a quick fix here. I can't. But know this. I've been thinking as we've been driving back, just as I'm sure you have. I know I love you. I don't know if I love Amy. There are times when I do, but lately there are more times when I don't. But I owe Amy and our relationship a chance, and if she wants to try and fix it, I've got to do that."

"I suspected you were going to say as much. But don't you see how that doesn't work for me? What do I do, sit around and hope your relationship fails? What does that make me out to be? No, Kelly. I don't want to do that." Susan took a deep breath. "Something happened last night. I'm not going to even try and explain it and I'm not going to apologize for it. It was mindless and emotional and completely irresponsible. So what I'm going to do is take control of it. I'm not in a relationship and I don't owe fixing anything to anyone, not even you. I want to get on with my life in Andover and I'll have that opportunity in another few weeks."

"So you're saying what? It's over."

"Kelly, it can't be over, it never started. We had a *one-night stand*. That's what we had." Susan hated the sound of those three words. But they were true. "We were two—I'm not going to say lonely, oh, hell yes, lonely—women who made love. Now let's just leave it at that."

"And the fact that I fell in love with you?"

"Doesn't matter."

"And if I can't stop loving you?"

"Doesn't matter."

"If I promise to leave Amy?" Kelly's eyes were begging again.

"I don't want that kind of promise. I've never been a wrecking ball and I'm not about to start now. Kelly, if you and Amy have problems, fix them, for God's sake." Susan could hear the defeat in her own voice. "Make your relationship work, and if you can't then get on with your life. But know this, I won't be in the background waiting to catch you because that ain't gonna happen."

"You decided all of that on the drive back?"

"Yes, no, I don't know. I just know I'm not going to be the one that breaks you and Amy up. I just won't do it."

"And if we're already broken?"

"I don't think that's the case. If you were already broken, you'd know. But I see the guilt in your face. You cheated on Amy and that's always going to be a problem between us."

"Susan, I love you. I don't know yet how to make this right." There were tears in Kelly's voice. "And you can say that what happened didn't matter, but it did. So I'm not going to say anything else." Kelly put her hand on the door handle. "Just that what happened last night was between two people who love each other. Now, that love has become problematic because of my personal life, but it doesn't diminish what happened between us. So you can talk about leaving and you can talk about putting everything on hold, but I love you, Susan." Kelly kissed her fingertips. "Someday, I'd like to share a tea bag with you."

Susan closed her eyes and willed herself not to cry. "You go ahead. I want to sit here a minute."

"Okay. If I can get a signal I'll call Laurie and tell her we're back."

"What reason are you going to give for being so late?" Susan looked at her watch.

"Four hours late."

"I don't know."

"Car trouble."

"Car trouble?"

"Tell her you had car trouble. Your tire was flat when we came out of the motel. I don't know, make it up as you go along. It's Labor Day weekend, not as many mechanics on duty. Tell her that."

Susan watched as Kelly drove out of the gravel pit. She rested her head against the steering column. The tears she had been holding back all day finally let go and she sobbed. She desperately loved Kelly, but what they did was wrong. Knowing how they felt about each other, they never should have been in that same room.

Why the hell hadn't she taken that bath? she asked herself over and over. Kelly probably would have been asleep by the time she was done. Why hadn't she gotten her own room? It wasn't as if she couldn't afford it. Hell, she never should have volunteered to go along. Kelly could have handled it by herself. But not Susan Iogen. No, she was known to everyone as the helper. Their being in the motel together was a blueprint for catastrophe and her rational mind had done nothing to stop it. She wiped away the tears and drove out of the gravel pit. She reached into her purse and got her sunglasses. The sun wasn't shining, but who'd notice.

She followed the dirt road back to the main highway and on to Kelly's house where the truck was backed up to the garage. Laurie's car was parked in the driveway.

"Susan, hi. Kelly told me about the flat tire. I'm so sorry." Laurie flung open the car door. She grabbed Susan and hugged her.

"I'm fine."

"I had everyone lined up hours ago to unload the truck, but they've all gone home." Despite the bad news, Laurie was smiling, clearly happy to see her.

"I told her we tried to call from the road, but I couldn't reach her on her cell phone," Kelly said.

"Damn things are useless here. Anyway, I sent everyone home. I have to get to work pretty soon. I called the rental place and told them I'd pay for an extra day. Everyone said they could be here tomorrow to unload. Susan, Kelly—look, I will make this up to you."

Susan could hear the distress in Laurie's voice. She felt guilty. "You don't have to make anything up to me. Really, for the most part the trip went fine."

"Fine? Fine is hardly the word I would use to describe Heather's little bitchy scene. I can't believe she did it—"

"Look, I agree with Susan," Kelly interrupted. "We got home with your furniture safely in tow so I don't think we need to go over that ground again."

"By the way, Amy was here looking for you. I told her—" Laurie paused. "Ironically, what I thought at the moment was a white lie—I told her you had car trouble, that's why you were delayed. Little did I know that's what really happened. Anyway, she asked you to come by the store when you got in."

Susan noticed that Kelly was avoiding her gaze. "Fine."

"I've gotta go." Susan said.

"Me too." Laurie gave Kelly a hug. "Thank you so much. Like I said, everyone will be over tomorrow around noon to unload. You won't have to lift a finger."

Susan extended her hand. "Thanks, Kelly. I enjoyed the trip."

"You're welcome. You going to be here tomorrow?"

"I think not. I have work to do."

"Good, I don't want you to help unload," Laurie enthused. "You've gone beyond and above, or above and beyond, whatever the hell that cliché is."

"You got time to run me home before you go to work?" Susan didn't look at Kelly.

"It's the least I can do. Thanks again, Kell. See you tomorrow." Susan followed Laurie to her car.

Chapter Thirty-two

Kelly watched Susan and Laurie leave and then went inside. She got a bottle of Guinness out of the refrigerator, opened it and downed half the bottle. Ordinarily she didn't drink beer because Amy hated the smell of it on her breath. She finished off the bottle and put it in the recycling bin. "Jasper, my love," she said to the cat that was now twined around her legs. "You got a house full of problems. Okay, my young feline friend, I've got to face the music."

Kelly drove to the store where the anti-LNG group was still meeting. Elizabeth's pickup truck was parked next to Maggie Beth and Terry's Subaru. At least she'd be surrounded by friends. *Just act normal*, she told herself. What the hell was normal anyway? Life had not been normal for the past two months. She thought about the night before and shivered. Never had any woman made such fervent and ardent love to her. Susan had been insatiable and, amazingly, so had she. Kelly looked down at her chest. She was

293

relieved to see the letter "A" had not appeared. She smiled to herself. One of her favorite novels while she was growing up was Nathaniel Hawthorn's *The Scarlet Letter*. She wondered if like Hester Prynne, once the others found out, she would have to wear the letter "A" on her chest. In Hester's day there was no excuse for adultery; today everyone had an excuse. *Thank God some mythical hand didn't just carve the letter "A" for you.* Kelly chuckled to herself. She wouldn't be alone.

She'd decided while driving back that she and Amy would have to talk, but not about Susan. Not yet, and not while Susan was within reach of Amy's anger. She paused outside the door to the shop. Did she love Amy? she asked herself for the one thousandth time that day. Did she really want to fix the relationship or was she hoping Amy would say no to a counselor, leaving Kelly guilt free to walk away? Hadn't that been part of the argument? Kelly wanted to see a counselor because she knew they couldn't fix their problem alone, and hadn't Amy rejected that?

"Hi, guys," Kelly said as she walked into the shop. The group looked as though it was in the process of breaking up.

"You're late," Amy said officiously.

"Car trouble."

"Cut her some slack," Elizabeth said to Amy. "You look beat," she added, embracing Kelly. "I'm glad you're back and you're safe. We were worried."

"Sorry." Kelly looked away. She felt as if Elizabeth's eyes had read her soul.

"We were worried." Maggie agreed as she also hugged Kelly.

"Where's Terry?"

"She woke up with some kind of bug this morning, so I made her stay home. We're almost finished here."

Kelly greeted some of the others who were folding chairs and picking up papers. She busied herself with helping them. She just couldn't look at Amy. She had heard the irritation in Amy's voice and knew she was in for an evening of explanation.

Amy said after everyone had left, "You didn't call."

"We left not talking. Frankly, I didn't know what to do."

"You could have called."

"Look, things went really crazy after we got there. I know Laurie told you. We didn't finish loading the truck until late, and by the time I got back to the motel I was exhausted. This morning I woke up and had a flat tire—it was just a major screw-up trip. I'm glad to be back and I'm glad it's behind me. All I want to do now is go home, take a shower and go to bed. Laurie said she rounded up a group of people to unload the truck tomorrow, so I'm not even going to think about that."

"Well, I'm glad to see you too," Amy said sarcastically.

"No anger tonight." Kelly felt defeated.

"I'm not angry. I was worried. No telephone call, no word from you. I didn't know if you'd fallen off the face of the earth."

"Well, I hadn't."

Amy started cleaning off the table. "I finally called Laurie. I felt embarrassed about that. She told me what Heather had done. Thank God Laurie was so preoccupied with the antics of her ex she didn't seem interested in why you hadn't called me."

"Look, I didn't want to get in a fight with you over the telephone. Frankly, I didn't know what to do and then when things went bad in Portland, I just figured I needed to get the job done and get back here."

"Well, I'm glad you're back." There was still a touch of irritation in Amy's voice, although it had softened.

"I'm glad I'm back too."

"I've been thinking a lot about what happened."

"And?"

"Just that I'm going to see the counselor with you, but not Thursday night. I figured you could go by yourself. Once this LNG stuff is over with I can focus on us, not that I think a counselor is what we need. I've said that before and I'll say it again. But I'll go, just not right now. I also think we need a long vacation. We've been wanting to go see the Grand Canyon. How about doing that in October or early November? Or how about a trip to

Jekyll Island, Georgia? Terry and Maggie said there's great golf there. It's a very slow time here at the store, so we could get away for a week—heck, two weeks."

"I'll have to check my vacation schedule." Hurt, Kelly turned toward the door. She wanted to escape there. She wanted to run and see Susan. She wanted someone to hug her and tell her that all of life's tangles would go away. She wanted someone to kiss it and make it better, like when she was a child and had cut her finger. She was relieved that Amy had put seeing a counselor on hold. Somehow it underscored their relationship—Amy had put them on hold.

"How about a hug?" Amy said as she put her arms around Kelly. "I did miss you. I'm not sure why we fought, but I'm sorry." She stepped back. "You smell like beer."

"I was thirsty when I got back. I drank just one," Kelly mumbled.

"Well, that will certainly take the romantic edge off tonight." Amy's words were laced with sarcasm. Before they had gotten together, Kelly had liked to have an occasional beer, but after they became involved Amy had made it clear that if Kelly drank beer, Amy would not make love to her.

But now Kelly felt relieved. She smiled to herself. How subconscious was that to drink the beer? She didn't want to make love to Amy tonight. She wanted to close her eyes and think about making love with Susan. She wanted to think about the way Susan sucked in her breath right before she had her first orgasm and the way Susan looked at her through sensual slumberous eyes afterward. Hell, she thought, she might even drink beer every night for the rest of the month, for the rest of the year, for the rest of her life!

Chapter Thirty-three

Déjà vu, Amy thought. It was Wednesday night and the select-men and townsfolk were again listening to the developers telling them about what a great opportunity they had facing them. It was the biggest town meeting ever. The school gym was packed. Television cameras were everywhere. Several reporters had asked her to talk with them after the meeting. The air was charged and people were energized.

Maggie Beth and Terry were seated behind her. Elizabeth was on one side of her, Kelly on the other. She squeezed Kelly's hand. Kelly smiled. She hadn't seen much of Kelly since the trip. Kelly said they were doing some kind of hospital licensing and she spent a lot of hours there. Her anti-LNG group had been busy putting the finishing touches on the petition that she now had clutched in her hand. They had collected more than four hundred signatures and Amy was pleased.

"So what do you think they'll offer?" Maggie whispered in her ear.

She and Maggie Beth had been playing a guessing game up until the meeting. Maggie Beth figured the developers would offer what the developers had offered in southern Maine, eight million dollars. That would mean islanders wouldn't have to pay property taxes for the next sixty years, a tempting offer. Amy's was the lone voice in the group who said she thought they would offer more. The rest had pooh-poohed her. "Lots more than the eight million dollars you expect," she whispered back.

"Could I have your attention?" The project manager had stepped to the front of the group. Amy looked around. The project manager and technical advisor were there; the public relations woman was not.

"Your friend's not here," she whispered to Kelly.

"No." Kelly frowned and Amy wondered if she was feeling okay. Kelly had been preoccupied after her trip to Portland.

"Could I have your attention?" He waited until everyone stopped talking. The selectmen were seated at the front table. "I want to introduce myself, although many of you know me. I'm Dean Creager, the project manager. This is Bill Leighton, our technical advisor. Susan Iogen, who ably carried us through several presentations, is a little under the weather tonight and could not join us . . ." He paused. "Tonight, we're going to discuss with you some of the things that we've discussed with the selectmen behind closed doors. As you know, Maine's Right to Know Law allows—"

"Excuse me." Amy stood up.

"Yes?"

"I have something to present to the selectmen."

"Could it wait until I'm through?" he asked.

"No, this is far more important than the bribe you're going to offer in the hopes this community will sell its soul to you." Several of Amy's supporters applauded.

"You are?"

"Amy Page."

"Well, Amy Page," he said, "why don't you present your petition."

Amy did not react. The developers were well aware her group had been circulating a petition and she knew that they had expected it tonight. "On behalf of the citizens of this town," she said as she approached the chairman. "I'm presenting this petition to you, the selectmen of Bleu Island. We ask that you put the question of whether an LNG terminal should be sited on this island before voters." She handed the numerous pages to the chairman. He nodded as he accepted it.

"Thank you," Dean said. "Now, if I could continue. We actually welcome this petition," he said to the group. "We feel that this is too big of a decision for a group of five men and women to decide. Anyway, getting back to my opening statement . . ." He looked pointedly at Amy. "We have, under the provisions of the law, met with your selectmen on several occasions to hammer out a deal. Tonight, I want to announce as a result of some very hard bargaining on the part of your selectmen we are prepared to offer you fifteen million dollars a year"—there was a collective gasp from the group—"adjusted for inflation for the life of the project."

Amy looked at Dean. A fox, she decided, who'd found the key to the chicken coop. Her anger was rising. She had anticipated ten million dollars, not half as much more.

"As a result," he continued, "the payment—and of course it's up to the voters how they want to allocate it—could mean that not only would the property taxes be paid in full for residents on the island, but also every single household would be paid a yearly stipend. You do the math and see that it will be a hefty sum for every man, woman, and child."

Amy couldn't bear to listen to the rest of the discussion. Her group would have to come up with yet another strategy. A few thousand dollars for every person who lived year-around on the island was a lot of money. There were as many as five and six children in some families. That would be a tidy additional income for some, vacation trips for others. She glanced back at Maggie. "Let's meet after the meeting, get as many of the group together as possible," she whispered.

Maggie nodded in agreement.

"Any questions?" Dean asked.

"I have one?" Amy turned and saw that Jim Bows, her friend who operated the schooner ship, had raised his hand. "What happens if you go belly up? We still guaranteed that money?"

"Absolutely. Your selectmen have really negotiated in your best interest—"

"Not as far as I'm concerned," someone yelled from the back of the room.

"In any case," Dean continued, "we've hammered out a one-hundred-and-eighty page contract with your selectmen, which, I might add, they have not signed. Anyway, they have required we post a bond up front to cover the cost of the removal of the tanks when the project is over. What that means is that we remove everything that the town doesn't want and restore the area. So if, let's say, natural gas goes bust, which it won't, we will see to it that there is enough money in a trust account that can't be touched by anyone, to remove whatever is necessary. Your selectmen have suggested that maybe they would like to keep the pier. It could be used for fishing and pleasure boats. In addition," he went on, "the selectmen also said they want us to set up a second trust fund for the total amount we've agreed to pay for all property taxes as well as dividend checks for the next sixty years. They've negotiated a hard bargain, but we've agreed to it."

"And how much will you be getting out of this? How many billions of dollars will you get from this?" Terry asked.

"Don't know," he said matter-of-factly.

"Well, you're going to make a bundle off of this, otherwise you wouldn't be doing it. This isn't a charity deal," Elizabeth added.

"No, but at this point it's hard to talk about what the profits might be."

"Not so hard if you wanted to," Amy shot back.

"Any other questions? Good. Well, ladies and gentlemen, it's up to your selectmen to decide when they want to schedule the vote. Now, I'm not speaking for them—" Amy noticed that Dean had turned to look at the chairman. *I bet, she thought*—"but, I think they are going to need some time to digest the petition. Probably refer it to the town's attorney and then decide on some kind of vote. Again, we thank you. We would welcome this vote. We've spent the last few months educating and informing the community and we're not going to stop now. For the next few weeks we're going to set up additional information meetings, and whether there's one person there or one hundred we're going to answer all questions. So if there's nothing else, I thank you."

"Meeting, my shop," Amy said to Elizabeth. "Get ahold of the rest."

Chapter Thirty-four

"What do you mean you don't want to meet with us," Amy said, clearly disappointed.

Kelly steeled herself. "Amy, I'm tired. I had a hell of a day at work and I just want to go home. You're not going to decide anything tonight." They were standing in the parking lot next to Amy's car. Amy, Elizabeth, Maggie Beth and Terry had mustered their supporters and agreed to meet at Amy's shop. Kelly knew that the fifteen million dollars had thrown Amy.

"How are you going to get home? You didn't bring your car."

"Barb's over there. She can give me a ride."

"Barb?"

"One of the nurses at the hospital."

"Go," Amy said dismissively. "I've got important things to talk about. I'll see you at the house."

Kelly turned, relieved. She saw Barb getting into her car and ran over. "Can I catch a ride with you?"

"Hop in."

"Thanks Barb," Kelly said as she opened the door. Five minutes later, they were in Kelly's driveway. "I appreciate this."

"Anytime, Kelly," Barb said. "See you at the hospital."

"Thanks." Kelly watched as Barb drove off. She walked to her car. She hadn't seen Susan since they had parted at the gravel pit. She'd tried to call her several times. Most of the time she ended up cursing caller identification. She knew that Susan could tell she was calling and just refused to answer. A couple of times she thought about going over to Susan's but each time stopped herself. She could not stop thinking about her. She'd sidestepped making love with Amy by saying she was exhausted, and Amy had been so preoccupied with the LNG project that she left early and came home late. By the time Amy got home, Kelly always made sure she was in bed pretending she was asleep. They'd had a few tiffs because Kelly hadn't been to any of the anti-LNG meetings, but even those hadn't amounted to much. Now, tonight, she was so disappointed when Susan hadn't been present.

I've got to see her tonight. It wasn't like Susan to miss a meeting. On her way to the Grange estate, Kelly wondered what she was going to say. She hadn't either fixed or gotten out of her relationship with Amy. Hell, she hadn't done a thing except to avoid confrontation. And she hadn't stopped thinking about Susan. *You're in love with her, Kelly Burns. You're desperately in love with her and at the same time a coward.* She didn't want to confront Amy. Why, why, why did she use Amy as an excuse that morning? Telling Susan that she wanted to fix the relationship. She couldn't fix it. It'd been broken for a long time, otherwise Susan would never have gotten into her heart. A counselor. Amy was right, she needed the counselor. Hell, she needed a shrink. She was the one with the problem. She was the one who needed her mind fixed.

She turned into Susan's driveway and frowned. Susan's car wasn't there, but Laurie's was. She stopped. The outside light flipped on and Laurie appeared at the door. *You can't leave now,* Kelly told herself. *Laurie's seen you.*

303

"Hey, pal," Kelly called through her window.

"Kelly, hi. What are you doing here?"

"Can't I pay a visit?"

"Come in, come in," Laurie said as she opened Kelly's door. "Actually, I thought it might be Susan. She's left."

"What do you mean, left?" Kelly tried to keep her tone neutral.

"Just that. You weren't around Monday when we unloaded. She helped and everything seemed fine. We came back here Monday night, had a quick dinner. Tuesday morning her car was gone. I thought she was at a meeting with the developers, something that happens regularly. I got concerned when she didn't come home Tuesday night. This morning I called the developers—boy, are they a hard nut to crack. At first they wouldn't say a thing. I told them I was a friend of hers from Boston trying to get ahold of her. They told me to look in Andover. They said she had had some kind of family emergency and had to go home. They didn't sound happy," Laurie was clearly anxious. Her speech sounded like a rapid-fire automatic weapon. "Come in, come in. How about a glass of wine. I thought you were at the meeting tonight. I should have gone. What happened?"

"Yes, I'd like a glass of wine. Yes, I was at the meeting and no, you weren't there. They offered the town fifteen million dollars a year, a lot of money. It could have an impact."

"Wow, I didn't think they'd offer that much. They really want to put one here," Amy said as she took two glasses out of the cupboard. "I gotta tell you honestly, I haven't been able to focus on this LNG stuff." She reached inside of her refrigerator and pulled out an open bottle of wine, poured two glasses and handed one to Kelly. "I've been worried about Susan. Did anything happen while you two were in Portland?"

"What do you mean?" Kelly could barely swallow her wine.

"I don't know. I think that thing with Heather upset her more than she let on. She was really quiet after she got back here. I knocked on her door several times and even though she was here, she didn't answer. I could kick Heather."

"Don't blame Heather. That was unpleasant but not earth-shattering. Could be she just needed to get away."

"Well, I thought that too. I feel like an absolute stalker. God, I hope there's nothing seriously wrong. What if she's sick?" There was misery in her friend's voice.

How could she tell Laurie the truth? How could she tell her that Susan wasn't sick but leaving behind a jerk who couldn't make up her mind about her relationship? She and Susan had had the most mind-blowing lovemaking in the world and she had turned her back on her. How could she tell Laurie that she was a heel and a jerk who deserved to lose Susan? "I'm sure if she was sick, they would've told you," Kelly said, sipping her wine.

"I guess." Laurie clearly wasn't convinced. "I love her, Kell. I love her and I'm in love with her and we haven't so much as held hands. Isn't that the most ridiculous thing you've heard in your life?"

"Not really." Kelly felt the sadness she'd held at bay all week engulf her. She was in love with the same woman. "Laurie, I—"

"I know you care about her," Laurie interjected. "She said you'd become real friends on the trip."

Kelly remained silent.

"I've called Information. No Susan Iogen is listed. Her business number is listed, but there's no answer there. I've called it every day. Finally, I reached Elizabeth just before the meeting and she had her home number. I didn't tell her why I needed it. God love Elizabeth, I didn't even ask her how she knew."

Kelly set her half-empty glass down. She felt if she swallowed again she'd choke. She wanted to ask Laurie for Susan's number, but what reason would she give? She wanted to tell her she loved Susan, yet she was too much of a coward. She was scared because Susan was gone, yet afraid of finding her. What would she tell her if she did find her? she thought. She not only hadn't told Amy, she was afraid to tell her. Afraid of the fight. She was a cad, a first-rate coward. "I gotta go."

"You haven't finished your wine."

"I have stuff to do."

"Okay. Amy at home?"

"No, they had an impromptu meeting tonight. The developers offered the town all that money, I think it caught everyone off guard."

"That's a lot of money."

"Agreed. Could convince people to vote for it."

"No question. Wow, I suspected there'd be some kind of offer, but not anything like that. I'll tell you, Susan is a consummate professional. She never hinted that they'd offer that kind of money." Laurie paused. "I wish I didn't have another four-day shift coming up. I'd drive to Andover, camp out on her doorstep. No chance I could switch with one of the other nurses?"

"You know better than that. If you want to do that you get one of the nurses to agree. Don't look to me to ask a nurse to work for you. I just won't do it." Kelly could feel the frustration growing inside her. She wanted to find Susan. Crush her in her in arms and tell her she loved her. Tell her she would fix everything.

Laurie was silent as they walked to Kelly's car. "I've asked. I couldn't find one to switch at the last minute." She ran both hands through her hair. "I didn't think that her leaving would have this kind of impact on me," she said quietly. "Well, I'm going to keep calling. I have to find her. If she isn't back by the time my four-day shift is over, I'm heading to Andover to find that woman."

Kelly nodded, afraid to speak. "I'll see you tomorrow at the hospital."

"Yeah, I'll be there. Unhappy, but I'll be there," Laurie said as she closed Kelly's car door for her. "I love her, Kelly."

Chapter Thirty-five

Susan ignored the ringing telephone. She could see it was Laurie calling her yet again. What if it was Kelly calling? Would she answer then? This was so uncharacteristic of her not to answer the telephone.

After they had returned from Portland, Laurie had not left her alone. All she wanted was to be alone to think about Kelly and the relationship that was not going to go anywhere. What a fool she had been to fall in love with someone who was not emotionally available. She wanted to think about what an ass she was for making love with a woman who was already making love with a woman.

On Monday, Laurie had insisted Susan go with her to Kelly's house to unload the furniture even though once there she wouldn't let Susan help. She went because she hoped to see Kelly. She knew that they wouldn't be able to talk, but she just wanted to be around her. When she got there, Elizabeth said Kelly and Amy had gone off on an impromptu picnic together. Something Amy had come up with. Elizabeth was evidently overjoyed for her friends, glad the two had gotten away for some alone time.

Susan could still feel the blinding jealousy she had felt that day when Elizabeth had told her about the picnic. She wondered if they had gone to that special spot where Kelly had taken her. She could focus on nothing else for the next two days. All day Monday, Laurie had been solicitous and entertaining. But she didn't feel like being entertained. She sat by the telephone Monday night and Tuesday. When Kelly didn't call, she phoned the developers and told them there was an emergency. She had to make a quick trip to Andover. They were not happy with her because she was going to miss the public meeting Wednesday night. She wondered if she'd have a client after being so irresponsible with the LNG people. Now, sitting in her townhouse in Andover a week later, she wished she'd never left.

The telephone rang again and she looked at the caller ID. It was Laurie. She ignored it and picked up her overnight bag. She had to go back. She had to face Kelly and she had to face the life she knew the two of them would never have together.

Seven hours later Susan pulled into the driveway, relieved to see Laurie's car wasn't there. She carried her suitcase inside. She'd called the developers from Andover and told them she was on her way back. They had set up a meeting for seven o'clock the next morning. She could tell from the sound of Dean's voice that he had felt jazzed after the public meeting. Things had gone well. She was relieved. There was no mention that she was out of a job.

Now, all she had to do was unpack and catch a bite to eat and go to bed. She pushed the red button on her answering machine. The first few messages had to do with LNG.

"Susan, hi, it's Kelly. Give me a call when you get in," the third message told her.

Susan looked at the time, it was a little after five o'clock. Not likely, she thought. Kelly hadn't said where to call her. She picked up the telephone. *No backbone, Susan Iogen.* She looked up the telephone number for the hospital.

"Hi, is Kelly Burns there?"

"She just left," the voice on the other end answered.

"Thanks." Susan hung up. Disappointment overwhelmed her. *Well, you're batting zero for zero,* she said to herself. She wasn't going to call her at home. What if Amy answered? What would she say? *Hi, this is Susan Iogen, I just had one of the most torrid lovemaking nights with your partner. We made passionate love until three o'clock in the morning. Is she there?*

Susan picked up the telephone on the first ring.

"You're there."

Susan could hear the relief in Kelly's voice. "Where are you?"

"Driving. I want to talk to you."

"Where?"

"I don't know. How about the gravel pit?" There was desperation in Kelly's voice.

How could she tell her she hated the gravel pit? "All right," Susan felt like a teenager again sneaking off to the backwoods behind her parents' house to kiss Bobby Olsen. "I'll meet you there in a few minutes." *Stay strong,* she told herself. *Tell her it's over. Tell her that it was a mistake. We were two women who for a brief six hours needed each other. I'm going to tell her I'm crazy and have been going crazy since Monday.*

Kelly was leaning against her car when Susan drove up. "I'm so glad you came." She opened the car door for her. "I . . ." Kelly grabbed her and kissed her.

Susan melted in her arms. She kissed Kelly passionately. All her Herculean resolve to stay strong and to ignore any physical contact just melted away the moment she saw her.

"I love you, Susan," Kelly said against her neck. "I want you and I love you. This is mindless and insane, but you're all I've been able to think about. I was so scared when I'd heard you'd left. I wanted to call you, but I was afraid. I called the cottage so many times, my finger is blue from punching the numbers."

Susan rested her head against Kelly's shoulder. "Kelly, this is crazy. You haven't done a thing about Amy, have you?"

Kelly looked guiltily at the ground. "No, I haven't. I know you won't believe this, but there hasn't been time. Amy is like a hostage to this LNG stuff. She can think of nothing else but LNG and winning. She's meeting right now with her group. They're pushing for a vote by mid October. I know I shouldn't be telling you this."

"Then don't," Susan said gently. "We each have our own strategy. Before, I would have loved to have had a mole in the group, but now it doesn't matter. All I care about is that the process has worked."

"Process?"

"Getting the information out, letting people make an informed decision, but that's not what we're here to talk about, is it."

"No."

"What are we here to talk about?"

"I don't know. That I love you, want you in my life. Beg you not to leave again. Beg you to give me time to fix this." Kelly paused. "I've never felt such gripping fear as when I'd heard you'd left." Kelly held her at arm's length. "Why did you leave?"

Now it was her turn to look guiltily at the ground. "Jealousy."

"Because I was with Amy? Nothing has happened, Susan, I can promise you that."

"That and the fact that the two of you went off on a picnic Monday. I just—" Susan stopped. She felt foolish talking about it.

"Picnic? We didn't go off on a picnic. Who told you that?"

"Elizabeth."

"Amy must have told Elizabeth we were going on a picnic. When she asked me to go, I told her I wasn't in the mood. So we caught the ferry to the mainland and went shopping, food shopping. Amy insisted I go with her. I didn't feel like hanging around while everyone unloaded the truck, so I went."

"Shopping." Susan laughed. "Well, that's a far cry from a picnic."

"I wouldn't have gone on a picnic. All I've wanted to think about was you. So we went shopping, but I had my own jealousy."

"Why?"

"The only reason Laurie didn't go looking for you is she's working a four-day shift. She told me that when that ended she was determined to go to Andover and find you. She was going to camp out on your office steps. I know she's in love with you."

"I'm going to have to deal with that." Susan stepped back. "I told you before I don't feel the same way about her." She felt miserable. "Boy, how complicated life has become." She shivered. The September night was chilly.

"Come sit in my car," Kelly said. "We've got to talk." She opened the door. "I've made some decisions," she said after they were settled. "Now, I haven't told Amy, but I will. I'm just waiting for this LNG stuff to end."

Susan looked at her expectantly. "That could take six months."

"I'm not willing to wait months, but I'm asking you to give me a couple of weeks, just until this vote is over. Right now all that anyone is doing around here is eating, drinking and living LNG. I don't want to tell Amy that I'm leaving."

"You're leaving?"

"Absolutely. I can't work at a relationship where my heart isn't anymore."

Susan reached out and touched Kelly's cheek. "I can't do this."

"What do you mean?" Kelly was clearly alarmed.

"I told you that I've never wrecked someone's home before, and I'm not going to do it now."

"You're not wrecking my home. My home was a train wreck before you came into it. Amy and I have been on two separate tracks for years. I've proposed counseling many times and she's found an excuse not to do it. Most of the time she's said we could work it out ourselves. We can't. This time Amy said she would do it, but I know she doesn't want to. This time the excuse is LNG. What I've realized over the past few days is if I were important to her, she would do both. She'd battle against LNG, but she'd battle to keep us together, not just pay lip service to the idea of a counselor. That just ain't happening and now, it's too late. I've fallen in love with you." Kelly kissed the tips of Susan's fingers. Susan could

311

feel a tingle inside. "I thought I had lost you. I didn't think I would ever see you again. I wanted to call you, but I was afraid. I wanted to go to Andover and find you but was afraid you would slam the door in my face. I don't know what happened, but somehow you've found your way into my heart and I love you. I want you in my life."

"God, I love you so much, Kelly. I was afraid of losing you. I left because I was a coward. I just didn't want to think about you with Amy. I knew that I couldn't go back to what it was like before. Our lives collided and I fell desperately in love with you." She pulled Kelly to her and kissed her. Her tongue explored Kelly's mouth. "I want you in my life," she whispered against Kelly's lips.

"Me too," Kelly said. "I want to make love to you. I want to feel you against me. I want to hold you all night and all day." She paused. "I love the way you look in my arms when I make love to you," she said tenderly.

Susan put her hand on Kelly's chest and gently pushed her away. "I want all the same things, but not in a gravel pit."

Kelly looked out the window, her face flushed. "You're right." She laughed. "It does seem a bit teenage desperate."

"Just a bit." Susan laughed. "I'm half expecting a tap on the window, the flashlight and the cop asking what we're doing. Now, that would cause quite a flap on this island. Tongues wouldn't just wag, they'd shake in anticipation of telling the story."

"Can I see you again?"

"How?"

"I don't know. What about this weekend? You could go over to the mainland, shopping, whatever."

"I'll try, although Dean and Bill sounded so relieved that I was back, they might not let me out of their sight. Any idea when the vote will be?"

"Someone said something about mid-October, that's what—" Kelly stopped. "Four or five weeks from now."

Susan nodded, thinking.

"Everyone seems in an all-fired hurry to get this over with."

"People are tired of it, people on both sides," Susan said.

"Probably."

"What about Amy?"

"I've got to tell her."

"You're going to tell her about us." It was a statement, not a question.

"Yes. You know. I never thought about this before, but Amy and I were slowly coming apart before you ever came into my life. Please believe that, Susan, because it's true. I was just drifting along thinking that everything was going to be all right. I accepted the fact that when things were good between us, they were always going to be good. Then that other Amy would come out and I would look at her and wonder why I ever fell in love with her. It doesn't feel right talking about Amy, but know that we had huge, huge problems before you came into my life."

"I've seen it."

"You have?"

"The few times we all were together, there was a tension between you. It was just below the surface. You'd say something and she'd either correct you or criticize you. I know—and this is before I knew I had feelings for you—I felt embarrassed for you."

"Funny, it must have been more obvious than I've realized. I always figured she did a pretty good job of hiding it from our friends."

"Not that good a job." Susan looked at her watch. "I've got an early-morning meeting. Kelly, I'm not going to meet you out here in the gravel pit again. I don't care how much I want to."

"This weekend, go to the mainland, we can have dinner there."

"Let me see how Dean and Bill have scheduled the weekend."

"I'll call you, I promise." Kelly leaned over and kissed her again. "I want you in my life and hang the consequences."

"Let's hope we don't have to hang them too high," Susan said as she kissed Kelly.

❧

313

The rest of the week seemed to go at turbo-jet speed. Dean and Bill insisted they meet every day. They also had meetings with the island selectmen and town manager along with the Port Bleu selectmen and town manager. The island selectmen finally announced the election would be October 15. They agreed to meet again on Saturday, but Sunday was still a question mark. The developers hadn't made a decision about Sunday so Susan didn't know if she had to work or not. They kept saying it depended on how well the week went.

On Thursday morning, Susan pulled up in front of the town office. She squared her shoulders before going inside. She knew Elizabeth was there. She had called her earlier to ask for a copy of the petition.

During the conversation, Elizabeth had been professional and Susan hoped she'd sounded professional too and not unhappy. There were three people she'd met on the island that she wanted to keep in her life, Laurie, Kelly and Elizabeth. Now she felt as if they all were wobbling on the edge of a cliff—Laurie because she didn't love her, Kelly because of their relationship and Elizabeth because Susan sensed she was sensitive enough to pick up changes in her friends.

Susan opened the door.

"I'm so glad to see you," Elizabeth gushed. She grabbed Susan and gave her the biggest hug her tiny little frame could muster. Susan smiled as she hugged her back. "I was worried. You weren't at the meeting last week and those two tight-lipped men you work for wouldn't say a word. Well, I grilled them." Elizabeth had her hands on her hips.

"I had an emergency at home. Got back Monday." She looked away. She felt guilty for lying to her new friend.

"Well, you're back now and I'm glad. And no more of that," Elizabeth ordered.

"No more of?"

"You leave, you best tell me. We've only known each other a few months, but you're a part of my life now. So I want telephone numbers." Elizabeth was serious.

She reached into her briefcase and pulled out her business card.

"Here," she said as she turned it over and wrote on the back. "Here's my home telephone number, my cell phone number, my home address and my personal e-mail address," she said as she handed the card to Elizabeth.

"Good." Elizabeth tucked the card in her pocket. "You okay?"

"I am."

"You back to stay?"

"Well, until the vote. After that I really don't know. My contract with the developers gets us to the vote. After that who knows."

"Well, it goes down in defeat, I know you won't be back. It passes, I expect they'll hire you."

"I'm not even thinking about that. Right now I'm just focused on getting us to the vote. October fifteen is not that far away."

"No, it isn't." Elizabeth paused. "I made a copy of the petition." She handed her a brown envelope.

"Thank you."

"I want to invite you to the house for Sunday dinner."

Susan sucked in her breath. "I can't. I think the developers plan to meet all weekend. How about Monday or Tuesday? Lunch or dinner? Your choice."

"Probably will have to be lunch. Amy's got us scheduled every night with meetings for the next few weeks. She did give me Sunday afternoon off, although the group is meeting. I think she thinks she might wear me down. I'm not used to doing this much meeting. I'll be glad when it's over."

"Me too. I'm sorry, Elizabeth, I wish we could have dinner Sunday, but I've just got to see what the developers want."

"I know you're busy."

Susan sensed that Elizabeth wanted to say something else. "Look, I've got to go," Susan looked at her watch.

Elizabeth took her hand. "I know it's hard being alone here. Just know this"—she touched Susan's cheek—"you have a friend here, and if you need someone to talk to, I'm here for you and no one has to know. I know I probably come off as this yakky silly old woman, but I'm there for my friends."

Susan hugged her. "First off, you're not a yakky silly old woman. You're a warm and kind dear friend whom I've grown to love. Second, I know that if I needed to talk with anyone, it would be you. Believe that, Elizabeth." Susan stepped back and looked her in the eyes.

"I felt that, but I just wanted to make sure we understood each other."

"We do."

"Good. Let's plan lunch on Tuesday."

"You're on—" Susan stopped when the telephone rang.

"Town office." Elizabeth said into the receiver. "Sure, I can get that for you. Hang on just a second." She put her hand over the telephone. "Noon? You want to meet here, or you want me to come to your office?"

"I'll pick you up here at noon."

"Sounds good," Elizabeth said as she turned back to the telephone.

Susan tucked the envelope Elizabeth had given her in her briefcase and left the town office. She thought about her conversation with Elizabeth. Somehow, Elizabeth had sensed something was bothering her. Susan got in her car and leaned her head against the steering wheel. Her life felt so out of control. Like the time she couldn't master the clarinet. Gosh, she hadn't thought about that in years. *How funny our brains are.* She chuckled to herself. Her elementary school had started a band and she'd been late getting to the meeting. The only instrument left was the clarinet. She had wanted to play the drums but settled on the clarinet because all of her friends were part of the new band. She remembered the day she'd first picked up the clarinet. Her music teacher gave her a personal lesson and sent her home to practice "Mary Had a Little Lamb." When she got home, she propped her music book on her dresser and started to play. All that came out of the end of the clarinet were shrieks and screeches. Her mother had yelled at her to stop playing.

That's what her life felt like right now. Instead of the harmony that had been a constant in her life, she had only discord and sour notes like that clarinet. She thought about Kelly. That disharmony was because she felt so guilty about getting involved with Kelly. *She's in a relationship*, she reminded herself for the one thousandth time. After they'd met at the gravel pit, Kelly had called her often from work. Instead of making her feel better, the calls just added to her resolve that although she loved Kelly desperately, she refused to be the other woman. She didn't want Kelly to choose between her and Amy. She had to tell her that again. Make her hear her words. That would only lead to problems years from now when Kelly might look back and wish she'd never been forced to make that choice.

Outside the town office, she started up the car. She was due back at her office for a meeting with Dean and Bill. They wanted a look at the petition. She turned onto Main Street. If the developers didn't agree to a break over the weekend, she'd call Kelly at work and insist Kelly figure out her life first. She had to tell Kelly that it didn't matter if she was going to end her relationship with Amy or not. She was not going to sneak around, not anymore. *Stay strong*, she told herself. *Stay strong.* She sighed. She loved her. She wanted her. But right now she couldn't have her. She may never have her. What if Amy decided to fight for her once she found out? Amy may not be the woman Kelly wanted right now, but Amy was in her life and Amy had been her life. Susan thought about Amy. If she were her, she would do everything to save their relationship even if it meant seeing ten counselors. But then, she wasn't Amy. "No, I'm not," she said aloud. She was swimming against a mighty current—the history of their relationship—and she didn't want to drown. Right now she had to tuck Kelly away in her mind. Kelly had problems to solve and they weren't hers. Bury it away. Kelly had to be hermetically sealed in her mind. Otherwise she was going to make stupid emotional decisions she'd regret.

She parked outside her office. Dean and Bill were already there. She inhaled deeply. She loved Kelly. She wanted her in her life, but she had to do what was right first, she thought. Kelly had to decide

317

what she wanted to do with the old before embracing the new. "And, my dear," she said glancing in the rearview mirror, "you are definitely the new." If a friend came to her with this ridiculous problem, she'd give her the same advice. Now, she almost wished the problem belonged to someone else and not to her. It would be so much easier. She had to tell Kelly and she had to tell her immediately.

"Susan, hi." Laurie suddenly was giving her a hug.

Susan felt disoriented. "Laurie . . ." She hugged her back. "I'm sorry, I was deep in thought."

"I noticed. I waved to you from across the street and you didn't even see me. I was just going to the store. Join me. Better yet, hang the store and let's have coffee."

"I can't. Dean and Bill are waiting for me." She nodded toward the office.

"Bummer. Oh, well, I'll see you Saturday night."

"Saturday?"

"Remember, we had a date."

"Sorry." Susan tried to cover up her confusion. "I've been really immersed in all this stuff since I've been back."

"I know. I've tried to catch you at the cottage. I called you a couple of times, didn't leave a message. You're never there. Of course, I was working the night shift so when you were sleeping I was working . . ." Laurie laughed. "You know what I mean. I thought we'd go over to the mainland and have dinner. Celebrate getting my furniture back."

"How about we stay here?"

"Good. I tell ya what, I'll cook dinner at my house. How does that sound?"

"Good. I'll bring a bottle of wine."

"You don't have to." Laurie gently touched her arm. "Just seeing you is all the spirits I need."

Susan smiled. "That's very nice of you." Inwardly she groaned. Why couldn't she fall in love with Laurie? Instead she fell in love with someone she couldn't have. *You're not exactly the sharpest tool in the shed*, she said to herself. "What time?"

"Whatever, just come over when you're ready. I got lots to tell you." Laurie grew serious. "Stuff I want to talk to you about. Anyway, it'll wait. See you then."

"'Bye." Susan watched as Laurie walked back across the street. How could she have forgotten their dinner date? Obviously her brain had disengaged and she wasn't thinking. She opened the door to the office. She'd have to tell her tomorrow night. No doubt Laurie wanted to discuss moving their relationship to yet another level. She'd have to tell her it wasn't going to happen. Susan hesitated in the entryway to the office. She couldn't tell her she was in love with her best friend. Or that they'd made spectacular love together. She couldn't tell her that. Susan sighed. For the next few weeks her job was to throw herself into work. She'd work until she dropped, and no matter what happened, she'd leave afterward. Leave Bleu Island and all its complications behind. The heavy mantle of melancholy that had drowned her all week was back. She felt disoriented as she walked into the office. *Put on a smile*, she told the business side of her brain. Bill was on the telephone. Dean was looking at some papers at the back of the room. "Hi, guys."

They spent the rest of the day working on strategy and agreed to run a second set of focus groups with some of the same people. Susan argued that they would probably not have many in attendance because a lot of people had already made up their minds. The two men were adamant and Susan finally conceded that Dean was right. A second set of focus groups might be just what was needed to convince the last of the fence-sitters. Bill reminded her about an engineer he'd been able to get ahold of. Susan knew he was the best in the business when it came to explaining how LNG worked. They'd hoped to include him in their first round of discussions with the first focus groups, but he already had a commitment. He had said he would be available in late September or October if they still needed him to talk to groups. It fit nicely with their plans. She could tell Dean and Bill were enthusiastic. The engineer agreed to spend as much time on Bleu Island as was needed to make their case. They wanted him because he was personable and groups seemed to adore him. Dean felt that his presence would get some new people to the table to learn. Susan said she would get some stories in the local newspapers announcing his visit.

Susan got up early on Saturday morning and went for a run. She then met Dean and Bill at nine and showed them two of the press releases she had written the night before about the engineer. They were in high spirits and after working a half a day they decided to take the rest of Saturday and all of Sunday off.

Now back home she picked up a book and put it down. She couldn't concentrate.

She needed to tell Kelly she had Sunday off. They hadn't talked since yesterday. Kelly had called her from the hospital before she'd gone home. Susan remembered how excited she was talking to Kelly and how disappointed Kelly had sounded when she told her she might have to work the whole weekend. She also couldn't tell her on the telephone that she never wanted to see her again, even though the woman she loved was going home to another woman. She didn't want to think about that.

She called the hospital, but Kelly wasn't in.

She turned on the television set. Tiger Woods was getting ready to swing. She watched for a minute and then turned the sound down. At least there would be someone else in the room besides her, she thought. What excuse could she use to call her at home? She returned to the problem that had been vexing her. *Hi, Amy.* She could just imagine the conversation. *Is Kelly there? I just want to tell her I have Sunday off and I'd love to meet her at some hideaway place on the mainland. I didn't think you'd mind.* Susan shook her head. Amy could be at an LNG meeting, but then again maybe not. She didn't want to risk it. She could call and hang up if Amy answered.

This is stupid. When the telephone rang minutes later, she snatched it up. It was Laurie.

"Susan, hi. I'm looking forward to dinner."

"Me to."

"How about coming over earlier? Say around three?"

"I can't. I'm working on a presentation here." Susan bit her bottom lip. Hell, she definitely was going to burn in hell for all the lying she'd been doing lately. "But I am chilling a bottle of wine."

"That's great. I know you're going to love dinner."

"I know it too. So I'll see you around five."

"Looking forward to it."

Susan hung up and continued to pace. After a half-hour, she picked up the telephone and dialed Kelly's cell phone number.

"Hi. Can you talk?"

"I can. I'm on my way to the hospital. Do you still want to get together on Sunday?"

"I do." Susan felt downright shy. How silly, she thought. "What time?"

"Four o'clock? There's this neat little restaurant on the mainland." Kelly gave her directions.

"I have some shopping to do on the mainland. I'll take the earlier ferry and meet you at the restaurant at four."

"Susan, I love you."

She swallowed. "I love you."

"See you at four."

" 'Bye." Susan hung up. Well, that was good, she thought. She sure told her off. Put her in her place. Made sure she knew she'd never see her again. She sure told her to repair her life, otherwise it was going to break her own. Susan picked up a pen and threw it across the room. She sighed, then went and picked it up. She felt horrid. New love was supposed to be young and fragile, she said to herself, this was duplicitous and dishonest. She put the pen next to her computer and picked up the comments Dean and Bill had given her about the engineer. Impressive, she thought as she added the information to the fact sheet she had started. They agreed she would be the one to introduce him.

Susan had the bottle of wine tucked under her arm as she knocked on Laurie's door just after five.

321

"I'm so glad you're here," Laurie said as she embraced her.

"Me too." Susan hugged her back. She handed her the bottle of wine. Laurie had on a forest-green blouse. Susan liked the color on her. Her jeans were dry-cleaner starched. "This is in celebration of your emancipation or whatever you want to call it. I hope you like Australian wine."

"Australian, French, Californian, New York. I like it all. And this is a celebration," Laurie gushed. "I've been sprung loose. Not just from Heather," she added hastily. "Truth be told, Heather and I should have ended it months after we started, not years. It didn't work from the beginning. Does that make sense? I know this sounds self-serving, but I'm celebrating my move here. At first I thought I just wanted to get away from Portland and big-city hospital nursing. I haven't been here long, but Kelly was right, people embrace you in a small community. I've met some of the most wonderful people. But I've missed seeing you. I worked those four days last weekend and they seemed like an eternity. I'm glad we could have dinner tonight."

Susan smiled to herself. Laurie sounded like the rat-a-tat-tat of a sewing machine. "Me too."

"Have you thought about staying? After the vote I mean?" Laurie handed her a glass of wine.

"To your freedom." Susan lifted her glass and clinked Laurie's. "I don't have the connection here you do."

"You could."

"It's different. I'm like the . . ." Susan shrugged. "I can't think of what kind of military unit does it, but I'm like the military unit that's sent in to do a quick mission and then I'm out again, and other people come in to do the mopping up."

"I'm not sure. I used to watch a lot of John Wayne, but I don't think it's the Green Berets. Oh, I know, a SWAT team."

"Anyway, whatever they're called. That's what I'm paid to do. So I never thought about staying here."

"Well, I hope I can change your mind." Laurie's smile was faint. "Don't say anything." She held up her hand. "First we eat. Here . . ."

She handed her the bottle of wine. "Please be seated. The one nice thing about a one-room house, you don't have far to go for anything. But I love the kitchen. Whoever designed it did it with an eye to efficiency. Anyway, we are going to have a very special meal. To celebrate my freedom and your success with LNG—" She stopped. "And other things."

Susan set the wine bottle on the table. It was the "other things" that worried her. It was the "other things" she knew she would have to talk to Laurie about. Tonight was the night, she thought. Tonight she'd tell her she loved her as a friend, but that was it. She wondered what Kelly was doing. If she and Amy were . . . *Don't think about it. Don't think about Kelly and Amy. Think about where you are. Think about Laurie and how much fun you'll have if you'd just relax.*

"We begin with lobster quesadillas." Laurie set down the platter. "And some salsa, guacamole and sour cream." She added several dishes to the table and sat down.

"They smell delicious."

"That's why your white wine was so appropriate. I hope you like them," Laurie said somewhat anxiously.

"I'm sure I will," Susan said as she reached for one. She spread salsa, guacamole and sour cream on top. "Oh, wow. This is wonderful, Laurie."

"Phew." Laurie helped herself. "This is the first time I've ever made them. I was worried. I can't tell you how many times I've ruined tortillas. I almost threw in the towel."

"I'm so glad you didn't," Susan said taking a second one. "This could be a meal."

"Just an appetizer. There's plenty more. Although I thought about soup tonight, I figured we'd have enough food."

"Thank you. Have you noticed, since we've been neighbors, we've spent a lot of time eating." Susan laughed. "I've had to spend more time running off the pounds."

"I've think you look great." There was an unclad fervor in Laurie's eyes. Susan looked away. "Anyway, that's just a start. Go

323

ahead and finish the last one. We're going to take a fifteen-minute breather while I serve up the rest of the meal."

"So how are things going at the hospital?" Susan asked.

"Good. Really, it's good. It hums along. Kelly is a good administrator. The staff really likes her and it's a good staff. Sometimes you get prima donnas on the medical staff, but not here. Everyone seems real comfortable with the setup. We all work. At times it's harder than at other times, depending upon how many patients we have in-house."

"It's not a big hospital." Susan remembered her research.

"No, twenty-five beds, plus three ICU beds." Laurie took several dishes out of the oven and set them on the counter. "It's small enough that everyone knows everyone. Unlike Portland, where nurses on the regular floors didn't have a clue as to who was working in ICU or the emergency room. This place is small enough that if there isn't a patient in ICU, the nurse comes out and works the floor. I really like that. Same with the ER nurse. A lot of time she's on the floor helping us out if we have a full load."

"That's convenient."

"It is. And they don't seem to mind. That's what I mean by no prima donnas. I like that. But what about you? You feeling okay coming up to the vote?"

"I am. The developers feel really confident." Susan thought about Dean and Bill. They were looking forward to it. The selectmen had set it for the second week of October. "Not overly confident, but good about the feedback they've been getting. They've worked really hard. I think they've done a lot better than those outfits that tried to site one down south. Dean and Bill actually came into the community. Lived here, got a feel for it."

"That's good, right?"

"Right."

"You have any last push?"

"Nothing big. We've set up some more information meetings. We have several full-page ads in the local newspapers talking about all the benefits. We want to do a round with some of the people we first met when we came into the community. They'll be our barometers. An engineer who does a good show-and-tell is coming to the island. He's going to meet with several groups." Laurie carried two plates to the table. "Whatever it is, it smells wonderful."

"Enchiladas. It's my fiesta night." Laurie's smile was smug.

Susan waited for Laurie to sit down before she took her first bite. "Laurie, this is wonderful. You have me beat as a cook hands-down."

"No way." Laurie said after a moment's reflection, "We've had some great meals and some great times. I hope they won't end."

Susan put her fork down. "They won't. I've enjoyed our friendship. In fact, if it hadn't have been for you, I would have been really lonely. You and Elizabeth. You two have made my life here wonderful and I will always be grateful."

"Same here, Susan. I've really enjoyed these past few months."

Susan felt uncomfortable with the serious tone their conversation had taken. "So any more"—she lowered her voice to that of a TV newsman—"things the public never hears, stories from the hospital?"

"No . . ." Laurie looked at Susan intently. "Isn't that strange. In Portland there were always all kinds of silly things happening. Not here."

"Well, fewer people. We have fewer characters here."

"Did I ever tell you the time the receptionist shaved a drunk's eyebrow off?"

"No, do tell me."

"This happened in Portland of course. A drunk came in, he"— Laurie pointed at her eyebrow—"had a cut right above his right eyebrow. Anyway, we had our hands full that night. There'd been a bad accident and we had a bunch of injuries, plus the hospital was full of patients. So the doctor asked her to prep the guy. She was young, had ambitions of going to medical school. She'd helped out before and had actually prepped some of our patients. Nice kid, eager to learn. Anyway, he told her to get the guy ready. He was a real Tony Soprano type, only with big bushy eyebrows." Laurie laughed as she recalled that night. "Anyway, the guy's so drunk he passes out on the table. So this kid does everything to the letter. She disinfected the wound, but then she proceeded to shave the guy's eyebrow to make it easier for the doc to stitch him up. There were a lot of emergencies that night, like I said. There had been a bad accident with multiple injuries, so the doc takes care of them first. When the doc comes back in the room there's this drunk on his back with this nakedness above his right eye. You see, eyebrows don't necessarily grow back. The doc nearly does a horse puckey in the middle of the floor. He looks at the receptionist and looks at the drunk without his eyebrow and just starts to laugh. He explains to her that the guy could end up with only one eyebrow. She was horrified, but the doc was laughing so hard, she joined in. He called all the nurses and the other docs in to look. They all just stood there and roared. The doc laughed so hard he had tears running down his face. He almost couldn't sew the guy up because his hand was shaking so hard from laughing."

Susan chuckled. "That poor kid. She must have been devastated."

"At first, she was. The guy looked absolutely ridiculous."

"What did the doctor do?"

"Put on a bandage large enough to cover the cut and the lost eyebrow. He let the guy sleep it off. When the drunk woke up a few hours later, the doc told him he'd have to leave the bandage on for days if not weeks."

"That's hilarious." Susan wiped her own eyes. "Somehow you can just picture this guy running around with just one eyebrow. What happened to the young woman?"

"I think she became an accountant."

Susan chortled. "I just love your stories. We don't have anything that compares in public relations. We're downright dull compared to you guys."

"Well, we see the very best and the very worst of the human condition. A lot of tension and stress, especially in city hospitals. So when you get something funny like that it just tickles everyone. More enchiladas?"

"I'd say no." Susan sat back and rubbed her stomach. "That was so good."

"You're not done yet. We have dessert."

"How about a breather in between. I'll help you clean off the table."

"No, you won't. That's why God invented dishwashers. I'll just add these few to the dirty ones that are already there and presto. It's like you have Hazel the maid working for you. Go sit on the couch. I'll be there in a minute. More wine?"

"No, thanks. I'm full of good food and wine. Thank you very much." Susan sat on the couch and tucked her feet under her and watched Laurie as she carried the dishes from the table. How many times had she sat here doing the same thing while Laurie was cleaning up in the kitchen. But this time it was different. Her thoughts kept turning back to Kelly. Why did she ever have to get involved with Kelly? Why couldn't it have been Laurie? Laurie with the funny stories. Laurie with the love of fun. Laurie who was going to turn serious any moment.

"How about some coffee?"

"That would be nice."

"Dessert is light, I promise you." Laurie came in carrying two cups. Susan hadn't noticed she'd already brewed the coffee.

"I need light."

Laurie set the cups down on the coffee table and sat down next to her. She took a small box out of her pocket and set it next to Susan's cup. "This is just a small welcome-back gift," Laurie murmured.

"I don't need a gift," she protested.

"It's nothing important. Well—" Laurie stopped. "It's important, just not that important. Ah, heck, just open it."

Susan picked up the small box and opened it. The sapphire stone glistened in the light. "It's beautiful." She took the ring out of the box. "It's absolutely beautiful. My birthstone."

"I know."

"How'd you know?"

"I have my ways. Your birthday came and went and you told no one."

"Birthdays, when you get to be our age, come and go and you don't care about telling anyone."

"Well, we're not exactly prehistoric. In fact, I haven't felt more alive. Susan, I really care about you. I know we've never talked about this, but I've got to say it. I think about you day and night. I'm falling in love with you."

Susan gently closed the box. She reached for Laurie's hand and put the box with the ring in it in her hand.

"What are you doing?" There was confusion in Laurie's eyes.

"I like you a lot as a friend. I . . ." Susan studied her. "I just don't love you in the way you want me to love you."

"Not even a little bit?" Laurie clearly was trying to keep her voice light.

"I wish I did, but I don't and it wouldn't be fair to you to even suggest anything else. I've valued these past few weeks, Laurie. You've made them bearable because you're so much fun to be with. I've enjoyed the nights we've cooked together. Enjoyed the conversation. I've enjoyed us on so many levels, but for me I just am not in love with you."

"And if we wait just a bit? Is it possible that might happen? That you'd fall in love with me. How could you resist my charms?" Laurie wiggled her eyebrows.

"Careful, one might fall off."

"I hope not." Laurie's laugh was forced. "Not a chance is there." She paused. "How'd this happen that I've fallen head over heels in love with you and you don't feel the same way. I have to tell you Susan, this is a first in my life."

"Well, I wasn't certainly going for any kind of firsts, but I just can't—" Susan took a breath—"let you believe that I may someday fall in love with you. That wouldn't be fair to either of us."

Laurie stared down at the ring box Susan had put back in her hand. She opened it slowly, took out the ring and placed it on Susan's finger. "This is a buddy ring. You look at this and you'll know you have a buddy and a pal out there."

"Are you all right with this?" Susan asked suspiciously.

"No, I'm not." There was sorrow in Laurie's voice. "But I would rather have you as a friend than not have you in my life. So I want you to have the ring. No strings. It's just something I wanted to give you. It's your birthstone and it may be two weeks since your birthday, but happiness to you always, Susan. That's my birthday wish for you."

Susan swallowed deeply. "This is one of the nicest things anyone has done for me in a long time." She felt tears spill over and she wiped them away.

"Don't cry," Laurie said kindly.

"I'm . . ." Susan said in a faint voice. "I'm overwhelmed by your kindness. Thank you, Laurie." She hugged her. "My life is rather complicated right now."

"I know. With all this LNG how could it not be. But I'm not going to add to your stress."

Susan wiped her tears on her sleeve. "Thank you. You're a wonderful woman, Laurie. You truly are."

"I am," Laurie said jauntily, breaking the tension. "So no more tears. You'll ruin my reputation. Someone might look in the window and see you crying, they'll blame me for breaking your heart." She paused, then said wistfully, "I have to say this once though. I fell in love with you the first day I met you. I've never felt that way about any woman and I doubt I'll ever feel that way again. I had hoped you felt the same way, but deep down in my heart I knew you cared, just not that way. I didn't want to admit it to myself. The ring is just what I said it was—a friendship gift for you and a reality check for me."

"I'm so sorry, Laurie. You're important in my life. You made me smile, you made me laugh, and for that I'll be grateful. But more importantly, I do care about you, I just wish it was the same way."

The two fell silent. "Well . . ." Laurie cleared her throat. "We are not ending this night on a sad note." She got up. "I have strawberry sham torte for dessert and we're going to fill up on sugar and celebrate our diversity."

"Diversity?"

"Yup." Laurie reached for Susan's hand and pulled her up from the couch. "Definitely diversity. I love a woman and you love a friend. It can't get any better than that."

Susan bowed her head. She wondered at the emotional response whirling around inside her. Here was a woman who loved her and she loved a woman who was not available to her. When she looked at Laurie, her smile was tremulous. She almost didn't trust her voice. "Thank you, Laurie. Thank you for this night and thank you for understanding."

Laurie's voice was serene, almost virtuous in its calmness. "I fell in love, no question. I'm going to tuck that love away in my heart and keep it. You will always be very special to me, Susan."

Susan swallowed and she could feel the tears again. She closed her eyes. She wanted to tell Laurie the truth. She owed Laurie the truth.

"You okay?" There was concern in Laurie's eyes.

"Just okay."

"Sugar. We both need sugar." Laurie said, pulling Susan toward the kitchen. "It was my mother's remedy for everything."

"Did it work?" Susan tried to capture Laurie's lightness. The moment of truth had passed.

"It did." Laurie reached for two plates and put them on the counter. "Susan, I will always be your friend."

"I know that. And you know you'll always have a friend too."

"I do and I like that." Susan cut two large pieces of the torte. She spooned strawberries on top and dolloped whipped cream all around the plate. "Now, this should do the trick. Put us right over the top. Send us to sugar heaven where sugarplum fairies dance on the tops of tacks."

Susan laughed. "You are too much." She smiled. "Thank you, Laurie."

"For what?"

"For being you."

Chapter Thirty-six

Kelly's whole body felt electrified, she was going to see Susan. That was all she could think about all day Sunday. Wishing her life away again, she thought for the hundredth time as she waited for the car ferry. So much for valuing today. She thought back to her Erma Bombeck resolve that still hung on her bulletin board. But even a few hours with Susan was worth wishing for, but then her mind seemed to be overwhelmed by thoughts of Amy. They had had several minor disagreements since the town meeting because Kelly no longer went to the LNG meetings. Funny, she thought, she no longer cared. She usually didn't get home from work until after she knew Amy had left for the meetings, and she was usually in bed pretending to be asleep when Amy got home from the meetings. In the mornings they talked briefly before they went off to work. Kelly could tell Amy was focused on the last few weeks before the vote and wasn't interested in anything else, not even what was going on in Kelly's life. All they talked about was LNG and the group's last-ditch strategy before the vote. The selectmen had set the vote for October 15 and now Amy and the rest of the group were busy ordering "Vote No" signs. Bumper stickers had appeared on several cars and Amy was even wearing a badge that the group had had printed up that had a red circle with a line through the LNG.

Kelly followed the cars onto the ferry. She turned off the engine and sat and stared at the water. She was relieved that Amy was so preoccupied. There was no movement toward making love. Now she was going to see the woman she had fallen in love with. They would have dinner and talk.

"We thought that was you!" Maggie Beth, a big smile on her face, was approaching her from the other end of the ferry.

Kelly jumped. "Maggie Beth, Terry, hi."

"Get out of that car and come join us. Where you going? Can you have dinner with us? I can't believe we ran into you," Maggie said.

"It's great to see you. Kelly followed them to the front of the ferry. Her heart was racing and her throat all of a sudden felt like the Sahara desert. She had a flashback to another time when she had been caught by her mother sneaking in the back door after drinking beer down at the sandbar with her friends. She was fourteen. She remembered how her heart raced that night at the thought of being grounded for the rest of her life. Now her heart was flying faster than a stealth bomber on a mission. "I thought you guys would be at the meeting today." Her voice sounded pitched even to her. She inhaled deeply and pulled her jacket around her. The September air felt cool on her skin. She shivered. Was she cold or was that just the icy finger of fear crawling up her spine?

"We planned to but we're playing hooky." Terry smiled. "A lot of us are today. God love Amy, she's so directed. People were canceling on her left and right and she said she was going to hold a meeting if only one person showed up. Maggie kept telling her that on the seventh day even God rested, but not Amy. Ya gotta admire that she's pursuing her goal. Anyway, we needed some parts for our boat. Timmy's coming by tomorrow to fix it. We could have waited until tomorrow and picked them up on the island, but if they didn't have one of the parts we'd have to call him and put off the repairs. We decided to come over to the mainland and make an evening of it."

"That's great." Kelly could feel her heart slowing down.

"Amy was disappointed, but I told her everyone needs a break," Maggie offered. "If we win this we're going to have her to thank. She's been the spark plug for this engine, believe me."

"She has," Terry added. "We're all committed to winning this, but Amy's been absolutely driven to the point that we're worried about her if we don't win."

Kelly could hear the concern in Terry's voice. "Amy will handle it if things don't go her way." She thought about what she'd just said. She'd handle it all right. Her own life was going to be hell for months. Amy would rage and then go off like those 55 Hiroshima bombs they talked about if a missile hit an LNG tanker. She'd be right in the middle of the fallout. *Hell, you're going to be the fallout.* She hadn't thought about that. What if they did lose? Amy would blame her because she wouldn't have anyone else to blame.

Kelly could hear it now. "You weren't there to help. It's all your fault. If you'd helped us more we'd have won. You weren't there when I needed you." She could just imagine Amy's rant. She shivered again, but this time not from the cold.

"You're cold," Maggie said.

"No, not really." Kelly turned to her friends. "I know I've been the absentee member of the group, but somehow I'm betting on the people of this island. I know the fifteen million dollars threw all of us. I know that that's a very tempting offer, but somehow I think we Yankees can't be bought for fifteen million dollars. It's just a gut feeling."

"Well, I hope you're right," Terry said doubtfully. "The developers have been good. They've used their time on the island meeting with—well, everyone who was interested enough to learn about the LNG project. What we don't know is how many they've convinced. A lot of the summer people have left, but Elizabeth said she's had more than three hundred requests for absentee ballots. I think that's going to work in our favor."

Kelly nodded. "Well, you guys have met with just as many people. What's your gut feeling?"

"Hard to say. If we believe all the people who said they're going to vote against it, we've won. But you know folks Down East, they'll tell you what you want to hear. Not out of meanness, just because they don't want to hurt your feelings."

"True." Kelly laughed. "We have that problem at the hospital with a lot of our senior citizens. The doctor will ask them questions and they'll just shake their head and say they're just fine. It's the nursing staff that picks up on all the symptoms and tells the doctors. Then if the doctor asks them if they had abdominal pains the night before, they'll say. 'Oh, that, that was nothing, just a little gas.' "

Terry and Maggie Beth laughed and Maggie said, "Well, I guess we're all guilty of doing that. Anyway, we'll see what happens. You can't predict what anyone will do."

"I can't get over the folks on this island when it comes to a lot of votes. Remember when Bill Clinton, George H. Bush and Ross Perot were running for president? This island voted overwhelmingly for Perot. I don't think it was so much ideology as it was just a vote for independence."

Kelly grinned. "I wasn't around then, but you guys made statewide news." She paused. "Look, we're being waved to our cars."

"So why are you going to the mainland?" Terry asked as they walked back toward their cars.

"Just to do some shopping this afternoon."

"Great, let's all meet for dinner," Maggie invited again. "It'll be fun."

"I can't. I'm meeting a friend from the hospital for dinner.

We're going to talk about a problem she has." Kelly could not look at her friends.

"That's too bad," Terry said. "It would have been fun just yakking." Terry, and then Maggie, gave her a hug.

"I agree, maybe next time." Kelly hugged them back. Her heart was racing again. Great, she thought. She was going to have a heart attack right here in front of her friends. Then when everyone asked what happened, they'd say the poor woman was on her way to do an act of kindness for one of her staff members and she keeled over. That was a heck of a lot better than saying she was on her way to meet the woman she loved and keeled over because she ran into friends who might inadvertently mention something to her current partner. She hadn't told Amy she was going to the mainland. She stopped at her car. "Anyway, guys, it's been great seeing you. How about having lunch on the island next week." She exchanged another round of hugs. "Good luck with finding the parts for your boat."

"Thanks," Maggie said. "We'll call you next week and set up a day for lunch."

Kelly watched them walk to their car. *Hell, you're going to burn in hell, Kelly Burns. Lying to two of the nicest women in the world.* She got in her car. What did she expect? She lived on an island. A small island. Why was she surprised when she ran into two familiar faces? What would she have done if Susan had been there. Wow, her heart was racing now. It probably would have ruptured if she'd run into Maggie and Terry and Susan had been in her car or standing next to her on the ferry. She hadn't thought about it, but she was glad that Susan had offered to take the earlier ferry. Kelly felt relief ripple over her. She'd almost been caught. No wonder her heart was racing. She was a stupid imbecile who was tiptoeing around like a teenager. She inhaled and ordered herself to stop painting ghosts on the wall. She didn't want to think about getting caught. She wanted to think about love. She wanted to think about the woman from Andover who had placed a footprint in her heart. That woman was waiting for her right now.

Kelly followed the cars off the ferry when Maggie Beth and Terry turned right toward the marine supply store, she turned left toward the mall.

She spotted Susan's car parked near the restaurant and pulled in alongside it. She wasn't going to tell her about Maggie and Terry. She had enough worry in her heart for both of them. "Hi," she said as she exited the car. Susan was standing next to her car. She had on a blue jacket. The blue seemed to reflect off her eyes and deepen the color. Kelly wanted to grab her and hug her, but instead she shoved her hands deep into her pockets. "You hungry?"

"A little."

Kelly felt suddenly shy around her. She wasn't quite certain what to do. All week, she had pictured them together. She saw herself holding Susan in her arms and looking deep into her eyes. Now all she could do was stutter and stammer and feel insecure. She also was surprised how meeting Maggie and Terry had jolted her. "Look, I feel awkward about this. Why don't we pick up some sandwiches and go someplace where we can talk?"

"Sounds good."

"Let's go in my car. There's a neat little deli not far from here," Kelly said.

"Fine."

"You okay?" she asked as they got in her car. She let the keys dangle in the ignition. She wasn't ready to go yet.

Susan gave a half-smile, "I feel just as awkward. I've never done this before and I don't have a frame of reference for it. That night in Portland, it just happened. Now I do feel like I'm sneaking around. I've never had to meet someone on the sly."

"Well, this isn't exactly on the sly." She started the car. *Tell her the truth*, she told herself. What if they ran into someone in the restaurant? She was worried. Why hadn't she told Susan about running into Maggie and Terry? Because she knew the answer, she was afraid of being caught. She turned right onto Washington Street.

"Well, if we weren't sneaking around we would have had dinner on the island."

"You're right. We're not going to have a fight, are we?" Kelly gulped as a quiver of fear shot through her. She didn't want to fight with Susan.

"No, but I agree we have to talk. I had a long talk with Laurie."

"When?"

"Last night. She gave me this ring."

Kelly touched the ring. It was a simple silver band with a fiery blue sapphire. Even in the cloud-covered light, it shimmered. "What does it mean?"

Susan twisted it around on her finger. The depth of the blue mirrored her eyes. "She called it a buddy ring." She smiled faintly.

"Was she all right?"

"She was," Susan said in a calm measured tone. "We got through the evening quite well. I know she was heartbroken, I saw it in her eyes. But she was brave. Put her feelings out there for me to tramp on." There was a touch of sarcasm in her voice. "I'm sorry. That was harsh and not honest. She put her feelings out there and we worked through them."

"I'm sorry you had to go through that."

"I'm more sorry for Laurie." Susan raised her hands in surrender.

"I am too. She's never been in this type of situation before. Usually, the women are declaring their undying love for her. It had to have been hard."

"It was."

"I'm sorry," Kelly said again as she turned into the parking lot at the deli. The lights from inside flooded the parking lot.

"This one's not your fault."

"I'm still sorry. It sure would have been a lot easier on you if I hadn't been in the picture," Kelly said feebly.

"Had you not been in the picture, I still wouldn't have fallen in love with her. I didn't feel that way about her from the beginning. I love her as a friend and I'm glad she's in my life, but I don't love her."

"I love you."

"I know." Susan gestured helplessly. "And that's the complication in both of our lives."

337

"I know."

Susan glanced around her. "I guess we should get those sandwiches."

"I guess." Kelly felt dejected. "You want to come in or do you want me to order for both of us?"

"Bring me their veggie sandwich and a bottled water."

"I'll be right back." Kelly hurried inside and ordered.

Where were they going to go? she wondered. She had felt cold on the ferry, the September air cutting through her windbreaker. There was a small park near the water, but if she'd felt cold, she knew Susan would be also. All she had on was a light jacket. She didn't know anyone on the mainland. She thought again about Maggie and Terry. What if they ran into them or someone else from the island? Someone would probably mention it to Amy. *So what's the next step, hotshot?* She was irritated with herself. Boy, if Susan didn't have a frame of reference for this, she surely didn't. She'd never cheated on her partner before. Cheat. She repeated the word. That's what she was doing, wasn't it? Cheating on Amy and asking a wonderful woman to be her co-conspirator. No wonder Susan was so quiet. She must have felt just as guilty.

"Look"—Kelly handed her the bag of sandwiches—"I didn't plan this out at all. And I'm feeling guilty about this and I can tell you are too. Do you just want to go back to the island and forget about this?"

"Yes, no, I don't know." Susan was clearly miserable. "I think we need to talk. I need to know where your head is. I need to know if I've fallen in love with someone who's not emotionally available to me."

"Come on." Kelly pulled out of the parking lot. "I know where we can talk." She retraced their path back along Washington Street. "I stayed here one time when we had a two-day conference here at the hospital. Several of the workshops went late into the evening and the ferry had stopped running." She turned into the driveway of the Eastland Motel.

"Do you think this is a good idea?" Susan asked, uncertainty in her voice.

338

"It's just a place to talk. That's all." Kelly got out of the car and went into the office. She returned a few minutes later with a key to a room. "We can eat, talk and then be back in time to catch the ferry. If you want, you can catch the early ferry and I'll hang around in town and catch the later ferry." She parked her car in front of the door. "It's okay, really. Nothing else has to happen."

"I know." Susan sighed.

Kelly slipped the electronic key in the door and the green light popped on. She held the door for Susan. Inside, Kelly put the sandwiches down. Susan was hanging back. "We've got to talk." Kelly felt a hoarseness in her voice.

"I know."

"But I've got to do this first." Kelly gently raised Susan's chin with the tips of her fingers and kissed her. "I've been thinking about this since that night in Portland. I've been dreaming about doing this."

"Me too." Susan put her arms around her neck and pulled her close. Kelly felt dizzy from the intensity of Susan's kiss. She folded Susan into her arms and rested her forehead against Susan's cheek. Susan's body seemed to mold into hers.

"I want you, I love you," Kelly's mouth found Susan's and she kissed her with the same intensity. "I know this is crazy. I promised myself this wouldn't happen. I know we have to talk. But I want you, I want to devour you."

"I want you so much." Susan kissed her again.

Kelly eased her onto the bed. She opened her jacket and kissed Susan's neck. "I love you so much." She could hear the desperation in her own voice. It scared her. Her need for this woman was terrifying.

Susan responded with another kiss.

Kelly stroked Susan's breast, then traced a line along her thigh and felt a tremor like the vibration of a violin string on a finger. She unbuttoned Susan's blouse. She inhaled deeply when she saw the black bra. What a beautiful sight, she thought. "You're so beautiful."

"I want to feel you against me," Susan said as she pushed Kelly's jacket off her shoulders. Kelly struggled out of it and threw it on the floor. Susan pulled Kelly's shirt over her head then unhooked her bra.

Kelly traced a line down Susan's nose, across her lips, down her chin to her neck then to her breasts. She caressed first one and then the other breast through the sexy black bra. She rolled on her side and rested her head on her arm. "I want to look at you, you're so beautiful," she said again.

She opened the button on Susan's slacks and eased the zipper down. She suspected that black panties would be waiting for her there. She wasn't disappointed. Her heart was doing a highland fling. She could barely swallow. She reached around and unhooked the black bra, got up on her knees and eased Susan's slacks down over her hips. She tossed the pants over her shoulder and bent down and kissed first one and then the other breast. She hooked her fingers on either side of Susan's panties and slipped them off. It had been days since they'd been together and all the romantic fantasies she'd held while they were apart exploded. Kelly looked deep into Susan's eyes and saw her own intensity reflected back at her. *I want to make love to you.* The words repeated over and over in her mind as she began to caress that spot that she knew would bring Susan to a climax. Susan's skin felt on fire. Kelly felt the response she wanted, the wetness and Susan drew in her breath.

Kelly felt a pulsing between her legs as her lips sought again the sweetness of Susan's breast. Then she began a slow teasing trail down Susan's stomach to the spot she had dreamed of after that first night of making love. Her tongue found the spot and she felt Susan open to her like a cactus flower in the night air. She felt the rawness of Susan's passion and then her climax. In one fluid movement she touched Susan inside and felt her vibrate. She was at one with Susan as her thrusts synchronized with the rhythm of Susan's body. They moved together until she felt Susan tremble and then explode as first one and then a second orgasm consumed her. Kelly collapsed next to her, feverish and scorched from their lovemaking.

"I want to make love to you."

"Soon, let me just hold you." Kelly folded her into her arms. "You're a spectacular lover," she said as she stroked Susan's hair.

"So are you." Susan replied sleepily.

"Close your eyes."

"I want to make love to you."

"You will. Right now I just want to hold you."

Kelly stared at the clock. Does that say nine o'clock? She swallowed. The last ferry was at ten. She eased her arm out from under Susan's head.

Susan stirred. "What time is it?" she asked groggily.

"Nine."

"You have to get back." Susan moved away from her to the edge of the bed and sat up.

"Don't leave me yet," Kelly whispered.

"Welcome to reality. You have to get back."

"I know," Kelly said as she touched Susan's naked back.

"I promised myself all week that this wouldn't happen, that we'd talk over where you were in your head with Amy."

"Me too. But when I closed the door I just had to touch you. I'm sorry. I know we need to talk. It's just . . ." Kelly sighed. "We haven't resolved anything, we've just complicated it more."

"I know. All week I planned to tell you that I wasn't going to get involved with you."

"You were?" Kelly said, alarmed. "I love you."

"And I love you, but we're walking into an emotional trap that's going to do nothing but break both of our hearts." Susan sighed deeply. "Let's not talk. Let's just get dressed and go."

"I have to take a shower."

Susan turned and looked at her. "Of course."

Ten minutes later Kelly opened the bathroom door, steam followed her into the room. She looked at the bag of sandwiches. "Are you hungry?" Her stomach had shut down. She wasn't hungry.

"No."

"Do you want to shower?" she said as she picked her clothes up off the floor and put them on.

"I don't have to." Susan had dressed. She sat in the chair looking at the emotionless room.

"You're angry." She watched the black clouds dance across Susan's face and felt so unhappy inside.

"Just sad."

"About us?"

"About life."

"I love you. Please believe that, I just have complications right now." Kelly knelt in front of her. She took Susan's hand and kissed her fingertips.

"You're going to miss the last ferry." Susan stood up and went toward the door.

"Susan, I love you. Just give me a chance to fix everything."

There was a heaviness in Susan's voice as she said, "Right now I just want to get through the rest of tonight." She picked up Kelly's sandwich and handed it to her. She opened the door.

Kelly tried to get Susan to talk as they drove back to the restaurant.

"I'm fine from here," Susan said as she got out of the car.

"Susan, I love you. Believe that. I just have to fix what I now have in my life. I want you, I want you in my life."

"I know."

"When will I see you?"

"Soon. But right now you have to get back to the island. Your ferry waits, madam." The lightness Susan was trying to affect in her voice fell flat.

Kelly sighed. The clock told her she had less than fifteen minutes to catch the ferry. *Hang the ferry. Stay here with the woman you love*, she argued with herself. But what about Amy? Even if she wasn't her life anymore it wasn't fair to let her just worry. Even after they'd had a horrific fight, she'd never not come home before. "I will fix this, I promise." Anxiety rose inside her.

"I know."

Kelly glanced at the clock again. She hated it as the digital minutes clicked one after the other. She wanted to freeze time. She had less than ten minutes to make the last ferry. She felt parched in her throat. "I love you." She touched Susan's face.

"Go fix your life and then call me."

"I will, I promise."

Susan stepped back from the car as Kelly put it in gear and drove out of the parking lot.

What are you doing? Kelly asked herself. She looked in the rearview mirror and saw Susan get into her car. *Why didn't we talk?* They'd agreed that they'd talk about the future. Figure out what they wanted. Where they wanted to be. Why didn't they stay with the plan? Why did they end up at a motel? She knew that would be a prescription for tragedy. She was afraid of getting caught, true. *Reality check, Kelly Burns.* They ended up at the motel because she wanted to make love to Susan. She couldn't stop chastising herself. It was as if she was consumed by her need for intimacy, hang the consequences. She got what she wanted and the woman she loved felt violated and alone. *Turn around, go back to the motel. Tell her you love her.*

What about Amy? She was afraid not to go home. How could she explain where she'd been. What she'd been doing. Was she afraid of Amy's anger, or the fear of getting caught? Five years of her life she'd spent with her. She had to tell her good-bye, but not over the phone and not from a motel room. *Go back and tell Amy the truth. Tell her you've fallen in love with another woman. Tell her. Tell her.*

Kelly got in line. She was the last car on the ferry.

Chapter Thirty-seven

"Where have you been?" Amy was waiting for her at the door when she walked into the kitchen. There was no pot of coffee on, no waiting glass of wine.

"I went over to the mainland."

"No note, nothing?" Amy's tone was accusatory.

"It was impromptu, I hadn't planned to stay so long."

"And you did what?"

"Thought I'd do some shopping."

"You hate to shop. But even so, the stores close at six o'clock on Sunday. What did you do with the rest of your time?"

"One of the nurses from the hospital needed to talk with me about a personnel problem."

"And you had to do it on a Sunday at Port Bleu?" Amy was staring at her.

Kelly went to the refrigerator. She needed a glass of wine. She'd eaten half her sandwich on the ferry and tossed the rest. "I'm having a glass of wine. Would you like one?"

"No, I'd like an answer."

"She called, asked to talk. Said it couldn't wait until Monday and said she wanted to talk off the island."

"What was so important she took you off-island?"

"You know better than to ask that question." Kelly gulped down her wine. "It's a *personnel* matter and I can't talk about it."

"Convenient."

"How was your meeting?"

"Don't change the subject," Amy snapped.

"Why the inquisition? I went over to the mainland. I'm guilty of not leaving you a note and for that I apologize."

"Did it occur to you that I might be worried? I got home from my meeting several hours ago."

"I didn't think about that. Your meetings have been going late. There are times you haven't gotten home until eleven or twelve at night."

"Well, this one didn't go as well as I'd liked. Maggie and Terry weren't there. I insisted Elizabeth take the day off—she was looking really tired. So it was just a small group. We decided to bag it around seven. I came home. You weren't here. I waited an hour, still no you, no telephone call. I called Laurie and she's now worried. I called Maggie and Terry, but they weren't home. I called Elizabeth, who hadn't heard from you. I called the hospital, and the receptionist said you hadn't been in all day. I was going to try your cell phone, but it was sitting there on the counter." The anger was unpronounced in her voice, but Kelly knew it was there just slightly under the surface.

"I set it down this morning and forgot it." Kelly poured herself another glass of wine. "I'm sorry. I didn't intend for you to worry. I just wasn't thinking," she said helplessly.

"That's pretty obvious. By the way, call Laurie. She said she was going to send out the search dogs for you if you weren't home in an hour."

"I'll call her." Kelly hoped the discussion was over, but when Amy didn't move, she picked up the telephone and dialed. Laurie burbled her concern and asked where she'd been. She told her

345

about going over to the mainland to shop. She didn't mention talking with one of her staff about a personnel problem. Mostly, she just listened. Kelly put the telephone down.

Amy stood with her arms folded. "Who else is missing?"

"I don't think she's missing, but Laurie hasn't talked with Susan and she's worried."

"Well, Susan's not someone I'm worrying about tonight. She told me how Susan had dinner with her on Saturday and told her to cool her jets. Laurie needs to forget about that woman. She's nothing but trouble and when the vote goes against her she and those developers will be out of here faster than Canada geese in the fall."

Kelly poured herself another glass of wine.

Amy picked up the telephone. "I told Elizabeth I would call her when you got home—she was worried too. Aren't you hitting that wine a little hard?" she said, dialing. "Elizabeth, hi. I hope it's not too late. Good." She frowned at the telephone. "Our wandering nurse is home. She had some stuff to do on the mainland. Yeah, I gave her what for. She's looking quite contrite. I'll tell her." Amy hung up.

Kelly finished the glass and rinsed it. She put the wine back in the refrigerator. She wanted to numb her mind so she would stop thinking about Susan. Susan, alone in that motel room. Susan with such sad eyes when she'd left.

"Elizabeth said you have to do penance."

"I'm not Catholic."

"She was just kidding. You've got to lighten up. I think penance would be a great idea. I think a few more hours of my yelling at you should do it. I'm still mad at you."

Kelly sucked in her breath. She didn't want to listen. She wanted to curl up in the dark and think about Susan. Think about what she was doing. Think about how dispirited her face looked when she'd left her. She wanted to call her at the motel, but Amy wasn't going to leave her alone. "How about we just go to bed."

"I was really worried about you tonight." Amy's voice had softened. "I know I sounded like the grand inquisitor when you came in, but I was so worried. I didn't know if you'd been driving somewhere and gotten hurt. I didn't know if you were in a ditch somewhere. And this may seem odd, but worrying about you made me realize that I don't want us to have problems. So when this LNG stuff is over, I want to go see that counselor—" She paused. "I'm not convinced it will help. I still say we can work this out ourselves, but I'm willing to try. I realized tonight how scared I was that you might not be in my life." She took Kelly's hand. "I know it's been tough around here the past few months and I've been hard to live with because of all this LNG stuff, but know this, Kelly, I love you and I want you in my life."

Tell her. Tell her the truth. Don't let her believe that you feel the same way. Tell her you love Susan. Tell her that you're a moron and an ass and she deserves better than you. Tell her that you've been unfaithful. Tell her it's too late to go see a counselor. Tell her that she treated you badly even before LNG. Tell her you don't want anyone to fix your relationship. Tell her you don't want to see a counselor because you're in love with someone else. Tell her! Tell her! Kelly was mentally kicking herself. She said, "I'm pretty tired, I'd like to go to bed." Android-like, she turned away. She tried to quash the emotional merry-go-round whirling inside her.

The two fell silent.

"Okay."

Kelly sensed Amy wanted to say something else.

"You go ahead upstairs. I'll turn off the lights."

Kelly turned toward the stairs but stopped when Amy touched her arm. "I love you, Kelly, I truly do." She put her arms around her and pulled Kelly's lips to hers.

Kelly turned her face to the side and rested her cheek against Amy's. "I'm really sorry, Amy, I'm tired tonight."

"It's okay. I just want to hold you," Amy said softly.

Kelly turned away for the second time that night. She could feel tears stinging her eyes. She wanted to shed five years of tears. *Why now, God?* Why did Amy want to fix the relationship now? Three weeks ago she would have clasped Amy's declaration to her heart. She pondered that incontrovertible truth—three weeks ago she would have immersed herself in Amy's willingness to see a counselor. She thought about the emotional ride she had been on in the past few weeks and how she now was skidding from the rapturous high she had felt hours before while making love to Susan and being in love with Susan to this depressing low. She took a deep breath, exhaled slowly then went upstairs to bed.

Chapter Thirty-eight

Ten days had gone by and Susan would not talk to her. After their rendezvous in Port Bleu that Sunday, Kelly had called at first every other hour. Then several times a day. Finally every other day. She begged her to meet with her, but Susan had refused. She even drove downtown hoping to catch her coming out of her office or eating at the SeaBleu restaurant. She just was not around. At first, Susan had used the excuse of hundreds of meetings, but lately she just said no. She was afraid to go over to her house—what would she say to Laurie? Kelly stared at the ceiling in her office. She had been doing that a lot lately, and lately her ceiling was boring.

Kelly knew Susan wanted to hear that she and Amy had broken up and their life together was over. But she could not say those words. After Amy's declaration that she was willing to see a counselor, how could Kelly not try? How could she turn her back on five years of history? Hadn't she been the one who had begged to see a counselor? They had so many problems, she'd given up the count. For the first time, Amy was willing to acknowledge those problems and said she wanted to face them together. Isn't that what she had been pushing for? she asked herself for the thousandth time. Wasn't that what she had wanted? So how could she now tell Amy that she didn't want to see a counselor? That she didn't want to save their relationship? How could she tell her that she was not willing to try? She felt like she was losing it. The self-flagellation had been going on for days. She couldn't be in love with two women. That was impossible, something Laurie would do.

She thought about Laurie. She knew she was hurting and wanted to talk to her about Susan's decision for them not to get involved, but she had sidestepped all conversations. When Laurie appeared at her office wanting to talk about Susan and how her heart was breaking, she pretended she was too busy. She had seen the look of disappointment in her friend's eyes. She had seen that look a lot lately, even in the eyes that stared back at her in the morning mirror.

Kelly picked up the telephone on the first ring. It was the receptionist. "Kelly, I'm terribly sorry. You'd asked me to hold all calls, but Elizabeth insists it's a matter of life and death."

"That's fine, put her through." Kelly listened to the clicks on the line and then Elizabeth's hasty invitation to lunch. "Elizabeth. I'm so glad you called. Yes, I'd love to have lunch with you. How about noon?" She looked at the clock. She'd been so caught up in studying the lint in her navel that she hadn't noticed that she had thought away most of the morning. "I'll meet you in about five minutes. Great."

Kelly turned on her computer. She hadn't done any hospital work since she had gotten in that morning. She was determined to do some work when she returned from lunch. She closed her office door and walked to the reception area.

"Kelly, I'm sorry." Kelly could see the worry on Loraine's face. "It's just hard to say no to Elizabeth. I remember when as kids we all went to her and Lois's house—no one said no to Elizabeth."

350

Kelly smiled. It was times like this that she wished she had grown up on the island, that she had known Elizabeth as a youngster. She had heard stories about the two women's annual invitation to junior classes to walk on the beach and talk about the ecology of Bleu Island. "It's fine, Loraine. Elizabeth is special and you can put her through any time. Any other messages?"

"You have several." She handed Kelly a stack.

Kelly hastily thumbed through them. There were several calls from Amy and one from Maggie Beth. There was also a call from Laurie. She was disappointed when she didn't see any from Susan.

"Do you want me to hold your calls this afternoon?"

"No, I'm caught up on my paperwork, so put them through. I'm going out for about an hour for lunch."

"Have a good lunch."

"Thank you." She handed the messages back to Loraine. "I'd appreciate it if you'd hold these until I got back."

"Sure, Kelly, no problem."

Kelly could see Elizabeth through the restaurant window. She was studying the menu. Kelly smiled. She knew Elizabeth would have the usual, no matter what was on the menu or what the day's special was.

Kelly nodded to several people she knew in the restaurant. It felt good, she thought, to walk into a place where people knew you and smiled hello. "Hey, old salt," she said affectionately as she sat down in the booth.

"Hey, yourself. I'm so glad you could join me for lunch. I haven't seen a lot of you lately."

"Been busy."

"We've missed you at the meetings."

Kelly stared down at her hands. "Amy's doing such a great job, you guys don't really need me."

"It's not about needing you at the meetings, Kelly, it's about seeing you. Y'know, there are people out there who think you're pretty special. Remember, we jumped out of a helicopter together and that created a special bond between us. I wonder if there's some kind of blood thing because of that." Elizabeth was teasing her and she chuckled.

"Actually, you're right." Kelly tried to keep her tone light. "We've shared something together on this island that no two other people have shared."

Elizabeth was examining her closely. "I really have missed seeing you, Kelly." She sat back when Carrie came up to their table.

"The usual, Elizabeth?"

"Nope, I feel like fish chowder today." Elizabeth's smile was triumphant. "Just to let you two know that I can handle change with the best of them."

"I'll have the same thing." Kelly waited until Carrie walked away. "I'm glad you called. I just haven't gotten out a lot lately and it's kinda nice having lunch with you. How's Maggie Beth and Terry?"

"Great. They've been working closely with the group. It's been a good few days. Hard to believe the vote is just two days away."

"How's Susan? Have you seen much of her?" Kelly bit her tongue. Why did she ask about Susan? *Because you're worried about her, that's why. Because she won't talk to you. Because she hates you.*

"No, not since the day she came in to pick up a copy of the petitions. Funny, too, we were supposed to have lunch." Elizabeth frowned. "She hasn't returned my telephone calls. I guess I'm going to have to track her down like I did you. I know she's holding focus meetings. I just don't want to go to yet another meeting, so I haven't gone. I'll find her. But I also have to admit I expect she and the developers are scrambling—I know we are. This is a big vote for both sides."

"How do you think it'll go?"

"Honestly? I don't know. Amy seems to think we've won. I'm going to hate to see that woman if it goes the other way."

"Me too," Kelly mumbled.

"Look, I know I'm just an old busybody. But are things all right between you two?"

"Yeah, fine. Has Amy said something?"

"No, gosh. She hasn't said a word about anything other than LNG. She's thrown herself into this like a dirty shirt headed for the washing machine. I've never seen her this driven before about anything. It has me worried. That's why I wanted to know if everything's okay between you two."

"Fine." Elizabeth's words nagged at Kelly's conscience. "So why are you so worried about her?"

"If we don't win, I'm afraid Amy's going to take this as a personal defeat. I do, Kelly."

Kelly rested her head in her hand. She was just too tired to take on yet one more emotional battle. "Amy's a fighter," she said weakly.

"I know, Kelly, but this one's different. Over the years, I've seen Amy when she takes on an issue. She's often preoccupied with it, but this one's distinct. Deep down she's really angry. It's as if she sees this as a personal vendetta. With the rest of us, we're in it to win, but we know if we lose our life will be altered, not broken. For Amy it's different, and lately she absolutely hates Susan. It's almost as if she feels like she's at war with Susan, like this is some kind of personal conflict. Ever since the party, it's as if Amy sees her as some kind of adversary and she has to beat her. Mention her name and she reacts with such bitterness. I don't understand it. Has she mentioned anything to you?"

Kelly sat back as if Elizabeth had slapped her. "I've been busy at the hospital so we haven't really talked. She gets home, I'm usually in bed. In the morning, she's out the door early. I didn't know," Kelly she lamely. "Why Susan? Why not the developers?"

"I don't know. I've asked her. I've talked with her a lot about this because I'm worried about her. Other than to say it's winning or nothing, she won't say." Elizabeth clearly knew more than she was saying. "Maybe because Susan's a woman. Maybe because she's a lesbian and Amy sees this as some kind of Judas sisterhood thing. I really don't know."

353

"I'll talk to her." Kelly stopped when Carrie put the steaming bowls of fish chowder in front of them. "Thank you." She picked up her spoon and swished it around in the bowl, making the steam spew even faster into the air. She needed to think. It felt like Elizabeth's words were burning a hole in her brain. First Amy and then Susan popped into her mind. She felt as though she was being strangled by all of her emotions. *Stay calm*, she said to herself. Elizabeth was a friend. Should she talk to her about this? Tell her about Susan? Tell her what a mess she'd made out of their lives. But how could she? Elizabeth was Amy's oldest and most cherished friend. She was her mentor. How could she tell her she had been cheating on her. She had to think. She dipped her spoon into the broth and raised it to her lips. She blew on it and took a taste. The richness of it made her think about Susan and that day on the cliff when they had eaten chowder like queens and talked about life like philosophers. Did Amy suspect? No, she thought. If Amy suspected she wouldn't be able to hold it in. There would have been an explosion. The entire island would have heard it. All of a sudden that huge sense of loss she'd been feeling about her life seized her. She couldn't breathe. She coughed.

"Are you all right?" Elizabeth said as Kelly coughed several more times. She could see the concern on her friend's face.

"Yes, just too much pepper." Kelly coughed again into her napkin and sipped some water. *Stay calm*, she thought. *Don't start to hyperventilate.* "I know Amy's driven, but she's a survivor." She still felt like she was choking. "I think she'll be okay if this goes against her."

"I don't know." Elizabeth also tasted the chowder. "This is good." She picked up several packages of crackers, opened the cellophane and shredded the crackers into the chowder. "I'm worried about her and I'm worried about you." There was a questioning look in her eyes.

"Me?"

"Yeah, you. Do I need to repeat something so simple?"

"Don't worry about me, Elizabeth, I'm fine."

"I didn't come here to pry, believe that, but I know something's wrong here."

"Wrong how?" Kelly continued to avoid Elizabeth's gaze.

"Wrong because you won't look me in the eyes. Wrong because Amy's so maniacal about this that I'm scared for her. Wrong because you haven't been around. Wrong because something's going on."

Tell her, she admonished herself. *Tell her the truth. Tell her. What's stopping you? Fear.* For the first time Kelly understood what was going on in her head and why she was afraid to tell Amy. That tidy excuse—wait until this LNG thing was over—was just that, nothing more than avoidance. She realized this whole thing with Susan was entwined in fear and not just fear of Amy's wrath. She loved Susan. She wanted to be with Susan. But fear clutched her. Fear that Elizabeth would judge her. Fear that Elizabeth would side with Amy and hate her. Fear that she would lose Elizabeth from her life. All of a sudden Kelly felt very sad about that. What would their friends think? she wondered. What would Maggie Beth and Terry think? Losing them would be very painful.

Kelly put her spoon down and looked at Elizabeth. "I love you. I count you as one of my best friends. I've known you for only five years, but I feel as if I've known you a lifetime. Elizabeth, I can't talk about what's wrong right now. Can you accept that? I just need to think about some things first. Is that okay?"

Elizabeth pondered the question for a moment. "Of course."

Kelly stared at her chowder. She wanted to tell her. *Tell her!* The voice in her head wouldn't leave her alone. She was tearing herself apart inside. The nucleus of her being had been severed over two women. She felt a loyalty to the past and Amy, yet she was excited about the future with Susan. *Tell her you're an ass.* "Thank you. I didn't realize Amy felt that way about Susan. I know she gets passionate about things, but I didn't realize she was angry at a public relations woman. This is new information and a bit over-whelming, I might add."

Elizabeth's smile was sympathetic. "Kelly, you don't have to say

355

a thing. Look, I love you as much as I do Amy. So whatever is wrong, I'm here to help make it right."

"Can we talk about something else? I don't want to start weeping in my chowder. It seems rather humiliating."

"Of course we can talk about other things."

"How about we talk about you for a change?"

"Well, one of my favorite subjects, but not very interesting right now." There was a smile in Elizabeth's voice.

"I do wonder—" Kelly said.

"About?"

"Life."

"That's a hard one. All of life is hard to talk about."

Kelly grinned. "Not all of life. Just a portion . . ." She stared at her chowder. "I'm dealing with, let's say, a hypothetical dilemma."

"Okay."

Kelly put her spoon down and pushed the chowder away. "One of those life type questions?"

Elizabeth followed suit and pushed her chowder aside. "Go on."

"Was there any time in your life when you wondered if it just isn't worth it. Throw in the towel. There's no value to life?"

Elizabeth chewed on the question. "Yes." Her answer was almost a whisper.

"Just that? Yes, with no explanation."

"Explanation? Well, yes, there's an explanation. I just need to think about how to answer." Elizabeth rubbed her temples. "When I was with Lois," she began very quietly, "every day had value. I know that sounds simplistic, but it's really true. I loved every single day we had together. We just had this marvelous connection. But after Lois died, I wondered what value my life had and I almost ended it."

Kelly sat back. No one had ever mentioned that Elizabeth had felt so despondent.

"No one knew," Elizabeth added briskly, as if reading her mind. "But after Lois died, days became lifetimes and I didn't want a lifetime without her. I lived, mostly because I was too much of a coward to die. That's why I'm running through life now. Jumping out of helicopters. Wanting more and more thrills. It helps disguise the day. Even now I have such regrets. Sometimes I think I love Lois more now than when she was alive. If that's possible."

Kelly felt as if she was eavesdropping on Elizabeth's life.

"I fill up my days with work and fun, but my nights are wastelands of emptiness."

"I'm sorry, Elizabeth. I didn't know. I feel like I should be doing something for you."

"You can't. I've accepted Lois's death, I just haven't gotten used to it. I haven't talked about how I feel to my friends because they'll feel a need to fill up my life with stuff. What they don't understand is, when you've lost your soul mate you can't fill up your nights with just stuff. Before Lois died, she told me she wanted me to find someone else. I got mad at her. Really, really mad at her. But I was the silly one. She was so sensitive. She understood better than I did the depths of my loneliness. But even in that throat-strangling aloneness, I didn't want to share my life with any other woman. I'll tell you something funny. I talk to her every day—I do." Elizabeth held up her hands as if to stop an onslaught of questions. "Please don't feel you have to rush to make my life better. I'm just telling you this to let you know I understand."

Kelly could feel the tingle of tears in her eyes. "Would you love me if Amy wasn't in my life?"

"Of course."

Kelly swallowed the mountain in her throat. "I'm glad." Relief washed over her.

"But you don't want to talk about it now, do you?" Elizabeth said gently.

"No."

"Kelly, I know this is going to sound simplistic because I've never been good at this giving advice stuff. Not in the realm of philosophy—that was Lois's gift. But know this. Whatever is troubling you now, indecision will only make it worse. But also know that your friends will always remain your friends. I guess that's why I called you today. I had this sense that you're grappling with something and you need to know that there are a lot of people who love you and also understand what you're going through. So don't feel you're alone. If you want to talk, you can talk with me. I promise you no one else needs to know, not even Amy."

Kelly wiped her eyes. "Thank you, Elizabeth. As soon as I can figure out what's going on in my life, I will talk to you."

"And also know this. And this is not a disloyalty to Amy. Her friends love her dearly, but we all know her."

Kelly read the unspoken words in Elizabeth's eyes. "I—"

"Can I get you anything else?" Carrie asked.

"No, I'm fine." Kelly studied her hands. The moment had been broken.

"Me too. No dessert for me."

They waited as Carrie removed the dirty dishes from the table. She set their bills on the table. "Take as much time as you need," she said with a glance at Elizabeth. "We're not that busy. So you don't have to rush."

Kelly watched as Carrie went back behind the counter where she busied herself with adding up another bill.

"Well." It was Elizabeth who broke the silence.

"Thank you," Kelly said.

"For what?"

"For calling me. For asking me to lunch."

"You're welcome." Elizabeth paused and then looked Kelly in the eyes. Kelly felt as if the truth of Elizabeth's thoughts were burned into her. "Kelly, don't fidget about the future, just decide what's best for your heart."

"I'm going to try, Elizabeth. I really am going to try. But right now I don't know what's best for my heart. All I know is I'm afraid to make a decision. Does that make sense?"

"Frighteningly, it does."

Kelly noticed Elizabeth glance at her watch. "Do you have to get back to the town office?"

"Not me, you're the one who said you only had an hour for lunch."

Kelly thought about her morning. "You're right. I've got to get back." She stood up and extended her hand to help Elizabeth.

"These old bones find it harder and harder to get out of these tight places," Elizabeth groused.

Kelly threw twenty dollars on the table. "That should cover it."

"That should more than cover it."

Kelly gave her a hug. "Well, Carrie seemed to know we were deep in conversation. She spent more time away from the table than at it. For that I'm grateful."

"Good waitresses and bartenders pick up on a lot of signals."

"You're right. We could probably take lessons from them." Kelly turned to Elizabeth and hugged her again. "Thank you, my friend. Thank you for being so sensitive that you knew I needed to talk. But thank you for not prying. Thank you for taking the time to be there for me, and thank you for being you. But most of all, thank you for loving me because I truly love you."

"You're welcome, and know this, Kelly, your friends will be there when you decide to talk about what's going on in your heart."

Kelly held the restaurant door open for her and walked her to her car. "Thank you."

Elizabeth rolled down the window and touched Kelly's hand. "You're loved, my young friend. Remember that."

Kelly went right to her office after she got back to the hospital. She picked up her messages and closed her office door and dialed Amy's number. Amy picked up on the first ring. "How about we both take the night off and have dinner?" She could hear Amy's protestations about the vote being just two days away. "Of course, I understand. I'll come over there. Do you want me to pick sandwiches up for everyone?" Kelly wrote names and the sandwiches they liked. "I will. I'll stop by Subway on my way over. See you around five."

She picked up the telephone again. "Loraine, is Laurie working today?" She waited while the receptionist checked. "Thanks." She picked up the telephone again and dialed Laurie's number. "Laurie," she told the answering machine, "I'm just checking in. Hope things are well with you. Give me a call when you get in. Let's figure on having lunch or dinner tomorrow."

Kelly sat back in her chair. She picked up the telephone again and dialed Susan's number. When the machine clicked on, she said, "I didn't expect you'd be there. Just listen. We need to talk and soon. So please give me a call. I know you're right out straight, but even just a quick call would help." She paused. "Be safe." She clicked off. Be safe? Why didn't she tell her she loved her? Why didn't she tell her that by talking they might be able to problem-solve this. *You're a first class-moron and she doesn't deserve to have you in her life. Nope, not you. You tell her to be safe.* Kelly shook her head. Why didn't she tell her she understood her sadness that night at the motel? Ask her for forgiveness.

Kelly picked up the telephone on the first ring. "Hello. Oh, Don. Sure, I'll come right over." She picked up her notebook and closed her door and walked toward the CEO's office. His secretary wasn't at her desk. She knocked softly on his door.

"Come in, Kelly, sit down."

She waited. He picked up a large report and handed it to her. "I just want to tell you the state licensure board was very impressed with us. We got good marks in a lot of areas. Some criticisms, all minor. Things we can handle in-house and simply. I just wanted you to know I'm pleased. You've been my director of nurses for what—six months now?"

"It seems longer, but yes, I guess it has been."

"I want you to know I'm pleased. You've done well, Kelly. You had some big shoes to fill. Sandy was loved around here."

"I know. I almost didn't take the job because of that."

"Well, anyway. I'd like you to read the report. Give me your feedback."

Kelly stood up. "I will. Thanks. I'm glad it went as well as it did."

"Me too. These things can be sticky. They come in here and sometimes see things we don't. But not this time."

Well, at least that part of her life was going well, she thought. She didn't know why, she certainly had not been a very good supervisor of late. *Get your act together,* she ordered herself. *Take control.* She bypassed her office and headed to the nurse's station. It was time she acted like she should. It was time to visit with people who made her life easy.

Chapter Thirty-nine

On Wednesday, election night, Kelly was with the opponents. They had all gathered at Amy's store awaiting the results of the vote. The polls had closed an hour ago and people were in various stages of anticipation. There was food on a nearby table, but no one was eating. Kelly knew that Amy had put several bottles of wine in her office refrigerator and had not told anyone. She knew Amy was determined they were going to celebrate tonight. She had to marvel at Amy's commitment to winning, but she also worried about what Elizabeth had said. What if they lost tonight? Kelly's concern about Amy had turned to fear.

For the last two nights, she had left work early to be with Amy. Amy was definitely appreciative, but also distracted. When Laurie finally called her back at work this morning, they'd talked for about a half-hour about what Susan had told her about not feeling the same way about Laurie. Kelly was surprised. Laurie was handling it very well. Although when she prodded, Laurie admitted she hadn't talked with Susan in days. Susan hadn't called her either.

At noon, she and Amy had gone to the polls together to vote. Elizabeth was there, but she was all business. They had to wait in line and Kelly marveled at the turnout. She had voted in only one presidential election on Bleu Island and that had been George W. Bush's bid for reelection. The polls were busy that day, but nothing like the lines today. Jefferson County had voted for Bush, the majority of Maine against.

"Did you get to ask Elizabeth how the numbers went?" Maggie Beth asked Amy.

"I didn't. I was afraid to talk to her. Afraid the proponents might think I was trying to influence her or something because she's a friend."

"Well, I asked her," Jeremy Kendell said. He owned the local marine supply store. "She said by noon they'd had more than three hundred voters. I expect we're going to set some kind of record."

"I think that's good," Terry put in.

"How so?" Amy asked.

"I think the more voters we have, the better it is for our side. All those people who for years have never voted in an election are out there today. I think it's because they care so much about this island, they want to vote to save it."

"I don't know." Maggie Beth shook her head. "I worry just the other way. That all those people who've never voted are voting for jobs."

"Did Elizabeth say how long they might be counting?" someone from the back of the room asked.

"No, she didn't," Amy answered. "She just said she had extra counters coming in tonight. The law allows them to at least sort the absentee ballots. They can open the envelopes, but they can't count them. They can only sort them into yes and no piles ahead of time. She said that would help."

"I wonder where the developers are tonight?"

"I heard they and some of their supporters are at the SeaBleu Restaurant." There was more than a hint of derision in Amy's voice. "They think they're going to be celebrating tonight. I expect your friend Laurie's there too."

"Laurie's working tonight," Kelly said quietly. She sensed a shift in the mood in the room.

"I think it's too early for anyone to think about celebrating," Maggie Beth said softly. "Gosh, I wish that telephone would ring." She looked longingly at the phone on the counter. Kelly knew that Amy had two people standing outside the polling booth waiting for the results; only the counters were allowed inside. The media was lined up outside the polling booth, also waiting. Once the vote was tallied she knew they'd rush to question the winners first, then the losers.

Kelly looked up as two more people came in. "Sorry we're late," Jim Bows said. His wife was with him. "We got hung up. I had to take one of my boats over to the mainland for repairs. We just got back a few minutes ago. Haven't had a thing to eat." He and his wife greeted several of the people in the room. "Kelly, hi," he said as he greeted her. "Sorry you haven't been around."

"Me too." She smiled at him. "I was here last night, but you were the lost soul."

"Problems with that boat. That's why we took it over today. Marcie and I"—he nodded to his wife—"we voted this morning and then took off. Y'know, I haven't seen you since—"

He stopped when the telephone rang. Amy rushed to pick it up. "Elizabeth. Hi." Amy turned to look at the group. Kelly could see the sparkle in her eyes. "We did? What was the vote? Oh, thank God."

Kelly looked around her. It was as if someone had flipped a switch and the entire room had become animated.

"We won, people." Amy cupped her hand over the receiver. "We won by not a lot, but we won. Thanks, Elizabeth. Come over after you close up there." She hung up and announced that the vote was 490 to 466 against LNG. "Wahoo." Amy pumped both arms in the air.

Kelly smiled. It felt like New Year's Eve.

Amy walked over and hugged her. "It's over, my love. It's over and we won," she said softly.

Kelly hugged her tightly. "You done good, Amy. This happened because of you. You should be proud of yourself." She could see the excitement in Amy's eyes.

Maggie Beth grabbed them both and hugged them. "We did it. You did it, Amy. You made this happen."

"Not me, we." Amy took off laughing to hug the others in the room. "I got wine." She went to the refrigerator. "I knew we'd win and I brought wine along to celebrate."

"You're amazing," Terry said. "You've had a confidence about this like no other. I know at times I lost hope. I figured we'd lose. But not you. I admire that. I really do."

"Well," Amy said seriously, "I just wouldn't allow myself to dwell on losing. Losing was not an option. Every time it made its way into my mind I just redirected my energies to the thought of winning."

"Well, if karma can make things happen, then your hard work and your positive karma made the difference," Jeremy said as he hugged her. "I bet they're crying the blues at SeaBleu." He laughed at his own pun.

"Reporters are here." Jim pointed at the door.

"It's your baby." Maggie gently pushed Amy toward the door.

Kelly watched as the television cameras and journalists fluttered around Amy. Oblivious to the frenzy, she answered each question. She clearly had learned how to handle the press. Kelly turned away. She thought about Susan, who had fought just as hard as Amy. She remembered their discussion on the beach when Susan talked about how important the contract was to the future of her company. But she'd been philosophic too. She wanted to win, but not at any price. She wished she could call her. Kelly wished she could go over there and hold her. Tell her she was sorry she'd lost. Tell her she wanted to fix everything. She looked at Amy; the reporters had left. Kelly felt a tug at her heart. They were headed to the SeaBleu. Susan would be the perfect professional, but there would be no radiant smile. The smile that tugged at Kelly's heart whenever she saw it.

She watched Amy float around the room hugging everyone. Then it hit her. Amy had said once this was over they would go see a counselor. Kelly felt like an anchor had been tied to her foot. The joy she was feeling just seconds earlier over the win turned to terror. Amy was buoyed. Energized. She was going to want to make love tonight. Kelly walked toward the other side of the room. They hadn't made love since her return from Port Bleu. They'd barely talked. Not now, she thought. She looked over at Amy again. She was pouring wine into plastic cups and handing them to everyone. She handed the wine bottle to Maggie Beth and picked up two cups and came toward Kelly.

"We've earned this, love." She handed a cup to Kelly. "To us." She touched Kelly's cup. "And to—"

"She's here." Just then, the door opened.

Elizabeth was all smiles.

Kelly watched as Elizabeth made her way across the room embracing everyone in her path. Elizabeth then turned to Amy and held out her arms. "You deserve a special hug." Elizabeth's tiny frame seemed to turn into a giant hug machine.

"Tell us what went on at the town office," Amy said, laughing. "Terry, get this woman some wine. She's had a hell of a day."

"It wasn't bad." Elizabeth accepted the cup and took a sip. "Oh, that's good. Better than the coffee we've been drinking all day."

"What are the selectmen saying?"

"Well, of course all the reporters were there. Even the three channels from Bangor. They were standing outside the town office with their cameras and microphones. Most of the selectmen weren't there. The chairman was. I suspect they made him go 'cause someone had to talk with the reporters. Give the town's reaction. He's been for it all along, but he was good. Very professional. One of the reporters asked him if this meant it was over— that's the part that worried me. He hedged. Said he hadn't yet spoken to the developers."

"What does that mean?" Maggie Beth asked. "Of course it's

over. We won. What, they're going to pretend this was like the Florida election, where the ballots were questionable?"

"I don't think so." Elizabeth's brow wrinkled.

"No. I know exactly what it means," Amy said. "There's just a few numbers separating us. I didn't take it in when you told me, but it's what—"

"It's a twenty-four vote difference."

"So, they may ask for a recount?" Terry asked.

"They could." Elizabeth pondered the question. "Although twenty-four votes is a lot. If it'd been three or four, then a recount would make sense. It's pretty hard. Most they could hope for is maybe ten ballots were questionable, that's about it."

"They're not going to ask for a recount. They're going to ask for another vote." Amy said the words with no particular emphasis. "You know how it is in Maine. Keep running it past the voters until they get it right."

"Can they do that?" Kelly asked.

"They can," Elizabeth answered. "The other side can get a petition. Ask for another election. It happens all the time. I remember one time in Lubec, they had some kind of issue. They kept running it past the voters until it just wore them down. They finally passed the measure . . ." Elizabeth paused. "Gosh, I wish I could remember what that was about."

"So this isn't over." Jeremy was clearly disappointed.

"Well, I for one am celebrating." Amy lifted her cup. "To us. We stuck together, we fought the good fight and we won. We're not going to worry about tomorrow." They all, including Kelly, lifted their glasses in agreement. "Now, I have more wine, and by golly we're going to celebrate."

Kelly talked with friends as more and more of them found their way to Amy's shop. She looked at her watch. It was ten o'clock. Amy had been drinking quite a bit of wine and Kelly could see she had more than just the afterglow of a win on her cheeks. Kelly smiled. What the hell, she thought. Amy deserved this night and she deserved to relax with some grape spirits.

"She sure looks happy," Elizabeth said.

"She does and so do you."

"Well, it's nice to have this over." Elizabeth paused. "For a while at least. I tried to call Susan, but she didn't answer. I wanted her to know that even though she lost, she did a hell of a job."

Kelly had been thinking about Susan all night.

"I was thinking of going over to the restaurant. I sense she could use a friend right now. You want to go along?"

Kelly looked over at Amy. "No, you go ahead. Tell her . . ." She paused. "Tell her I'm sorry."

"I will." Elizabeth gave her a hug. "I'm sorry too. I'm not going to tell Amy where I'm going. I don't want to interrupt the joy that's on that face, and she just wouldn't understand."

"It'll be our little secret." Kelly watched as Elizabeth told Amy she was leaving. She saw her say something to her. Amy smiled and looked over at Kelly and smiled again.

Kelly spent the rest of the evening walking around the room and talking with friends. She kept touching her cell phone, hoping it would ring. She had hoped Elizabeth would call her and tell her how Susan was doing. It was well after ten. She had to go to work in the morning.

"We gotta go," Maggie Beth said to her. "We're pooped. There's no other word for it." They picked up their jackets from the pile near the counter. "I told Amy we're having a get-together at our house next weekend, kind of an after-the-party party."

"Good, I'll be there. Sorry, I've not been around much—" Kelly said, trying to explain her weeks of absence.

"Don't be silly," Maggie Beth said. "When Amy said you were in the middle of a state licensing thing, we understood. I remember those years when I was on the board. Everyone's biting their nails but walking around like it was business as usual."

Kelly laughed. "Well, something like that."

"Anyway, we'll see you Saturday night." Maggie Beth looked around the room. "Looks like a lot of folks are certainly enjoying that wine." She nodded toward Jim, who had his arm affectionately around Amy's shoulder and was talking to her. "You know Amy and her sense of space. Not that Jim means anything by it," she added hastily. "Just that Amy hates to be touched."

"You're right. I better go rescue her." Kelly grinned.

"Agreed." Maggie Beth and Terry laughed with her. They both hugged her. "Anyway, we'll see you in a couple of days."

"Sounds good." Kelly watched as they left. Others were also saying their good-byes. Kelly went toward Amy.

"Kelly, hi." Jim gave her an unsteady hug. "I was just telling this friend of ours how proud I am of her."

Marcie grabbed his arm. "He's not had any dinner. So these few glasses of wine have made him unusually happy." She smiled affectionately at her husband. "It's time for us to go," she said.

"You're right, hon. Sorry, ladies, I did sip a wee bit too much." He hugged Amy and then Kelly. "I'm so glad you're back, Kelly. I was kinda worried about you. I saw you with that LNG lady that night outside the restaurant and I was worried you'd gone over to the other side. I thought you were going to come in and have dinner. I was going to invite you to join us. But you two left."

Kelly looked at Amy. She could see her jaws tighten. "I just ran into her that night." She took a deep breath then exhaled slowly. "We had dinner. One of those bump-in things." She could feel her chest tighten. She was in the middle of a full-blown anxiety attack.

"I told Marcie about it, she said the same thing. Come on, hon, we got to take this tipsy guy of yours home." He leaned on his wife's shoulder.

"We'll talk later," Amy said between clenched teeth. Her smile was malevolent. Several more people hugged her as they said good-bye.

Kelly walked to the other side of the room and began to pick up some of the chairs and put them away. Jeremy began to help her. Some of the others were cleaning up the food on the table. *Your ass is grass, Kelly Burns*, she kept saying to herself. Her cheeks burned. She was mortified. Occasionally, she'd glance over at Amy, but Amy didn't look her way again.

"Anyone who wants to take home the leftovers, do it," Amy said as she began to help with the cleanup. She grabbed some plastic bags and put several dishes inside. She came over to Kelly. "Look, I'll see you at the house. Right now I don't want to look at you."

Kelly could tell from Amy's tone there was no room for discussion. "Okay."

Kelly picked up Jasper. It was after eleven o'clock. She was going to get very little sleep tonight. "This is it, little buddy. I have a feeling after tonight you're going to have only one mother." When she had gotten home, she packed her things in her backpack. It was sitting on the chair. She hadn't thought about where she was going. She set Jasper down when she heard Amy's car. She stood with her back against the counter.

"That night you came home from the mainland, you smelled of fresh soap, like you'd just taken a shower. I didn't think much about it at the time because I was so relieved you were home. You were with her, weren't you?" Amy said as she opened the door.

"Yes."

"How long has this been going on?"

"It happened when we went to Portland."

"That's not true," Amy said firmly. "These things just don't happen. It's been longer than that."

"I was attracted to her from the beginning. Is that what you want to hear?" Kelly could scarcely breathe.

"Why didn't we talk about it?" Amy's tone was measured, controlled. She sounded almost reasonable.

"Because we rarely talk anymore, we mostly argue," Kelly said somewhat defensively.

"So it's my fault? This one's not my fault," Amy said as she answered her own question.

"I'm not saying fault. I just am trying to tell you why I couldn't talk about it."

"How many times?"

"How many times what?" Kelly didn't mean to sound sarcastic. "Look, I'm sorry. Let's just talk about now, can we?"

"No." Amy bristled. "We have to talk about how we got to this point. I deserve that much."

The two fell silent.

"Amy, I'm not sure what happened." Kelly's eyes filled with tears. She turned away. "I just know that I felt an attraction for Susan. Things happened."

Amy sat down in one of the kitchen chairs a sardonic grin on her face. "'Things happened,'" she mimicked. "Things don't just happen, Kelly," she shot back. Kelly could sense the anger boiling in Amy.

Kelly wiped the tears. "All right, Amy, let's talk about truth. You're going to think I'm blaming you for this, but I'm not. But this happened because things haven't been right between us for a while now."

Amy was smiling like the poker player who held a royal flush. "When I was driving over here, I tried to figure out how quickly you would blame this on me. That this was my fault."

"It's both our faults," Kelly countered.

"Okay." Amy folded her arms across her chest. Amy looked at her and held her gaze unflinchingly. "Tell me how it's both our faults."

"How many nights and days have we spent lately not talking to each other. Living like roommates?"

"I explained that," Amy exclaimed. "I told you this LNG thing was important and you saw how important it was tonight. We won. But if we hadn't fought hard, we'd have lost. I begged you to be patient. To understand the pressures I was under. But you wouldn't. You immediately fall into the arms of a bimbo."

Kelly's anger flared. "Don't blame Susan for this."

"Well, if I can't blame Susan and I can't blame you, I'm certainly not going to blame myself." There was a low growling fury in Amy's voice.

"Us, Amy. Put the blame where it belongs, on us."

371

Amy jumped up and stood within inches of her. "No, Kelly, you want to blame me. You want to use the things I've said as a hammer. You want to beat me over the head with that. When all I've done is tell you the truth about your life and about the things you do."

"Truth, Amy? Well, your truth hurts Your truth slices through my brain like a saber." Kelly tried to choose her words carefully. *Don't let this escalate. Try to keep it controlled,* she told herself.

"But I don't mean anything by it," Amy sputtered furiously.

"You do." Kelly got up and stared out the window. "You say exactly what you mean. You just don't take into account how they feel to the other person. I'm not going to do a she-said, she-said. We've talked about this before and you promised things would change, but they didn't."

"That's what I'm trying to say—my words are just that, words. How they make you feel is your problem, not mine. Your inadequacies put the spin on it, not what I say."

Kelly turned and stared at her. "You really don't get it. I know you don't believe that because if you did, then you'd be just as caustic with our friends. You'd tell them how to improve themselves and their lives. You would be just as critical, but you're not, Amy. And do you know why?"

"No, but I'm sure you're going to tell me."

"Yes, I'm going to tell you." Kelly could feel all the years of frustration building, all the criticisms moving from isolated chambers in her brain to one large room. "Because if you did you wouldn't have the friends you have. And either consciously or subconsciously you've figured that out. If you said those kinds of things to your friends you wouldn't have any."

"That's crap. I treat you the same way I treat my friends." Her voice was a whiplash.

Kelly looked sharply at her. "No, you don't. But what's really sad about this?" Kelly fought hard to capture the tears that were again getting ready to spill from her eyes. "You care more about what your friends think of you. And that's sad. You don't care what

372

your partner thinks of you. Your partner is your verbal punching bag." Her brow furrowed.

Amy shrugged. "That's unfair. We've always gotten past those tense moments before. You didn't run out and have an affair with a bimbo." Amy waved her hand in the air as if trying to grab hold of the word.

"Stop calling her that," Kelly yelled.

"Well, that's a word that certainly hurts," Amy challenged.

"Stop calling her that," Kelly said more quietly. "This isn't Susan's fault. It's mine. I did this. Yes, we've gotten past those arguments before. But it's always a temporary fix. Then something sets you off and you pick at me. You pick and pick. All I want from you is the same respect you show your friends. You get mad about something, take it out on that person, not me. If you get mad at yourself, take it out on yourself, not me. We all have frustrations, we all get angry. I do, but if I do something stupid, I don't yell at you. I yell at myself. You should hear the conversations that go on in my head when I've done something that's made me angry. It would amaze you."

Amy sat back down in the chair. "So I say stuff, it doesn't mean I don't love you."

"When you get mad at me you don't love me. You don't even like me. Sometimes I don't even know where it comes from, you've blindsided me so many times."

"You're a real ass sometimes, do you know that?" Amy's anger was surfacing, Kelly could feel it. "Most the time you know when I'm upset."

"I don't, Amy," Kelly exclaimed. "Our first year together—hell, it was our first few months together—something happened. I can't even remember now, but I told you then that you treated your friends better than you treated me. We talked about it and for a time things were better, but then you fell into your old habits and I gave up."

"I remember that fight and I've tried to change."

"You haven't, Amy." Kelly stopped, suddenly bone-weary and

exhausted. "What's always amazed me is that you truly do not believe you have to take responsibility for your words. You really believe you can say anything you want to me and I'm supposed to accept it for whatever reason and go on loving you. I don't think you get it."

"That's not fair, Kelly. I've worked at it."

"But not enough to really change."

"Now, that's not true." Amy's voice flared with contempt. "I told you I'd go see a counselor." An ironic smile briefly crossed her face. "The Sunday you were with Susan, I was thinking about how much I loved you and how much I wanted to save our relationship. I said then I'd see a counselor. Wow, little did I know what you were doing."

"Don't go there, Amy," Kelly warned. "This is not Susan's fault. Do you remember what else you said?"

"Please tell me. It obviously stuck in your mind."

"You said you'd go, but you still didn't think we needed it. You did it to placate me."

"Don't you dare attach to me what you think I meant." Amy shook her head. "Or whatever the hell that means. I didn't do it to placate you. I did it because I realized I loved you and I knew you felt strongly about that."

"Did you just hear what you said? Because *I* felt strongly about it, not *we*." Kelly inhaled deeply. *Get control of yourself*, she thought. *If you don't you're going to start crying. Don't cry*, she ordered herself. "You just don't understand how we've come to this point. Why I wanted to see a counselor. You really don't."

"No, I guess I don't."

"Amy, I can't please you. Whatever I do, I can't please you. We needed a counselor to point that out. Point out to you what's going on in your mind that you see only the negative in our relationship and point out to me why I can't seem to get past some of this stuff."

"See only the negative in our relationship? That's not true. I tell people all the time how important you are. How proud I am of you. I tell people about the wonderful things you do for me, for us."

"I'm sure you do. I don't care what you tell other people. I want you to value me. Tell me about how wonderful I am. But you don't. You're too busy burying me under a ton of criticism."

"You're not making sense."

Kelly blinked back the tears. "Last Thanksgiving. We had something like thirty people coming? We'd had a quick breakfast and then you fixed the turkey. We worked side by side in the kitchen, we were really in sync. And I thought, wow, this is the way couples do it and we finally were clicking as a couple. Because in the past, when you had the stress of putting on a big dinner for friends, I knew at times I got in your way. I would do something you didn't like and we had problems. But it was different this time. After the turkey was in, we got all the new dishes out and we set up tables. I just loved it and I loved you. No disagreements, everything was just perfect. We'd finished up and you'd taken your shower first, then I went and took my shower. I'd bought this new blouse and a bottle of Chalimar perfume. You know how I hate to shop, but I wanted to surprise you. Anyway, I came downstairs all excited. You were doing something at the stove and you turned around looked at me and in the most unpleasant tone said, 'Ugh, I just hate the smell of that perfume.' Amy, you undid that day for me. I felt so self-conscious about myself I went into the bathroom and tried to wash it off. You didn't even notice." She paused. "Our friends arrived and you were in your element. You didn't even have the sensitivity to understand how you'd hurt my feelings. I felt bad about myself the rest of the evening."

"That's it? You sleep with another woman because I didn't like the smell of your perfume months ago?"

"No! Please leave Susan out of this. I'm leaving, Amy, because you don't like *me*. It's taken me a long time to figure this one out." Kelly was tired. "You don't like who I am or what I wear or what I bring to this relationship. You don't like me." She could feel the knot tighten in her throat. She swallowed hard. *I'm not going to cry.* She repeated the words like a new mantra.

"That's crap," Amy scoffed. "Do you know what the real issue is here? You just won't forget the past."

"You're right, I don't forget. Harsh words are hard to forget."

"I—"

Kelly held up her hands. "Let me finish, Amy. Please let finish my thought." She clenched her fingers tightly against her palm. "That day, you'd apparently been frustrated and I didn't realize it. I'm going along blithely thinking this is a wonderful day, things are clicking between us, but that wasn't what was going on. That day, I realized in all the days and months and years we've been together that things go on in your head that changes you within a nanosecond. Somewhere in that gray matter where you go, I become the object of your frustration. There are times when I've known you're angry with me and I've known how to deal with them. The problem is that most of the time I don't know when you go to the dark side of your brain until the words spew out of your mouth like molten lava and burn me. It's those times that I'm not prepared for. It's like you're Dr. Jekyll and Ms. Hyde. You didn't dislike the smell of my perfume, there was something else going on that had upset you that day and you let loose with that criticism."

"How little you know me," Amy said, red-faced and angry. "You've never once understood me. I told you about my childhood, how I grew up."

"So we both had lousy male figures in our lives. Two men who had bad tempers and who thrived on criticizing others. The trouble is, you became your grandfather. At some point, Amy, your childhood has to stop being a crutch. We see people around us every day who had worse childhoods, but they grew up to be decent people."

"Now you're saying I'm not a decent person?"

"Amy, you're looking for any excuse to turn this into something else. You are a decent person; you're just not decent all of the time with me. And to use your childhood as the excuse for your acid tongue just doesn't cut it. You've talked about your grandparents— your grandmother adored you, your grandfather was cold and indifferent—but you had someone who loved you. I know your mother was gone because of her job, but she loved you. You've told me that lots of times. Look at people who grow up in homes where their parents have abandoned them, where they've been physically or mentally abused. Some do become their parents and do the same thing as adults, but not everyone. Amy, I didn't have an easy life growing up. My father was verbally and physically abusive, and I could have so easily become that man, but I didn't. Call it an accident, a freak of fate, but I didn't."

"So, you're a better person than I am. Well, bully."

Kelly sighed. "I don't need your sarcasm now."

Amy shot her an irate glance. "I accept the fact that I say things that upset you," Amy said more calmly. "But have you ever thought the problem might be that you just can't accept criticism?"

"That goes both ways. But when I tell you that something upsets me, you react with anger. You won't accept the fact that something you said might have irritated me. So I've stopped telling you and I just eat your words. But you're right, they roll around inside of me. You call it pouting. You discount my feelings. But you know, Amy, I could have said things about what you wear or how you eat or about how you decorated your house, but you know what the difference is?"

"No."

"They were just things and because I loved you, they didn't matter. I remember that time on the telephone when you told Maggie Beth about—" Kelly stopped. She was just going to make this worse.

"About what?"

"No, I'm not going to go there, because it doesn't matter."

"Go there, this is your day to do the biting. Talk about acid tongue." Amy's defensive anger was escalating.

I am not going to let her change this into something it is not, Kelly thought. *I am not going to play let's match criticism.* If she did, that's what they'd both remember. "No, Amy, I'm not." She inhaled sharply. "Why hurt each other more? It doesn't matter; I'm trying to tell you why we're at this point in our relationship."

"I know why this won't work. It's because you screwed another

377

woman," Amy hissed. Her anger now boiling over. "A bimbo! You ass, you did this! You slept with another woman and now you want to push it off on me. Blame me for your being nothing more than a common cheat," she screamed. She turned away. Kelly could see her clasping and unclasping her fingers as if trying to get her hands around her anger. When she turned around her face was red. Her eyes were glazed. Her mouth hung open.

Kelly's tone was measured. Her words, she realized, were her razor of reality. "We've been broken for some time now," she said quietly. "Blame Susan, blame me. Blame the goddesses, but . . ." She shook her finger at her. "Believe this, we're so broken now, we can't be fixed."

Amy pushed Jasper, who was rubbing against her leg, away from her. "Would you have told me if Jim hadn't brought it up about seeing you and Susan together?"

Kelly sensed Amy's mood had shifted yet again. She did not trust the calm. She had seen it before. "I don't know."

"Well, at least that's honest. And would you have gone through the counseling?"

"I don't know that either."

Amy rubbed her chin against Jasper's head. "How does Laurie feel about the fact that you've been sneaking around seeing Susan behind her back. Screwing the woman she loves?" her voice was thick with disdain.

Kelly felt her anger boil. She felt like a piñata that Amy kept whacking and whacking at until she exploded. "Wrap yourself in that, Amy, pull it around you like protective clothing," she fumed. "Use it as an excuse to ignore the real reasons we're breaking up." She picked up her backpack and walked out of the door. "I'll get the rest of my things later."

"I'm changing the locks on the door," Amy yelled after her.

"Do what you feel you have to do. Everything I care about is in this backpack." Kelly turned around and looked at her. "Got it? Everything I care about is in this backpack." She kept her voice flat. "And by the way, I hate olive oil on rolls." She saw the confused look on Amy's face, the frown. Funny, she thought, that night at the restaurant had meant nothing to Amy. She shook her head. And for her, she now realized, it had been a watershed night.

Kelly willed herself not to slam her car door or fly out of the driveway. Her heart was pounding at double its regular rate. Where should she go? She couldn't get to the mainland because the ferry had stopped running hours ago. She didn't know where Susan was. Plus she couldn't go to her now that it was after midnight. Her life was just too screwed up. She drove down to the marina and parked her car. She was glad it was October. The usual press of people that walked along the marina on a summer night were gone. She walked along the rocks to a spot where she could sit and stare at the water.

Kelly shivered. She looked at her watch. It was twelve-thirty. She didn't want to go to the only motel on the island—tongues would wag in the morning. She got in her car and put on the heat and headed back through the downtown area toward the hospital. She could go to her office, pretend she had work to do if someone saw her. More than likely no one would see her. She had a key to get in the front door and at this hour there was no receptionist on duty. She'd sleep in her office and then head for the mainland in the morning. She'd leave Loraine a note, tell her that she was calling in sick.

Then she saw the street sign and turned her car onto the Shin Pond Road. She followed the road for miles until she came to Maggie Beth and Terry's driveway. She drove past. There was a light on in their living room. She knew they were up late. *Don't do this*, she thought as she backed her car up and turned into the driveway. Maggie Beth and Terry were some of Amy's oldest friends. Kelly felt as though a magnet was pulling her toward their house. Oh, well, she thought, they may as well hear the bad news from her. That way they could tell her kindly to her face that they were Amy's friends. She realized she would regret that very much. She had felt such a strong connection to both of them.

Kelly saw the porch light come on. Terry was walking toward

379

her. "We're sorry," Terry said even before Kelly could open her mouth.

"She called." It was more a statement than a question.

"Yes. We invited her here to talk, but she was going over to Elizabeth's."

Kelly backed up toward her car. "I'm sorry, I shouldn't have come here. I . . ."

"Kelly, you're our friend and you will always be our friend. Maggie and I talked about this before."

"You knew?"

"Come in, it's cold out here."

Kelly looked around as if hoping to find an answer. "I don't know. I—"

"What's taking you so long?" Maggie yelled from the door. "It's cold out and you two are about to freeze. Kelly Burns, you get your butt in here."

Terry linked her arm through Kelly's. "Have any doubts now?"

"No." Kelly smiled wearily. She felt bone-tired.

Maggie hugged her. "You okay?"

Kelly nodded, afraid to speak.

"You're in luck, I made a pot of spaghetti tonight. I'm going to get some out and heat it up for you. I bet you haven't eaten except that stuff at the gallery. That wasn't food."

"I—"

"Don't argue." Maggie meant it. "Follow me." Kelly followed her up to the second floor. "You can sleep in here." She reached into the linen closet and pulled out a towel and washcloth. "If you want to freshen up before I feed you, go ahead take a shower, whatever."

"No, really, I'm fine." Kelly reached for Maggie and hugged her. "Thank you, but this is just for tonight. Somehow, tonight, I really didn't want to be alone." She laughed. "Plus I had no way of getting off the island."

"For tonight or for however long, you have a room in this house, woman," Maggie said matter-of-factly.

380

"Maggie, I'm not going to say anything negative about Amy. I expect she told you about Susan."

"She did."

"Don't judge Susan, please. This isn't her fault. There've been lots of problems in our house."

Maggie looked down at her hands. "Amy jokingly calls us her oldest friends from away, and she is our dearest friend and we love her. But we also know who she is as a person and we know what's been going on between you two. She's a wonderful woman, and we love her to death. We were hoping your relationship would be different. But you don't have to talk about it or anything else for that matter." She paused. "Just know this. Terry and I talked about this months ago and we agreed that we wouldn't take sides and you both would still be our friends. We've only known you for just a few years, but time isn't a measurement of friendship—who you are is, and you're going to remain our friend."

Kelly felt the tears well up in her eyes. She wiped them off her cheek. "Thank you. When I walked out tonight I really feared losing my friendship with you and Terry and Elizabeth. That thought scared the hell out of me."

Maggie hugged her. "We love you. Now, freshen up. I'll see you downstairs."

Kelly put her backpack on the bed. She looked longingly at the bed. She just wanted to lie down and pull the covers over her head. Pretend that this had been a lousy joke and tomorrow it would be over. She swallowed. She could feel the tears again. She put the towel against her face and sobbed.

Chapter Forty

"Amy, I've loved you like a child since you were that gangly little kid who appeared on Lois's and my doorstep." Elizabeth was sitting in her kitchen, her robe pulled tightly across her chest. She had made tea for both of them. "I've watched you break up from short-term and what you would call your long-term relationships and never said a word. But I'm going to risk the bond that has existed between us all these years to tell you the truth."

Amy turned on her defiantly. "You're taking Kelly's side in this. She sleeps with Susan how many times I don't know. Sneaks around like a wolverine and you're going to take her side." She couldn't keep the anger and surprise out of her voice.

"Her sleeping with Susan was wrong," Elizabeth said ruefully. "But your problems are deeper than that and you know it and I'm willing to risk our friendship to say that." She picked up her tea and sipped it. "Amy, you have a love-hate relationship with your partner. You love Kelly, but I've seen how you've treated her. I've watched you criticize her to the point where I would have liked to have popped you one. I've watched you put her down in front of our friends. I've seen you embarrass her in public. And how canny of you to know she'd never ever say anything back to you in front of people. She'd silently take it and you would go on as if nothing had happened."

"Has Kelly come whining to you? I know you two had lunch a few days ago."

"No, Kelly has not said a word to me. This is something I've seen and not just with Kelly, but with every woman you've been involved with. I don't know why Kelly slept with Susan before getting out of the relationship with you. I don't like that. But I think I understand it. Five years of frustration finally erupted and she and Susan were together and something happened. Blame it on the full moon if you want, but it happened. Unfortunately, you now feel like the victim, which means you're not focusing on the real nut of the problem."

"I knew you'd take her side. You don't have a clue as to our relationship." Amy jumped up. Spike, who was sleeping at Elizabeth's feet, jumped up also. He growled at Amy.

"Sit down." Elizabeth's words were like a flash flood engulfing her. Amy sat down. "Lie down, Spike." Elizabeth's voice was soft, coaxing as she petted his head. Spike lay down. "You're going to listen to me because if I don't say it no one will. I know this isn't going to come out right, but it's what I know." She paused. "It's what I've seen. Amy, you've said things that have hurt Kelly. It's as if you needed to test her love by verbally assaulting her and because she took it, it somehow proved she loved you. But you keep pushing the boundaries. I'm not a counselor—"

"No, you're not."

"Be quiet and listen to me," Elizabeth said without missing a beat. "Lois saw it too, not with Kelly, but with your other partners."

"I don't believe you."

"Believe it. Lois was the no-nonsense one of the two of us and she wanted to talk to you about it after you and Angela broke up. I told her it was none of our business." Elizabeth shook her head. "Now, Kelly comes along and it's déjà vu. Amy, I love you, but you've got to fix you or you're never going to find what Lois and I had. You're going to keep pushing the one you love away."

"You're taking her side when you should be angry at her. She cheated on me." Amy was almost yelling.

"I told you I didn't agree with that." Elizabeth reached down and stroked Spike's head again.

"You don't have a clue as to how I treated Kelly."

"I do. Remember that time you two were here for dinner and I was talking about remodeling that extra room Lois and I used as a guest room and turning it into a family room." Elizabeth pointed to the room just off the dining room. "At the time I mentioned how I never liked having the television set in the living room and I was thinking of moving it in there. Anyway, Kelly agreed with me and said she thought it was a great idea. You got upset with her. You saw her agreement with me as a challenge to you. Because your stupid television set is in your living room. So you kept picking at her, demanding to know why. When she refused to explain—do you even remember this? She finally said you should ask me because I was the one who brought it up, but you wouldn't do that. No, you just kept picking at her and picking at her, demanding an answer." Elizabeth put her hand on her chest. "I was embarrassed for her, and I should have said something, yet instead I changed the subject. You took her agreement with me as a criticism of you. She wasn't saying that because your television set is where it is you were wrong, she was just stating her preference."

"This is ridiculous. So I questioned her about a TV set. So what."

"You don't get it. What that little exchange said to me, Amy, is that you feel insecure about your decisions, and because Kelly innocently had a viewpoint different from yours you saw it as a challenge to you. So when Kelly mentioned her preference, you had to bully her in front of me. It's your way of protecting your identity."

"I don't have to stay here and take this. I came here for comfort. I didn't come here for a lousy Dr. Phil rendition."

"No, Amy. But I've been wrong in keeping silent all these years. Not because I want to say things that hurt you, but because I know that unless I tell you, you're never going to see the other side of you. There's the good Amy and the insecure Amy who says mean things, and as long as you allow that bad Amy to exist, you're never going to stay in a relationship."

Stung, Amy said, "I'm out of here, I don't have to listen to this crap." She jumped up and started for the door. "I came here for help. I turned to you looking for kindness and love and instead I get a lecture. What kind of friend are you?"

"A good friend, only I should have been a brave enough friend to tell you sooner. Kelly loved you and you're never ever in your life going to find someone so devoted to you. You had a chance to have that same wonderful life that Lois and I shared, but you blew it. If I were you and it wasn't too late, I would run back to her. Beg her to come back. Promise to see a counselor, whatever."

"She cheated on me, and if Jim hadn't said something about seeing them, I probably would never have known."

"What she did was wrong. I said it before and I'll say it again. But if things had been right between you, it never would have happened. You don't cheat on someone you're passionately in love with. We've talked about this before. If your relationship hadn't been broken, Susan never would have come into Kelly's life, because there wouldn't have been room in her heart. But her heart was hurting. You did that, Amy Day, you did that and until you fix that, you're never going to really love a woman."

Chapter Forty-one

Kelly hung the decorated wreath next to her door. She had been living on the mainland since October. She gave her notice at the hospital shortly after she and Amy separated, but Don refused to accept it. So every morning she got up and took the ferry to work and the ferry home again at night. She hated the small apartment she'd found near the town's marina, but inertia had a stranglehold on her life. She missed Laurie. After their fight, Amy had called Laurie and told her about Susan. Laurie's reaction mugged Kelly's thoughts every time she recalled that day. Laurie had been restrained the morning she had appeared at her office, her typed resignation in hand.

Kelly tried to explain, to tell her she didn't mean for it to happen.

Laurie put the resignation on Kelly's desk and raised her hands up almost in surrender, as if bewildered by the entire incident. Her voice was impassive, her gaze unflinching as she said, "I loved you.

I trusted you. I know Susan and I weren't in a relationship so I don't blame her. But I do blame you, Kelly. You cheated on our friendship and I'll never forgive you." She then walked out of her office and out of her life. She'd heard that Laurie had gone back to her old job in Portland.

Susan had also disappeared from her life. She and the developers left the island two days after the vote, but Elizabeth said proponents of the project were eager for a second vote. Apparently for the time being everyone had decided to take a breather.

She'd had dinner with Elizabeth several times. She never talked about Amy and Kelly never asked. That was true of Maggie Beth and Terry too. No one talked about that night, although Kelly knew their breakup was all over the island. People didn't know what happened, so those who didn't ask made things up. Kelly heard that the stresses of the LNG battle had caused them to break up. She smiled at that one—how close to the truth was that?

After she left the island, she settled into a routine. She got up, went to work and returned at night to sit in her apartment. Lassitude was her best friend, inertia her partner. Those nights she stayed on the island to visit with friends, she usually stayed with them until the morning. Lately, she'd decided to spend more time alone.

Thanksgiving had been just another day. She knew Amy would have Thanksgiving at her house again this year. It didn't matter if Kelly was in or out of her life, Amy would never miss a beat when it came to holidays. Elizabeth insisted they spend Thanksgiving together, but Kelly had lied and told her she had other plans. She told her a couple she had met on the mainland had invited her to their house. She knew Elizabeth felt guilty that Kelly would be alone and that was why she had made the offer to spend the day together. Kelly knew it was the right lie. Elizabeth and Amy had spent Thanksgiving together forever and Elizabeth needed to be there again. To be a part of Amy's life.

Afterward when she and Elizabeth had had dinner, Elizabeth let it slip she'd spent Thanksgiving alone. When Kelly had asked her why, all Elizabeth would say was that's the way she wanted it. Kelly remembered the guilt she felt. The one person who continued to love her had been alone on Thanksgiving and it was her fault. Even though Elizabeth refused to talk about Amy, Kelly sensed not for the first time that somehow their breakup had caused a rupture in Elizabeth and Amy's friendship.

Kelly sat at the computer in her apartment, typing her resignation yet again. It was just a formality. Don knew she'd been looking for another job and when she found one at a hospital in Lewiston she had told him. She was scheduled to start work on January third. Although Don had refused to accept her first resignation, this time he said he was happy for her. He too had heard the rumors about the breakup but never asked what had happened.

She smiled to herself. This year she got to break the rules. It was Christmas Eve and she had scheduled herself to work the floor. She had also scheduled herself in for Christmas Day. Her nurses were happy, especially those who had to work the holidays.

She finished the resignation and printed it out. She looked at the clock. She had two hours before she had to catch the ferry to the island. She returned to her screen and started yet another letter to Susan.

Dear Susan.

What to write, she thought. She held the backspace key down and erased the two words. She closed the file. Microsoft asked her if she wanted to save it. She clicked on no and turned off her computer. She'd written Susan letters, sent her e-mails and called her home and her office. The silence coming from Andover was unbearably loud.

Elizabeth said that she and Susan had remained friends. It was Elizabeth who told Susan about Kelly and Amy's breakup. It was Elizabeth who had tried to get her to talk to Kelly, but she had refused. Kelly didn't blame her. She had royally screwed up.

Kelly picked up her backpack, locked the front door and went to her car. So what if she was an hour early getting to the hospital. Hours didn't matter much to her anymore. Ironically, as small as the island was, she and Amy had not run into each other. Kelly never deviated from her schedule. She went straight to work and then back to the mainland. She didn't shop on the island or stop for gas. She limited her time there. If she had dinner out with Elizabeth, it was always on the mainland. Maggie Beth and Terry often met her on the mainland too.

She drove to the hospital and parked in the lot. It had started to snow. She raised her face to the sky and let the snow float down onto her face.

"Merry Christmas."

Kelly spun around, her eyes wide. "Susan." She swallowed. "Where . . . How . . ."

She could feel Susan's shyness. "I wanted to see you."

"I don't know what to say." Kelly looked around helplessly.

"Maybe we could go inside. I've been sitting in the parking lot a while."

"Of course. Sorry." She fumbled with the key that unlocked the front door. "Let's go to my office." She followed Susan in. The receptionist's desk was dark. "Come on." She unlocked the door to her office and stepped back so Susan could go in. She closed the door. "Can . . . I hug you?" she asked, afraid Susan might run away.

"Yes." Susan stepped forward and hugged her.

Kelly folded her into her arms. She closed her eyes and willed the moment to last forever. Susan's face felt cold against hers. "You're chilled. Let me get you some coffee."

"I'm fine." Susan unbuttoned her jacket. "Elizabeth told me you'd be here. Although I think she had the times messed up. She said you were working the morning shift."

"I was, but I changed with one of the other nurses—that way two of them got to spend Christmas Eve with their families."

"That was nice."

"Well, I could do it now that I'm leaving."

"I heard."

"Elizabeth." Kelly smiled.

Susan nodded.

"Where'd you go?"

"I ran away."

Kelly could just barely hear her words. "Susan, I'm so sorry."

"I'm sorry. Elizabeth told me what happened with Amy. You went through such hell. I felt guilty. If I hadn't gone to Portland, it never would have happened."

"It would have," Kelly said fiercely. "Only it would have been a different time. I fell in love with you."

"And I with you."

Kelly took a deep breath then exhaled slowly. "I'm afraid I'll do or say something that will make you run away again. I'm afraid, Susan." She hung her head to hide the tears.

Susan stepped forward. "I love you, Kelly. I don't quite know how to fix this, but I love you." She put her fingers under Kelly's chin and gently tipped her head up and kissed her.

Kelly pulled Susan against her. Their kiss was fervent yet familiar. "I love you, Susan. Please tell me you're in my life."

"I am," she said against Kelly's lips. "Can we make this work?"

"I don't know, but I want to make it work."

About the Author

Diana Tremain Braund continues to live on the coast of Maine in a house that overlooks the water. She and her dog, Bob, who is now six years old, take long walks on the beach. This is where she comes up with ideas for Bella Books.

You can e-mail the author at dtbtiger@yahoo.com.

MURDER AT RANDOM by Claire McNab. 200 pp. The Sixth Denise Cleever Thriller. Denise realizes the fate of thousands is in her hands.   1-59493-047-3 $12.95

JUST LIKE THAT by Karin Kallmaker. 240 pp. Disliking each other—and everything they stand for—even before they meet, Toni and Syrah find feelings can change, just like that.
1-59493-025-2 $12.95

WHEN FIRST WE PRACTICE by Therese Szymanski. 200 pp. Brett and Allie are once again caught in the middle of murder and intrigue.   1-59493-045-7 $12.95

REUNION by Jane Frances. 240 pp. Cathy Braithwaite seems to have it all: good looks, money and a thriving accounting practice . . .   1-59493-046-5 $12.95

BELL, BOOK & DYKE: NEW EXPLOITS OF MAGICAL LESBIANS by Kallmaker, Watts, Johnson and Szymanski. 360 pp. Reluctant witches, tempting spells, and skyclad beauties—delve into the mysteries of love, lust and power in this quartet of novellas.
1-59493-023-6 $14.95

ARTIST'S DREAM by Gerri Hill. 320 pp.When Cassie meets Luke Winston, she can no longer deny her attraction to women . . .   1-59493-042-2 $12.95

NO EVIDENCE by Nancy Sanra. 240 pp. Private Investigator Tally McGinnis once again returns to the horror filled world of a serial killer.   1-59493-043-04 $12.95

WHEN LOVE FINDS A HOME by Megan Carter. 280 pp. What will it take for Anna and Rona to find their way back to each other again?   1-59493-041-4 $12.95

MEMORIES TO DIE FOR by Adrian Gold. 240 pp. Rachel attempts to avoid her attraction to the charms of Anna Sigurdson . . .   1-59493-038-4 $12.95

SILENT HEART by Claire McNab. 280 pp. Exotic lesbian romance.
1-59493-044-9 $12.95

MIDNIGHT RAIN by Peggy J. Herring. 240 pp. Bridget McBee is determined to find the woman who saved her life.   1-59493-021-X $12.95

THE MISSING PAGE A Brenda Strange Mystery by Patty G. Henderson. 240 pp. Brenda investigates her client's murder . . .   1-59493-004-X $12.95

WHISPERS ON THE WIND by Frankie J. Jones. 240 pp. Dixon thinks she and her best friend, Elizabeth Colter, would make the perfect couple . . .   1-59493-037-6 $12.95

CALL OF THE DARK: EROTIC LESBIAN TALES OF THE SUPERNATURAL edited by Therese Szymanski—from Bella After Dark. 320 pp.   1-59493-040-6 $14.95